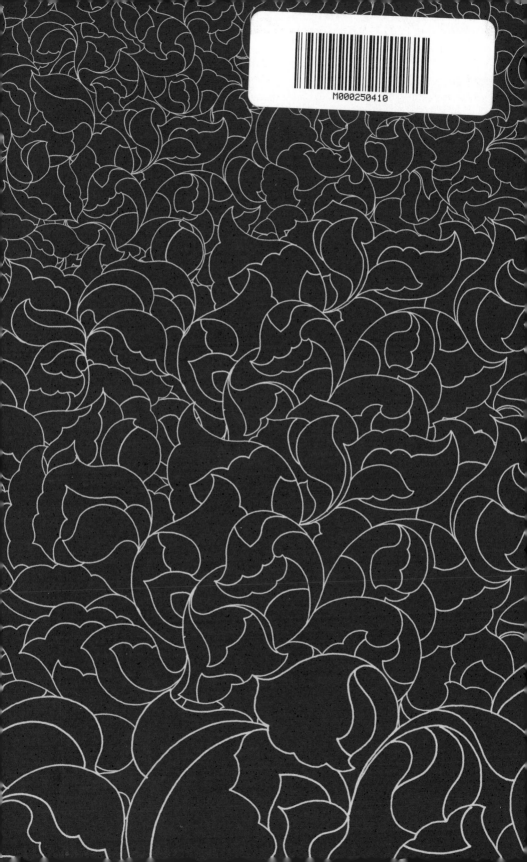

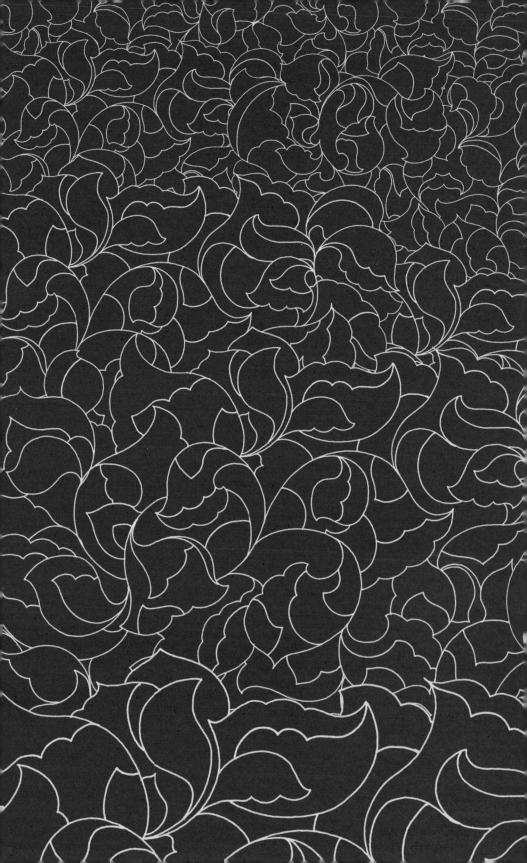

X

X

⤿ the erotic treasury ⤾

Edited by Susie Bright

CHRONICLE BOOKS
SAN FRANCISCO

Pages 366–367 constitute a continuation of the copyright page.

Library of Congress Cataloging-in-Publication Data:
   X : the erotic treasury / edited by Susie Bright.
      p. cm.
   ISBN: 978-0-8118-6402-2
   1. Erotic stories, American. I. Bright, Susie, 1958- II. Title
PS648.E7X15 2008
813.008'03538--dc22

                                        2008010680

Manufactured in China

Design by Suzanne M. LaGasa
Cover Illustration by Hannah Stouffer
Typeset in Caslon and Avenir

10 9 8 7 6 5 4 3 2 1

Chronicle Books LLC
680 Second Street
San Francisco, CA 94107
www.chroniclebooks.com

Contents

Introduction
Susie Bright

When I first conceived of a treasury of erotic stories, the phrase that crossed my mind was "an embarrassment of riches." I thought like a pirate—chests of gold, emeralds, rubies, and pallets of pearls spilling out everywhere. Goblets overflowing in a smoky haze.

For this volume I invited a group of authors who were worthy of such excess, writers who'd rival Scheherazade in their storytelling prowess—writers who could tell a tale as if their life depended on it. I'm honored to present these gifted poets, any of whom would make Mata Hari look slack. They made me laugh, they aroused me, they twisted my mind and my sheets before I could protest.

All these stories are about lovers: heartbreakers, foxes, maniacs, romanticists, and virgins—freaks, love bunnies, hell-raisers, and utter bandits. You'll have a hard time separating one gem from the next. Share them with someone you love, or share them with someone who just happens to be by your side. I have a feeling they're likely to shower you with gratitude.

༄ BROADS ༄
R. Gay

JIMMY NOLAN HAS A THING FOR BROADS—loud, brassy women who sit with their legs open and drink beer straight from the bottle—women who always say exactly what they're thinking and for better or worse, mean what they say.

Jimmy Nolan has a hard time meeting broads. He's not quite sure if this is the result of geography, circumstance, or personal limitation. Jimmy's ex-girlfriend Marissa was the antithesis of a broad—pale, thin, precise, and polite, with a watery voice and weak handshake. She says that Jimmy isn't the kind of guy broads go for. More than once during the course of their three-year relationship, she turned up her nose when Jimmy ogled a broad passing by.

Jimmy Nolan would like to think that he *is* the kind of guy broads go for. He likes his steak rare, enjoys a cold Budweiser, and has a hearty laugh that echoes in any room. His problem, however, is that he models himself after caricatures of who he thinks broads would go for. And unfortunately for Jimmy, he's a nice guy. He opens doors and covers his lap with a napkin at dinner, never interrupts a conversation, and always says *please* and *thank you*.

Then there are his hands—slender, almost delicate hands, finely veined, the skin stretched smoothly over bone without blemish.

It's his habit of placing his napkin on his lap that first got the attention of Greta, a waitress, a broad among broads, at his favorite diner. Greta's charmed by Jimmy's manners—how even when he comes in only for coffee and a Danish, he still takes the time to use his napkin properly. Greta doesn't claim to know much, but she knows men. She knows that their hands and their minds wander, and that they will say most anything to get into the pants of a broad like her. Knowing so much about men is exhausting for Greta. Each day, when she sees Jimmy Nolan, Greta is grateful to see the kind of man she knows nothing about.

Jimmy long ago decided that his hands were the bane of his existence. Women like Marissa coo and fuss over them; they yearn for Jimmy's lovely hands to toy with their tender bits. Marissa's favorite thing was for Jimmy to lie next to her in bed, gently sucking one nipple while he stroked her clit with one finger in small, fast circles, until the pleasure was so sharp it hurt. She couldn't get enough of Jimmy's middle finger—until, of course, she met someone who was happy to take Jimmy's place. In Jimmy's experience, the women in his life often find someone who can take his place. And broads, they take one look at Jimmy Nolan's hands and decide that hands so fine would crumble inside their bodies. They hardly pay him any mind at all.

Every night, Jimmy Nolan takes a bath. It's a ritual he's perfected over the years. At exactly 10:35 P.M., after the evening news is done, he runs hot water until the tub is three-quarters full and adds a capful of musky bath oil. He sets the radio to KSZU FM, a jazz station—real jazz, not that new stuff—and after stripping naked, sinks into the bath with a heavy sigh, enjoying the swirls of steam that fill the room. Jimmy bathes with his eyes closed, his long dark hair clinging to the ceramic edges of the tub. He fantasizes about trashy and brassy broads—imagines their mouths and breasts and thighs and eyes. In more explicit detail, he imagines Greta—a tall brunette with thick thighs, large green eyes, and her small yet perky breasts.

Jimmy doubts that Greta knows his name, but he leaves her a generous tip every day. He compliments her on the way she manages to dangle a cigarette between her lips and hold a conversation, all while pouring coffee. As he thinks about Greta, he wraps his hands around the rigid length of his cock—which is not at all delicate—and slowly strokes himself. If he closes his eyes, he can pretend Greta is there, with him, sliding into the tub, sighing as she relaxes. Jimmy knows that Greta has long days. What she needs at the end of that long day is a hot bath and a man like Jimmy Nolan waiting for her.

In his mind, she sits across from him, smiling her slow, easy smile. She arches her leg just so, and traces Jimmy's body from shoulder to shoulder with her big toe. Jimmy massages her foot, then her calf. Greta moans, whispering, "That feels so good."

Greta's skin is slick, smooth, and he can feel the tension in her muscles as his hands move higher. Greta slides lower and pulls Jimmy toward her. He imagines her full lips, brushing against his neck as she straddles his lap and slowly lowers herself onto his cock. Jimmy breathes slowly; he wants to make the moment last. He wraps his arms around Greta's strong frame, and smiles to himself as she perches her chin over his shoulder.

Her ankles lock against his back and then Greta fucks Jimmy just like a broad should. She is exuberant, loud, and her thighs squeeze him so tightly Jimmy can hardly breathe. Jimmy rises to meet her thrusts, enjoys the wet sound of their bodies slapping together, water spilling onto the tiles. When she's about to come, Greta grabs hold of the sides of the tub and lifts herself a bit, so that her breasts bounce against Jimmy's face. He wraps his fingers in her thick, damp hair. She tells Jimmy to open his eyes and stares at him, her lips parted.

Afterward, when the fantasy of Greta there in the tub with him has faded, there is a small constellation of grayish come floating somewhere over his torso. Jimmy smokes a cigarette, thankful that his hands prove themselves useful on occasion.

Jimmy has tried asking Greta out on a date. He's certain they share a connection. Greta has a habit of resting her hand against his narrow shoulder a little too long, smiling a bit too brightly when he passes through the grease-smudged doors, taking a seat across from him when there's a lull. During these lulls, Jimmy and Greta talk. He loosens his tie, rolls up his sleeves, and flexes his forearm. They banter about work and politics and movies and life and always, Jimmy reminds her that his name is Jimmy Nolan. He knows that she has one kid, no husband, no boyfriend. She drinks Heineken, exclusively, likes clubbing when she can get a sitter, voted for Ralph Nader in *the* election, and plays a mean game of golf.

What he does not know is that these conversations are the highlight of Greta's day. When she's home, after she's put her kid to bed, she stares out her bedroom window, looking past what's there, and tries to recall every word Jimmy Nolan has ever said to her.

On a very ordinary Thursday, after working late, Jimmy Nolan decides to stop by the diner, add a little variety to his routine. The place is nearly empty when he takes a seat at his regular booth. Greta is still working, and she looks a bit more worn than usual. Her long hair is unkempt, wayward strands creeping out of the ponytail that draws her features back. Light shadows line her eyes and Jimmy imagines that this is what Greta must look like when she first wakes up—drowsy and succulent.

Greta smiles when she sees Jimmy, leans against his table, and drawls, "Jimmy Nolan, is it tomorrow already?"

"So you do know my name?"

Greta cocks her head to the side and fishes her notepad from her waist. "What can I get ya?"

"Coffee. A burger, rare, with everything and a side of onion rings."

She pens his order, chewing on her lower lip, then taps the top of his head with her notepad and heads back to the kitchen. Jimmy watches her go, the way her hips rock back and forth. He hopes she knows he is watching. Greta hopes Jimmy is setting aside his polite ways long enough to watch. When she brings his food, the only other customer in the place, a tired-looking trucker with nicotine-stained fingers and a dent in his lower lip, pays his bill and leaves. Jimmy realizes that save for the short-order cook watching TV in the kitchen, he and Greta are alone for the first time.

Greta sets Jimmy's plate before him and takes a seat, pouring some ketchup on a napkin before sliding a finger through an onion ring and twirling it in the air. "At last," she says, winking. Greta takes a bite of the onion ring and wills Jimmy Nolan to take an interest in something other than casual conversation with her.

Jimmy feels a blush creeping from his chest up through his neck and into his cheeks. He turns away and coughs as he assembles his hamburger— bun, ketchup, mustard, burger, mustard, ketchup, lettuce, tomato, onion, bun. The pickles he eats separately, one by one.

"You play with your food the way I used to play with LEGOs," Greta remarks.

Jimmy shrugs. "I know how I like my food."

Greta takes another bite of the onion ring she has stolen. "That's good," she says. "That you know what you like."

Jimmy can't help but grin. "Long day?"

Greta swings one leg out to the side, her blue skirt slowly inching up her thighs. "Every day is a long day."

Jimmy nods as if he can understand what it's like to stand on your feet for ten hours. He brings his burger to his mouth, notices his hands, and blushing, quickly takes a bite, dropping his food and hiding his hands under the table.

Greta rubs her chin thoughtfully. "I could try and devise a scheme to get you in the bathroom, but I already know how to unclog a toilet."

Jimmy leans forward, one leg twitching uncontrollably. "Why do you need to get me in the bathroom?"

Greta stands, smoothing her outfit. "Follow me."

Again Jimmy watches her walk away, stares down at his plate, and at the empty space across from him. He practically trips over his own feet as he extricates himself from the booth. His leg still twitching, he makes his way to the bathroom and pauses, studying the two doors before him. After a quick debate, he curses himself for quibbling with himself about which door she's behind and decides that Greta will be in the ladies' room. Greta is sitting over the sink, her ass against the faucet, legs slightly spread.

"Took you long enough."

"I got lost."

Greta laughs and Jimmy shivers. She has a vulgar, voluptuous laugh, one that echoes like his. She reaches out and takes hold of the narrow length of his tie, pulling Jimmy closer. He stumbles forward, falling into her, his nose pressed against her cotton blouse. He takes a deep breath. She smells like grease, tobacco smoke, lipstick, and a perfume he's never smelled before—a perfume only broads wear, he thinks. Shyly, Jimmy takes hold of Greta's waist and looks up at her.

"Jimmy Nolan," she says.

Taking a deep breath, Jimmy brushes his lips across Greta's. He memorizes every faint groove, the way her full lips come to a point in the middle and never seem to close completely. It's been a long time since he's kissed any woman, and an even longer time since he's had the opportunity to kiss a woman properly—wetly, with lots of tongue, hard enough to leave his lips swollen the next day. The tip of his tongue slips past her lips and he traces the hard edges of her teeth. Her tongue is thick and flat, salty. Greta's legs spread farther apart and she wraps them around Jimmy's waist before clasping the back of his neck, letting her long fingernails dig into his skin. Jimmy Nolan tries to become the kind of guy broads pick up in a diner. He undoes her ponytail and wraps her soft, thick hair around his fingers. He growls, Greta arches, and her breasts press against the flat of his chest.

Pulling her head back, Jimmy drags his fingers from the tip of Greta's chin, along the column of her throat, to the top of her blouse, hurriedly undoing each button, one of them flying off in the process and landing on the floor with a loud ping. Greta is silent, but she kisses Jimmy with an intensity that frightens him. Beneath his slacks, his cock is hard against the soft fabric of his boxers. He brings his mouth lower, sinking his teeth into Greta's neck, pulling at the tight flesh and tracing the red marks he makes with his tongue. He wants Greta to stare at herself in the mirror in the morning, draw her fingers over the bruise he will leave. He wants the world to know Jimmy Nolan was here.

Jimmy looks up for a moment. He almost doesn't recognize himself in the mirror. His face is flushed, a sheen of sweat covering his forehead and upper lip. His eyes are flashing, nostrils flaring. Greta tugs his tie again, and Jimmy takes her small breasts into his slender hands, enjoying the weight of them as his fingers follow her curves, squeezing softly. He pulls each of Greta's nipples into his mouth, suckling them. The textures of her body against his tongue send shivers down his spine, and thighs. Greta presses her nails into his shoulders. Jimmy starts to nibble her nipples with his teeth. He persists until Greta is moaning and grinding against the hollow sink beneath her. Jimmy rests his nose against Greta's breastbone. She smells different now.

He doesn't bother removing her skirt. He knows how broads like it when they're being fucked in bathrooms. She instinctively raises her ass as he shoves her skirt up around her waist. He can hardly control himself as he slides her panties, a purple, silky thong—the kind a broad wears—down her legs, leaves them dangling from one ankle. Greta takes hold of one of Jimmy's hands, and one by one, pulls his long fingers into her mouth to the third knuckle, lathing them with her tongue, grazing them with her teeth. She makes loud, sloppy sounds that remind him of her kisses.

"You have beautiful hands," she whispers. "The first thing I noticed about you."

Jimmy is startled. He looks at his hand in her mouth, imagines reaching into her body, reaching past the viscera in search of something he can't quite put to words. He can't help but say, *thank you*. Greta takes the hand she is sucking, pushes it down the center of her body, leaving a wide, moist trail. She firmly plants his hand against her cunt and stares at Jimmy.

"You have beautiful hands," she says again.

Jimmy nods silently and lowers his mouth between her thighs, licking the warm spaces between his splayed fingers. Greta shivers and Jimmy shyly spreads his fingers, exposing the downy strip of her pussy lips. Sliding his tongue between them, he licks upward. Her taste changes from subtle to thick and sharp along this intimate geography. Her clit, when he reaches it, is softer than he imagined, but sensitive, her thighs trembling each time his tongue passes over.

"Your hands," Greta says hoarsely. "It's your hands I want."

He rises slightly and leans forward, resting his forehead against the upper swell of her breasts, and slides two fingers inside Greta as he presses his thumb to her clit. She's tight—tighter than he expected—and her wetness slides around his fingers like warm water. Greta is tracing his shoulders with her fingers and has carefully wedged one of her feet between their bodies, pressing the arch against the hard length of his cock. For reasons he can't explain, Jimmy Nolan notes her flexibility.

Jimmy slides a third finger inside Greta. She adjusts, spreading her legs wider. He twists his hand and arches his fingers upward, exploring the silky smoothness covering hard bone, the way her cunt curves. He tries to find the deepest, pulsing part of her, though he is not quite sure that such a thing is possible.

The opening of Greta's cunt puckers around his fingers. Taking a deep breath, Jimmy lets his pinky slip inside of her. Slowly, at first, he begins to fuck her with his fingers, sliding them in to the third knuckle, then pulling back, then sliding back in. There is a sound—a soft, squishy sound that Jimmy Nolan hopes he will never forget. Greta begins rocking her hips, and she moans, a high-pitched, squeaky moan that borders on laughter. Her thighs are slick with sweat. The bathroom reeks of disinfectant, grease, and sex.

Greta pounds Jimmy's back. "More," she says tersely. "More."

Jimmy fucks Greta harder. Faster. The muscles in his arm burn from shoulder to wrist, but he doesn't stop. He presses his thumb against the palm of his hand and slides his entire, delicate, finely boned hand inside Greta's cunt. His fingers curl into a fist and Jimmy Nolan thinks it is a marvelous feeling, the sensation of Greta's insides clinging to his hand. Greta lifts Jimmy's chin with one finger and forces him to look at her. Her expression is serious—one of intense concentration. Her eyes are cloudy, her lips open wide. Jimmy holds her gaze, grabbing Greta's ass with his other hand, thrusting his fist in and out of her with strokes that make her whole body tremble. Her moans are louder, throatier now. Jimmy doesn't know how much longer his arm will last, but he keeps fucking Greta, rolling his fist around inside of her, rubbing his knuckles against the soft, doughy pad just below her clit, his own hips rocking in rhythm with hers. His cock is throbbing and he knows that soon, very soon, he will come all over his boxers, and he'll have to walk home in the wet spot.

Greta throws herself back, her head hitting the dirty mirror. Jimmy blinks. Her cunt spasms around his hand, wetness oozing over his wrist, trickling along his forearm. He leans down, licking some of the moisture.

"Don't stop," Greta says through clenched teeth.

His hand feels raw, knuckles chafed. Jimmy catches a glimpse of the two of them in the mirror, their bodies entwined. He likes what he sees. After a final, husky groan, so low Jimmy can hardly hear it, Greta's body stills. He tries to pull his hand out, but Greta shakes her head.

"Not yet," she says.

They sit there, leaning against one another for a long while. Jimmy can hear the cook cleaning up the kitchen, leaving out the back door. They are silent, save for slow, heavy breathing. Finally, Greta kisses Jimmy's chin and nods. Slowly, Jimmy slides his hand out of Greta's pussy. He traces the soft, exquisitely soft folds of Greta's pussy lips with his narrow pinky. Greta takes his wrist again, pulls his hand to her lips, kisses the open palm, then closes his fingers over the memory of her lips. He smiles widely. Jimmy Nolan is dizzy, delirious. He is slightly incredulous that he has a broad like Greta in the palm of his slender, almost delicate, hand.

ᏚᎧ YES ᏚᎧ

Donna George Storey

THE FIRST TIME YOU SEE HER, she's dancing with another guy. She's a good dancer, which means what she's basically doing is fucking out there on the dance floor. But she's not fucking him. Her body is moving all on its own, her hips thrusting into air, her back rippling like silk, sucking the music up through the floor. She *is* the music. You can't take your eyes away from her ass and that bare band of skin above her jeans, shimmering with a fine film of sweat.

She turns and sees you staring.

You don't believe in love at first sight or auras or telepathy or any of that hippy-dippy shit, but at that instant a voice—not yours but a woman's voice, and how the hell that got inside your head you'll never know—it whispers to you.

Yes.

Later you run into her by the metal tub where they're keeping micro-brews on ice. She smiles. You take the opportunity to talk a little, make her laugh, get her phone number. She asks you to walk her to her car. The neighborhood's a little scary at this time of night, she says. As a reward for doing your Boy Scout duty, she lets you kiss her, long and hard, against the door of her Mini Cooper.

It's all so smooth and easy, you even start to think parties aren't so bad after all. Or maybe all those years you spent guarding the keg and stumbling home shit-faced drunk and alone because all the smooth-talking assholes got to the pretty girls first were just practice for this night, the one time you got it right.

The sex starts out great, and you have a feeling it's only going to get better.

It does. Each time you learn something new. How she gets all hot and squirmy when you stroke the soft crease of her elbow with your fingertip. How she almost sobs when you push her knees up to her chest and go in deep—but then afterward strokes her belly tenderly and tells you how good it feels to be sore there, like you're still inside her.

Then there's the time she asks you to come on her face. She's shy about it at first, mumbling into your shoulder about a fantasy she's had for a long time, but she'll understand if you don't want to try it.

Of course, you do.

As you straddle her chest and take your cock in your hand, it feels like something you've wanted, too, since before you can remember. It makes you rock-hard to see her spread out beneath you, a meadow of smooth neck and cheeks and forehead, waiting for the rain. She's playing with herself as she watches you, with a look that's horny and curious and scared all at the same time. Her face is bright pink, and you can smell the seashore scent of her and hear that beautiful squish-squish of finger on sopping clit. You time your strokes to hers and it's like you're touching her and she's touching you. She seems to know when you're about to shoot your wad because she closes her eyes and tilts her head back like a kid playing in a summer storm. When the first party streamer of come pelts her cheek, she sucks in her breath, then lets out a whimper with each new spurt. When you're done, she's a mess—beads of spunk in her hair, a shiny little puddle in the hollow above her chin.

She's still playing with herself and you reach down and start smearing the slick, soapy stuff all over her cheeks and lips. You give her nipples a coating, too, plus a pinch for good measure, causing her to arch and quiver. Then you start to feed her, spreading your spunk over her lips so she can lick it off, drop by drop. She tells you afterward that she loves the taste of your semen when she's turned on. She says it's like rolling around on a newly mown lawn, licking a dish of vanilla crème pudding that she snuck from the kitchen while it was still warm. Sure her clothes are getting stained and her mom's gonna be mad she's eaten dessert before dinner, but it's all so slick and creamy and deliciously naughty, she doesn't care.

You love it, too. The way she moans and sucks your finger like it was a cock when she comes. The way she opens herself to you, a little more each time.

You think how a new woman is like a pack of baseball cards. You tear open the wrapper, your whole body aching with the hope that maybe this is finally the one with the 1952 Topps Mickey Mantle rookie card waiting inside. But time after time, all you get are common ones, hardly worth tossing in the drawer.

Now you look down and see her face, all shiny with your spunk. Her eyes are shining, too. You remember the chicks who winced at the mere mention of swallowing, who wouldn't even go down on you at all, and you see before you old Mickey in mint condition, holding that yellow bat over his shoulder as he gazes heavenward into a golden future. And you wouldn't trade this for all the money in the world.

The next time, her little surprise for you is to bake cookies, not from a mix but special ones with white chocolate and raspberries and fancy liqueur. She says white, sweet, creamy things make her think of you.

You pretend to read the paper while she stirs up the batter and hums like some TV mom from the fifties. But she's not wearing an apron and pearls. You can see her nipples through her shirt and she has on the same jeans she had on the night you met, with a wide leather belt that makes you think of a slave girl you saw in a history book in school. Back then you wanted to do all kinds of nasty things to the girl in the picture, things you didn't have a name for.

You know what to call them now.

She waves you over, scoops up a swirl of batter on her finger, and licks it off slowly with the pointy tip of her tongue. She offers you a fingerful and you take it in your mouth. It's sweet—all butter and sugar and a healthy dash of booze—but that's not what makes you dizzy. It's the taste of her underneath, her flesh and her spit, which has the same faintly musky taste as her pussy. She told you once she smells different to herself, tastes different, too, since she met you. As if you've marked her.

That's the flavor you're searching for on her skin.

You think of taking her right here, lifting her up on the counter. Or bending her over the kitchen table, doggy-style. But that little voice, the one you've learned to listen to, whispers again.

Wait.

So you pull away and slap her ass and say, "No more fun until you clean up these dirty dishes."

She pouts, but her eyes twinkle, and she gets right to work, humming her happy homemaker tune.

You walk to your bedroom. Already the plan is taking shape. You remember a story she told about her college boyfriend, who begged and begged her to let him fuck her ass, until she gave in, but it was lousy. He was too rough and it hurt and he was a real wuss about the mess afterward. She'd never done it since, and wasn't sure she ever wanted to again.

In your book, if a guy begs a woman to let him fuck her ass, he should at least be a gentleman about it. You promise yourself you won't be like him.

You won't beg.

You open the drawer where you keep your condoms—plain, lubricated, flavored, for her pleasure—pick out a plain one, get the bottle of lube, and tuck them in your jeans pocket.

She's bending over to put the last mixing bowl in the dishwasher—she really does have a beautiful ass—and sure enough, the place is spic and span. You come up behind her and wrap her in your arms. She sighs and starts to turn around. That's when you squeeze her just hard enough to hold her in place.

"Put your hands on the counter and bend forward," you say. Your voice comes out deeper. Firm but kind, part-drill-sergeant, part-favorite-uncle.

She snorts. "What?"

"You heard what I said. Are you going to be a good girl? Or do you want to hear what happens to bad girls who don't do as they're told?"

She giggles, but leans forward anyway. It won't be long before you'll have her making other noises.

You pull her shirt up over her breasts, glad you don't have to struggle with a bra this time. As you flick her nipples, you enjoy the silky sway of her flesh, ripe fruit dangling from a tree. "Can you feel it in your pussy when I touch you here?"

"Yes." Her voice comes out tight and small.

"Is it making you wet?"

"Yes."

"I want to check. I hope you're not being a bad girl and telling me a lie." She shakes her head.

You feel for her zipper, then yank her jeans and underwear down to her knees. You slide your hand between her legs. She wasn't lying. You play with her for a while, just to feel the lips swell and her clit stand out hard like a little diamond.

"You are wet. Very wet. Too bad. It's such a waste."

She freezes, mid-moan. She doesn't say it, but you feel the question in her body.

That's when you take out the lube and pop open the top. You squeeze a few drops on your finger and smooth it along the valley of her ass.

"Don't," she cries, lurching away, but she's hobbled by her jeans and only manages to fall against the counter.

You hold her and hush her and tell her it's okay.

She whimpers, but you know she's back with you because she leans forward to offer her ass again.

"We're going to take this slow since it's only your second time. I understand the first time wasn't so pleasant for you." All the while you're stroking her soft crevice very gently, then circling around the puckered entrance. "Is this pleasant?"

She lets out an "ah" from deep in her belly. Her shoulders are heaving. You move your other hand back on clit duty. She's drenched down there.

"Push your asshole open for me. That's right. You do want this, don't you? You want me to fuck you in the ass."

Her little cry and the gush of her juices in your hand is answer enough, but you wait for the word, the sweet sibilance of it: *Yesss*.

You've gone in the back door before, but never like this, so carefully, like it was a sacrament. You pour out more lube. You anoint her with it and she opens, little by little. You slide a finger in and leave it there until she softens even more. All the while you keep tap-tapping her clit until she's shaking and panting and begging you to do it, then you roll on the condom, oil up, and knock lightly against the entrance.

She gasps, but it slides in easy once you get the head of your cock through the doorjamb. Later she tells you she's never felt so full, as if your cock were pressing all the way up into her skull.

"Try to move now," you say, low and soft in her ear. "Nice and slow. That's a good girl. You like it, don't you? You like the things I tell you to do."

She's in the zone, now, beyond words. Her back is flushed and her head nods—yes, yes, yes—each time she thrusts back onto you.

You work her clit faster as her ring of muscle grips and glides up and down your cock. It's tight and good, but it's not like her pussy. Beyond that sweet rubber band at the opening, there is nothing. It makes you understand fisting—a weird gay thing you tried not to think much about before—but you understand now, because you want to be so deep inside her you can nestle right up against her beating heart—but for now her pretty pink cock ring will have to fill that hunger. That and the voice in your head—*Oh, god, you're fucking my ass, you're fucking my ass and it's good, oh, it's good*—and when she comes you really feel her spasms, milking you, squeezing you, and then you come, thrusting freely, hurting her maybe, but she's crying out, "Yes, yes, yes," and you know it's okay.

In the beginning you don't really plan any of it. Sometimes you just take advantage of a lucky set of circumstances. Like the night your old friend, Sean, stays over on his way back from a year at his company's Asia office. She offers to make dinner, and you say yes, because you like showing her off to your friends.

She bakes her special desserts again. You both call them Fuck-Her-Ass Cookies now, although she offers them to Sean as Raspberry Surprise Bars. When she goes off to get the coffee, Sean follows her with his eyes, like he's still hungry.

"Do you realize I haven't had any action in almost a year? Nothing. I barely even talked to a woman. It was just too depressing to pay for it. Oh man, it's been harsh. But you seem to have a pretty good thing going here."

You have to agree. She's perfect, just like that old saying—a lady in the living room, a whore in the bedroom. And sometimes the other way around, too.

It's then you get your next idea.

You pour him a little more brandy. You want him to be drunk, to think only with his dick. Since you met her, you don't drink much. You don't need numbness, it's sensation you crave, so clear and sharp it cuts into your flesh. Your dick is still important, sure, but sometimes it's your head that throbs with a tight ache, filled to bursting with dark, nasty longings. All you have to do is touch her, even look at her, and suddenly it's not trapped inside you anymore.

And so, after the fuck-her-ass cookies are eaten, you suggest some after-dinner games.

The two of them frown and you know what they're thinking: Poker? Charades? Truth or dare?

What you have in mind is a little of all three.

"This game is called Secret Desires, and the lady always goes first," you explain as you pull the long chiffon scarf from your pocket with a magician's flourish. Sean looks clueless, but she blushes because she knows you use that scarf for one thing—to tie her up sometimes when you have sex.

You walk behind the sofa and look down at her. Her chest rises and falls in quick, shallow breaths. She leans her head back and meets your gaze, her eyes so big and wet and open you could fall right into them. But not yet. You make the scarf into a blindfold, knot it tightly around her eyes, and go sit in the recliner, leaving the two of them alone on the sofa.

Sean blinks stupidly, but there's no hiding that bulge in his pants. She is every man's dream sitting there, a scarf over her eyes, chest heaving, red lips moist and slightly parted.

"I'll tell you a little secret about my girlfriend, Sean, old buddy. She likes to show off. You should see her when we go to parties. She's practically spilling out of her shirt and her jeans ride so low you get an eyeful of cleavage there, too. I don't know why she looks so prim and proper tonight. Let's let Sean see the real you, sweetie. Why don't you take off your blouse for him?"

She sits there, without moving, for the longest five seconds of your life.

You realize you're holding your breath. Even after all these months, you can never be totally sure you've gotten it right. You lead her to the edge of the cliff and give her that nudge, but she decides if she'll fly or fall. And wherever she goes, she takes you there with her.

Slowly, very slowly, her hand moves to the first button. You let out a sigh of relief and shift in the chair to adjust your boner.

She inches her blouse over her shoulders and pulls her arms from the sleeves. At your command, she takes off her bra, too, and sets it carefully beside her on the sofa. Eye candy's the word for her now. Her breasts are so pretty and tasty looking, the aureoles like disks of raspberry candy on the creamy skin.

"Why don't you show Sean what you like to do to your nipples when you're alone and feeling in the mood?"

"Jesus," Sean murmurs.

She's being a good girl, doing just what you ask, rubbing her palms in slow circles over her breasts, twisting the stiffened tips between her fingers. It's not just an act, either. Her chest is flushed and she's squirming and sighing.

"This is great, honey. Sean is really getting a better sense of you as a person," you say. "But I don't think he understands yet how much this is turning you on. Why don't you take off your pants and show our guest how wet your pussy is, too."

She winces under the blindfold and flushes a brighter shade of pink. But a second later she's shimmying out of her pants and underwear.

"Spread your legs," you say.

She obeys.

From where you're sitting, you can see her pink folds glistening with moisture.

Sean's eyes bulge. The cords stand out in his neck.

"Spread your legs a little more," you say. "That's right, let's get a good stretch. Now I want you to play with yourself. That's the part you like best, isn't it? Showing guys how horny you are?"

She lets out a little "oh" of shame and desire. Her hand moves slowly, as if she were dragging it through water, to nestle between her legs. Will she really do anything you ask? Part of you wants to stop now, send Sean off to bed with his fist and his dreams, but that voice fills your head again.

More. I want more.

"Yes, you've gotten our guest quite worked up with your show, you horny little slut. I'll bet he wouldn't mind at all if you bent over and sucked his cock now. After all, that would only be polite."

She nods, as though in a dream, and moves closer to him, groping her way like a blind person.

"Kneel between his legs," you tell her.

She crouches and fumbles for his zipper. Sean snaps out of zombie mode to help her pull his pants down. His cock springs free. He's big, but not so big you have anything to worry about.

She doesn't seem to need directions anymore, because right away she starts licking his shaft with the flat of her tongue, quick, teasing little laps. Then she tickles the sweet spot beneath his swollen cock head with the tip of her tongue. He groans and paws her hair.

You're enjoying the view, the way her jaw muscles bulge and her cheeks hollow out when she takes him between her lips. She's definitely making an effort to do her best. You wonder if her eyes are closed under the scarf and if she's pretending she's someone else. Or he's someone else. You wonder if it's turning her on as much as it is you.

Sean is going crazy, humping up into her mouth, his face all twisted up with lust, and finally he gets the words out that have probably been on his mind for some time. "Hey, is it okay if I fuck her?"

"Absolutely, but remember, we're still playing Secret Desire, so you'll use up your turn." You laugh, tossing him a condom.

Then you add, "But no anal, okay?" You want to keep that part of her for yourself.

"Yeah, sure, no problem," Sean mumbles. He's not going to press his luck.

You wait just long enough to see what he's going to do. He lays her out on the sofa and gets on top. She grunts softly when he enters her, then she turns her head toward you, just like the night you met. And just like that night, you sense the connection, through the scarf, through the hot, damp air of the room. She feels you watching, and that's the only thing that matters—she tells you later this is exactly what was going through her mind.

Sure, Sean is the one pumping away on top of her and kneading her breast like it was bread dough, but he's doing it for his own pleasure. He isn't thinking of her.

That's the difference. You're always thinking of her.

You silently thank your dear friend Sean for being such a boring, predictable fuck as you get up and walk out of the room. No need to stay for the finish. By which you mean his finish, not hers.

Because, of course, you've saved your Secret Desire for last.

You go to your bedroom, undress, put on your robe, brush your teeth, take a piss, and lie down on your bed to get ready for your turn. Voices drift from the living room. Oddly enough, they sound friendly, like a real couple in the afterglow. She laughs. Your cock stiffens—you'd lost some of your hard-on while you got ready for bed—and you realize you're angry, too. You gave that bastard permission to fuck her, not talk to her, and you're tempted to call to her to get her ass in here right away. But you wait, your skin getting hotter and your cock harder, until she comes into the bedroom. The scarf is gone and she's dressed, but her expression is naked with excitement.

You know she's saved the best part for you.

First you tell her to lock the door. You don't want Sean nosing around for an extra pillow. He's taken enough of your hospitality for tonight.

She strips and joins you on the bed, pressing her wet crotch against your thigh like a little dog in heat.

"Did you like my game? Did it make you hot?" you ask, in that deep, smooth voice she likes.

She nods into your shoulder.

"Did you come for him?"

She pauses, as if she's wondering what the right answer is. But of course there is no right answer.

She shakes her head.

"I'm disappointed in you," you lie. "You've been very rude to our guest." You lift her on top of you. She plants her knees on the bed and lowers herself right onto you. No condom, just skin against skin, your cock nestled in the warm, wet glove of her bare pussy. "The next time I give you to someone, I want you to come for him. Do you understand?"

She nods, grinding her crotch against your belly, desperately, as if she's afraid you'll tell her to stop before she reaches her climax. But you won't. Not this time.

"Do you promise? I want to hear you say it." Of course you're not sure there'll be a next time. There are other places you want to take her, new places where no one's ever been.

She's thrusting now, jerking her hips the way she does when she's close.

"Yes, I promise," she whispers.

"I was right, wasn't I? You are a show-off. You liked playing with your tits and masturbating for him. You liked making him hard." You spank her, slow and steady. With her cheeks spread in a straddle, you can land every few slaps on her sensitive crack. She makes a low animal sound and pushes her ass out to receive the next blow.

"Yes."

She says your words are as good as your hands or tongue or cock at turning her on. It turns you on, too, to open her with your voice and slip inside her head. It's like wandering through a forest in the nighttime with huge stars winking in the trees like jewels.

"You liked fucking him, too. You liked it because I told you to do it. You'll do anything for me, won't you?"

Your chest swells with the possibility of it, because you can do anything together. You can push her over the edge and catch her at the bottom, soft and safe in your arms. You can watch her dance and be inside her all at the same time, because you are the music she's dancing to now, faster and faster.

She cries out a response, but you know it's the answer to another question, the one that matters more than anything. Because it's the sweetest sound a man can hear, a woman you love coming around your cock, moaning, sobbing, sighing, and whispering that one magic word.

Yes.

✥ A PERFECT FIT ✥

Katya Andreevna

IT WAS ONE OF THOSE DAYS. I spilled coffee all over my desk. The copy machine broke down. While I was receiving a twenty-three-page fax, the paper kept jamming and the machine printed the same page over and over. As soon as the church bells next door struck six, I was out the door and headed, where else, but to Macy's, the largest department store in the world.

My feet slapped against the pavement as I overtook slow-moving commuters. I dipped into the street to cut around a pack of them, all smoking, and slipped into a moving revolving door. Inside, the cool air and the perfume enveloped me. I charged past some dazed tourists to the escalator and jogged by several women with shopping bags and a kid drooling on the handrail.

I hit the designer shoe section and, slowing, breathed deeply. I started cruising at the far end, keeping the truly expensive shoes for my climax.

A pair of oxblood pumps drew me. *Too preppy,* I thought, but the warm color of the leather made me stroke them and hold them close to my face so I could take in their rich scent. Then a pair of blue suede loafers caught my eye. I checked to see that no other shopper was looking and rubbed their soft skin against my face. The delicate perfume filled my head. I closed my eyes and drank in the leather-laden air.

I felt someone looking at me, but I didn't turn to confront the eyes at my back. *Probably just some store detective*, I thought, and kept moving toward the even more expensive footwear.

Then I saw them. The heel was probably higher than I could comfortably wear, but it was exquisitely crafted. Chunky and solid, yet elegant, the heel, which arched toward the instep just slightly, would leave a half-moon print behind the delicately pointed toe. The rich burgundy leather called out for my touch.

I approached slowly, studying the play of light on the subtle sheen that complemented this pair. I leaned toward them as if greeting a dog that I didn't know, hands at my sides, ready for rejection. I could feel my heart beating in my sex as I moved a hand to meet them. I caressed the heel with one finger and gasped. The leather felt as smooth as fifty-year-old port, as soft as wet labia. My hand closed around the heel gently. Realizing I was still being watched, I lifted one shoe, as if to read its designer label, and inhaled deeply.

"What size would you like to see, ma'am?" a husky female voice asked me from behind.

"Seven, please." I smiled at the salesgirl, a tall brunette. Her eyes pried into me, but she acted cool.

"Would you like to see anything else? You know, we're closing soon." Her dark eyes held mine. I shook my head, still clutching the curve of the heel.

The salesgirl was back before I knew it with a glint in her eye. She directed me to a seat and opened the box with a flourish. Slightly larger than the display pair, the shoes looked bolder and more powerful. I slipped out of my flats.

The salesgirl lifted one burgundy shoe out of the box and, with her other hand, took my arch. The firmness of her fingers made the pulse between my legs grow stronger. She slid my toes inside and smoothed the shoe over my heel, allowing her cool fingers to linger briefly at my ankle.

I gazed at the perfect shoe on my left foot. The salesgirl stepped back, wiping curly hair from her forehead. I followed her lead to the mirror near the cash register. She held the other shoe out to me. As I reached for it, she pulled away. A slight smile played across her chestnut-colored lips. Again I reached. And again she withdrew.

"Tsk, tsk," she said, holding the shoe out. "Patience." I stood my ground. She moved closer. My eyes focused on the shoe, but I saw her high breasts rise and fall with her breath. My bare foot on the carpet seemed glued to the spot. My eyes climbed, cautiously. Her face was utterly still, but I detected movement behind her deep eyes.

Slowly, she directed the shoe at me. She touched the tip of my breast with the toe and began to circle around my nipple. I closed my eyes as my nipple hardened and poked against my silk top. She pinched it firmly through my shirt and led me into the storage area. I was surrounded by shoes, boxes and boxes of them emitting their opium. She applied the toe of the shoe to my other breast.

Air rasped through my lungs. I clutched a metal shelf, my knees were so weak. Where had this woman been all my other visits? I kept my eyes closed for fear she would stop. I heard a register across the floor beginning to cash out.

I reached down and took the shoe from my left foot. I cradled it to my face, pressed it against my cheek. This leather had an unusually sweet bouquet that went right to my head. The salesgirl's cold fingers covered my hand, loosening my grip from the burgundy prize. All the while she held my nipple firm.

"No. I want it." I whined as she dragged the shoe from my cheek.

"Show us how much," she said.

She held the shoe around the middle, just in front of my mouth. I leaned forward and kissed the delicate leather, then unleashed my eager tongue. I licked the toe as she moved her hand downward. I ran my tongue along the side and dipped it into the crack where the upper meets the sole.

"Yes, baby," she hissed through closed teeth as I squatted to the floor. I lay down on my stomach and thoroughly explored that crack, tracing it with my tongue from the point of the toe to the back of the heel. Her breathing grew deeper and more rapid above me.

Kneeling in her short skirt, she rubbed the crescent of the heel along my bottom lip. Momentarily I wondered if another salesperson might see us, but then the shoe in front of me absorbed my attention. At first I caressed delicately with just my lips, but soon I began swirling my tongue around the heel, pondering the slight metallic flavor of the inner part of the heel and its contrast with the rich burgundy leather that wrapped its curved back. She moved the heel deeper into my mouth, then drew it away so my lips could barely reach its tip.

"Down," she said as I turned over and moved to sit up. She moved my hand from where it had drifted between my own legs. "Lie still," she commanded.

My cunt absorbed her words and burned with them. I lay flat on my back and closed my eyes. All was quiet for a moment, so still, in fact, that

I wondered if she had disappeared from my side. I held myself down on the floor, my mind racing, anticipating what was to come.

She laughed slightly, a rich, throaty sound. The heel caressed under the arch of my foot and across my instep. I felt my toes parted. She ran the heel between my first and second toes, back and forth, and I gasped.

"Sh-sh," she replied and began to trace the bones around my ankle with that heel. She moved up my calf slowly, then teased at the back of my knee. I twitched on the floor, trying to keep my body still as she had commanded.

"You want it, don't you?" she asked in a low, steady voice.

I moaned. "Y-yes," I stammered. My heart beat fiercely in the damp space between my legs.

Abruptly she pulled up my skirt. She played the heel over my knee then moved up, stroking my inner thigh. She rubbed my groin with the whole shoe and my hips rose involuntarily. She passed the shoe across my belly, along the bikini line. I was afraid to look at what she was doing; afraid if I did she would stop.

I moaned loudly as she dipped the heel under the waist of my panties. She brushed my bush hairs one way, and then the other. She slid the heel slowly down till it was just at the edge of my slit. I shifted my hips so I could feel its slight pressure on my clit.

"Please," I whispered hoarsely, looking up at her. My face was flushed and I felt sweat breaking out all over my body. I had never been so excited. "Please," I repeated.

She pushed on the heel a bit, making my clit, and my whole being, jump. She ripped down my panties. The sole grazed my bush, exciting every hair follicle. She ran the delicious shoe between my thigh and outer lip. The soft leather felt perfect against my delicate skin. I thought I would either come right then or die from arousal.

"Yes, now," I pleaded. My burning inner lips parted. The crescent heel slipped between the folds of my waiting flesh. Then withdrew.

"Do it. Do it now," I croaked. I couldn't stand any more.

"Certainly, madam." She laughed again. And then it was inside of me, that perfect leather-covered heel. Something in my chest loosed and my limbs flopped on the floor as if a spring that had held me together had finally come undone.

She pumped the heel into me. My head rocked from side to side. She placed the shoe's mate in my hand and I held it against my cheek.

"Deeper," I cried, and she plunged. The sole of the shoe massaged my clit while the heel pressed ever inward.

The words "yes, yes, yes," poured from my lips as I sucked in the scent of the shoe's mate. This time, as she slid the heel deep inside me, she twisted the shoe and pressed it hard against my G-spot.

"Harder," I whispered.

She rammed the heel inside me, holding at the top of the upswing. Her speed and force increased and all I knew was my smell, the pulsing between my legs, and the shoe, the perfect shoe inside of me where it fit so well.

My body had begun to tense and tremble. The air entering my lungs came in short gasps. I raised my head slightly, gazed at the salesgirl's face intent on her work. Beyond her a mirror held the scene: I lay legs parted, the heel of the perfect shoe disappearing into me. I watched the heel slide out and then plunge. All my muscles jerked, my spine arched up, my head fell back.

The heel still inside me, I dropped against the floor, turning my flushed face to the other shoe. My ears began to ring.

She slowly pulled the shoe from between my legs. Patting my bush with one hand, she placed the shoe next to its mate on the floor. She stood. Towering over me, she smoothed her skirt and straightened her employee name tag.

"They're a perfect fit," she said.

"Yes," I croaked, scrambling up from the floor. "The heel's not too high?"

"They look great . . ." she paused, "on. They suit you."

"Yes," I said, smiling and pulling out my credit card. "Yes, they do."

ॐ PARTS FOR WHOLES ॐ
Monmouth

First Movement

Let's begin with my finger. My index finger, to be exact, held snug in the anxious grip of a rectum that is unaccustomed to the intrusion.

If she thrusts down, it'll dislocate my finger.

The finger is there by invitation. Which doesn't mean that it hasn't encountered any resistance along the way.

"We go all the way," she had whispered, voice a little shaky. "Whatever I say, you can't take no for an answer."

"No, please . . ." she pants now, breathless.

Let's move on to her eyes. Lovely, translucent, gray eyes—sharp, intelligent. Blind. They can see nothing now, wrapped in her own satin-lined blindfold secured around her head with an elastic band and a black nylon stocking. When I undressed her, I unrolled the fragile garment so carefully down her thigh that she was startled to feel me wrap it around over her blindfold. I tucked the knot under her ponytail.

She has her hair up because I like to see her lips. Plus, it's useful—I know how she hates it when the blindfold slips.

Outside, walking along like two perfectly normal pedestrians, she'd stopped in front of a shop window and taken out her lipstick. We'd smiled at our reflections in the glass as she'd begun to apply it. "You love seeing me do this, don't you?" she'd asked. I'd laughed, because I'd had nothing clever to say about being so obvious.

Now for her hands. At this moment her fingers are still a bit sticky, slick with her own juices and my saliva from when I told her to sit up straight, take them out of her dripping cunt, and hold her hands out in front of her.

Waiting, arms extended, she gasped when she felt my lips enfolding her wet fingers. Her fingers still in my mouth, I slapped the soft, leather cuffs on her wrists. First one, then the other.

Now they carry her weight. She is on her knees in bed, wrists connected with a steel clip, hooked to a length of chain fastened to the wooden frame of the bed. She has already pulled at it a few times to test the security of her restraints.

Arching her back, stretching like a cat, she pushes against my finger. Not bucking. Not dislocating. Driving me deeper inside of her a full inch above the knuckle.

"You know how far I can go," she'd said to my reflection in the window. Lipstick hovering. "Tonight, let's pretend as if we didn't know."

Let's look at her lips. Puffed, blood-filled, perhaps a bit sore. The lipstick is worn off—a couple of slutty smudges that suggest that I may already have had my way with her kneeling on the floor, wrists chained to a bedpost, sinking my aching, hard cock into her hungry, warm mouth.

No hands allowed.

Just soft, red lips encircling my shaft, dripping with saliva, my hand grasping a tangle of her hair. Cock hitting the back of her mouth. Deep, muffled moans, from the pit of her belly.

This is behind us now, in the moment of the finger buried inside her. I am waiting for her to push once more, grinding down all the way so that there is nowhere for my finger to go, but back out again. It will be replaced with something harder, larger.

Second Movement

Let's start again, this time with the urgent throbbing between her legs, the sensitive, engorged nub of nerves and blood twitching in between the lips of her pussy. She's glistening with moisture. She's blind, feeling my hand reaching around her hips (yes, the finger is still where it was), when she lets out an encouraging, barely audible, "Yes . . ."

My hand comes to rest palm down on the swell of her belly, just above the mound. Pressing lightly I can feel the contractions—her crotch is throbbing, open, begging to be touched. I keep my hand perfectly still, the tips of my fingers grazing the topmost hairs. No indication that it is going anywhere soon. Another twitch.

This whole time I have not touched her pussy. Neither has she.

I keep it that way. I turn my finger slowly, buried almost all the way in her anus. First one way, then the other. By the end of the second half-turn, she has taken it all the way in. There is no farther to go. I begin to withdraw.

"No, no, no . . ."

"Yes." Seriously, calmly. "Just keep relaxed, stay open, stay like this . . ." I kiss her raised buttock, nibbling a little.

I place a second finger alongside the first. The longer, middle one. I add another dab of lubricant and press back inside the tight, resistant opening. Up to the first bend.

She growls from somewhere near the pit of her stomach. Then she lets out a high-pitched aah and pushes herself back with enough force to ram my fingers all the way up her arse as far as they will go.

Then stop. Her head hanging down, lower lip between her teeth, biting in concentration. Slowly, I bend my fingers to push at her perineum, the wall of skin, muscle, and veins, looking for the sensitive spot on the other side.

"Aaahhh!" she *pushes* the sound out of herself.

I have a photo of her blindfolded, lying naked on her stomach, a pile of pillows wedged under her hips. Her head is raised toward the lens, and in the background her bottom's raised into the air. I took this photo on a phone camera. She heard the "click." "Did you take my picture?" she asked, a hint of anger.

"Do you trust me?" I asked.

She shook her head. I put her phone back into her bag.

When we kissed goodbye, I told her to check her phone for pictures.

Her ankle has a slender black snake circling it twice. This tattoo has always seemed to me like an invitation to place my hand on top of it, and grasp firmly—either to hold her still, or to spread her legs. Now, her tattooed ankle is beating against the mattress. She doesn't seem aware that she's doing this. Her hands are restrained with the cuffs, she's on her knees, back arched, pushing herself back on my two fingers buried in her arse. The thumps of her foot against the bed urge me on.

I press my fingers in as far as they'll go, and begin to rotate my hand slowly.

She lets out a long, steady hiss.

The worst thing I could possibly do to her right now is pull my fingers out, rip off her blindfold, untie her, and tell her she's had enough for tonight. She would claw my eyes out.

Instead I reach back and grab her by the tattooed ankle. Next time there'll be cuffs there, too.

"Stay still." I begin to remove my fingers from her tight hole very slowly. She knows what's next, and begins to whimper quietly, "No, no . . . don't go there. . . . That's not right. . . . Please fuck my pussy instead. . . . My pussy wants you. . . . Not there . . ."

I ignore her. I calmly describe what I'm doing, how I'm rolling on the condom, how hard my cock is, how big she's making it by begging like this. How cool the lube feels against my fingers. When I swipe a dab of it on her red, protruding anus, she stops protesting for a moment and lets out a long, deep sigh.

I'm ready. But first the little egg-shaped vibe. It's hers—about the size of a hen's egg, attached to a battery pack with controls. When I slip it in between the glistening lips of her pussy, it's the first time I've touched her there.

"What are you . . . ?" The "on" button shuts her up. The lowest setting, a gentle hum in her loins. I take my time, stroking her buttocks, massaging her rosebud with my lubricated thumb until I think she's ready. When I nudge my cock up against the opening, I can feel the soft vibrations of the egg inside her. Arching up suddenly, she drives herself against me. To keep my balance, I push back, and my cock is inside her, the head popping in, past the outer muscle. Still, still—my hands on her buttocks steady us. No hard and fast entry here. I am throbbing, my cock filling and stretching her, sinking farther inside.

The vibrating toy is right underneath the shaft of my cock, pushing it forward against the front of her cunt.

Her first orgasm comes without warning, shaking and screaming beneath me. If not for the restraints, she would have thrown me right off her back.

I lean forward, grab a pillow, and put it under her hips. Then I push us forward so she's resting on her stomach. It's been only a few minutes, but her arms shake with the strain. Prostrate on her stomach, she stretches out under me, spreading her legs even farther, riding the down wave of the first orgasm into the next. I begin to fuck her slowly, driving my cock in and out in long strokes, her tight, twitching arse enfolding me.

She buries her face in her pillow bunched against the headboard, and some last vestige of civilized neighborliness gives her the good sense to scream into it. If it hadn't been muffled, the sound would have brought someone knocking at the door. Her convulsing orgasmic frenzy feels so good around my cock that it just makes me want to hold back, to relish this a bit longer. But she's moaning in a way that suggests that she won't be able to take it. I pull her up again a bit roughly, and fuck her just the way I like—long strokes in and out of her tight bottom.

There is always a moment in these games when self-control vanishes. I drive in and out of her with no thought of whether she is getting any pleasure from being handled like my helpless fuck toy. I know that at this precise moment there is no restraint.

I recover from my orgasm and release her wrists. She's all right, stretching, feeling for me. The blindfold is hers to remove when she's ready—with permission. Right now she wants to be held, enfolded in the dark.

⸎ MILK ⸎
Michael Dorsey

MOSCOW IS BEAUTIFUL IN THE SPRING. All cities are beautiful in the spring, but Moscow is more beautiful because, after the Russian winter, Muscovites need it to be. And when overcoats and boots start to come off the women of the world, and ankles and knees and even thighs come in view of the desperate men of the world, Moscow's women are the most beautiful in the world—because they have to emerge from under more layers of shapeless clothing than the women of other great cities, and the miracle of being able to walk down the street and see a thousand different shapes and sizes of breasts pressed against a thousand different blouses and sweaters—that miracle has been longed for ardently through the dark and bitter months gone by.

This year the women of Moscow are more beautiful than ever. They have to be. The winter has never been harder. So many people are out of work. The homeless are everywhere. Food is scarce. The women are unbearably beautiful. Desire hangs shimmering in the air. This can only mean that there will be a great many more mouths to feed next winter, but now it is spring, and the people want to shake off the grim months behind and live again.

Still, the lines are long, and they are everywhere. Lines for bread, lines for sausage, for shoes, for milk.

Milk. When there was nothing else through the long, dark years to keep the country alive, there had at least been milk. Milk and vodka. Some prefer the vodka, but others cannot think of their home, of their nation, of life, without thinking of milk.

There is a young man now, going from line to line around the city. There are no lines at the milk stores today because there is no milk. The supplies were gone by noon, and it is now nearly three. But there are lines in front of certain garages and apartment blocks where the black market dealers operate, and any one of them could be selling milk.

He hurries from line to line, staying just long enough to find out what is being sold, then hurries on to the next line. He isn't joking or talking politics or showing off to the women, who are ethereally beautiful right now. Everyone has begun to notice it, even the old men are aware of a musky imminence floating in the rays of the late-day sun.

The young man is tall and well built, good-looking enough that the women notice him, smile at him. He is as pale as milk himself. He grew up in the Ukraine but was chosen to become an engineer and brought to Moscow. He knows no one in the city, and isn't likely to. Shyness has led to loneliness and an overwhelming thirst that seeks to fill the empty place. Not a thirst for vodka. He longs for milk. It is the only thing that takes him back to where he wants to be, to the Ukraine, and to his childhood, and away from a city he doesn't like or understand.

The government gave him an apartment and a tiny stipend, and in theory he is still waiting for a call, one that will never come, telling him where to go and what to do to be an engineer. He has no reason to stay, but no reason to go—things are not any better where his parents are. So he stays, and aches, and tries to drown the ache in milk. All the money he has, or can get, everything that he can sell or trade, has gone for milk. Like any drunk, he cares about nothing but getting another glass, another bottle, and he stumbles around the city in a daze, thinking of nothing but pure, sweet milk.

Today he has chased the black market dealers through every district and found nothing. It's almost dark, and the lines are breaking up. People are going home. Some have succeeded in finding what they wanted. Others have found each other. It's been the first really warm day of the spring, and everyone seems pleased and hopeful, even those who go home with empty arms. The young man turns toward his apartment building, out of habit, and plods along, numb with failure and desire.

A very pretty young woman approaches him. Her face is almost hidden behind heavy makeup, but she is young and can still shine through her own inept artwork. She has on a tight red sweater and even tighter blue jeans.

The day is cooling off quickly, but she has left the sweater unbuttoned, so that all can see how the sweater presses her breasts together and lifts them up, asking to be touched and kissed. The valley between them is pink with the cool breeze, and her nipples have hardened against the cloth of the sweater. She smiles up at him.

"Would you like to see my apartment? It's very pretty. I live alone."

"No, no. I have to meet someone."

Before he can race away, she catches his hand and presses it against her breast.

"It wouldn't cost much. Not for you."

"I have to get some milk."

She is as surprised by this as he is himself, and she draws her hand away. He stands for a moment looking at her but, unable to think how to explain himself, turns and flees. The one time he looks back, she has already approached another man. They are both laughing, but surely, he thinks, about something else. The other fellow's hand is already inside her sweater, warming one of her poor chilly breasts.

He makes no haste, but soon reaches the square, plain block of flats where he lives. He pauses for a moment just outside, with a dim sense that somehow something will happen to prevent his having to go in unsatisfied. Nothing happens except that the breeze whips up, cooler than before, and he goes in.

Most floors of the building have as many as six separate apartments, but on his floor there are only two. His own is quite small, and he knows from this just how large the other is. There are as many doors on his floor as on the others, and he assumes that once there were as many flats. He knows nothing about the couple living there. He has seen the man many times, rushing in and out, always well dressed, graying, purposeful. They nod but they don't talk, and both of them like it that way. He has seen the woman only a few times, through the open door of the apartment, once in the street outside, from the back, walking away.

Maybe the man is a member of the government. He must have some sort of influence, an influence that has grown, and as his power has grown, the apartment has slowly swallowed up its neighbors, the walls separating them inside coming down one by one, the doors onto the hallway no longer used. One day soon, the young man thinks, these people will want his apartment, too, and will demand it, and it will be given to them— unless the man has lost his prestige with the change of government.

The young man is in the hallway outside their door when his legs suddenly become useless with a lack of purpose and refuse for a moment to continue. He leans against the door of the couple's flat, the one door they still use. He isn't listening, isn't doing anything at all, and yet he can't help hearing from behind the door the soft crying of a baby. It isn't a plaintive crying, but the self-soothing crying of a baby putting itself to sleep, and still more softly and distantly he hears the cooing of its mother encouraging its efforts, soothing and gentling her baby off to sleep. He has heard a baby in the building before, but the flats are old, the walls are thick, and he never knew that it was so nearby, that right across the hall from him a mother and a child were going through all the rhythmic rituals that are such a distant memory for him. His cheek is pressed against the wood of the door, and his hand caresses its grain. Without a sound he too begins to cry, not painfully or loudly, but with all his soul.

Without thinking, he knocks on the door. He is startled by the sound and wonders where it comes from. Before he understands that it was he who made it, the door opens. There stands the woman. He has never been so close to her before. She is small, with wide hips and big breasts, swollen now with milk for her child. She is wearing a sweatshirt with the name of an American rock-and-roll band, and blue jeans that show the shape of her legs and thighs. She is over thirty, much older than the young man, but her face is soft. She looks just a little surprised. His face is wet, but he forgets that. He is a little confused, but the woman doesn't seem unkind.

"I . . . I heard the baby."

"I'm sorry. He's asleep now."

He wants to say more, but doesn't know what.

"Do you have any milk? I couldn't find any. I looked everywhere."

"I may have some powdered."

Again, the moment of confusion.

"No, never mind. Thank you."

His legs still won't move, and he stands looking at her, the tears standing in his eyes. She takes his shoulder and brings him into the flat. As soon as she touches him, he is able to move again. She quietly shuts the door, and with no sound and in a single gesture she lifts the sweatshirt over her head. Her breasts are white as milk, as soft as milk, heavy with milk. Her nipples are big and thick and dark. As soon as the shirt is off they begin to wrinkle and reach toward him. She lifts her right breast with her hand and looks at him. He is again paralyzed. As though the breast had been rejected, she lifts the left one and looks at him. Then she understands that he cannot move without her, and she puts her hand behind his neck, to draw him toward her.

She has to reach up, he is so much taller, and as she pulls him toward her, she also pulls him down, until he is on his knees before her. His mouth is then just level with the purple nipple he is offered, and he closes his eyes and opens his mouth. She pushes her breast against his lips, and he begins to drink. Her milk is sweet and rich, much better than any he can remember. He throws his arms around her now, his strength returning, and pulls her against him. He sucks too hard, and she gasps and pulls his hair to make him be gentle. He stops for a moment and looks up, not drinking but with his tongue still pressed like a question mark against the tip of her breast. She smiles and pats his hair. Again he closes his eyes, and resumes more gently.

There is so much milk, it seems at first that it will go on forever, but at last it stops. Still he keeps on, gently biting and teasing her nipple, licking her breast all over, whimpering softly, pressing his face against the softness of her. His hand comes up to her right breast and kneads it, squeezing until a jet of milk spills out across his wrist. He looks at his wrist and licks it, looks at her breast, and starts to lick his way across to it, but she stops him.

"No, it's too late. My husband could come home anytime."

He looks up at her from his knees, the confusion again settling over him. He looks around, as if to see where he is, and then he hugs her waist, pressing his cheek against the dampness of her breast, wetting again the tears that have dried there. She pats and gently pulls his hair with both hands, hugs him to her, then pushes him away.

"Come again in the morning. He will be gone all day."

He is again in the hall, not quite sure how, but his legs are once more moving and they take him into his own apartment and his own bed, where he lies all night, not sleeping but nonetheless dreaming. Maybe it isn't even a dream, it is so simple. He dreams of milk, and of the breasts and face of the woman who gave it to him, and he dreams of having more.

In the morning he is alive and awake, well rested as if he had slept. His mind is clear, and all he wants is for the first few hours of daylight to pass so that he can return to the woman. He hears the man leave, but makes himself wait another half hour to be sure he won't return, and then he walks boldly across the hall and knocks. She opens the door at once.

Today she is dressed in a leather skirt and nylons, a silk blouse that he cannot quite see through. He can see her nipples, already standing up hard against the fabric, rubbing against it every time she moves, making them impatient and irritable with a need like a persistent itch. When she opens the door, she makes a small, pleased sound, and he sees a small, dark spot where a drop of milk has escaped onto the silk.

In the time when he wasn't dreaming his single dream during the night, he wondered about this moment. Would she want him to kiss her? Did she want to talk? Could anything ever be as simple and clear as the day before? He has no experience in these things and doesn't know what she might expect. As soon as he sees her, the doubts begin again, but before they can overwhelm him she has again drawn him inside and shut the door.

Once more without a word she reaches for her blouse. At first her hand grazes the button, but then she hesitates a moment. With the silk still covering them, her hands begin to caress her breasts, rubbing the silk against them and irritating them still more. He watches for a few seconds. Then his own hands reach out and brush hers gently aside, taking their place and moving around and around in circles, lifting the heavy flesh and letting it fall, feeling its weight and bounce, squeezing the hard tip and feeling it get harder still. There are spots on the silk over both breasts now, and both the man and woman have begun to breathe hard, to make small sounds, to sigh and catch their breath. She reaches again for the button, and he pushes her hand away again, more firmly this time, and himself unbuttons her blouse.

As the silk falls away he sees her breasts once again, as full and beautiful as they had been in his mind all night. He had almost feared that his mind had exaggerated, but nothing could move him more than the way they hang, soft and heavy and fat with her womanhood. He had drunk the day before until her left breast was half the size of its friend, limp and empty, but here it is again as proud and full as it had been, and as he looks at it, he, too, begins to swell.

His patience gone, he falls to his knees again before her and buries his face against her until the milk begins to spurt from her too-full breasts. And then he licks it up from where it falls, on her belly and ribs, making his way back up until he once more reaches the nipple and drinks. This time he knows just how hard he can suck without hurting, and he begins to tease. He pulls a little harder and a little harder until he hears her start to gasp and feels her grip on his hair tighten, then he becomes gentle and she sighs. If he becomes too gentle, she beats her fists softly on the back of his head and finally presses him against her until he responds by sucking harder.

It doesn't take long, though, until the breast is empty again, and he begins again to bite the nipple and squeeze the breast with his hands to punish it for bringing his supply of milk to an end. He hasn't eaten anything since he first saw her the night before, except the milk that she gave him, and he has a hunger now like never before. He bites and licks her stomach, holding her tightly as he had done the night before.

"The other one. It needs you, too."

It is only the third time he has heard her speak, and he has not spoken yet. His voice sounds rusty as he replies: "You need something for the baby."

"My husband is black market. I do nothing but eat. There's plenty for the baby. Why do you think I'm so fat?"

"No, not fat. Never fat. Look at you, you're beautiful."

"That's not what he says. He promises me there will be no more babies. He hates me because I am a cow."

"No."

"Come sit by me on the sofa. Put your legs over the arm and lean back with your head in my lap. Touch my other breast. Milk me."

Before he disappears once more into his milky dream, he smells something new—the deep, mysterious smell of her womanhood, still hidden in nylon and leather, reaches out to him. Before he can find out what it is, she pulls his mouth to her other nipple, moans and sends him back to the secret place they have made together. All too soon this breast too is empty, his stomach is full, and he sinks from this dream into the sleep he denied himself all night, his head falling against her lap.

She strokes his hair and pats him, content for now to let him sleep and renew himself as her breasts, empty now and just a little cold as their damp nakedness is left exposed, themselves begin to renew and refill.

He dreams a different dream now. His desperate desire for milk was the only thing in the world for so long, he had been unable to imagine anything more. Now that need is satisfied; not for the moment, but forever. And yet he isn't satisfied. In his new dream he is chasing something, something dark, a shadow, something he can't quite see but feels he has to catch. He wakes with a start, his face slick and sweating where it has rested against the leather of her skirt. She sees that he is upset and reaches to comfort him as she would her baby. Her breasts have begun to fill again, and she lifts one of them for him, ready to give him what she has, to soothe and comfort him, but he wrinkles up his face and fusses, just as her baby will sometimes do. He turns over, as if to return to sleep, and buries his face in her skirt.

He smells the leather and is wide awake again. He opens his eyes, but all he can see is black, the black leather of her skirt, just like the dark shadow that he chased in his dream. His mouth is wet and a little saliva drips out as he opens it to lick the leather, taste it, chew it. But the leather isn't what he dreamed of. Now he smells her, through the leather, and knows that what he smells is what has replaced the dream of milk. He wants it as he has never wanted anything, and he begins to bite and chew, trying to get through the leather at what is hidden underneath.

She puts her hands on his shoulders and pulls him hard against her, her back arching. She makes a long, low sound that isn't a word, and pulls harder on his shoulders as if to pull his whole body inside her. He loses his balance and slips from the sofa onto the floor, losing touch with her for a moment. Again he is on his knees. She puts her feet on his shoulders and sets her knees apart. The stockings end at her thighs, with a white lace belt above them, holding them up. Nothing at all separates him from her open center.

The smell of her is overpowering. It is new to him, strange, but familiar somehow. The dream of milk is very far away. Her legs are dark where the nylon covers them, pale and smooth at the thighs, and where they meet is a dark, heavy tangle of hair. In the middle of this tangle are her lips, slightly parted and shining with moisture. That is where the smell comes from, and that is where he has to be. He leans toward her slowly. She lifts her feet from his shoulders and lets him approach. He inhales slowly, savoring her smell, and then he is right in front of her, and the smell fills him until he is the smell of her. And he kisses her, so softly that his lips barely brush hers, her hair just touches his cheeks. The moisture that clings to her is slightly cool from being exposed to the air.

As he kisses her he whimpers, and she grabs his hair and pulls it. He makes a louder noise and drives at her, no longer gentle. His tongue slides up and down across her open lips, lapping at her wetness, trying to swallow it, to swallow her. He reaches inside her with his tongue, wanting to go deeper, to reach her womb, to reach the woman inside her. His nose is pressed hard against her lips, his head rocks back and forth, inhaling her, and somewhere far away he can hear her cries and shouts, can feel her pulling hard against his hair. Something small and hard is pressed against his cheek as his head slides from side to side through her wetness, and his tongue goes looking for it. He kisses her, harder now, sucking against her soft wetness, his tongue flicking in and out, darting around looking for that small, hard spot, finding it, rubbing it. When he touches it her back flies up, her feet slam on the floor beside his shoulders, and her pelvis rises in the air before him. He clings to her as to his life. She is standing now, her knees still wide apart, her hands pressing his face against her as she screams and falls back against the seat, panting.

The tip of his tongue continues to press and surround the little button of flesh, feeling it throb and tremble. His hands are on her hips, and he can feel the trembling spread from where he kisses her to every part of her body. The tiny quiver against his mouth is a shaking in her hips, a heaving of her chest and shoulders, and a wild thrashing of her arms. Her breasts are bouncing wildly and her cries have joined in a long, deep, guttural scream that rises and sinks and ends in a faraway sigh. He presses into her again, and she spasms again all over, wails, trembles, goes limp. Pleasure has become pain, and she slams her legs shut around his head to make him stop. His tongue retreats and instead he showers her with little kisses, sliding his lips, his nose, his cheeks back and forth in her slick darkness, laughing.

He finally is able to pull himself away from the warmth and soft-ness, and looks up at her, smiling. She is smiling, too, but tears are silently streaming down her face. She puts her hands under his shoulders and lifts his face to hers. As they kiss, she places her hand on his waist, slides it down, and finds him hard and straining toward her. She runs her hand up and down against the cloth that holds him back, and his legs become weak again. He sinks onto the cushions, and their eyes finally meet on a level. She kneels in front of him, and as she touches him again, the image from his dream becomes clear, the shadow slips away, and he knows what he was chasing.

He starts again to laugh, at himself. Here he is, twenty years old. What kind of fog has he been wandering in for . . . what, years now, that he should be surprised now at his own clear, simple desire? Where has he been for so long? And what great luck has brought him here now?

She has stepped back from him and he isn't sure why, until he, too, hears a sound in the hallway. No one ever comes here but the two of them—and the third, her husband. She looks alarmed.

"He has never come home in the daytime. Never. Go back through the rooms. Some of the doors still work. Just try them."

She kisses him hastily and pushes him through the door to the next room. Before he can turn and find out where he is, he can hear her opening the windows in the first room, and no matter what the danger, he can't help laughing again. How could she get the smell out of the room? It seems to him the whole world is full of her scent.

But he must find his way out. He is in a small, narrow room, almost like a hallway. He tries the first door he sees. It's locked. The knob won't even turn. He quickly moves on to the next. Here is the baby, sleeping peacefully. He has only heard it the one time. It certainly must be a happy baby with such a mother, spending most of its day in the peaceful dream of milk. He steps up to the crib and pats the child. It starts to stir and fuss, and suddenly less bold, he hurries into the next room. It is the bedroom of the couple, dominated by a great, heavy canopy bed. He hesitates a moment. He doesn't want to leave. He wants her to join him, right now, under that canopy, and soothe the ache that has settled in his middle as his hardness, undiminished by fear or flight, begs him to finish what he has begun. Should he hide here and hope the husband leaves again at once? He hurries on. He passes through two more rooms, outfitted with chairs, desks, tables, and wonders why they have bothered with so much furniture, as no one ever comes to see them. How can two people use so much space? He realizes he must be quite far from the door the man entered through by now, and he begins to try the doors that he thinks must join the hall, with no success. Still the rooms go on.

Soon, though, there is no more furniture. He passes through three rooms that are filled with boxes of all shapes and sizes. The man is certainly in the black market, as she said, and not shy about living with the evidence. Teams of men must have been needed to bring in so many things, and yet he has never noticed anything. Such a fog I have been living in. And then a door opens for him, and he is back in the plain hall of his floor, quite near his own door.

It is another sleepless night. He isn't afraid. What has happened to him has stirred something very deep in him that will never really rest again. His luck has been so absolute he feels that it will protect the woman as well, and tomorrow she will come for him and they will finish his education, his awakening. All night he can hear the coming and going of many feet, and he smiles. This must go on every night, and I never hear anything. Remarkable.

The long night fades away at last, but still he waits. It has been silent for hours, but surely it is best to wait until she comes. Finally he can wait no longer, and opens his door. From where he is, he can see the door to her apartment, standing open, and on the sill of his door are two things. The first is a folded paper. He picks it up, unfolds it, and reads: "I have no time. My husband thinks the police know where he is. He is taking us away. I don't know where. You are a beautiful young man. Remember me."

He still doesn't know her name. The other object is a small jar full of milk.

❦ FOOTPRINTS ❧
Elle Molique

I MET HIM AT A JAZZ CLUB IN HOLLYWOOD—Lucky Seven. The club's gone now, another California dream that burned itself out after a few months of money-draining idealism. He was a young jazz guitarist who'd seemingly been dealt a perfect hand and had a successful career by twenty-one. I, on the other hand, had recently crawled over thirty and was freshly divorced, having struggled for years to gain some respect in a male-dominated field. Everyone expected a chick to be a singer or piano player in the jazz scene. Being a female professional saxophonist made me an anomaly, or, at the very least, a lesbian. Consequently, I was often loveless in a sea of sensitive, egotistical males who felt the need to prove themselves worthy of legacies like Miles Davis, Wes Montgomery, and John Coltrane.

He stuck a business card in my hand after hearing me solo with the house band one Wednesday night during a jam session.

"You sound good," he said. I had no idea who he was, and I'd have had to hear him play before I'd have considered keeping the card. I didn't even bother to look at the name.

"Thanks," I said, and flipped the card through my fingers.

"You gonna stick around? I'm up soon."

I hesitated. I hated hanging out while these young boy jazzers tried to intimidate each other off the stage. Even worse were the really bad players who never improved but showed up at every jam session like clockwork. My ace in the hole was that I could move my fingers faster than most heavyweights, though it felt more like wind sprints than music a lot of the time.

Still, this kid had a cute little baby face.

"Okay, man." I tried not to look put out by the request. I didn't want to come off as jaded as I felt, but I'd been in the business too long. The only reason I still came to the jams was to keep my chops up. I had a little bit of a name around town, but so did everyone else. It didn't mean shit, because you could make up your résumé as you went along. No one with any power cared if you could *play*, anyway; they just cared about who you'd played *with*. The new kid's exuberance was surprising.

"Cool," he said, smiling at me and looking me in the eye.

He tried to be cool, but I knew where his nerves were. No matter how well you thought you could play, your balls would be heaved up on the block as soon as you hit the stage. Everybody in the room critiqued each note. The kid glanced down at my feet before he turned toward the stage. My 6½s were deeply buried in socks and black leather Dr. Martens knockoffs. I was kind of tall at five foot seven to have such small feet. It made me clumsy at times, especially in high heels. Still, they were dainty and unique. There were guys out there who'd appreciate that. I'd always wondered what it would feel like to have someone move out of the regular erogenous zones and electrify me from another part of my body.

I walked toward the bathroom, but I wasn't in any big hurry. It was jazz. The average song lasted over six minutes. I'd be back before he finished his solo.

The trumpet player running the jam got on the microphone: "Please welcome to the stage . . . *Rick Bonetta!*"

The whole room applauded like crazy. I'd always wondered what that guy looked like. He was this wunderkind guitar player who'd taken over New York. Sometimes came back to Cali to hang out with the session players. His dad was John Bonetta, the famous film composer. John's claim to fame was writing the scores to almost every after-school special in the late seventies. Dubious honor really, but he'd made a lot of money off the royalties. That went a long way in L.A.

"Shit . . ." I said to myself. I don't know why it had taken so long for me to put it together. I looked down at the card he'd given me. His name was featured in small print. Phone number was, predictably, written in pen instead of printed on the card. New York cell. Working musicians were pretty much a bunch of talented transients, commuting from coast to coast. An image of shadowy footprints tracked under his name. I got the joke. It referred to the overplayed Wayne Shorter blues tune "Footprints."

I rerouted myself back to the main area of the restaurant. There Rick was, smiling hugely as he tore up the stage with some delicious bebop lines over a tough Charlie Parker tune called "Donna Lee." He was a player, not a hack. More important, I was actually *enjoying* his playing.

He ended with a tasteful quote from a Cannonball Adderley solo I particularly liked from the 1958 Jazz at the Plaza performances in New York. Wow, this kid was good. He could tell from hearing me play *one time* that Cannonball was my idol. He'd also picked one of my favorite solos to swipe a lick from. If he'd bought me a rose or a box of Godiva, it would not have had the same impact.

The applause was unanimous, which was unheard of in a West Coast jazz club. He walked over to me after a few bows and waves at the audience.

"You're flirting with me," I said, flitting my eyelashes at him. I'd never felt so much like a girl. I liked it.

"That would be correct. Don't take this the wrong way, but I've never heard a chick play anywhere near Cannonball. It's . . ."

"Kinda hot?" I finished. His face turned red.

"Yeah," he said, finishing off an embarrassed laugh.

"I'm—"

"Stella Kartson, I know," he said, shaking my outstretched hand.

"You play your ass off, too, man. Good ear . . . specially since you are so wet behind them," I said, jabbing him about his age a little. His quick success, though well deserved, was a little meteoric for my tolerance. I'd had to fight for my place in the jazz pantheon, even on a local level. He'd lived up to the hype, though.

"I may be young, but I can . . ." he started.

"You can what?" I challenged.

"Please you," he said, rather directly.

"Really?" I said, moving a little closer. Men didn't often put their cards on the table with me, much less throw them at me like this.

"I adore women," he whispered in my ear, the words sliding out of his mouth wrapped in the warm tone of truth.

"You and pretty much every guy in this room," I whispered back, rolling my eyes cynically over the throng. A subtle heat was creeping up between our bodies. My nipples popped under my bra. He threw some of the energy at me that he'd put into his guitar playing. I threw it right back at him. Still, his head hung down a little. He seemed almost shy. It didn't make sense. I hadn't shot him down yet. Then I caught it. He was looking at my feet.

"Um . . . see something you like?" I asked.

"Sorry. I . . . I didn't mean to stare," he said.

"Most people have the decency to look me in the tits when they talk to me," I said.

He cracked a smile but kept looking down. "Six and a half medium. You're embarrassed about your toes being small and curvy, but you shouldn't be. The pigeon-toed thing is kinda cute." He paused, deep in thought. "Oh, and you have low arches."

"Jesus. Remind me to put that on my business card," I said. Then I remembered *his* card. There was much more to this footprints thing than just the song.

Another masochistic player made his way toward the stage with his stick bag. I'd heard this guy play drums before. The old fart couldn't keep time with a Swiss watch strapped to his face, but he loved to play. It would soon be a bloodbath of snickering whispers fit for a fashion critics' luncheon. I couldn't watch.

"Are you pretty open-minded?" he ventured.

"I like to explore certain things," I said, wishing I felt that way about music at the moment.

"Like what?" he asked, looking me in the eye again. In that look was the sliver of a distant hope that I might be able to see the real him through the brain-bleeding distortion of American social cinema.

"Like . . . people's deeper desires," I said.

"Really?"

"Try me," I whispered.

He stared at me for a minute. The carnage was in full swing onstage. The pianist, a studio musician who'd played on countless jingles and sitcom sound tracks and frequently subbed on *Jay Leno*, was furiously smoking menthols and trying not to break his gin glass to slash his wrists. We grabbed our instruments and left Lucky Seven.

I followed Rick in my Toyota, threading through the mountains that butted up against Hollywood. L.A. was full of strange people who lived in the nooks and crannies of the pompous desert peaks that forced a false supremacy on the valleys. Rich people lived in the hills. Musicians fraternized with the porn stars down below. I was surprised as we wound our way through Laurel Canyon to an area that I knew, even with a record deal, a jazz musician couldn't afford without outside help.

His car stopped in front of a three-story yellow house surrounded by wild, twisting eucalyptus trees, offset by carefully arranged rock gardens. He motioned for me to park next to him.

I got out of the car. He took me by the hand and led me into the house without a word. It was completely dark. Dusty lavender incense hung around the edges, evidence that candles had burned, if not recently.

"You live *here*?" I asked.

"Um . . . sort of. I stay here when I'm in town. Friend of my dad's owns it. He's on location in the Czech Republic shooting a movie."

"That's a pretty cool deal, no?" I said, a faint bitterness creeping into my voice. "I live in a tiny apartment in the gay ghetto in North Hollywood."

"Yeah, I've got a cushy situation, I realize. Got the same kind of thing in New York," he said, twisting the knife a little. I couldn't tell if he was doing it on purpose or not. He slid his hands along the wall, finally hitting the light switch. A pair of warm candle sconces barely lit the room enough for our forms to cast shadows on the hardwood floor.

"Things come easy for you, don't they?" I said. Beating around the bush was tedious.

"Yeah, and *you* are smokin' hot. A lot comes easy for you that you don't realize," he said back.

Was this going to turn into a philosophical face-off? My blood was turning to Tabasco rather quickly. "Yeah, thanks, but . . . that only gets you so far. It can work against you just as easily. Nobody wants a chick to be smart *and* stacked. It's like you cheated or something."

"Same kind of thing is true for being a famous composer's son. Nobody thinks I did any of it on my own."

"Yeah, but you *are* talented. I really liked your playing," I admitted, despite his having pushed my buttons.

"And I *felt* yours," he said, pressing me up against the wall.

I kissed him, just to remove any doubt. He gave his mouth to me, deferring to my trained embouchure. Playing saxophone had some amazing advantages. I'd never need a face-lift and I could French like a Parisian. He tasted *so good*. I pushed the kiss a little deeper. His mouth acquiesced to my lead, yet his body kept me where I was.

I knew he wasn't going to try to push the foot issue on me at our first encounter, so I pulled one of my shoes off to see what he would do. He shuddered a little, completely aware of what I'd done. I held the back of the other one down with my toes and slid my foot out, keeping our kiss locked the whole time.

I'd been in my shoes since the morning. My feet were damp and musky. I rolled one of them in its sock to loosen it. I stepped on my loosened toe with my other heel and pulled my foot out. I pinched my big toe and its neighbor together with my now naked foot to pull the other sock off.

I stood there barefoot, my feet cooling under me. He pushed me harder into the wall. Out of nowhere, he broke the kiss.

"You okay?" Usually *guys* asked that question. I knew he was a few years younger that I was, which, in my experience, could be intimidating for him. I actually gave two-tenths of a shit about the male ego when I got this close.

"I don't know," he said, sitting cross-legged on the floor. I followed suit. He just stared at my pretzel-positioned legs.

"Have you followed through with this kind of thing before?" I asked.

"Um . . . not really." He looked like he wanted to cry.

"Have you even tried?" I asked.

"Regular sex is fine with me," he said quickly. "I can live without . . . *this*," he said, pointing at my legs, then quickly pulling back his hand like he'd stuck it in a fire. He seemed to be getting younger and younger by the second.

"Why should you?" I asked.

"I'm embarrassed," he said.

"You play jazz! What can be more embarrassing than your first time onstage trying to play a solo when you barely know what the hell you are doing?"

"I don't know. It's just something I've had trouble with," he insisted.

"What do you want?" I asked, looking him in the eye. It was a hard question. It's easy to *want*. Not so easy to ask for it.

He waited. The words were probably screaming in his head, but the gatekeeper of his mouth would not let them out.

I slowly stretched a leg toward him, pointing my toe. I would have to go on instinct since this was all new to me, too. I knew that if I could just get him started, his fantasies would map it out for us. He uncurled his legs, leaning toward me. He kissed the arch of my foot, holding my calf with the grace of a ballet dancer. A shot of energy traveled up my leg, grounding itself in the spontaneous wetness of my crotch.

A moan blossomed in my throat. He took it as encouragement and licked my ankle. I wrapped my foot around the side of his face as his lips found their way under the leg of my jeans a little ways up. I pulled my foot back, grazing his lips with my toes.

"No toes. Not yet," he said. His voice was hoarse. He broke himself away from the spell of my feet, pushing me onto my back and straddling me. He spread my legs apart with his knees, dropping his weight onto my body. The hardness I felt in his pants was flattering, but it ground the seam of my pants into me. I moved my pelvis to put him in a cozier cleft. The adjustment clicked our energy into place. He unbuttoned my shirt with his hardworking fretting hand. His right hand, with long, perfectly manicured nails for when he played classical or flamenco guitar, was kept as idle as a rich Victorian widow. He could think with his fingers, sliding his hand under me and unhooking my bra with half a pinch. His pampered hand sampled the feel of my breast like it was an imported bonbon.

I pushed him off of me and stood up, throwing off my shirt and bra. I walked around the room with the cocky sureness of a shirtless, muscle-bound construction worker. He sat on the floor watching me prowl around him. I pulled his T-shirt off from above. He reached up, unbuttoning and unzipping my pants. He pulled them down over my muscular thighs, slipping his fingers underneath my panties from below. He tasted his fingers, then put them back into me. He was pushing my buttons again, but the good ones this time.

I wriggled out of my pants and stood in front of him in my pink cotton bikini underwear. He smiled. I walked up to his face and put it in my crotch, holding him there with my hand at the back of his head. He breathed into my underwear, sliding his bottom teeth over my covered clit. The friction made me tingle. I lifted my knee to the side, opening my legs so I could push his nose deeper into me. I loved riding his face like that. His tongue searched for a way to get through the last of my cloth packaging, lashing around the crotch of my underwear like an angry snake. I pushed him onto his back with my foot, stepping on his chest.

His breathing sped up. Instinct took over completely. I dragged the inside of my foot up along his neck to the side of his face, slid my toes along his cheek, and stepped on the side of his head. His nose and mouth were smushed lovingly beneath my arch. He groaned underfoot.

I kept him there for a minute.

"Take your pants off," I commanded.

"Yes, ma'am," he said through his squished lips. I wasn't sure if I liked *ma'am*, considering the difference in our ages, but I sensed that he wasn't mocking me. It felt like a deep show of respect. I let him up so he could do what I said.

He enjoyed obeying me, kicking off his shoes and socks as quickly as he could. Off came his jeans, just as fast. He was wearing soft cotton boxers. *My favorite.*

We both stood there in our underwear. He pushed me against the wall again, back where we'd started, only much more naked. His tongue traveled down my neck to my breasts. He held them together to feel their soft warmth surrounding his face. He sucked both my nipples at once, starting a new flow of juice between my legs. He made tiny bites down my stomach to my underwear. Reaching around to my ass, he slid his fingers into my panties and pulled them down my legs at an angle, my wetness leaving a trail on my inner thigh. They landed at my feet. I stepped on the little wet heap. He quickly licked the juice off my foot. Licking slowly up the inside of my leg, he made his way back to my clit. My head flew back, hitting the wall. I swung one leg over his shoulder, locking him into his task. He picked up my other leg and put it over his other shoulder. I held on to the doorknob with one hand and the bookshelf with the other, the strength of pure pleasure holding me up. I let myself slide down the wall so he could eat me on the ground. His tongue flicked across my folds with the random beauty of a modern jazz solo, his intensity matching my body's every response and building on them until we'd gathered so much energy that I couldn't hold it back any longer.

I let go into his mouth, grabbing him by the hair and pulling his face into me, opening my orgasm to him. I trusted him because I knew he was giving me parts of himself that he'd never given anyone else. *He trusted me*—the ultimate aphrodisiac.

"Did you really come?" he asked, breathless.

"Oh, yes," I breathed, extremely satisfied with his performance. Faking orgasms wasn't in my repertoire.

He moved his body along my wet legs and laid his head between my breasts. I hugged his head for a minute. He seemed content to have made me come. That wasn't enough for me, though. We'd gone this far. I wanted to see at least some of his suppressed fantasies make it to light. I brought his face up to mine and kissed him, sucking the glaze off his lips. I reached down to his underwear. He was semi-hard after his tongue workout. I wanted to see him explode.

I laid him down on the floor on his front, his head to the side, one ear to the ground. I stood over him, my feet on either side of his head. I wiggled my toes by his mouth. He licked at them. We were both new to this, so I tried to give him a way to get to his desires. *An opening.* I lifted my leg so he could get underneath my foot. He kissed the sole. He turned over onto his back and looked up at my naked body. He closed his eyes and felt up the back of my thighs.

I stepped over him and sat on the ground. He sat up, facing me. He sucked in a deep breath and scooted back a little, getting himself into position. He took my foot in his hands and slid my big toe into his mouth. It tickled, all the way up to my ass. I calmed my excited leg down and leaned back to pull his boxers off. He was hard as a rock now. He put my second toe in his mouth with the big one, savoring the salty taste, feeling the ridges of my toe prints with his tongue. I spit on my hand and started feeling up and down his cock. He moaned as I stroked him. He took another toe in his mouth. The pressure was starting to build in his balls. His tongue was catching every bit of taste off my tiny toes. The fourth toe, my little crooked one, hooked itself on to one of his bottom teeth as he sucked on the quartet. He took another breath, his eyes rolling back as I continued my attentions to his hard cock. He would surely blow if I got that fifth one in; I knew that as well as I knew my blues scales.

I looked him in the eye. He nodded as he madly sucked my toes. I let him take in the tiniest toe, the pinky. He'd gotten the whole set into his mouth. His eyes closed in a pleasure and peace I'd never seen in a man before. He sucked my whole foot as I stroked him, licking the ball of my foot in rhythm with my strokes. He pulled my foot out of his mouth. I touched his taut sac with my free hand. He licked at my toes, sucking at the group of them and pulling off like they were a double Popsicle as I found his sweet spot and jerked him with both hands. Three long, low moans vibrated my foot. I stroked faster as the pace of his moans sped up. He closed his eyes and went silent.

He came so hard that I could *hear* the semen coming out of him. He squeezed my immersed foot with his hands, then fell back, dropping the wet object of his desire onto his chest. His load sprayed into my hair, onto my hands, and all over my bare tits. Tears accompanied his hoarse gasps, years of pent-up frustration draining away in an instant.

I cleaned myself off with his T-shirt. He tried to sit up, but decided against it. I looked around the room. We hadn't really gotten fully into the house. I laughed. He smiled as he lay there.

"You are amazing," he said.

"Why, thank you."

"No, not just that. I've heard about you—your sax playing—even in New York," he said.

"Really?" I asked. I couldn't keep my own tears from jumping out of my eyes. I'd worked so hard for so long.

"Yeah. It's a tough business. Everyone's struggling; they just make it seem like they've got it together," he said. "Oh, and you should wear strappy shoes if you want. Your feet are cute. *Real* cute," he added, smiling at me.

"I guess *so*," I said, holding up his sticky T-shirt.

I kissed him as he lay there, in bliss. Here I was, trying to give some kid relief from his demons, and he ended up giving me relief from mine. Shit, I might even start wearing high heels.

೫ A CLEAN, COMFORTABLE ROOM ೫
Pam Ward

SALLY HAD BEEN DRIVING LONG AND HARD FOR ELEVEN HOURS ALREADY. When she saw the blue glow of the deadbeat motel she decided to pull in. She'd seen the Blue Star Motor Inn's giant sign from the highway. "Clean Comfortable Rooms for $16.99." Sally turned off at the exit and drove to the squat stucco building. It had about ten units connected under one slim roof. Nothing but road dirt and concrete. A loud Coke machine sat out front.

She got out and walked quickly to the office. As soon as she stepped in, she was hit with the harsh scent of canned meat cooking. The office looked more like a living room. There were two TV sets, a small black-and-white and one color stacked together. There was a small stove and a giant, brown refrigerator with a big dent in it. There was an ironing board and a rotary phone hooked to the wall. A hefty man in loose-fitting over-alls sat in a La-Z-Boy covered with duct tape. He looked about sixty-five. His bald head gleamed from the neon. His numb eyes were glued to the set. The man broke into a wide smile as Sally walked in.

"I'm comin'," he said, walking laboriously to the front desk. He had one of those beer guts that hung like a sack of rice. His breath was heavy. When he got close, Sally noticed a gray possum wrapped around his neck. Its wet eyes were watching her.

"What can I get you?" He grinned, revealing a gummy row of gapped teeth.

"How much for a room?" Sally had left in the middle of the night and had only twenty-eight dollars in cash on her. She needed a room before she could hit the ATM in the morning.

"We got some go for thirty-five and some that go for seventeen. Depends. You by yourself?"

"For now."

The man chuckled to himself when she said that. His double chin jiggled. "Well, I guess I can let you take the cheaper one." He sighed deeply. He seemed disappointed he wasn't getting a bigger sale.

"Can I see it first?" she asked.

"Sure, sure. Wait a hot minute. Let me get the keys." The man ducked behind a torn curtain.

Sally leaned across the front desk while she waited. She tapped her long fingernails across the wood. *I hope he doesn't take too long*, she thought. She wanted to hurry up and get to her room so she could lie down. She opened her purse and took out her lipstick. She smeared the deep red on. Sally looked toward the blue glow of the television. *Rosemary's Baby* was on. Rosemary was struggling down the street with a heavy suitcase. She looked pale and worried.

Suddenly there was a horrible racking cough, coming from the dark corner of the room. Sally leaped. It sounded like a hyena. She squinted to see. There, next to the stove, was a wide-shouldered man in an undershirt. Sally hadn't noticed the man before. He blended into the dim corner of the room. He couldn't have been more than twenty. Was probably the older man's son. Sally watched him bring a bottle of whiskey to his lips and drink a messy swig. He licked around his mouth and watched her. He was staring at Sally's large breasts. His gaze never rose above her neck.

Sally was wearing a jean jacket over a thin black slip. She'd just shoved the flap inside her pants. Her bare feet were in pink thongs. To avoid the man's gaze, Sally walked outside toward the Coke machine. She wasn't going to stay in there with some wild-looking fool drooling at her.

She slipped in three quarters and the red can came rumbling out.

"Oh—there you are darlin'," the older man said, walking outside. "I'm fixin' to get that room ready."

Sally leaned against the hood of her car. It was a warm Arizona night. You could see every star from here. Sally heard a rattling sound behind her.

She jumped. It was just a corn chip bag stuck in some weeds. Sally was dead tired and her nerves were shot. She hoped he wouldn't take too long.

The man was back in less than ten minutes. He was carrying an old bucket.

"Well, it's all spic and span. Got it real nice for you."

Sally hoisted her large purse over her shoulder. She followed the man to the room.

"Here we are, little lady." The man stood firmly in the doorway. Sally had to brush past him to get in. He smelled like hard liquor and farm animals. As soon as she stepped in the room the fumes hit her. It had that rank smoke smell. A scent so thick it was embedded in all the walls, rugs, and drapes. Smelled like it would never go away. Like somebody smoked in there year after year and never once opened a window. The wallpaper was peeling off, the bedspread was a hideous floral orange and the corners had cigarette burns. "I'll take it," Sally said.

The man had her fill out a tiny white slip asking her name and license plate number. Sally fumbled around with her purse and finally counted out seventeen dollars. She handed it to him.

"Now, my name is Edmond. Let me know if there's anything you need, sugar." He leaned over to hand her the room key and his huge body trapped her against the doorjamb. Sally fell back and dropped her purse. The man bent down slowly and handed it back to her. "Watch yourself now. Looks like you need some shut-eye."

Edmond walked outside to the lot. He looked hard at Sally's car. It had about five layers of dirt on it. "I can wash that car there for you, if you'd like. Have it looking real nice. Real sweet. I know how to suds a car down. It's all in the motion you know. Got to go in a circular rhythm, keep your hands rubbing round and round and round. Don't have to press too hard to get a shine." His bald head looked hideous in the lamplight.

"Sleep tight," he said, walking off. Sally watched his lumbering stride go back through the office door. He looked back at her before going in.

Sally shut the door. *Banjo-playin' motherfuckers*, she said to herself. She slid the extra lock across the frame. She took off her jacket and laid it on the bed. Sally was beat down. She'd been driving for half a day already. She pulled the blanket all the way back and examined the sheets. They seemed clean. She took off her shoes and pants, then peeked through the drapes.

The road was real quiet now. It was 11:45 P.M. There was only one other car in the lot. She walked to the small bathroom. Some of the tiles were missing. A shower curtain hung limp on a metal rod. The toilet paper roll was half-gone. Sally took a hot shower and wrapped herself in the thin, frayed towel. She sat on the edge of the bed. She wished she had one cigarette. Something to take the edge off. She clicked on the TV. *Rosemary's Baby* was still on. She watched the set while sipping the rest of her Coke. She looked around the room. There was a small refrigerator in the corner. She pulled it open. There were four beers strung together on a pale vein of plastic. The last person in there must have left it and the owner hadn't noticed it.

Sally didn't drink. She didn't even want to be tempted. Not now. Not after everything that had happened. Sally hadn't tasted liquor for three years straight. Not since that rainy night long ago. She dialed the front desk.

"Hello, ma'am. Room all right?"

"Yes, it's fine, but I found a six-pack in the fridge. I really don't want it."

"That's all right, ma'am. I'll send Leon down to pick it up."

Sally put the receiver down and put her pants back on. *Leon must be the fool who didn't have the decency to look me in the face, she thought.*

She was buttoning the front of her jacket when she heard a soft knock on the door.

Sally peeked out the small hole drilled over the doorknob.

It was Edmond again. "I'll just take the beer off your hands myself. Leon's busy right now." *Busy?* Sally thought. *That man wasn't doing nothing but jackin' off to* Rosemary's Baby. Edmond crossed the room, looking around it quickly. He walked over to the refrigerator and jerked the handle. He snatched the cans away as if Sally might change her mind. They clanked against his wad of keys. He stood next to her for a moment. She could smell the sour seeping out from his pores. She had emptied a few things from her purse, and a pair of black four-inch pumps was standing erect next to the TV set. He stared at them, too. Sally put one hand on her hips.

"Well, I guess you have everything," she said, using that fake sweet tone she reserved for work. She sure didn't miss Sizzler. Only thing she got from that job was a handful of bad steak knives.

"Yes, ma'am, I reckon I do. I'll just take this on back to the front. Let me know if you need anything else, hear. You be safe now, pretty little thing like you got to watch herself. Lord knows what's out on that road."

Sally started closing the door slowly. He could see her red lips and giant cleavage through the crack. The man took two steps but didn't leave. He reeked of cheap booze. Sally saw a dirty ring around his neck where the possum had been. She inched the door further in and accidentally touched his hand. It was hairy and rough. He looked down at her. His forehead was sweaty and large. Slowly, the corner of his lips curled up into a crooked smile. "I'll take this on, now," he said stepping out. "Call again." Once his feet cleared the door, Sally closed it shut and locked it tight. *Country fools*, she thought.

She waited a moment before taking her jacket off. She went into the bathroom and washed out her slip and hung it on the shower rod. If she left the window open it ought to be dry by morning. Sally lay on the bed naked. Damn, she wanted a cigarette. She searched the room. Nothing. She thought about the last smoke she'd had with William. It was right after they'd made love. Damn, that man was good. He sure knew how to serve it up. She remembered how he cupped her breasts and sucked both nipples at the same time. How he begged her to climb on top of him, plunging himself deeper and deeper. How he tugged her hair just enough, just until her body was one huge arch. Until she felt like pure steel. Like one hot metal rod. Like she might just snap. Sally loved the way he screamed her name when she violently came. Yeah, she'd sure miss her some William.

Sally began playing with her breasts. She slid her hand down to her things. Damn, it was hot. Buck-ass naked and she was still sweating. Sally thought if she got off she could get to sleep. All that road coffee had her fried. She tried and tried but only ended up in a frustrated knot under the sheet. Her long hair was glued to the back of her neck.

She yanked the sheet back and thought about Leon sitting in that office in the dark. There was something peculiar about him. Something backwoods mixed with wild. *Too much inbreeding, I bet.* But there was something else, too. Something simmering like a pot of hot greens on the stove. Sally thought about the cigarette pack rolled up in his sleeve. His thick, muscular arms and that tight six-pack stomach. The way his eyes ate her breasts. The way he leaned in his chair with his legs cocked out wide. The worn look to his jeans. The hard tips of his boots. The boy looked pure country. A bona fide hick. All wild-eyed and woolly haired, too.

But it wasn't like she was in the backwoods. Flagstaff was just five miles away. Sally remembered what the gas station attendant had told her. "Be careful on them roads honey," she'd said. "Some of these small towns are more common than the Deep South. Watch out."

Sally took a bag of pretzels from her purse. She was hungry. Besides the Coke, it was the only thing she'd had in hours. She opened her wallet.

She only had eleven dollars left. Her tank was already close to the red line. She had to get some cash fast.

Edmond walked back inside the office and opened the cash register. "Sure is a pretty gal up in thirteen." He counted the money and put it back inside. Leon didn't even look up. His eyes were fastened to the set. He watched Rosemary's naked body being shoved against the long table. She was struggling frantically. The men were holding her legs down.

Edmond slumped his large body back in the La-Z-Boy. It was stuffed with old copies of the *Phoenix Gazette*. The newspapers filled the deep hole in the seat. "Yes sirree. A real live citified gal. Should have seen them patent leather hoofers she had up in there. Um, um, um." Edmond wrapped the possum around his neck, but it squirmed so much he let it loose on the ground. It ran to a dark corner of the room. He pulled a handkerchief out and patted his sweaty brow.

"I don't know what a lady like that is doing out here in the middle of the night. Did you see her clothes? Look like she just shoved her nightie in her jeans and took off. Must be another one of them women had a fight with their boyfriends. You see she wasn't carryin' nothing but the clothes on her back. Man oh man. If it wasn't for boyfriend fights and city folks cheatin', we'd be out of business."

Leon didn't say anything.

Sally lay across the bed. *Rosemary's Baby* was still on. She watched as Rosemary's slender body moved crazily against the hard table. The men pounded her down, took turns thrashing away, while naked old ladies chanted and held both her legs. Sally clicked the TV off. "Demonic shit," she said out loud to herself. She slid under the sheet and got a whiff of the dank smoke lodged in the bedspread. "Damn," she said. "I wish I had just one cigarette. Something to take the edge off." Sally dug around in her purse even though she knew there was nothing. She wished she hadn't dumped her ashtray out at the gas station. Probably was one butt she could have gotten a good toke from.

Sally scanned the tacky room. It reminded her of all the lonely nights in that hard apartment with William. All those dinners alone. All that waiting and waiting. Looking through windows for hours. All the cars going by, her ears straining hard. Waiting for his rumbling engine. Staying up half the night, smoking pack after pack, wondering when he'd pull in. She thought about all the crazy fights they had had in that room. All the broken-up dishes, her clothes ripped in half, the big plates of food that had gotten tossed at the wall. She played back the scene of their last blowout.

It was right after she had let him move back in. She'd come home early and found him in the apartment with her coworker. They'd looked like two little kids stuck in a crosswalk right before a bus had mowed them down.

"Shit," Sally said out loud. "I could sure use a cigarette now."

Suddenly there was a sharp rap at the door.

"Excuse me, miss, but I just wanted to see if you needed anything before me and Leon closed the office down for the night. I'm fixin' to go get some fish up at Rusty's. Wanted to see if you wanted some. You was looking kinda hungry when you checked in."

Sally peeked from the hole. Edmond was right there. She could see the hard hairs poking from under his dingy shirt. She could hear Leon's thick, angry cough.

"No thanks," she said through the door. "I need to get some rest. I'm really tired. Thanks for asking." She checked the knob to make sure it was locked. She could see them both step back.

"Well a little shut-eye never hurt nobody. But you sho' don't need no beauty rest." Edmond laughed real loud at that. Leon stepped forward. Sally noticed a pack of Marlboros bulging out from his sleeve.

"Cigarettes," she said under her breath. The nicotine pull yanked her beyond the point of caution. Sally cracked the door. "Mind if I have one to puff on?"

"You can puff on two." It was the first thing Leon had said. He said it really slow. It sounded so sexy. His body was young. Strong and well built, but his face looked like twenty miles of bad road. He snapped the box open and shook the pack until one slid toward her. Sally pulled it out slowly as Leon brought a flame up to her face. His whole hand was a spider web of black tattoos. He had a fresh scar across his brow.

Sally didn't want these two men inside her room, so she stood in the doorjamb and eased the door closed behind her. "I don't like the smell of smoke while I'm trying to sleep," she said, stepping farther out. She leaned against the door, facing her car. Her huge breasts gleamed under the moon.

"Where you from?" Edmond asked, taking out an old pipe and pushing some tobacco in it.

"Los Angeles," she said, blowing her smoke out rapidly.

"I knew it! You can always tell city folks. Spot y'all a mile away. Y'all stay in a hurry. Where you headed?"

"The Grand Canyon," she lied. She figured they'd make her out to be a tourist passing through.

"Yeah, I reckon we get a lot of folks wantin' to see that. Been out here nineteen years and ain't laid eyes on it yet. Ain't nothin' but a big hole, I hear. Lots of red rock. Folks line up for it all day. Standing there in the hot sun. Taking pictures and whatnot. Yesterday they said a lady fell the whole two hundred feet to the bottom. Got knocked straight off the trail by one of them loose rocks. Said her scream ricocheted for miles."

Leon almost smiled at that.

"So where are you from?" she asked, bored. Her eyes were on Leon.

"Why we from right here," Edmond said. "Never been nowhere else. Never wanted to go." Edmond adjusted the straps on his overalls and looked over at Leon. "He don't talk much."

Sally tossed her butt toward her tires. Leon flipped the pack open again.

"You might want one for later," Edmond said slyly.

Sally pulled two cigarettes out. She put one in her front pocket. Both men stared at her heavy chest. She tried to close her jacket but she was so top-heavy, it flapped open again.

Leon jerked one of the beers from the six-pack. He handed it to her.

"No thanks, I don't drink," Sally said, waving the can away.

"Why not? Nothing wrong with a cool drink every now and then," Edmond told her.

Sally was trying to finish her cigarette. She wanted to get back inside. "I don't touch it now. Did though, had a little problem with it."

"Yeah," Edmond said. "If you keep messing with the stuff, nine times out of ten some kind of problem will come up."

Sally remembered her last episode. All the horrible crashing of glass. She watched Edmond drink huge swigs and follow it up with Wild Turkey shots.

"Never learned how to keep away from it myself," he said. "You married?"

"Kinda."

Edmond laughed heartily at that and even Leon, who looked like he'd never smiled in his life, looked at least less mean.

"I guess I'm kinda married, too," Edmond said laughing, stealing a quick glance at Sally's wide ass when she bent down to pick up some matches lying in the street.

"You can have my lighter," he said. "I got a bunch of 'em at home." Sally glanced up at him. She could see he was torn up now. There was a hint of delirium to his eyes.

"Listen, it was nice meeting you both," she said, stepping back.

"Wait now . . . you want some of this?" Edmond took a small package of crumpled foil from his back pocket. "Best weed around. Y'all can't get this in the city." He handed the package to Leon, who carefully rolled three fat joints.

It was really getting late now. Sally didn't want to spend one more minute with these two. And she wasn't about to blaze up in a parking lot in the middle of the night with some hicks. But Leon took the large joint and lit the shit up, right there over the hood of her car.

"Well, I'm goin' on to Rusty's," Edmond said. "Whatchu want boy?"

Leon held up two fingers and said, "Kaafish."

"Catfish sandwich and fries?" Edmond looked at Leon a long time.

"Umm humm," Leon said.

"You be careful out here, boy. Don't want nothing like what happened last time, you hear?" Edmond walked toward a gray pickup. He hoisted his large body inside.

Sally got up from the curb, taking her last cigarette with her. She'd only planned to talk a few minutes to be nice. Her feet were getting cold now. She was ready to go back inside.

"Well, good night," Sally said to Leon, getting to her door quickly and slipping the lock shut. She watched him from the peephole. Leon was blowing the smoke out real slow.

Sally finally breathed out easily. She washed her face and hands and got into bed. She tossed and turned but couldn't sleep. She tiptoed to the door again. Leon was still out there. He was stretched across her car. One leg hung over the rims. His hand was rubbing his flat stomach. *Oh hell*, she thought.

Sally cracked the door open. "You want to come in?"

Leon smiled and walked inside. He closed the door behind him. Sally sat back on the edge of the bed. Leon sat right beside her. He handed her the lit joint. She inhaled it deeply. It was some strong weed. Leon leaned over and picked up one of her black heels. He was rubbing his fingers over the shiny, smooth leather. "You want me to put these back on?" she said sweetly, touching his wide arm.

"Um hum," Leon said. *Must be the quiet type*, she thought. Sally got up and went into the bathroom. Her black slip was almost dry. She pulled it over her head and wiggled out from her jeans. She slid the pumps back on. When she walked out, Leon was standing just outside the door, waiting for her. His shirt was on the floor. His slick chest was nothing but muscle. He picked her up and pressed her against the wall. She wrapped her legs around his slender waist, and he kissed her crazily, carrying her to the bed. He gently laid her down, covering her neck and breasts with his mouth. He was so tender and sweet. Sally ran her hands over his huge back and through his thick black hair. She could feel his belt buckle against her navel. He was grinding more rapidly now. With more fever. Sally playfully moved away. She wanted this to last.

Leon pulled her back toward him. He straddled her and started kissing her down her legs. When he got to her shoe, he pulled it off and tossed it across the room. He smiled big and lavishly sucked each toe. Sally moaned inside his bushy hair. She grabbed a handful and bit into his earlobes. Leon was bucking like a wild bull now. He pulled her slip over her neck. He grabbed her panties with his fist and snatched them from her leg.

Leon got out of his jeans fast. "Slow down, cowboy, I'm not going anywhere," Sally grinned at his naked body. He had the ass of a twelve-year-old boy. She squeezed it while he put himself inside her. He rode her a long time. Real slow. Groaning and going strong. He was breathing faster and faster. Suddenly he yanked it out and burrowed his head between her thighs. Sally thought she would die. Her whole body was hot. Her thighs were pure steel. Leon put it in again, slapping her wide hips until she couldn't hold back anymore. Her whole body jerked into a maddening spasm. Leon was making a guttural sound. The next thing she knew she was asleep.

Sally was half-awake when she found him thrashing away again. He had entered her from behind. He was breathing real heavy, almost wheezing against her. He had her doggy-style and she could smell the hard whiskey from his mouth. She went to grab his head and found he was totally bald.

It was Edmond. He was fucking her like a mad dog. She flipped over and all his weight fell against her chest. His heavy gut made it difficult to breathe. He pinched her breasts until she screamed. Sally tried to squirm from under him. She tried to roll over but she was pinned down. His wide thighs held her legs apart. Edmond bit hard into her flesh. Sally yelled in pain.

"Shut up!" he screamed.

He wadded a washcloth and shoved it in her mouth. She dug her nails into his huge back.

Just then, the front door flew open. Leon came across the room and grabbed Edmond off of her. "Sta . . . Sta . . . Staaaaaap!" he yelled. But Edmond socked Leon across the face, tearing open his new scab again. "You trying to tell me what to do? After I raised your lil' ass! Your own mama don't want ya." Red blood poured down Leon's brow. He threw a punch at Edmond but missed. Edmond smiled wickedly at Leon and smacked him across the mouth. Leon looked like he might cry. "Sta . . . Sta . . . Staaaaaap . . . it," Leon stuttered.

"That's right, start bawlin', you big baby! Ha-ha! What's that you say, boy? Huh?" Edmond laughed in his face. "Look at you. Got the body of a man and the mouth of a two-year-old. Stammering and carryin' on. Can't say one sentence to save your natural life." Leon's lips started quivering. He was starting to drool on one side.

Sally looked at Leon. She had figured him for the quiet type. She didn't know he was simple.

Leon ran up and rammed Edmond with his head. Edmond snatched the lamp from the table and bashed Leon's skull with it. He fell to the floor and didn't move. Edmond looked crazier than ever. He came over to Sally and slammed her back against the bed. She squirmed with all her might and they both rolled to the shag carpet. The TV was right there in her face. The news flashed a story about a man found with his throat slashed in Los Angeles. An unidentified woman was shot with him.

". . . killed in his own home. Police are looking for . . ."

Suddenly Edmond's foot caught the TV cord and he ripped the set right from the stand. It crashed down and went black.

Edmond was laughing crazily and licking Sally's face. It was then she turned her head and she saw it, her black purse right next to her forehead. He wasn't holding her hands, so Sally stretched out her right arm and rummaged through the contents. She finally felt the cool steel. She took the gun out and blasted him in the face. She fired four times, until he slumped over.

Suddenly it was dead quiet. Sally held her breath. She could hear her heart beating. Her whole chest heaved up and down. Suddenly there was another sound, a scratching from behind the TV. She looked down and saw the gray possum dart underneath the bed. Sally grabbed her clothes and got out. She took Leon's Marlboros and both men's wallets. Combined, they had seventy-eight bucks. She snatched the large key ring and went to the front office, opened the cash register, and found another hundred and a half. She took all the candy bars and bags of chips. She got back in her car and roared off. Sally clicked the radio on.

"Manhunt for possible female murderer. Sally Jones has been missing for two days now. Her husband was found murdered in their Compton home."

Sally punched the lighter in and headed up toward the interstate. *Damn*, she thought. *In two days, I killed three people already. There has got to be a better place to live.*

❧ INSPIRATION ☙

Eric Albert

YOUR BREATH'S HEAVY, your breasts heave. It won't be long now.

"Story?" you say, your voice a falling leaf.

I slowly surface. I'm fresh from the chapel on the ground floor, still knee-deep in prayer. The monitor is beeping cheerfully.

"What?" I say.

"Story."

I heard you right. "Like a filthy story?" But I already know what you mean.

I fumble about in my head for the list of things that make you hot. Everything I find feels dry and foolish. You cough, then choke. I reach across the bed rail and pat your hand as if it helps a damn.

And, just like that, the images appear, the words tumbling toward my tongue.

"Your whim is my command," I say. Then I begin.

I'm at work, bragging on you to the guy next office down: "My girl loves it up the ass, gives it anytime I want."

"No fucking way," he says. "My wife won't take a finger there. A hundred dollars says you're full of shit."

"You're on."

I use his phone, call home, get you, and let him overhear. "I want your best hole when I get back. Be ready." I hang up, no goodbye.

"He'll lose," you say.

"I know, hon. Let me tell it."

You take off your jeans and panties, buzzed with horniness. A bit of lube and you've slipped in the little gray butt plug. When you walk, your small, flat rump pokes out from under your shirttail, and the butt plug's base pokes out from between your cheeks.

You spend the rest of your day at home in just your top, an eye on the clock for when I'll return. Each hour, you swap the current butt plug for a bigger one. The increasing size keeps you constantly aware of your asshole, and what's to come, and what's to come in it. You like this preparation, gradually stretching yourself so I can instantly enter you.

Eventually, you're wearing the huge butt plug, one and three-quarter pounds of chromium steel—

"Love it," you say.

"Yeah. Pipe down."

Yes, it's the steel butt plug, custom-lathed to precise specifications by a mutual friend. Most women couldn't stand up with this inside; the weight would immediately overpower them with a CLONG! and a dent in the floor.

You're not most women, though—your ass muscles are strong from countless hours of late-night holding, gripping, squeezing. But even you can hardly concentrate with this monster in your rear; it's a relief when you hear me at the door.

You ditch the plug and plunk yourself down on the front hall floor, resting on your knees and tits, arms stretched out past your head, rug musty in your nose. Your ass is up, way up, and your hole gapes open, remembering the steel's thickness. Your tender tissues feel cool air as the door opens.

You picture what I see. You shiver. "Do it," *you call out.* "Fuck my fucking ass!"

"Sounds good, sweet pie," *I say.* "But what about my friend?"

You jerk your head up, crane to look back over your shoulder. You've never seen this guy in your life.

He's never seen you either, but he knows he's out a hundred bucks.

"Told you."

I tell him, "Get in front, get out your dick." *He almost tramples your hand as he races for position. He kneels, fumbles with his fly. His hard-on bounces before your eager eyes.*

I say, "You want your ass fucked, you show him a good time." *At once your mouth's all over him, licking, sucking, balls, shaft, everything; you do it for me, you do it for you, you do it for all you're worth.*

He's locked in place, eyes focused on your butt, which is still high, framed by the bottom of your shirt. I squat beside your shoulder, watch you work.

I glance at him. "You like the way my girl drinks dick?" *His eyes stay glued to your ass as he answers,* "Angel. Cock-sucking angel."

"Yeah. Pay up." *He can't believe my words, but I recognize a good bargaining position. I tell you,* "Don't let him come until he's square." *You nod your head, his prick.*

He gets it. "Fuck you, man, you're fucking twisted." *He goes into his pocket, pulls out bills, hands me five.*

"For fifty more you get her throat."

That earns me a look. His hand's back in his pants. I tap your head once, soft. By the time I've knelt behind you, pants and briefs cushioning my knees, your lips are jammed against his zipper. Show-off.

"Who, me?"

I squeeze your hand.

I shove my cock up your ass with a thrust. You gasp, I think; hard to tell.

I look along your body and meet his eyes. We'll have a lot to talk about at work. I say, "Stay deep—it makes her hole sweet as hell." *He nods solemnly and laces his hands behind your head to anchor you.*

The butt plugs have done their job; I go straight from zero to ninety. My crotch whams your cheeks, my balls echo against your lips, my whole prick's happy. I am seriously fucking your ass.

No need to hold your hips—the cock up front keeps you right here. My frenzied humping forces you to swallow the final half inch of his erection. Maybe that's why he's closed his eyes and started moaning.

Or maybe it's the way your throat's convulsing on him. Your body's shuddering, too. It's been just forty seconds but time passes slowly when you're jammed between two dicks and the oxygen stops.

Your hole goes tight. I push on through to heaven, full-fucking your slick tube as it molds itself to my prick. I'm using you, owning you, loving you, knowing you.

I can't hold back. I yell at him, "Come on. Down her throat." *He goes off and your body writhes, your asshole jerking wildly as it pumps out my semen. We collapse on the rug and all is silence except for you coughing, gasping, gagging.*

I stop. You're laughing silently. I know how much that hurts, but damn, it's good to see.

Your voice trickles out. "*Gagging.* Oh, you."

"I work with what I've got."

Your hand bats mine. "Excited?"

I lean over and brush your nose with a kiss. "Yes, sugarplum. You know what stories do to me."

"Make him happy."

I snort. "Come on. The place is crawling with nurses."

"Don't care."

"Well, I do. They tell me to leave, I'll have to kill 'em."

You extend your tongue. Hell. We both know I'm going to do it. In what universe have I ever won a battle with you?

"Okay, okay." I get up and close the door, which has no lock. I grab the chair by the other bed and push it over so I'll have some warning. I hope.

Back at my station, I grip myself through my jeans. I'm fully erect. I squeeze, thumb and two fingers, just below the head. Relax. Squeeze. Relax. Squeeze.

Your eyes drift closed. Wrinkles pile up on your brow like storm clouds, then disperse as the spasm passes. I see the face behind your face, the face I fell for back when we were whole.

Maybe you've fallen asleep.

"You close?" you murmur.

Maybe not. "You *sure* you want me to finish?"

"Cunt tease."

I lean forward. My fingers work. Your hand gropes for my other wrist and circles it. "Here goes," I say, and pulse against the unyielding Formica chair, my body emptying into my jeans.

I slump back. "Satisfied? These are the only pants I brought."

You grip my wrist tight, tighter than I thought you could. "Taste."

"You know we can't do that."

"Taste." Your whisper's fierce.

"Nothing by mouth," I say, as if you don't know your own chart.

Your eyes flick open and fix on mine. "Fuck. That."

Right. I unzip my fly and poke two fingers through the gap in my briefs. They come out sticky and I hold them up for you to see. Your face is shining. I paint your chapped lips, and they stretch into a smile that leaves me breathless.

೮ಾ FIVE DIMES ೮ಾ
Anita Melissa Mashman

"You want me to do what?" I asked, surprised, looking down at the silver coins on my naked stomach.

Patiently he explained again.

"Stand in the middle of the room, with your legs spread. Then put your hands together, over your head, palm to palm, with a dime between each pair of fingers and your thumbs."

Pulse beating fast, I thought, *What interesting little game does he have in mind this time?* I looked at the Cheshire grin on his face and said: "Anything you say, lover."

I walked across the bare wooden boards where he had rolled up the fluffy rug and stood, legs spread, nipples tightening with excitement as I wondered what he had planned. I carefully balanced a dime on the tip of each finger and the thumb of my left hand. Then I put my right hand over the left, fingertip to fingertip, and raised my arms over my head. He took his time walking over to me, although his erection advertised that he was excited, too. He put one hand on my waist and began to walk around me slowly as he explained.

"No matter what I do, no matter how you feel, don't let go of the dimes."

He was behind me now, his left arm wrapped around my waist and his right hand lifting the long hair from my neck. He whispered in my ear:

"If you drop a dime, and you can be sure I'll hear it on this wooden floor, everything stops . . . everything."

Then he kissed my neck and nibbled on my ear as his hands caressed my breasts. I moaned in dismay. Already my hands were sweaty. He kissed my neck more, sucking, nibbling, as his hands teased my tight nipples. He stepped back a bit and ran his nails lightly over my back, tracing tickling, exciting patterns, moving teasingly near my sensitive armpits. I shook with the effort to keep my arms up when every nerve screamed for me to protect myself from being tickled. He stepped in front of me again, standing almost nose to nose as his hands rested lightly high on my sides.

"Nervous?" he asked, barely moving his fingers as I shivered.

"Please don't . . ." My plea hung in the air, unfinished, as his hands slid down my round stomach and between my legs, where my swollen labia dripped moisture.

"Well, somebody's excited," he said and softly stroked my vaginal lips. I felt a tightening in my lower stomach, almost painful, as I responded, tilting my pelvis forward, desperately holding the slippery dimes above my head. He bent his head and sucked on my nipple, flicking it with his tongue as his fingers stroked and burrowed in my hot, wet cunt. My knees trembled and my arms shook with strain, but I held on to those five coins. I could feel moisture running down my leg, sweat or sexual fluids, I didn't know. His lips left my breast and he glanced up at my shaking arms and my equally shaky grin.

"Good girl," he said and kissed me, our tongues meeting and dancing. The fingers of his right hand rubbed gently round and round my clitoris. Then his left hand slithered down my sweaty back, between my buttocks, and gently stroked my anus, too. I almost came then, fingers rigid, thinking I would just die if I dropped a dime.

Abruptly he stopped, moving directly in front of me, his hands on my hips.

"No, no," I pleaded. "Don't stop, please. I haven't dropped any coins."

I pushed my throbbing crotch against his stiff, satiny erection, wanting him to be as aroused as I was. My lover just smiled, sank to his knees, and began to kiss my labia, teasingly. I closed my eyes, trying not to let the growing heat weaken my grip as he gently parted my vaginal lips.

"Oh, yes," I breathed as his tongue touched my clitoris. Tremors began in my thighs and I came then, crying out, as he took a long, sucking bite.

The dimes fell in a silvery shower as my exhausted arms fell forward, and I caressed my lover's head.

Slowly I calmed down, my knees felt stronger, the cramps left my fingers. I bent over, picked up the dimes, and put them in my lover's hand.

"Your turn," I whispered in his ear.

๖ BACKHAND ๙
Ernie Conrick

LOSING IN THE QUARTERFINALS was the worst part of the U.S. Open. The next worst thing was that it all took place in Flushing Meadows, Queens—no comment necessary there. The next worst thing was that it was painfully hot. The next worst thing was that Oleg, my hockey player boyfriend, ignored me because his babushka was in town and he was ashamed to be seen with his seventeen-year-old blonde *devochka*. I think that in English you would say that he has no balls.

But Mariana made up for all of it. I don't need to say a thing about her, really, she was a legend in women's tennis before I even picked up a racket. I'm still not sure I like her, even after what happened, but I am sure that I do respect her for not giving a shit about being a six-foot-two-inch Slavic dyke when it was still hard to be anything but a proper lady. And I respect her for what she did for me—although that's fucked up in its own way, as you'll see.

Mariana is an intimidating presence, tall, towheaded, piercing blue eyes that look out from a severe brow and pointed eyebrows. Even at forty-four, her body is rock-hard, or at least the muscles are. As for her skin, it's simply spent too much time unprotected under the sun, like the skin of all tennis players, and is leathery and tough like a hide, as if it had been skinned from her body, treated by a tanner, and then reattached. Nevertheless, a defiant sensuality shines through those forty-four-year-old wrinkles so that, even as I made a concerted effort to ignore her, I, on occasion, could not help but glance quickly at her from the sidelines and admire the knots of muscles on her calves, or the severe shadow of her jaw.

Of course, she hated me immediately. Rather, I should say that she hated me in a very particular way that is unique to women, and possibly unique to Mariana herself. Whenever her eyes would fall on me either during a warm-up or in the locker rooms, I would feel a cold disdain, cold and hard like I imagined her heart to be. She got to where she was by a Nietzschean effort of will, and she could see quite clearly that I was where I was (financially at least) with the generous help of my figure, my long blonde hair, my party-girl image, and the pictures of me on the covers of fashion and sports magazines looking kittenish, coquettish, and just plain slutty.

From my own point of view, the only people who complain about it are people who can't do it themselves, but I will admit that I've had more press coverage than the top ten women in the world, and I've never been ranked higher than twelfth. I don't blame her.

She first spoke to me as I walked off the court about two days before the Open. I was having a great day on the court, which bothered me, because I thought I would curse my game if I was too good during the warm-up. I feel better when I am less than my best until the day of the matches. Somewhere in my mind, I believe that you get only so many good games, and you need to save them up for the right time.

"Your name is Anna?" she asked as I walked off the court.

I nodded but stayed silent.

"Anna Gramovitch?"

We both smiled weakly at each other. I rubbed a towel up my arm, across the upper half of my chest.

"Do you know who I am?" she asked, gaze following the rag as I slid it across the back of my neck.

"A variant rival to a man," I answered.

There was a pause as she drove her hard blue eyes into mine.

"Let me tell you something. . . ." She leaned close. "Think more about your game, less about hockey players."

I rolled my eyes and headed for the locker room, but Mariana fastened an iron grip around my triceps and held me in place. "Gravenfort will eat you alive if your return is not better." She looked me dead center.

"*Spasibo*," I said. She was old and ugly and retired and irrelevant. I ripped my elbow from her and walked away.

When the Open started I was a victorious tornado. I removed the much-acclaimed but slow and lumpy Gravenfort 6–2, 6–3. Next, I eked out a win over the younger Neptune sister, Valariana, with a perfect shot down the baseline, followed by a perfect backhand and a series of equally perfect serves (even though the press keeps claiming that I cannot serve). She pouted and looked at me like an enraged lemur, but I met her most irate behavior with professional sportswomanship.

The crowd naturally championed their faltering poster girl, but nevertheless, a vocal minority could not resist my golden charm and made their support known.

After my win (4–6, 6–4, 6–4), Valariana's father told reporters I was the product of a Nazi eugenics experiment. Despite these remarks, I noticed he never took his eyes off of the Nike Swoosh on the front of my tennis dress. I suggested that perhaps she would do better next time if she would rid herself of those swinging braids, which surely affect her peripheral vision and make her look ridiculous. I even offered to braid her hair like my stylish coiffure, but this placated neither Valariana nor her rabid sire.

I was looking for Mariana after my victories to remind her that her prediction about Gravenfort had gone horribly wrong, but I did not see her either during or after the matches. I did see her once briefly in the company of Terri Fierce, that amazon with the prominent beak. I wondered what was going on there, but decided that I didn't want to know anyway.

My performance was faultless up to this point. I was in the quarterfinals and faced Christina Hinges, who was, in my opinion, a bit rusty, having been sidelined for six weeks with an ankle injury. Prior to this I had defeated her twice in a row. I fully expected to make cheese out of this little Swiss girl with my obnoxious forehand.

And so, the night before my quarterfinal match, when I should have been at the hotel resting, I was confident enough to accept Oleg's apologetic invitation to dinner. He was very gentlemanly, and obviously wanted to make up to me. Apparently his babushka did not like Ukrainians or some such nonsense. I really didn't give a damn what this old woman thought, but was irritated that he would hide me like that from his family. I was, after all, an international tennis superstar and sex symbol with millions of dollars in paid advertising endorsements. You'd think that the boy would be able to get around some fossilized prejudice in the old bag's head.

Despite his best efforts, though, our date was a disaster. If he wasn't talking about his mother or his grandmother, he was going on and on about his team's owner, some brain-damaged millionaire named Henry Quillgreen. According to Oleg he had taken most of the money meant for the hockey team and given it to a man who promised to develop barrel rides for tourists over Niagara Falls.

The long and the short of it was that Oleg might be traded to Calgary. When he said this I just looked at him. He must realize that if he moves to Alberta the most he will see of me is the pictures on the Gatorade bottle. I told him he could either make his peace with the Jew or forget about me.

"*Ach*, listen my little fish . . ." he said, leaning in close, "I was just mentioning it to let you know what is going on in my life, that is all."

"Well, now I know."

"Don't be angry, Anna."

"How can I not be? You are such a disappointment."

There was silence for a long time. I drank a Vodka tonic, then two.

"Anna Petrovich," he sighed after a thoughtful puff on his cigar. "You cannot be unhappy with me for long. I have quite a gift for you back at my place, you will—"

"Then I must remain unhappy with you for a while longer, because I am not going to your place tonight," I answered firmly.

"Anna . . ."

While this depressing scene was going on I tried to forget about Oleg by sucking on my drink. I sucked too much and presently felt dizzy. The candles and the glasses and the Caspian beluga swam before my eyes. It was at that moment that I felt a pair of icy blue eyes on me from across the restaurant. It was Mariana.

I almost didn't recognize her at first; she was sitting with two other women at a table across from us wearing a long, sleeveless black dress, flat shoes, and a string of pearls. I chuckled to myself, thinking, "Who has ever seen this woman dressed like this?" At the same time, I must admit that, far from seeming out of place in her clothes, she had a gawky, long-legged elegance to her. The dress made her look even longer than she was, so that she seemed to grow out of the ground like a vine.

Catching her eye, I smiled at her and raised my glass. Her lips tightened around her teeth and her body seemed suddenly rigid, as if she were getting ready to leap right at my throat. I saw her mouth move as she said something to her companions, who looked over their shoulders at me and giggled simultaneously. Then she smiled widely and winked at me.

I took another draft of my Stoli. It all seemed amusing at the moment, to have two famous athletes both flirting with me at the same time, one male, one female. I smiled back at her.

As the evening wore on, Oleg became more unbearable. He wanted to know why I wasn't coming back with him to his apartment. The fact that I was in the quarterfinals of the U.S. Open was apparently not a good enough reason. It occurred to me that he didn't even take my career seriously. Unable to endure him for much longer, and far more buzzed than I should have been the night before a match, I excused myself while he asked the waiter for the humidor.

In the marble ladies' room I looked at myself in the mirror. I looked somewhat tired and sad. Most people do not know that one of my eyes is not straight, it looks off to the side a bit. Maybe this allows me to see the ball coming better, I don't know. But in the mirror it almost seemed as if each eye were connected to a different brain, a different personality, a different person.

I can look at myself only one eye at a time, strange to say. It is always my straight, left eye. This is my strong eye and it seems like the me with which I am familiar. My right eye wanders a bit away from my nose. I have to tip my head to look in this eye, and when I do, I am not sure who I see.

My head throbbed. I loosened my braid and combed my locks with my fingers. I flicked some of my hair in front of my right eye so that it no longer looked back at me. That made me feel prettier. Then I played with the straps of my gown and the pendant that hung around my neck. Looking down I could see my cleavage and the slit in my skirt that ran up my thigh.

I once told an interviewer that my skirts were not shorter than the other players' skirts, it was just that my legs were longer. Looking at myself in the mirror again, I ran my hands from this slit, up over my pelvis and my tummy, to the spot right below my breasts. The papers were right: I was a gorgeous blonde goddess.

I ran some water on my hands, then wet my cheeks and brow. I learned over the marble sink into the mirror until I was inches from my own face. My thong nipped my pink anus as my haunches extended. "So this is what it looks like to kiss me," I thought. No wonder the boys pay so much attention. My single eye was captivating, luxurious, and intoxicating. My hair was coiled a bit and fell like flames over my chest, while my arms were supple and long, tan from the sun with tiny white hairs standing erect. I pouted my scarlet lips, then licked them with my shy tongue. Without even knowing what I was doing, I closed my eye and kissed myself.

The tip of my nose turned up as my lips pressed against the cold glass. "Mmm," I said.

I stayed that way for a moment, my hips swaying back and forth against the marble sink top. Then my eye, my wandering right eye, saw through the falling strands of my hair, into the mirror and around my shoulder.

Mariana was staring back from the mirror like a wraith in the shadows. She did not move.

I smiled shyly.

"Such a pretty girl," she said in her Czech accent.

"Thank you," I laughed, still leaning over the marble sink.

She slid up behind me, "If only you were not such a brat." And she slapped my ass; she slapped it a shade too hard for it to be a joke, and her hand lingered there without moving.

I straightened up and felt my buttocks tighten and sting against her wide, strong hand. Looking at us in the mirror I said, "I get paid to be a brat," and lowered my eyes.

"Not by me," she said in a low monotone, sliding her hand up to my lower back.

She pulled me toward her—or maybe I lost my balance on my heels— or maybe I just voluntarily settled back into her encircling arms. I really can't be sure. Her arms were around me and all over me; she was all hands, like some Buddhist bodhisattva clawing at the Shakti on his lap. One hand was on my thigh, playing with the slit, another on my waist. A third hand slid up my side to my neck, a fourth cupped my breast, a fifth ran lightly across my nipple, and a sixth pulled at my dress. A seventh hand lifted my hemline several inches; an eighth pulled my hair with a tug so that my chin was forced up to a forty-five-degree angle. Her lips were rough and cold on my neck, like a hairy bug crawling leg by leg toward my ear.

I heard the door open from the dining room. Startled, I stared open-mouthed into her eyes.

"Please," I whispered.

She wouldn't have stopped unless I'd said something, I am sure of it. And the irony of it was that here I was, the bad girl of tennis, pleading with Mariana to not start a scandal. She had no reason to stop—what did she care, she never hid a thing from anyone. But she did stop for me and smiled almost awkwardly. When the door opened and two Japanese women walked in, she played like she was my older aunt helping me to braid my hair. Wisdom is where confidence meets reality.

The two girls came to the mirror beside and chatted in rapid-fire Japanese. Mariana winked at me in the mirror and squeezed my shoulders with her rough hands.

"Good luck," she said, and turning as if she were leaving a military review, she walked out the door.

When she had gone, I looked in the mirror at myself again, this time into both eyes at the same time. I looked different.

Contrary to my expectations, it was a well-oiled Christina Hinges that showed up to the quarterfinals. To make matters worse, I had a hangover. I was the worst of all possible combinations. I felt as if I were playing in some sort of vacuum without air or noise. It was like an ocean of pain, where the crowd would roar, then hush like waves; and in the interim there would be a hard silence punctuated with my groans and Christina's girlish grunts. My returns were clunky, my backhand weak, and my serves inevitably missed the mark. I tried to salvage my game in the second set, but I could only concentrate for short moments at a time.

It seemed to me that the spectators rose on top of each other like layers of an inverted ziggurat. On top of the highest layer there seemed to be another layer, but this time of opaque entities of oppressive humidity called clouds. They piled on top of each other, up into the air, hanging over the rim of the stadium, looking down on us, pressing in on us like schoolboys trying to see a school-yard fight. Lecherous little boys, looking and pointing and whistling and finally spitting—first one drop, then two, then a barrage of thousands, all spitting on me from above. They called a rain delay.

I sat on the bench during the interim, looking at the small squares of space between the strings of my racket. Olga, my coach, asked me repeatedly what was wrong. She told me to wake up and to stop dreaming.

"Are you in love, Anna Petrovich?" she asked.

I shook my head.

Somebody whistled in the crowd. "Come on, Anna!" yelled a deep voice. I turned my face and saw that it was Mariana. She was sitting about three rows behind, between her two companions from the previous night, and wearing the exact same dress. She clapped her hands twice and an almost involuntary smile tugged at the wrinkled corners of her mouth. It seemed to me that she was making fun of me, trying to sabotage whatever concentration I could manage.

In the next set I was so angry that I consistently overhit the ball and faulted on the serve. Hinges was swinging like the doors of a whorehouse on payday. The coup de grâce was delivered by the line judge, who obviously hated me and called every shot for my opponent. When I protested, she ignored me, and the crowd cheered, as if it were just more entertainment for them.

They said in the paper that I refused to shake hands with Christina after the match. I really don't remember, but I think that perhaps it was Christina's dirty hands, more than my anger, that made me pass her by. She should wash them more often. I have nothing against sportswomanship, but I am not going to get a disease just to be nice, the press be damned.

People would not leave me alone on my way to the locker room. They shoved microphones in my face and leaned in front of me, and Olga would not shut up. I just wanted to be left alone. In my dressing room, I asked Olga to please leave me alone, but she kept talking about my backhand as if I gave a shit. Finally I yelled and threw my racket at the wall. She may claim all she wants that I threw it at her, but she just wants to get on TV. Finally, she let me be, and I cried on the carpet between the locker and the massage bench.

I didn't hear Mariana come in. I just heard her voice between sobs and heaves of my chest.

"You were not even trying, Anna Petrovich," she said, "you were thinking of something else . . . or perhaps you have been having too much fun."

I sat up. I hated her.

"You must really decide what you want to be," she said, "a champion or a party girl."

"You were there last night, too."

"Yes, but I am not playing today." She sat down on the bench in front of me, sitting on her hands.

"Is that what this is all about?" I asked. "You want to shame me? Does that make you happy, Mariana?"

"Yes, of course," she answered, with again the hint of smile that came from that borderland between altruism and cruelty.

I cried and lifted my hands to my face. She tried to pull me toward her, to press my head against her lap, but I shoved her away. She tried again.

"Go away," I said in a high and quavering voice, "what do you want?"

"For you to be a good girl," she answered, and crossed her arms in front of her chest.

"And how do I do that?" I cried more, to the point where I could not breathe. I wanted her to pull me to her, but she kept her arms crossed. I reached for her and my slender hands grasped her dress at the knee, then I knelt forward onto her lap, between her iron thighs. I wanted her to touch me. "I want to be, Mariana, I want to be." And, sobbing, I wet the cloth between her legs.

I pressed my face to her lap, and she pressed her lap to my face. My tears soaked her dress through, and then the cloth changed and it wasn't her dress anymore—and it was wet but not with tears.

I looked up at Mariana's face. Her eyes were fierce, severe, and wary. I lowered my eyes to her wet cunt. Her callused hand slapped her thigh sharply, like a ringmaster ordering his bear to dance. Looking up to her to make sure I understood, I pushed aside her underpants and felt her soft brown hair on my lips and nose. I inhaled deeply and took her scent deep inside me. For the moment, I forgot about tennis. To forget about tennis even for one moment feels like those first minutes after my braces were removed, so long ago. It felt strange and easy and finally natural.

As a thirsty pet rodent taking a drink from a water bottle moves the metal ball with its tongue to release the moisture behind it, so I lapped at Mariana's wet cunt. She stood, and lifting her dress with one hand, ground her softness into me from above. I inserted my tongue and, curling it upward, probed her moist, pelvic void. I imagined that every time I licked her, my tongue caught drops of her greatness.

My lips found her hooded clit and I placed it between my teeth like a champagne grape. I sucked her clit, gently flicking my pink tongue in a horseshoe-shaped swish around the hood, then back again; wax on, wax off.

She enveloped my face with her iron thighs so that my next breath must have come from deep inside her. I licked and licked and licked her wet cunt. I closed my eyes and tongue-fucked her with lightning quickness over and over again until my face was awash in her juices. Mariana's hips bucked against my tongue, trying to escape, but I pushed forward and pressed my lips desperately against her swollen labia.

She shoved me from her half-gently. I looked into her eyes and she still had the same fierce expression.

"Lift your arms, Anna," she commanded. When I complied, she removed my tennis dress with a single motion so that I was naked on the floor before her, nipples hard, my pale white haunches that turned to brown thighs, and my downy blonde hair between my legs wet and heavy. While her cold blue eyes appraised me, I unbraided my hair and shook my head so that it fell on my spine and tickled me.

She knelt in front of me so that our knees touched. Her rough hands traveled up my legs to my waist. She kissed me once, lightly on the lips, and then . . . crack!

She slapped me hard, not playfully, with the back of her hand. I was not expecting this and was stunned for a moment. Angry, my brows knit and I tried to rise. She pushed me down again.

"Stop it!" I squealed like a kitten, trying to rise again. Her thick arm caught me and I spun around as I was pushed toward the locker. Behind me now, she curled one arm around my waist and hooked my ankle with hers in a grapevine such that I could not rise.

"Stop it!" I repeated, "get off of me!"

"Shh," Mariana whispered, "shh."

I tried to rise but could not. When I felt her fingers work into my pussy and wiggle inside me, I was furious.

I screamed like a girl.

"Shh." She added another finger.

I yelled again and tried to rise, my hips inadvertently pushing against her. I bucked.

"Shh, be good," Mariana purred, as she finger-fucked me.

I screamed again, but softer and lower.

"Shh." She slapped my ass hard with her free hand.

My screams were no longer really screams.

The door rattled and I could hear Olga's voice on the other side.

"Anna, are you okay?" she asked.

I meant to say, "Help me, I am being attacked!" but all I could manage was, "Olga!"

"Anna, open the door," Olga yelled.

I meant to say, "Help! She is crazy!" But Mariana's hand kept moving in and out of me and she kept whispering "shh" into my ear, and I didn't say anything.

"Anna, do you need help?" Olga yelled. Mariana yanked my hair so that my head jerked back. She finger-fucked me hard and fast.

"Anna! I am going to break down the door!"
Her fist entered my hot insides.
"Go away, Olga!" I yelled.
"Anna!"
"Shh."
"I am okay, just go away, Olga, go away!"
Olga went away.
"Shh." "Good girl," whispered Mariana, fisting me.
I shuddered and cried; hips and hair flailing. Mariana's fist slammed into me over and over again until I didn't know what was happening. I came so hard that I was almost unconscious. I didn't hear Mariana leave and she didn't say goodbye.

After this experience I decided that it was, perhaps, time to end my affair with Oleg. He was heading to his babushka's place near Brighton Beach, so I invited myself along, telling him that I had to talk to him seriously. I could have ended it all over the phone, but I didn't. It was more authentic to speak to him face-to-face.

When I arrived, his grandmother's apartment was in turmoil. His grandmother, hearing that I was arriving for dinner, decided to display her mastery of American cooking by making us a lobster dinner. After locating a seafood store, she was surprised to find that the creatures were sold while still alive. She bought the poor fellow nevertheless. The old lady had it in her head that all fish, live or not, should be prepared in the same way: covered in bread crumbs and butter, and baked in the oven on a cookie sheet at 350 degrees. And so the creature's eight kicking limbs were doused in melted butter and covered in crushed Ritz crackers, after which he was placed, much against his will, on the middle rack of a very hot convection oven.

Shortly before I walked through the door the lobster, subjected to such conditions, began to scream. It is true, they can scream. Not only do they scream, they make the most pitiful, plaintive moaning noises that you have ever heard as the exoskeleton is heated.

The old lady had run out of the kitchen and was pacing up and down in the dining room.

"Shut up! Shut up, you little shit!" she said over and over again.

Oleg was in a state of indecision before the oven, holding a skewer in one hand and a pot holder in the other.

"Anna, the thing keeps yelling at us . . . this is not supposed to happen." He had a look on his face that I have never seen before, like a little boy afraid to jump in the swimming pool.

"Ahhhhhhhhhhhhhooooooooooooo!" screamed the lobster.

I opened the oven. A smell like burning pitch came out. The poor little crustacean had crawled off the pan, dragging its charred body into a corner in the back. Its antennae had fallen off and the stubs waved frenetically in the smoky air. Its eyes had burst, leaving him blind, and a whitish blue foam came from its mouth. Inside the thick rubber bands, the creature's claws clicked together, straining to free themselves.

"Ahhhhhhhhhhhhhooooooooooooo!" it cried.

Babushka looked over our shoulders, "Still it is not dead!" she exclaimed.

Now Oleg crouched next to me. "I will kill it," he claimed, and took several tentative stabs at the bug with his skewer. The lobster pulled back instinctively. Oleg tried again, but the angle was impossible.

In the end, it proved very resilient. Oleg finally removed it with tongs and brought it out to the driveway, where I smashed it with a shovel repeatedly until it lay still, heaving a final, tiny groan.

"I do not think it would be good to eat now," his grandmother remarked with a grimace, and disappeared inside.

Oleg and I sat on the steps and stared at the smooshed body of the lobster, still smoking in front of us. There was a long pause.

"I'm sorry," said Oleg at last. "Dinner has not gone as planned. . . ."

I nodded.

"Anna . . . did you have something to tell me?" he asked.

I shook my head. "No," I answered. I rested on his shoulder and sighed. I felt so heavy and tired.

"No," I said again, "but Oleg dear."

He raised a questioning eyebrow.

"Next time I will cook."

ᕤ BEYOND THE SEA ᕥ
Susan DiPlacido

IT'S NOT THE HEAT. It's the humidity.

I was born and raised in the Florida heat. A water baby from the start, I was surfing by the time I was a four-year-old boy, and by the time I was twelve, people were already calling me Rip. You don't spend that much time at the beach without being able to appreciate a hot day. Back when I was on the tour, surfing my way around South Africa, Portugal, and the Philippines, heat was a given. I could always take it.

But I never took to the humidity. That was different. That came in unexpected spots. France. The Northeast. Some of the tropical places. It'd seem worse at night; that dense, lung-crushing closeness that left your skin sticky.

That's what it is here on the USS *Lurline*, a cruise ship in the Caribbean.

Humid. Sweaty. Inescapable.

It never seems to let up.

But I can't complain. This gig's better than a washed-up ex–pro surfer deserves.

Carl, the pool deck manager, nudges me, shaking me out of my daze. He's just another glorified deckhand, but since we work at the pool together, he likes to think he's my boss.

"Show a little life, Golden Boy," he growls under his breath, and checks his watch. We're greeting passengers as they debark the ship for the day on this particular island, reminding them to come hang out at the pool when they're tired of the beach.

So I oblige. Smiling, nodding, pressing my hand against the passengers', feeling the film of sweat and Coppertone. Glad-handing and greeting. That's what I do now, along with giving surfing demos on board twice a day in our patented Wave-Life surf pool.

After the accident, most people expected I wouldn't surf again. Except other surfers. They expected I'd heal up and then hit the waves.

I guess you'd call this a compromise.

A pretty blonde lingers in front of me. "Thanks for the lesson, Rip," she purrs. She brushes her hand down my arm. Her skin is soft and dry, but it picks up the slick of mine as her hand travels down my arm.

"Give it a try," I tell her as I hand her a brochure for a board rental shop.

"Anyway you'd be able to join me?" she asks, tilting her head. Cat eyes, with a mischievous slant. But the heat is making her perfume too strong. "Maybe a little private lesson. Or demonstration. On a real beach."

Before I can answer, Carl laughs.

"What's so funny?" the blonde asks. Her brows knit together, reminding me of Cindy. Cindy also used to insist on perfume, even on the stickiest of days. I hated that. These passing resemblances to Cindy are what always make my once-formidable libido tank. No matter who the woman is, I always notice something in her that reminds me of her.

"I don't surf beaches," I tell the blonde.

"But," she says, "you're a world champion."

"*Was* a world champion," Carl corrects her.

"I had an accident," I tell her.

"Oh," she says. Her eyes flit up and down my body, looking for obvious scars, even though she'd just seen my relatively unscathed skin when I put on a show in the Wave-Life on the Fiesta deck. By the time she finishes her brief inspection, I can see the change in her eyes. She's made her judgment, and deemed me to be a coward.

And now she walks away.

Carl slaps me on the shoulder. "You could've at least walked her to the beach, Rip."

"We're not supposed to get intimate with the passengers."

He laughs even harder.

"She wasn't my type."

"She's not your type, just like the ocean isn't the type of place where a surfer belongs." As he moves to brush past me, he collides with a couple of cruisers heading back up the walkway. He jostles with a dark-haired woman, who clings to him briefly before straightening herself and pushing away. Her sunglasses fall to the ground.

"S'cuse me," the brunette says as she reaches down for her shades. But as she leans, Carl does too, knocking his forehead against hers.

While Carl holds his forehead, I nab the shades before they get kicked away. "Here." I offer them to the woman.

"Gracias," she purrs as her fingers ease them out of my grasp, her skin never making contact with mine. I can't smell a trace of perfume. Her eyes lock with mine for a full two seconds. But then she slides the shades back on and says nothing more, to either me or Carl, and turns to head back to the ship. Her dark curls bob below her shoulders. She's not wearing Juicy Couture, but it could've been her ass that inspired the brand.

I don't realize I'm staring until Carl slaps my chest. "Do you see that?"

"I see." She's wearing khaki shorts, with a glorious set of long, strong, tan legs carrying her, and that juicy ass, quickly away from us.

"You see her trying to tango with me?" Carl asks me.

"I saw." Up ahead, the crowd thickens and closes around her.

"She wants Carl to dock in her port, Golden Boy."

The sweat gathers on my forehead, a couple of beads starting to trickle from my scalp. I swipe them away as I turn back to face the land and let the breeze cool my back.

That afternoon, I'm next to the Wave-Life with about twenty people gathered, dudes and chicks who didn't bother to go ashore or who already came back on board. I keep the talk short, 'cause no one wants to hear what I've got to say anyhow. It's mostly just, "Show us how it's done, Rip!" from the couple of guys who remember me from the Wild Cherry Splash ThirstAde commercial I did five years back when I was still riding the wave from my first world championship.

I tell 'em a couple basic things. Get 'em to lie down and pantomime paddling out. Maybe if anyone's interested I'll get them in the other pool later and do it for real. But for now, with the talk gassed out, I grab my board and hop into the Wave-Life.

The water's heated, but it's cool enough. It's the only time I ever feel relief from the sticky, thick atmosphere. Even though it's "surfing lite," it's still better than not surfing at all. My brain shuts down and my body takes over. I've been doing it so long I can't even tell if it's training or instinct, but finding the perfect balance and riding it out in the Wave-Life seems easy. Effortless.

I'm in one of those endless recycling grooves when a blur of red catches my peripheral vision. I track it, and that's when I see her again. Carl's chick. The one he nearly ran over earlier; she's standing to the side of the Wave-Life, watching. Her khakis are off, and she's wearing a red bikini, eyes still obscured behind those dark glasses. She takes off her shades and smiles at me. Just as I'm flirting with the idea of what trick I can pull, she reaches in a beach bag near her feet, but it's nestled even closer to the feet of another girl. Casual, her hand slips inside the bag. Instead of looking inside, she locks eyes with me again, this time bringing her forefinger to her lips, gesturing for silence. As she rises back up, she pulls something from the other woman's bag. I wipe out.

My board does a full flip, sending me crashing to the bottom of the pool, planting my face into the granite. Since the pool is only three feet deep, I know not to panic. But even though the water has the bleachy smell of pool water, even though my ass and knees drag the bottom, I still freak out.

My head clouds as water fills my nose and an overwhelming memory freezes me. I thrash as the water keeps churning. I guess it's the impact of my foot hitting the pool bottom, but that's when I pull it together and simply stand up.

"There he is, ladies and gentlemen!" Carl shouts. "Your two-time world champion, Rip Cruz, bested by our own Wave-Life surf pool!"

People are clapping and laughing, but as I pull myself out of the pool, I remember what made me crash in the first place. Carl's in my ear, saying, "What the fuck, Rip? You hitting the rum already today?"

"No," I say, water streaming down my face as I turn to find her. But the girl in red, she's gone.

It's well past sunset and I'm nested on the highest deck, a secluded spot when most people are either at a buffet or in the nightclub. Mid-July, the air isn't cool, but there's a killer breeze that whisks the moisture off my skin nearly as quick as I can work up the sweat. I crack a new bottle of Captain Morgan's as I glance up, searching the stars. We're smack in the middle of exotic rum territory; I could get some local brew. A little cooler than this spiced stuff. But that'd require me to get off the ship, and that always seems like too much of a bother. I take a slug, letting the spice slip around my tongue before the telltale heat slips down my throat, working all the way to my belly.

"You on iceberg watch up here?"

I turn, and there she is, the woman in the red suit. She's still wearing the bikini, but her khakis are back on, her wavy hair dancing in the breeze.

"Evening," is all I can think of to say to her.

She reaches out and takes the rum bottle, slips it from my hands. She doesn't even give the label a look. She just raises it and takes a long, deep pull off it before passing it back to me.

"Yeah, help yourself," I say.

But she smiles at me, grabs the bottle again, and takes another long pull, not grimacing as she swallows.

"Gracias," she says as she passes it back. That's the second time.

I can finally see her face clearly. Rounded eyes and thick lips, but not wearing any makeup. She's not beautiful, exactly. "I saw you earlier," I say. She smiles wider, but doesn't bite. "What were you doing?"

She just tilts her head. Not blinking, looking me directly in the eye. Unexpectedly, she wraps her arms around my neck, presses her body close, and kisses me on the mouth.

Uncomfortable, I push her back. Indignant. Asking, "Who are you?"

"Isabella." She says it as though that answers everything. It doesn't.

I try again. "Where you from?"

"Originally? Puerto Rico." She doesn't have a thick accent.

"Yeah? I'm half Puerto Rican."

"I know," she says. "We take pride in our world surfing champion. Even if you do come from Miami." As she says that, she cuddles into me again, giving me that same smile she flashed at the pool.

"You stole something from that girl's purse," I say. "Earlier today."

She starts to unbutton my shirt.

"Uh," I say. "Or did you just drop something? You had to get it out?"

"That's much more likely. Isn't it, Ray?"

"Ray?" I ask.

"That's your name. Ramon Cruz."

"How do you know my real name? How do you know about my surfing?"

She laughs. Says, "You're loved in Puerto Rico. They still play your commercial."

"Yeah?" I ask. "You've seen that?"

Her hands slide down my chest, down to my sides as she presses her hips into mine. I have to admit, it's not unpleasant. She's so close I can't help but smell her, but instead of the sickly-sweet cloy of perfume, her hair smells like she was in the sunshine all day. She kisses me, hard. Her tongue slips out.

Cindy, she never kissed like that.

But I haven't kissed anyone since Cindy. I've had offers, sure. Plenty. But it's against policy on the ship to get intimate with the passengers. At least, that's the excuse I use.

I mean to pull away, but her tongue parts my mouth and slides against mine. She tastes like the rum, spicy warm. She pulls me closer. She grabs my wrist and plunges my hand down her shorts, between her legs, deftly moving aside her suit so that my fingers glide against her sex. Slippery hot, she sighs heavily in my mouth as she presses my fingers against her clit and grinds herself against my hand.

It's been a long time since I've felt a woman like this. I let her guide me, stroking her strongly until she starts to squirm and pant into my mouth. Then reality hits, and I pull away.

"What?" she asks, a raspy edge to her voice.

"We don't even know each other!" I say, feeling like a teenage girl.

Her smile goes away. "Why are you here, Ray?"

"I work here."

"But, why? Why aren't you surfing?"

"It's the middle of the night!"

"You know what I mean."

"I had an accident, you know."

"I know," she says, her voice softer now. Then she moves back in. But instead of taking my hand again, this time she curls against my body and her hands start pawing at me.

Well. Okay. Not pawing, exactly. More like massaging. My cock responds immediately. She rubs the length of me through my shorts, while she takes my mouth again. Her hand dives under the trunks, takes hold of my bare-skinned cock, and squeezes just so.

I can't breathe.

She says, "There now. You can go first." Stroking me, sparking me, tempting me, "Or we could both do this."

"Wha-what?"

Pressing her chest against mine, she offers, "Do you want to fuck me, Ray?"

"Holy fuck."

Before I can answer, she shucks her khakis and bikini bottom, pulling a condom from her back pocket before she tosses the shorts onto the deck. She hops onto the railing, situating her ass and beckoning me to come over.

My cock is still hard and hanging out in the breeze for anyone to see. I should feel ashamed, or embarrassed. But it's the most cooling and refreshing feeling—and the most perversely, wickedly hot I've felt in years.

I go to her. She coaxes the condom down the length of my cock, but I make the mistake of asking her again, "Why're you doing this?"

She looks me in the eye. "I'm rescuing you, Ray." My cock fully sheathed now, she takes hold of me with one hand and guides me toward her. Her hand snakes up my neck, fiddling with the hair at its base. I'm aching to plunge in.

"Ray," she pleads, her hand gliding along my length. I can see her nipples harden beneath her suit. I can't resist. I push aside the fabric covering one tit. Her skin is so soft. I squeeze; she's real. She's stroking me, totally jacking me off, sinfully good. I run my thumb over her pointed nipple. "You're something else, Isabella," I tell her. It startles me that I used her name, this stranger seducing me on the upper deck.

I blame the rum. But it's not the rum, or the situation; it's what she said, still lurking. I take my hand off her tit and stiffen my back as she tries to pull me all the way inside her.

"Just fuck me, Ray," she sighs.

I'd love to. I'm dying for it. But this chick knows my name, knows about me. Something tells me it won't be so easy.

"What do you want from me?" I ask her.

"I just want you," she pleads, opening her legs wider, drawing me closer, pressing the tip of my hard-on against her clit.

"Then what?"

She looks me in the eyes as she says softly, "I want you off this boat."

"Why?"

"You're wasting yourself."

A bolt of heat goes through me. I tried my whole life to be the all-American boy, but no matter how hard I tried to conceal it, I couldn't ever kill off my Latin temper. I pull back from her. "I'm taking a break."

"Oh," is all she says.

"Getting my footing."

"On a ship? Those are some sea legs, Cruz."

"Finding my balance."

With that, she slides off the railing and arranges her suit, hiding that plump tit from my sight.

"What?" I demand.

"Nothing," she says. "I was wrong. I hoped you'd be into me."

Just like that, that fast, she's fucked me up again. Two years of peace and solitude, and this broad charges in and I'm at war. I'm into her. And I'm so *not* into her. She's not that hot to be risking shit for.

"Who the fuck are you?" I ask again, suddenly aware of my dick hanging out in the breeze. I pull off the rubber and tuck my still-hard and unsatisfied cock back inside my shorts. But she doesn't answer me. She pulls on the rest of her clothes and walks down the deck, into the night.

Itchy, restless, I slug the remainder of the Captain's on my way back to the cabin. Carl's zonked out, but I keep it down and control my breathing as I slip under the sheet and mechanically set to work on myself in the cramped, thick room.

My head's hazy enough, and it's a well-worn routine, except the visions in front of my eyes are different tonight. I raise my free hand to my nose, smell her all over me.

Briny, like the ocean. I should've washed it off, washed her off. But I didn't.

It takes longer than usual, probably because I held off so long. But then I turn on my side, smell my fingers again, imagine thrusting myself into her, and I come unexpectedly, quickly. It's a release, a relief. But it's not completely satisfying.

The next morning, Carl's banging around our cabin wakes me early. "The fuck you doing?" I ask him.

"I can't find my watch," he says. "You seen it?"

"I'm sleeping, dude."

"I know I had it yesterday."

I stop at the breakfast buffet to grab a muffin. Across the dining room, I see Isabella at the ice cream bar, piling up a bowl, loading it with whipped cream. As she's walking across the room, she stumbles on a chair leg but holds tight to her sundae, both of them hitting the floor in a graceless splatter. I can't help but laugh, especially as I see her smiling sheepishly. But before I can move in to help, there's a small crowd of people around her. She's got whipped cream on her face, her one hand covered in goo. But as a man helps her rise, I see it, even though it happens quickly. Her free hand, the clean one, it slides into his jacket pocket and then into her shorts.

My blood boils. Yesterday, that girl's purse. Carl's watch—she ran into him yesterday. I know I need to say something, do something. It's one thing to be ripping off the passengers, but another to try and play me like she did and think I'm not going to catch her pulling all this shit. But then Carl's behind me. "Rip, let's move."

"Wait," I tell him.

"Gonna be late for the morning class, Golden Boy," he says and steers me out onto the deck.

Later that evening, we've pulled out of port and are cutting through the waves, heading for yet another exotic city with more flawless surf. I could go for cover in the safe harbor of my cabin, but I'm not down for the confines of that yet. So I decide to spend some quality time with my best friend, Captain Morgan, as I watch the sunset.

I find a secluded little nook on the Aloha deck to take it in. I unscrew the cap and take a long pull, letting the spice fill my mouth before the heat scorches a path to my belly. Cindy and I, we used to flop on the sand and watch the sun sink beneath the horizon nearly every evening when I was home from tour. Back then, when I was in serious training, it wasn't often that I'd unwind with a drink. Or ten, like I do now.

Back then, that's when everyone expected me to party. I mean, I wasn't a lawyer. I was a surfer. But once I met Cindy, once I got serious about winning a title, all that bullshit seemed to fall away as we settled in. I didn't have time to be the bad-boy Latin surfer. I wanted to be the all-American champ.

Everyone romanticizes their past, especially when their present is shit and their future is bleak. But I don't have to romanticize. World travel, world titles, and a world-class girl in Cindy. I had it all until I came home from a competition in Hawaii and found Cindy fucking her ex in our bed.

My heart broke, and something else, too. I walked out and hit the surf. Just past dawn, it was quiet out. To this day I'm still not sure what caused the wipeout, but I got rag-dolled around underwater and then sand-dragged till I crashed into the reef. I was cut to ribbons, reef rash, three broken ribs and a couple fractured fingers, not to mention a concussion.

But I lived. The weird part was, I didn't care.

I never went back to Cindy, or the ocean, again. Sometimes I think I loved the *idea* of Cindy more than I loved her. I loved being the all-American boy who had it all, a winner. And then I lost it all.

It wasn't big news, my accident. Even a two-time world champ, when it's a surfer, just doesn't garner much stardom. But I had that Wild Cherry Splash ThirstAde commercial while things were still good, so that when it was time to make some cash, I was lucky enough to get this gig. And to keep me company, I've got Carl to bust my balls during the day, and Captain Morgan to fill the lonely nights.

I take another deep slug from the bottle as the summer sun sinks beneath the waves. Even with the sun gone, the heat from the liquor mixes with the balmy night air to send a flush to my face.

Most staff, when they're not working, are supposed to stay out of sight. But given the ambassadorial nature of my work, I'm allowed free rein to see and be seen as I please. I drain the last of the bottle and make my way down to the Fiesta deck, stroll along the promenade, heading for another bottle of rum. As I'm passing the jewelry store, I see Isabella inside.

She's partially obscured by a man hovering close, but it's her all right.

This time she's dressed in a short, silky black dress. She turns to smile at the man, an older guy, who must be in his sixties or seventies, dressed in an expensive suit. Her hair is still a loose tangle of waves. She points to something inside the case and the clerk unlocks it. She pulls out a necklace, and even from my vantage point out in the hall, I see it glint and shine as it catches the light. The clerk hands it to the man, and that's when I see it happen.

As the guy drapes it around Isabella's neck, she points farther down the case, and when the clerk bends down to open it, Isabella reaches up to help adjust the necklace for the man. Quickly, deftly, his fingers graze her palm, the chains of the necklace slip off her neck. But before the clerk looks back up, the man has the necklace again centered and in place, and he fastens it behind her neck.

I slink back, unable to look away but peeking just through the edge of window glass. Another woman, who was browsing separately, passes behind the couple, her large purse slung over her shoulder. Isabella reaches back, quickly touching the woman's purse, and the woman pretends not to notice. But I see the telltale glimmer in that split second as the necklace— the real one—leaves Isabella's hand and glides unnoticed by the staff into the second woman's purse.

By then, the clerk has a bracelet out of the case. As the clerk holds the bracelet, she pushes the counter mirror closer to Isabella.

On the opposite side of the store, a young girl who'd been browsing the costume earrings moves toward the door and then stumbles, spilling out into the hallway near my feet, setting off the store alarm. I reach down to help her up. The clerk, she tells the girl to hold still just as another clerk appears from the back.

The young girl is apologizing, holding out the earrings, stepping back inside the store. Isabella, I can feel her eyes on me. It's not the slow, diffuse heat of humidity; her eyes are searing me. As the clerk from the back comes to help the girl with the earrings, the woman with the purse brushes past us, out into the corridor, walking quickly up the promenade.

I should stop her.

But I don't.

I blame the rum. Or my own stupidity. After all, I'm a surfer, not a security guard.

But I know it's not the rum's fault. It's Isabella's dark eyes, fixed on me.

The clerk from the back gets the young girl settled, while the other one flutters nervously behind the counter and finally gets the alarm turned off. Isabella waves off the bracelet and then turns around for the clerk to remove the necklace. Once the necklace is off, she and the older man sail out of the shop. She ignores me. Up ahead, the man turns left, and she turns off to the right. That's when I take off in pursuit. I'm still not sure how I'll confront her, but I know I have to. I expect to have to chase her, but when I round the corner she reaches out and takes hold of me.

The glare is gone, replaced again with a shy smile, her dark eyes sparkling. "What do you think you're doing?" I demand.

Her smile grows, but her only answer is to press herself close and plant a deep kiss on me. This time, she doesn't taste like rum.

I pull back, but before I can question her, she takes hold of my hand and leads me out onto the deck. "Stop it!" I shout, pulling my hand away from hers. She halts, appearing genuinely wounded.

"I know what you did," I tell her. Lowering my voice, "You're a thief."

"Not a thief," she corrects me. "Technically, I'm a pirate."

"Fuck you."

"Ray," she coos, wrapping her arms around my neck. She kisses me again. Warm, soft. I push her off immediately.

"What're you doing?" I ask.

"What's it feel like?" she mumbles as she nuzzles my neck.

"Who was that guy?"

"Oh," she smiles up at me. "Were you jealous?"

"No," I scoff, but I know I say it too loudly.

"He's a friend."

"Why are you here? Why are you doing this?"

"I came on this ship to steal expensive jewelry and to date Rip Cruz."

"You're fucking crazy," I tell her, this time pushing forcefully, getting her off me.

She laughs. Then she turns, motions with her finger for me to follow.

"I could call someone right now, you know."

She shrugs. "I'd be gone before they came to your rescue, Ray."

I snort. "What're you gonna do? Jump overboard?"

"I love the water."

"You'd drown."

"I bet you didn't worry this much when you were surfing."

I hadn't even realized I was following her, but that stops me dead in my tracks, the blood rushing to my face as I spit back, "I still do surf."

"Okay, Ray," is all she says, but she keeps walking. In the ebbing twilight, I realize she's leading us to the upper deck, where we were the other night. Once there, she leans casually against the rail, her face nearly obscured in the shadows.

"I still surf," I tell her again. "You've seen me."

"I've seen you on a board in a pool. Not in the ocean."

"Same thing. Basically."

"Mmm," she sighs. "Kind of like sex without romance."

"Tell me about it! You've been throwing yourself at me."

"There's moonlight. There's the ocean. There's mystery. What's not romantic about that?"

"You're a criminal!"

"Oh, Ray."

"That's another thing. No one calls me Ray. They call me Rip."

"And do you like that?"

I never thought about it, really. Even Cindy called me Rip. In retrospect, that should've been a clue as to her true feelings.

When I don't answer, Isabella says, "I bet you've tried really hard to be what other people want your whole life. To be the good boy. Don't you ever want to be the bad boy?"

"Look," I tell her. "We're not talking about me."

"Good!" she says, lighting up, sliding herself into my arms. She's warm, but not unpleasant. She sighs against my mouth before she kisses me, and then her tongue is licking at my lower lip. I try to pull back, but she holds tight. Asking, "Don't you like me, Ray?"

"You're a thief."

"Other than that. You really don't like me?"

I don't know. I like her kissing me. Frankly, as much as I tried to act indignant, I'm not bothered that she's a thief. It kind of turns me on. I tell her the truth. "I haven't been with anyone in a long time."

Her hand snakes down to my crotch, rubbing me, half-hard already.

"Since the accident," I tell her.

"Mmm," is all she says. Then, "I bet you miss it as much as you miss the ocean."

I consider telling her the real truth. That I almost didn't come up. I didn't want to.

She unbuttons my shorts, reaches inside, and takes hold of me. Halting, she brings her hand to her face and licks a few times, then starts pumping me gently, slowly. I should push her away. But I don't.

Stroking me, she leans close again, whispering in my ear, "I like you so much, Ray."

"Oh . . . man," I sigh. "Why? Because I was a winner?"

"Mmm." Her soft hand, pumping me, I'm fully hard now and it's feeling good. I give in to it. "No, it's because of how you surfed," she says. "You weren't trying to win the waves. You just became part of them."

"I loved it," I admit.

"Why'd you quit?"

She's making me crackle now, getting hotter. Her breath in my ear. I shiver. Admitting, "Because I loved it."

"Something else hurt you," she whispers, her hand gripping tighter, moving more quickly.

"Don't—" I try to tell her, but my heart's beating too hard.

"Rip," she sighs, and I suck in a breath, open my eyes that I hadn't realized I'd closed. Then, softer, "Ray."

"Oh. Fuck."

"Do you want to come?"

She has no idea.

"If you'd let me," she tempts, "I'd love you that much." She drops to her knees, takes me in her mouth.

I come. Fast. Hard. I come right from my core and shoot into her mouth, shuddering as she sucks and pulls, emptying me.

I'm done but still reeling. She rises up, still holding my cock, whispering. "Next time, my turn." She lets me go, exposing me to the cooling breeze and drops a promising last kiss on my mouth.

I wake up with a thick tongue and fuzzy brain. Carl shouts at me that I'm late for the early surf demo on deck. Once I roll out of bed, I don't bother with a morning shower. I can still smell Isabella on my shirt.

On my way to the pool, I see her run by in the corridor ahead, in the black dress again. I shout her name, but she doesn't answer. What's going on?

When I get to the hall, Carl jogs up to me. Asks, "You see a woman come this way?"

"Huh?"

"I didn't lose my watch! That bitch stole it! She's been pickpocketing everyone on board!"

"No." I deny it.

"Have you seen her?"

"Black dress?" I point him down the hall back where I came from and then follow Isabella's real path myself. I catch up with her on the stairwell leading to the lowest deck. "Isabella!" I yell again.

"In a hurry, Ray!"

But I catch up, take hold of her arm. "Where are you going?"

"I have to go, Ray."

"You disappeared last night—I owe you one, remember?"

"Then come with me."

"What? Where?"

"Wherever."

"You can't jump off this ship, Isabella."

"Watch me."

"Oh fuck," I say. "You'll drown."

"Listen," she says. "We'll just tread water for a while, then they'll come get us."

"Who'll come? Are you fucking crazy?"

From a distance, I hear a voice shouting. "C'mon! She's down here, Carl!"

"Shit," I say, looking over my shoulder at him as he starts his approach.

"You've been doing it for two years, Ray," she tells me. "Treading water. It's time to move again."

"I, I—"

"Keep her there, Rip!" the guy hollers to me as he picks up his pace.

She kisses me. Hard, deep. But there's no panic or desperation in it. It's warm. Passionate.

Now I hear Carl shouting, "I want my watch back!"

Pulling back, she looks me in the eyes as she says, "You don't need to find your balance. You never lost it." And with that, she pushes away from me and takes off running.

"Isabella!" I shout.

"Get hold of her!" Carl yells.

She climbs up onto the railing, and I can't believe what I'm seeing. Standing there, she lingers just long enough to turn to face me.

"Don't!" I shout. But just as I'm close enough to grasp her wrist, she holds a finger in front of her mouth, gesturing for me to be silent. She lets my hand go, leaps.

"Goddammit!" Carl shouts.

Below, I can't see her.

"My watch!" Carl shouts.

I turn to look, see his distressed face.

"Decent piece of tail, too," he says. "Such a shame."

"Shh," I say to comfort him. My finger in front of my lips, like she did.

Then, I climb up.

"Jesus, Rip!" he says. "It's not that important!"

"Yeah, it is." I find a perfect balance up on the railing.

"She's not that hot!" Carl says.

But really, yeah, she is. Besides, I owe her one.

"Golden Boy!" Carl shouts. "You trying to kill yourself?"

"No, finally," I tell him. "Just the opposite."

Headfirst, I dive in.

৩৬ SLOW DANCE ON THE FAULT LINE ৩৬
Donald Rawley

FAITH HAS NOT SPOKEN FOR WEEKS. Not to the nurses or her husband's doctor, her mother, or closest friends. Since Ted's heart attack, people have known not to call; she would pick up the phone and only listen, then quietly put the receiver down. Now when Faith walks into a room, there is the acute exhaustion of her silence. She is there to listen, nod her head, understand. There is nothing more for her to say.

She is silent with terror. She has felt the succinct, flat drop of abandonment for the last five years, and now it has assumed form. Faith is forty and her husband, Ted, is forty-one. She reasons she is young, that she had never foreseen or predicted anything. She is still beautiful and now deserted.

One month ago Ted had a heart attack, and the doctors now have given him days, a week at most, to live. Faith can only remember their shoes, never raising her head to the incorrigible hospital white that has followed her now for a month like a hot ending, where light obliterates breath and water and flesh.

It happened at dinner, at a nothing little place in the Valley they had stopped at after a screening at Warner Bros. It happens to everyone just like this, Faith had thought. You are sitting on the toilet, having dinner at a fast-food restaurant, putting bleach into the washing machine, and you go, or start the slow process. He had slumped onto the food, his hand pushing chow mein onto the tablecloth. She had gone wild, remembering nothing until after the sedation, when Ted was lying in bed at home, next to a nurse, the stink of his dying crawling through the long halls.

Ted was an agent at William Morris and Faith was an agent's wife. She had never worked. She was addicted to a certain amount of Valium and Percodan; they softened the edges. She had coped for twenty years to make sure she was everything Ted wanted her to be. Valium helped. Perfection helped. A smooth face. A smooth house.

Ted had big-star clients and a big house and they were in astonishing debt. There were two mortgages and payments were late. Their matching Jaguars had been bought on time and letters had come in for repossession. Out of seventeen cards, only three were not at the limit. No health insurance. No life insurance. No savings. She had paid for the hospital with a credit card. She was drawing money on the last credit cards to pay for the nurses. She had put the Jasper Johns up for sale, but the dealer had explained it was a minor piece and there were no takers. She kept her jewelry. She wouldn't sell her jewelry. Now she wore as much of it as she could.

Neither had any family, children, good friends. Faith had stopped talking when she realized she would be left with nothing at his death. Maybe her clothes. The days were a game; she shut everything out, helping with Ted's catheter and bedpan, cleaning the mucus running down to his lips, under his pink, upturned eyes and calcimined lids. Ted's organs wouldn't work. She would touch the sponge to the pale ash of his skin, falling inward like dry-rotted wood, then walk past the nurse into the bathroom.

There she would wash her hands repeatedly with liquid soap, spray herself with Chanel No. 19, redo the makeup on her face several times. Once she masturbated, with the nurse in the next room. The makeup had to be right. She tried to speak to herself in the mirror, but that's where the numbness was. Now it was three Valiums a day, sometimes four, and the wait.

She noticed only the sky, began to study it each evening and tried to reeducate herself on color. She noticed her face, the immediate world before her, where her feet walked, how to close a door quietly like it had never been opened. Every evening she got into her silver Jaguar and drove along Mulholland Drive, watching the sky. Certain dusks she was bewildered, questioning; other times, impatient. It made her feel like a child in her deadened flesh; it made her feel something.

She remembered as a little girl watching skies and asking things her parents couldn't answer. Then, as an adult, she hadn't paid attention for over twenty years. There were stars, and sunsets. Each moment became an aphasia and a halt. Winds would shift and stutter, smelling of other lives.

It is her birthday today, and this October in Los Angeles is over one hundred degrees. There have been brush fires destroying new construction in the northern Valley mountains, and the Santa Anas have begun to light the sky with the char of oil and bundled wood. It is an arsonist's sky, Faith thinks, sore, inflamed, and livid.

Storm clouds are coming in fast, leaking wet lavender and coarse gray violets into the edge. She sees aubergine and peach light in the west; a blue she remembers on Mexican tile. She takes the curves of Mulholland slowly, staying close to the yellow line. On her car radio she hears there will be an electrical storm tonight; no chance, no percentages, the storm is already here.

She parks on Mulholland and lights a cigarette in her car. Her hands are numb and her left leg has fallen asleep. She will wait for the thunder and lightning. She has all the time in the world.

It begins with heavy, dusty drops of rain and the sound of the elements colliding, rumbling, like an elevator dropping. Then white light in veins, like the veins of a man's arm running from the wrist to the shoulder, then nothing. If God is a man, then these are his arms; if God is a woman, then these are her lover's, Faith reasons.

She wonders if, at this moment, her husband has died. If she should be there, or here to see him rise. She wonders if the nurse is frantic and cursing her. No one knows how tired she is, and in her soothing air-conditioned car she tries to cry, thinking the storm will let it out. It is dangerous sitting on the top of a mountain in a car during an electrical storm. It is dangerous not to be able to feel.

Faith massages her leg and decides to drive down into the Valley, from here a shallow pond covered with fireflies and damp air. At dusk she will drive through alleys full of pillowless couches, dead plants, and stacks of magazines. She understands why pretty things get thrown away.

Faith has driven for an hour, past tract houses and sex stores, magnolia trees and carpets of ivy. The storm is getting stronger. Lightning frames inconsequential things she normally wouldn't see when she drives: plaster elves and birdbaths, dogs turning corners, women counting money in glassed-in motel offices, the moments when street lights turn on.

Children stand on front lawns and gape at the storm, then squeal, running around in circles. People are driving strangely, making wide left turns and almost hitting curbs, stopping for no reason and yelling at the driver next to them. Faith is hungry, thinks she should stop for a taco, but there are too many fast-food stands for her to be able to make a decision. The possibilities of taking one firm step in any direction are endless; she will keep driving tonight until the car runs out of gas. She doesn't know what else to do.

She is on Victory Boulevard headed into the flat gape of the West Valley, when, just out of Reseda, she sees a carnival on a vacant lot. It's a cheap one, with ten or twelve rides, and has been set up overnight. Each ride is lit with blinking lights and moving up and out into the sky at a different angle and rhythm. She thinks of big bands in the forties where men stand up and point their horns up and down, tapping their polished shoes, polished as Ted's doctor's shoes walking down deliberate and well-understood corridors.

She puts on a tape of Harry Connick Jr. and drives onto the dirt lot where she can park and watch the carnival. She turns the air conditioner off and rolls down the windows, letting the tropical blast of night air clean the car out, make it part of the scene. She turns the headlights off and watches people move in the dark toward the lights of the carnival.

The odor of smoke hovers in the trees, distilling the blinking neon. It is the burnt oil from the giant, rocking machines. There are no families here, only some scattered Mexican couples and women she reasons are just like her, walking through the electricity, stumbling to the lights, the rock and roll, the cotton candy, and chili dogs. They are alone, walking toward anything that gives light, anything that carries a pulse.

And then there are the men. They stand by parked cars, just beyond the streetlights, combing their hair with one knee up, attentive and silent, their silhouettes dark bronze and featureless.

They are homosexual, Faith thinks: I've seen them before. Two days ago, she had been at . . . she had been at a park at dusk, driving, stopping and thinking, when she had seen them, hanging around rest rooms under palms and at the edges of orange-tree borders, absolutely still. Then combing their hair and checking their watches, walking in and out of the rest rooms in a monotony, into other men's cars, where their heads would disappear, then back into the scalding Valley sun. She had watched for hours that slow evening, falling asleep, then waking up when a bum had knocked at her window.

It was a hunt. She wondered if tonight she was hunting, if carnivals like this are made for the hunt, where people who are lost come to eat. She only wanted the numbness to last forever. She would go on every ride twice, there was enough money. Today.

This is an October of fire that travels by wind and men she cannot see. Faith looks in her purse for Valium, cigarettes, and money. Checking, checking. Her lips must be repainted. It's her birthday. She takes a Valium and lines her lips, runs her hands through her hair, and realizes she can't feel her hair, lights another cigarette, and slowly gets out of her car.

She does not know why she is here except she cannot sit in Ted's room anymore with a nurse she will never see again. The house will be taken away from her, put up for sale, and there aren't even pictures of it, or scrapbooks. They never kept scrapbooks, considering it unsophisticated. There would be nothing by Christmas. Only a sense of something torn, drawers emptied, and new cities, hotel rooms, and planes.

Her high heel catches on a rock and she falls down, then gets up and steadies herself. The men in the shadows say and do nothing. She can hear only the shifting of boots, a car door quietly closing behind her. The wind of the storm pushes her beige silk dress against her body. There is no front gate, no entry to focus us; the rides are scattered and form a messy line that reaches to the back of the dirt lot.

She thinks of all the places she's never been to, of living naked in the trees, sleepwalking through gardens and beaches and trains with private rooms. She realizes she has never traveled with her husband to a destination that is completely foreign. At the front booth of the first ride she hands the girl ten dollars for ten dollars' worth of tickets. There are no smiles, and Faith assumes they are both silent women.

The half-empty carnival is full of color and movement, defying the regular flashes of lightning. God is taking pictures tonight, Faith thinks. Each ride has its own music playing, and Faith decides not to choose, but walk to the first one and keep going down the line. Until she reaches the last ride. That one she will ride until her money runs out. Then she will drive until her gas runs out. Then she will lie down and sleep.

Faith walks past revolving, empty kiddie rides; scratched teacups, tiny boats, and sports cars in Day-Glo glitter under dirty pink-and-yellow tents. They are attached to the motor by chains. There isn't a carousel with beautifully painted horses, or anything remotely innocent here. This is a carnival for children used to chipped toys. And they are home tonight, listening to the thunder.

She gives a ticket to a freshly scrubbed man with jowls and gin blossoms, pink as a pig. He runs the Tilt-a-Whirl and straps her carefully into the red oval chair. She feels secure now. Complete and ready. She will spin hard in a silence until there is no world around her. This is good.

She feels she is on the edge of the Pacific, her face the hue of cold mist. Her feet tense. She can feel something. Of becoming another element, of tasting salt and anything that gives life, controls the moon, and eats away cliffs.

It is at this moment that she sees a man staring at her. Standing against the ticket booth to the Octopus, a black iron, pink-lit spider ride, he is ugly and damned and he smiles. The ride heaves and sways in jagged stretches, like any animal used to crawling on ocean bottoms, drinking the life around it. The tiny cars at the end of each of the Octopus arms spin under the electrical storm, up and down to the Rolling Stones' "Sympathy for the Devil." She can see there is only one couple on the ride. The woman has curly, jet-black hair and it is falling in her face. She is screaming, exquisitely frightened, and her boyfriend or husband or brother is laughing, his arm around her and his hand massaging her breast.

Faith feels like a fool sitting on the Tilt-a-Whirl, numb and dazed in her beige silk dress with her hands in her lap and her legs crossed as if she were at a cocktail lounge. But this is what she wants; to be out of place, foreign, traveling in circles. She focuses her eyes so she stares past him but can watch him without effort.

The man staring at her doesn't have a shirt on and his shoulders are dirty, watery from the sudden shift of rain that breaks the static in the air like urine. She wants to watch this man and knows she can. The fat man is making her sit here, strapped, until more people show up for the ride.

The man staring at her is the most muscular man she has ever seen. Not a bodybuilder, but just huge and hard, with tattoos crawling up his scarred arms. She discerns women riding dragons, skulls and hatchets and clouds covering his shoulders. There is an eagle in flight across his chest, one of its wings touching his nipple, which is pierced. She looks at the ground, then looks up again, sees he is still watching her.

She sees his eyes, sable brown and feminine, almond-shaped with thick lashes. The rest of his face is horrible, as if he's been in an accident. The kind of accident men get into when they get loaded and fight each other. His nose is flat and flared, smashed up and broken, and his lips are bulbous, brooked under a pencil-thin mustache. He is bald and pock-marked, with oversize ears that point up at an obscene stance. His head is too small for his body and his eyes are too large for his pitiful face. His arms and hands are immense, muscular, and he is swaybacked. She knows he is younger than she is. He doesn't make sense to her. She is used to men who are easy to decipher, size up, control.

He spits, stretches his arms above his head in a sudden wave of rain, and lets his muscles flex, then yawns, scratches his armpit, and grins at her. His two front teeth are silver. One of his eyebrows is half-singed off. Then he looks down at his crotch and up at her, licking his lips. Faith is not frightened. She is surprised. She watches him from across the dirt lot and is entranced, thinking of the same fascination she experienced watching her first pornographic film, for those beginning minutes, until the repetition began to bore her. It's those beginning minutes when every-thing is alive, Faith thinks. She realizes he has broken through. She is too tired to smile.

The Tilt-a-Whirl begins to gyrate and wheeze, spinning in half circles, undecided. The Mexican couple are in the car next to her. The ride picks up and she suddenly likes the way her back is slammed against the metal, the circles that hit hard. What is the music? Bonnie Raitt is singing "Tangled and Dark," but only the pulse of the song comes through as the wheels of the Tilt-a-Whirl mainline and spike sparks and oil. She likes the incoherence and cacophony. She understands it. She wants everything she can understand.

When she gets off the ride, her legs are weak. He is at the gate. Smil-ing as though they are friends.

"You are one beautiful woman. And that car blows me away. I saw you come in, you know. I watched you. You going on all the rides tonight? I can tell. Got nothing better to do, do you? I'll go on them with you."

Faith walks by him. This silence is making her mad. Nothing will form in her mouth. Her vocal chords sting. She turns around and stares at his chest, his arms, and pockmarked cheeks. His bald head, covered with drops of rain.

"Bet you think I'm a carny, don't you? I'm not. I live around the corner. I'm easy to find, baby. In the trailer park around the corner. There's only one."

Faith tries to breathe. Her chest is tight.

"Let's go on the Fire Wheel. You want to? Come on. Maybe lightning'll hit us. Maybe you'll touch me. Maybe I'll tell you poetry men tell women who are lost at night. Come on."

His voice is soft and basso hoarse. He effortlessly puts his arm around Faith and walks her over to the Fire Wheel, almost lifting her off the ground. For some reason she closes her eyes. Then she knows. It is to feel another man's arms around her, record the sensation.

"You're stoned, aren't you? Bet it's some kind of rich lady's drug. You got a couple for me? Give me some later and I'll fuck all night. Dare me."

His muscles are surprisingly soft or it is soft skin wrapped around stone, she is not sure. The Fire Wheel looks like an angel-food-cake pan with leather straps and caged sides. Faith can see it turns around furiously and glues people to its sides. Centrifugal force. It is orange and withering black, children's Halloween colors. Candy corn and papier-mâché.

She doesn't know why this man is touching her or his name or if Ted is dead. She is completely disconnected, a visitor to eight-thirty at night, a place that will be gone in the morning. She is not frightened. She is going on all the rides.

He grabs two tickets from the roll clutched in her hand. "I want you real bad, lady, I got a hard-on right now and you're not saying a word. You let me around you and I like that. When we get on, I want you to let me touch you."

Faith stares at his giant's back, at his ass when he pushes ahead of her like a child.

"Come here. You can use the straps if you like. Nah, don't use them. I want to be able to crawl all over you. Look, we're the only people on the ride."

He positions her next to him. Faith feels dizzy from the fourth Valium she took in the car. She might faint and suddenly she doesn't care. She knows she will be picked up. This unnamed man's shoulders are a foot higher than hers. He looks down at her and smiles. He strokes her hair. She stares straight ahead.

"You're soft."

His hands are huge and cracked; the calluses and blisters on his palms catch in her hair. He lets go and she closes her eyes again. When she opens them, he is rubbing his chest with slow, even strokes, pinching his nipples and then rubbing his chest again, rapidly. He doesn't look at Faith, but whispers in a musical tone: "Feel the eagle on my chest. Touch him. Can you feel his wings? Can you feel his feathers? He's flying. Feel him."

He takes Faith's hand and places it on the center of his chest. She doesn't feel anything except the coarseness of tattooed flesh and his heartbeat. He takes his hand away from hers as a taunt. She quietly leaves her hand there.

"Feel my nipples. Each one. Slowly. Do it."

The ride begins to lurch and slowly rotate. It builds its speed with a precision that takes Faith's breath into spasms; a cancer that is colorless and suffocates. She is thrown once again against the cage wall. One of her shoes has come off and has inched up toward her shoulder. The man has pinned one arm and leg over her; she can feel his erection on her hip, extravagant and moving with the same force as his limbs.

"See how it feels, baby. To be pinned to a wall and not be able to move. And I'm right here on you, around you."

The Fire Wheel has tilted up at a forty-five-degree angle, and they have lost gravity at the cut-rate carnival. Rain comes, then a white endurance, electric and brief, and they continue to spin, stuck to the wall, and he keeps whispering in her ear, things she cannot understand.

She does not know where he will take her, if he will be violent, if he is diseased and rambling. She is shaking her brains, she is having a good time, she is young.

"I can keep you this way forever if you like. I can keep you against a wall, allow you only your breath. We don't have to leave. We can stay this way all night, curled in midair, anything you want."

It is almost one A.M. and they have been on every ride: the Paratrooper, the Round-Up, the Tilt-a-Whirl, the Zipper, the Fire Wheel, the Cliffhanger, and the Octopus. She doesn't remember the rest. He has whispered obscenities and hung them like doves at her neck. He has held her like a father, made her touch his genitals, and touched her vagina through her briefs, rubbing her pubic hair with his immense hands until it hurt.

He's licked her brassiere through her silk dress until there are great spots on the front that stink of his breath. He has made her close her eyes most of the night.

On solid ground her legs give way. He buys her a beer with quarters out of her purse and she does not care. She takes another Valium, thinking soon she could be someone else. He lights a cigarette and holds it to her lips. As she smokes through his hand, she smells semen and tobacco and an utterance of night that can cure, the perfume of men and chants she has suddenly heard, as if they were delivered.

Then they are dancing in the parking lot, her Jaguar door open, Harry Connick Jr. singing on the tape deck. She does not remember putting it on. The men in the shadows are there, watching, sitting on their cars. Certain cars are rattling where they are having sex. He is holding her against him with both arms and her feet are dragging the ground. She is coherent and calm. She is listening.

"I'm the poet, baby, who's waiting for you."

He's ugly as a tropical flower with overwaxed leaves that fight for sunlight in the steam. She wonders if there are tattoos on his penis, if he sat, drunk, in front of the tattoo artist, keeping it hard as he wiped tiny dots of blood away as the ink went in.

"Baby, I can take you to a place where there's an earthquake every day. In the desert between the Salton Sea and the Mexican border, where rocks move and men make women shake."

He lets his mustache brush against her earring, then along the ridge of her ear.

"I'll fuck you so hard and so often the only smell you'll know is me, the only God you'll know is me, the only food you'll want is me. I'll keep you wet all day and crying for me at night. I'll lick and clean you like a dog and I won't let you out of my sight."

His breath smells of tequila and chocolate mints. Faith can feel it on the fine hair of her cheek. He brushes his lips against hers and she smells marijuana, motorcycle exhaust, flames. The storm has not let up, the fires have not ceased, and the carnival is still buzzing in the pitch.

"I'll teach you how to suck my beautiful big cock and lick my balls. I'll teach you over and over until you get it right. I'll save all my come for you, baby. I'll fuck you in the ass and eat your pretty pussy while I'm fucking you. I'll comb your hair while you sleep and play with your titties while you dream of me, so you're wet when you wake up."

Faith rolls her head and looks at the sky. She must look at the sky. It will have answers. It will explain to her what season it is, why she is still alive, where she is.

"I'll make you laugh. I'll feed you snakes and wild birds. I'll make you jewelry from Indian beads and quartz. I'll teach you how to slow dance on the fault line, with fire under our feet, where we could drop if the earth shifts. I'll teach you the music of rivers and canyons. I'll drink your sweat and paint you in the sand."

Faith almost speaks. Then closes her eyes.

"I'll take you to Mexico and South America and we'll get lost in towns with four-room hotels. We'll put on shows and teach the whores how to do it. We'll travel only on nights with no clouds so we can see the moon. I'll love you."

Faith begins to back away from him. His voice growls. His chest becomes tight. He squeezes his cock through his pants.

"Look at it. It's yours. I live in a trailer park. I eat out of cans and write poetry on paper towels. I need money and I need you."

Faith watches this man, this child animal with a broken nose and pierced nipples, and she knows he is a narcotic, the hesitation before the rush, and she is waiting. Waiting to feel it on her skin, waiting for the blood to seep through Ted's brain and then into his lungs in the ancient language of lightning.

"So what do you do, little lady with a silk dress and a silver car? I'll give you everything. Stay with me tonight and don't go back. I'm desperate and alone. We're all alone. Forget where you came from. Let me fuck the words out of your throat."

She can hear the gasp of two men in the shadows. A car has stopped shaking. Thunder.

"What's the matter? Can't you talk? You're not deaf. Or mute. You're just playing with your own little balls of shit."

"My husband's dying." Her own voice surprises her. It must belong to someone else. It sounds hollow and pinched like a Hollywood woman, an old woman who cannot be taught. Faith reasons she is already a widow and has been for many years. She steadies herself and pulls away completely from him.

"Let him die. Kill him. Kill him for me. Put the son of a bitch out of his misery. I'll give you my address. I'm easy to find. If you want, I'll kill him for you. I'll be gentle. You want me to use a pillow, a gun, a knife, just let me know. I'll fuck you after. I'll fuck you so hard you won't care. You won't be afraid anymore."

Faith listens to the silence, staring at him. He looks like a child.

"I got nothing to lose, lady, and there's only one thing I want. I want a woman. I jack off all day long. I can do it for hours. I don't care what I have to do to get you. I'm lonely and I want a woman to love me. You."

Faith turns the ignition key.

"Come back to me when he dies."

It is her birthday. Faith checks her lips in the rearview mirror and slowly pulls out of the lot. She will have to remember where she is.

A week later Ted is dead. Two weeks after that Faith has bought two tickets to Cancún, converted her jewelry into dollars and pesos, put the house up for sale, and declared bankruptcy. She now talks, only about business, facts, essentials. Los Angeles is covered with the linen of crisp winter flowers and a warm midday sun, the haze of the Pacific and the sense that things are real, if only for a matter of days.

She has bought an extra ticket for the man at the carnival. If she cannot find him, she will cash it in at the airport. She has everything she owns in one bag, has bought a supply of Valium that should last a month or more. The Jaguar has been turned in and she has a rental car and she is driving through Reseda, trying to remember where the carnival was, which allotted dirt park was singed by it.

There is no trailer park. She keeps driving, looking for something that would be part of him. She is driving too fast. She rolls around a corner and suddenly finds it. It is early, and dawn comes in a henna flame. She has watched the sky every day since Ted's death and she has promised herself she will watch it in Mexico. It is now her companion.

Faith considers what will happen in Mexico. That one day she will wake up with this man, whose skin is a childhood taste, like sickness and cough syrup. That it will end. He will walk into the jungle, wait for another woman, and hunt. She will start swimming in the Caribbean and not stop. Or maybe not swim at all.

The trailer park is just as he said it was. Around the corner, but there were a hundred vacant lots. She drives slowly down the narrow trailer-park drive, past Chinese lanterns and tiny fences. She stops the car and gets out and walks in the early A.M. shiver. He said he was easy to find.

She sees a sleeping blanket with a mass huddled in front of the office trailer. She walks over to it and looks down. She kicks it. She doesn't care. As the bundle moves over, she sees his face covered with blood that has dried. He has been fighting.

They will sleep in Mexico, clean and oiled. She will rub his body in the sun, watch the eagle writhe under her thumb, the woman on the dragon glittering on her palm. She will absorb his desperation until they are both without language or thought.

He opens his eyes and looks up at her. He is naked under the sleeping blanket. He has lost his clothes. He smiles.

❧ COLD ASS ICE ❧
Chelsea Summers

Step outside and it feels as if you've entered a hot, wet oven. You're the pat of butter on the baked potato that is Gotham. It's hot, hot, heat, wet and hot, and it cleaves to you, sweat pressing your skin and enervating you with its doughy-moist succubus embrace.

You need to go somewhere the sun don't shine. You need to find your place in the shade. You need to embrace your inner Arctic. You need to stick an ice cube up your ass.

Maybe you try it on your own the first time. Maybe you go out and you buy a bag of ice because the cubes in your fridge just seem like you'd be shoving a square peg in a round hole, which you would. So you go out to the delis and the bodegas, the grocery stores and the mini-marts, you search high and low for those cubes shaped more like a child's cartoon smile than a shoe box. You find a bag, you plunk down the outrageous $2.50, and gleefully you bring them home.

You stow the bag carefully in your freezer and you survey your bathtub. You consider the switch-twitch at the knot between your labia and then you consider the ring on your tub. You are suspended, momentarily, between desire and laziness, between disgust and yowling erotic need.

You clean the tub.

You stop and you admire its creamed-butter sparkle, and then you go to the freezer and you open the bag of ice. You pick out a singular, perfect, crystal-smile cube. You put it, a quick, cold moment, in your mouth. You exhale and imagine you can see your breath in the freezer's polar air. You take the ice cube to the tub.

You realize you still have your clothes on, so you put the cube in a cup, store it in the freezer, go to your bedroom, take off your clothes, and tiptoe back to the kitchen. You don't know why you tiptoe, there's no one home, no one but pets to disturb, and they've borne witness to so many of your indulgent perversions that they're not even curious. But tiptoe you do.

Undressed, you get the cup out of the freezer. You add a second cube, just in case.

You go to the bathtub. You squat ungracefully and you recline clumsily. You extend your legs up the wall, so that the faucet sits between your splayed thighs, like the face of a grotesque lover. You consider for a moment running the tap with that gentle, flickering stream that, when you place your pussy exactly below its cascading fall, you come in a few wet minutes, your hips undulating a silent liquid adulation to your Neptune lover.

You consider it, but you don't do it. Not yet.

You take a cube, you rest it against your asshole, and you feel the immediate pucker of the ass-kiss, that quick inward convulsion, that wrinkle-crinkle in and up. And then with a deep breath, surely, remorselessly, unmercifully, you use your index and middle fingers to push the ice cube into your ass.

The shock of the ice. Its silver sliver ice-nine-esque core radiating. Like the plunge into a mountain stream from the inside. A swift, round shot of pleasure/pain/pleasure. Your breath inhales ragged-like. You imagine it's not unlike the sensation of crack, only pure body.

You lie there in the tub, the ice melting in you, your breath quieting its rush-rush pants. You can almost see the cube rounding and erasing, turning into a little puddle of water. You can almost see it and you can feel the pain easing into a pure goodness.

You find that your hand moves between your legs, and you rub your hard little knot of a clit, your legs up the wall, the ice melting in your ass, you rub and you rub, and you imagine your lover watching you, maybe with his friends, all of them crowding in at you in the bathroom, perched on the sink and on the toilet, peering down at you with encouraging eyes, commenting favorably. And as you imagine this, and as you watch the ice melt, and your hand rubs your little hard knot, and the heat bears down on this glass city, wrapping it in stillborn siroccos, as your heels scooch uncontrollably down the vanilla-cream tiles of your shower, you come.

Or perhaps you just get on your hands and knees before your lover, hand him the cube, and tell him, "Stick it where the sun don't shine." And turned away from him, you smile secretly as he does just that.

🕉 MUST BITE 🕉

Vicki Hendricks

I THOUGHT I'D SEEN EVERYTHING AND SURVIVED IT—and I was fucking sick of it. I'd been dancing in Key Largo for four years, since age twenty-one, and men were nothing but work to me. I enjoyed women's company—but since women were a dead-end economically, I was looking for a dick with major dollar signs flashing. I was ready to pack up for Miami because summer in the Keys was such poor pickings. Then came my lucky night, the night Rex turned up.

Sleaze, the manager, came into the club's dressing room to get me, so I knew he'd got a tip.

"He wants the monkey," Sleaze told me. "That be you."

"The monkey?" I caught my breath. "Who is he?" Spunky Monkey was the nickname Pop had given me back home in Indiana, but he was long dead and nobody in the Keys knew the name.

"Guy in his forties. Big guy. Wad of cash."

"He asked for Monkey?"

"Yeah. You used the trapeze last number, right?"

I nodded.

Sleaze jerked his thumb toward the bar.

"Cool." I tossed on a robe over my bare shoulders and moved my ass out. I had a real acrobatics performance and I felt appreciated when it wasn't wasted on a bunch of drooly burnouts. The usual crowd didn't care if you could keep time with the music as long as they could smell your cunt. Tips were lean at Reefers, and a special request meant I could set my own price, the best kind of reward.

I was compact and muscular, and kept up my gymnast skills from junior high. Being called Monkey was a compliment, although, as a red-head, I had less body hair than most of the girls. With my big blue eyes, I didn't really look like a monkey.

Rex was facing toward me from the bar, catching my titty action as I walked, what little there was. Attractive, considering he was close to fifty. Had a tan face, salt-and-pepper hair, and a hard, smooth jaw. About twice my size, sitting down. I was barely a hundred pounds, the smallest chick during off-season. I took my stance in front of him, legs wide, hands on hips, robe thrown back on my arms. It was how I met all the big boys.

"I'm Darlene. Lap dance?"

"Let me look and decide."

He'd seen all there was since I'd already swung naked with my legs wide-open a foot over his head. But I turned around and bent over, lifting the robe to my waist. The thin chain of the G-string didn't cover my little shaved mound from behind, and I got wet feeling his eyes hone in.

Pop had always told me it was a good thing to enjoy your work because that's mostly what life is made of. Too bad I didn't enjoy it quite enough.

I bent farther and looked between my legs. His mouth was half-open, and I got a sudden need for his tongue, like I would come the instant it split me.

"I'd like a date," he said.

I stood up and turned around. "I don't do dates." I always lied to get the price up.

"Never?"

"Not much."

He grabbed my arm as I started to walk away and showed me three hundreds. I asked for four. His place. After work. He'd wait outside.

When I came out a little after two, it was raining and smelled like a jungle, musty and thick, mosquitoes swarming the light under the awning, waiting to bite, tree frogs with their creepy grunts. There was one car, sparkling under the low, streaming palms, headlights shining through the downpour, beacons to my fate. He pulled up, and the passenger side opened. I slung my ass on the leather seat.

"Cool Mercedes."

He smiled at my thin, wet shirt and held out his hand for me to shake. "Rex."

He turned left behind Shell World, and we passed Blue Fin Marina, then snaked down a long, private drive. It was dark. Dripping vines and fronds dragged across my window, and the Mercedes bumped along slow. He pulled under a concrete block, two-story stilt house, and when I got out, I could hear the lapping of water out back, and caught the scent of rotten eggs that reminds you when it's low tide in the Keys.

He motioned me up the stairs on the side and flicked on a light. We passed sacks of feed and huge, empty cages, scratched mirrors, a rope ladder, chewed-up rubber toys, and a large doll, her eyes following me. Rex crooked his finger at me in my direction and I climbed the stairs, wondering if I'd get a chance to see what this was all about. He seemed to have a rule about not talking. I could handle it.

Rex opened the door to a Florida room with a built-in bar, lots of shiny bottles on the shelves, sparkling mirror tiles. He picked up a glass. I shook my head. I'd had too much of that sickening champagne at the club. He put his finger to his lips, and I followed him past two closed doors with small, barred windows, tiptoeing. Sounds of huffing, snoring, and heavy movement came from inside. Must be renting out rooms to crazy old farts, I thought. He led me upstairs to the loft. The rain had stopped, and clouds drifted over the moon outside the balcony window.

Rex wasn't the usual trick. He didn't act cool or order me around. He took me in his arms and kissed my neck, breathing hot, and held back my hair to uncover more skin. Normally, I would have broken it off and set some rules, but I was geared up to think that something interesting could come of this, with all his bucks. I dropped my snotty whore act and let myself go. He held my head back and planted the softest kisses on my mouth. His breath was sweet, no garlic, no rotten teeth, no cigarettes. I wondered how he was with mine. I kissed him back and he had to cut it off to get a breath.

He stripped me down so softly, I felt like I was the one who had paid. I held on to the dresser as he knelt in front of me, his fingers opening me up, and tongued my clit. I felt myself melting, legs going weak. He pulled me on top of him and slithered his hard cock into me, smooth and wide.

I let him do everything he wanted. Not for the money, but because it felt so good—slow hip-slapping, deep penetration, me on top, his fingers pulling at my cheeks. One finger went into my ass, sending tiny jolts of

pleasure into my tight cunt. I pulled myself astride to take him even farther in, gripping as I raised myself to the tip, then bouncing down, feeling
every inch of him smooth and hot. I lifted my ass and turned toward his
legs for the reverse cowboy, the view of my ass that makes them all come.

But he turned me back around. "I need to see your face."

He sat up and lifted my ass to his lap with his strong arms, looking me
straight in the eye. I let my world dissolve. Slow, wet, and warm, he rocked
me, up and down, teeter-totter, over and over. I was loose as a rag doll, but
he held me close and kept me moving, until I came from his cock, something that didn't happen very often. In all the years since Pop had turned
me out, I'd never felt so appreciated by a man.

That night he made sure I'd want to see more of him. He knew how
good he was, and the attention I needed. I'm sure he'd searched for a girl
like me in all the local places, with my athletic build and helpful personality, my need to get out of that disgusting club. A nickname like Monkey.
When I told him how he had hit on that, I saw the light come into his
eyes. I was a perfect fit.

The next morning I opened my eyes to bright sun sneaking through
the blinds. I was surprised at the clean, tropical style of the bedroom. No
mismatched furniture with broken arms or rings from glasses, no scary
stained sheets, not even a scratchy couch with burn holes like most Key
Largo guys seemed to own. The bed and nightstands were heavy-duty
bamboo, stuff I'd buy if I saw it in a thrift shop. He had orchids and other
plants outside on the balcony.

"Nice place," I said when I saw his eyes open.

"Want to stay?"

I tried to calculate a price for the day.

"Come on. Let me show you around."

I started to climb out of bed, but my foot got tangled in the sheet and
he caught me before I fell. His hands went straight to my hips. I couldn't
resist that tongue. He dug right into the pussy, and it was an hour before
we dragged ourselves out.

"Now you stand behind me when I open the door," he said. We were
outside of one of the two doors on the first floor. I stepped back so I could
only see his big body. "Hey, guys," he called out. "I have somebody for you
to meet." He turned to me. "It's okay. They're relaxed."

He stepped aside. I knew these were not going to be humans from the
sounds I could hear. There they were, four monkeys, two of them nearly my

size, looking at me. The smallest one had a finger in its mouth, like a child. The ceiling was high, must've been two stories, and there were trapezes mounted on beams. The windows were barred. A few piles of shit were off to the sides, and one wall had a hole punched through the plasterboard, exposing more bars inside the wall. I could see through a barred door in the middle of the wall that there was a bigger monkey in the next room.

"Hear no evil, see no evil, and speak no evil?" I asked, pointing one, two, three. "I'm not sure of the order."

"They're not quite that well behaved."

Two of them came over and I reached down to take the hand held out to me. The long fingers were warm and light, like a sweet pair of leather gloves.

Rex touched their heads gently. "These are spider monkeys, females, Itsy and Bitsy."

"Went up the waterspout?"

"You got it, but don't give me credit for those names, either. The other two are Mack and Sweetums, male and female."

I could see what seemed to be penises hanging from three of their asses, but no balls. "Females?"

"Spider monkeys have elongated vaginas. It makes mating impossible, except when they're fertile, every four years. Rape-proofing."

"The boys must get horny."

"Mack masturbates often—although not as much as Big Man." He pointed into the next room.

Sweetums stayed back, but Mack came up and took my hand, putting my fingers into the coarse hair on his back. I started to scratch and he leaned into it. "Don't let him get carried away," said Rex. I took my hand off, and sure enough Mack grabbed my wrist and forced my hand back between his shoulder blades.

"They're willful." Rex pried the long fingers from my wrist and disentangled the legs and tail clutching my thigh. He took Mack's wrists in one hand and pushed his body back with his shoulder. Mack arched and squirmed, making shrill shrieks. Rex tossed him into the mattress in the corner.

"Dash!"

I broke for the door and Rex pushed it almost closed behind us, but not quite, because he had to stop and tuck a small hand inside. "They like you," he said. "A lot. I knew it. Be careful what you start."

"Don't they usually like people?"

"Not really."

"So where did you get all these monkeys?" I could hear the other one rumbling around, wanting attention.

He locked the door and opened the next room. A monkey was waiting for us and took my hand in his warm grip. "This is the chimp, Big Man. He's an ape, not a monkey. He was named when I got him. You'll see why."

"I do already," I said. "He's as tall as me."

"That's not what I mean." He used his fingers to sign words as he spoke to Big Man. "Darlene—friend," he said. Big Man puckered up his lips, but I couldn't quite bring myself to kiss him.

Rex took my hand and motioned me to walk out in front of him. Big Man glared but didn't move. Rex turned and signed. "Bye, bye. Breakfast time." He shut the door and locked it.

"You taught them sign language?"

"No, when we bought Big Man they told us he understood signs. I learned some words so I could talk to him, but he never talks back. I think he understands, though."

"What about the spiders?"

"They don't pay much attention."

"Big Man must be bored."

"I entertain him. One chimp is hard enough to handle. Come on. I'll get their breakfast."

Rex led me into the kitchen. It was huge, with two stainless steel refrigerators. He opened one filled with vegetables. "I knew they'd take to you."

"I like them, too," I said.

I was starving, but I didn't say anything because the animals were waiting. They were hungry and dependent on Rex, and it was my fault that breakfast was late. I insisted on helping. We set everything out on the long preparation table and sink. I washed pounds of carrots, celery, and bags of apples, while Rex rinsed heads of lettuce. We divided the vegetables onto two trays and poured the monkey chow into the five bowls with their names.

Together we served them, first Big Man, then Itsy and Bitsy, Sweetums and Mack. I stood outside the window and watched them eat. Big Man sat and stuffed his face with a head of lettuce, pieces falling from his open mouth, making a big wet mess on the floor as he chewed, showing us how starved he was because we'd stayed upstairs fucking. Itsy and Bitsy chowed down, too, occasionally glancing over their shoulders at me. I knew the feeling, your meals being in someone else's control. Been there.

Rex sponged up the water and dirt we'd left on the countertop while I made the coffee.

"So where did you get them?" I asked him.

"It was a business."

"Monkey business?"

He laughed. "You got it."

"Circus?"

"No, a petting zoo of sorts, with some shows. The stage and big cages are still outside. It was my ex's idea, Julia. She taught them the tricks and it was fun—for a while. We never made money, spent it all on food and vet care, but she had money anyway. The Monkey Hut was her hobby. You want some bacon and eggs?"

"Sure. And then she split?"

"She left me the place and investments so I could take care of the monkeys."

"Ouch," I said.

"She was generous. It was my fault. We never talked."

"She never complained?"

"She might've."

He put a skillet on the stove and went to the second refrigerator and pulled out a package of bacon and a carton of eggs. "They'll smell this," he said. "Ignore the noise. I don't give them meat. Spider monkeys are vegetarian, and Big Man gets too wild. He wants it all."

The bacon had barely started to sizzle when there was a loud howl. Others took up the scream, and then there was pounding, like one was beating a tray. The screeching got louder and one of them started banging on the door.

"Metal doors?" I asked.

"Yeah, don't worry. They'll settle down in a minute."

It took about five minutes, but I thought, fuck, Rex is a kind man to care for all these animals, and I could live in a place like this. He could even make me come, unusual for a man. By then I didn't have any romantic notions. I'd settle for a nice home, some monkeys to play with. I was sure I could still get out now and then with my girlfriends. So Rex was devoted to monkeys, and I was the new monkey. That must have flickered in his mind when he saw me, and I had nothing against it—if enough money came my way.

Over the next month, Rex picked me up almost every night. I got on well with everybody. Rex and I took care of their meals together, and I scratched backs and gave treats. "The kids" brightened up every time I came into their rooms. At dusk, I fixed the strawberry yogurt, oatmeal, and flan combination that filled out their dietary needs. They'd stick their little faces into it or squeeze it through their fingers and lick it off. I felt appreciated, more than I'd ever have expected, more than most of my life.

I told Rex if he installed a big trapeze in the spiders' room, I could swing with them. He had it up in two days, no surprise. I climbed up naked and went into my act, swinging with my ass on the bar, then dropping to hang by my knees. But before I got any farther, Mack swung over and whipped past me, switching from hands to feet to tail and flinging himself to the other trapezes and back again. I couldn't compete. He scared me, coming so close, but he was perfect in his moves. Sweetums joined in and soon they were both swinging fast and switching hands, feet, and tails, synchronizing with each other. I pulled myself up to watch.

"Don't stop," Rex hollered. "I want to see you, not them."

I hung by my arms and swung a little. I pulled my legs above my body in a split across the bar, like I'd done that first night he watched me perform.

Rex came over and gave my cunt a greedy stare. The trapeze was just high enough for him to lick my pussy, no accident, and he slurped it a couple of times as I swung toward him, before he grabbed me. The monkeys kept cavorting around us, but he ate me like a starving man, ignoring them. I hung limp on the trapeze, feeling nothing but my aching clit. When I opened my eyes, all four spiders were watching, and Big Man was grunting in the next room. I didn't mind giving the show.

I wasn't sure who thought of marriage first, but things moved fast. A captain friend of Rex's married us on his sailboat, and we put on a party at Reefer's. Sleaze got in some decent champagne 'specially for me. I was glad to be saying goodbye to that place, and all the sucking up that went with it.

We'd planned on a honeymoon in the Bahamas for a few days, but on the morning after the wedding, Bitsy got sick, and we had to cancel. Rex was afraid to leave her with the sitter, a teenage boy that was supposed to stop by. She didn't look that sick to me, no puking or diarrhea, but she just lay on the mattress and held her stomach instead of eating her breakfast. Rex said that was a sure sign. When we'd cancelled our flight and looked in on her, she'd gotten up and was eating the remains from Itsy. I thought for sure she'd faked her illness, but it was too late to worry about it. Rex promised we could try again soon, but the kids didn't like everyone, and they needed lots of human interaction every day. It wasn't any big deal. The monkeys were more fun than most people I knew.

I had them spoiled in the first week. I started giving them an extra treat or two each day, a cookie or a few crackers. They loved french fries, too, but I was careful not to go too far with the grease. None of them would keep a diaper on. I hadn't counted on so much shit. It seemed to pile up more and more, maybe from the treats, or else Rex was falling down on the cleaning. I hadn't bargained on it, but I started pitching in on shit detail. They were mine now, too, and they would cuddle and kiss me when I sat with them.

"Why not use the big cages outside?" I asked Rex one day. "We could squirt them out easier."

"We used to. You can't keep neighborhood kids from sneaking around, sticking their arms inside."

"The monkeys seem so tame, even Big Man."

He shook his head. "One time Mack grabbed a handful of a girl's hair. He just wanted to smell her shampoo—he does that—but he's so strong. She told her parents he tried to scalp her. The father came back with a gun. Lucky I was home."

"That's crazy."

"Yeah, but when they get that look, like a war going on inside—watch out. One second everything is nice, nice, love, love—and the next, 'Must bite! Must bite!' flashes in their eyes."

"They're always so sweet to me."

"So far. You can't predict when somebody will get jealous. Especially Big Man."

Within a couple months, I was doing more than my share of the work, but, hey, it was appreciated. By the third month, things started to get a little tedious. Rex had been unemployed for a couple of years, living on the investments. Now with me around, or so he said, we were running short. I wondered why he hadn't figured that out earlier. He didn't ask me to go back to work, but the Mercedes was on lease, and it had to be turned in. We were stuck with the old pickup that was used for carting the monkeys in cages to the vet and bringing home bags of feed.

Rex started giving sailing lessons at the Yacht Club. Now he was gone most of the day, and every morning during prime feeding time. "Not working" was far more labor than I had imagined. Still, I got to drink piña coladas and lie around in the sun all afternoon on my own private beach.

Sometimes my best girlfriend from the club would come by to keep up her all-over tan. Danielle was luscious with her tiny, shaved mound and vanilla double-Ds. We'd loll naked on a quilt on the little beach, sucking face, pressing our tits together until somebody's fingers would start to travel—usually mine. She'd flip to her back and spread her legs, and I'd open her like an envelope, with one finger to her juicy clit, and let the breeze dry her pink edges so I could tongue them wet again.

We ordered in, pizza or sushi, and by sundown we'd have rubbed our clits raw. Rex had met her and must've figured we fooled around, being dancer types, but he never said anything. I gave him whatever he wanted, and he did his part.

At first, we went out to dinner most nights. There was so much food prep for the monkeys that the whole day would be taken up by food if we cooked dinner. There were lots of nice seafood places, and we had our favorites. At night, we'd sit at the huge window overlooking our bay and listen to music, gazing out at the stars and the water. He had a light behind the house, so we could see the palms blowing and the sparkle of waves. On the first night of a full moon, he turned the light off, and we sat there in the dark and waited for the moon to come up. It cast its glittery trail across the water, and I thought it was a magic road leading right to me, where I had found my jackpot.

Sometimes we'd put on Mack's leash and take him out with us behind the house, where he could be fastened to a rail left from the tourist attraction days. He really enjoyed the fresh air, and he would sit in a palm that slanted near the edge of the water. He'd flirt, throwing me kisses, and I'd unhook him and let him cuddle next to me and pick through my hair.

Our eating at nice places and stargazing got less and less over the months. Rex started to watch TV sports in the den a few nights a week. Sometimes he went out with his buddies, leaving me there to sip my drink and count the stars alone.

One night I thought one of the spiders was using the other as a punching bag. When I opened the door, Itsy and Bitsy were grooming each other, Mack and Sweetums were swinging, and Big Man was racked out in the other room playing with his toe, the door between the rooms closed as we generally left it. They all looked up at me, like, "What's your problem?" It was all a trick to get my attention.

These ruckuses began to break out more often. I'd go in to check on them and scratch backs, bring treats. Mack or Big Man would often sit there and masturbate, looking me straight in the eye. Sometimes the females would finger themselves.

I could sign a few phrases I'd learned to Big Man, but he only stared at me. He was stubborn. They were bored, poor things, him especially, because he was smarter and more isolated. I wanted to swing with them and get some exercise, but when I mentioned it to Rex, he said that was too dangerous if he wasn't home. I knew he was right. I saw them when the softness in their eyes turned flat and hard, like there was something wild ready to break out. That's when I'd race for the door.

Rex went out two nights in a row one week and I was really pissed. He had a friend down from Miami, but I was almost mad enough to head over to Reefer's and see some of the regulars. I started to get dressed, and then I thought about them—the regulars—and remembered the smell of that place. I wasn't that bored. Big Man was making a racket as usual, so I pulled a chair into the hall where he could see me to quiet him down. I knew the best way to stop boredom, so I slipped off my shorts and panties and put my favorite finger on my button and gave myself a nice twinge. Big Man seemed to know what I was doing. His eyebrows went up and he whimpered. When I started to breathe hard, he began to huff. He was jacking off, standing on the other side of the door. I wondered if this was a bad idea, but I didn't stop. I was almost there. I came and moaned out loud, and Big Man wasn't far behind. I was glad I hadn't left him alone. He was my friend.

I put on my shorts and got another drink. Big Man was whining, so I took a look and decided to let him out. He was calm, and he knew what the leash meant, so it was no problem to hook him up and lead him to the back patio. After he sat for a while in his palm, he came down to sit on the bottom of the lounge chair and I gave him pieces of ice from my drink. He stood behind my back and groomed me. I don't know what he found there, but his cool fingers picking through my hair was like a massage. I wasn't sure if Rex would like the idea, so I didn't mention it. It wasn't like Big Man would try to escape. He'd been born in captivity and he knew where his meals came from. He was more civilized than most of the regulars at Reefer's. It became our little secret. Every time Rex left, Big Man got out.

As the nights turned cooler toward Christmas, Big Man would sit next to me and doze off with his head on my chest. He'd wake up drowsy and look at my face. Nice, nice! glowed in his round eyes. But the animal was always close. Sometimes he'd jump, as if I'd hit him, and his lips would curl back. *Must bite! Must bite!* was fighting to take over his brain. I'd get out of his way until he settled down. He wasn't so different from the guys at the bar. You never knew with men.

I started to get suspicious of Rex. He didn't have much time for sex or monkey tricks, started spending every day at the Yacht Club. Since the snowbirds were down, it made sense that he had more work, but I thought he might be seeing another woman. If you think it, it's true, they always say. Maybe his chick was a snowbird, and this was their yearly rendezvous. I had my own girlfriend, but I didn't like that Rex was sneaking around and leaving me home peeling bananas all day. I wondered if that had been his plan all along, find some sucker for the monkeys so he could be with his winter girlfriend. Maybe she didn't like monkeys and I was his chance to make a break. Maybe that was what his wife did to him.

The difference was that Julia had had money. She'd left him with investments and the house, and had still had enough dough to take off. He was pretty much stuck with me, unless he wanted to leave with nothing. I started to think I could do without him fine, but even if he left me with the place, finances would still be lousy. I'd have to take care of the monkeys and go back to spreading my ass.

Finally, one night Rex stayed home with me, and we had a drink on the patio like the old days. I had several drinks. Big Man was making a ruckus inside, and I knew why, but Rex ignored it.

He finished eating, made himself another scotch, and got comfortable back out on the lounge chair without a word of thanks for the dinner I'd made. I sat down on his lap anyway, giving it one more cheerleader try. I massaged the back of his neck, licked his lips, and ground my ass a little into his groin. He kissed back without any pressure, his eyes glazed. I sucked on his neck and he pushed my face away, going back to shallow kisses, his arms straight at his sides, hands flat on the couch. Things had changed, but it wasn't my fault. I gave up on foreplay and undid his belt and zipper, slipping to my knees on the floor, thinking I could work him up for a good ride at least. I sucked him till my jaws cramped. Finally, he pumped me for a couple of minutes before his cock fell out.

I didn't make an issue of it because I didn't want to hear any lies. I tried to act normal and talk about all the cute things the monkeys did that day. Then I asked an important question. "What will the monkeys do if something happens to us?"

"I guess you'll be here when I'm gone," he said.

"Great. I can't handle them."

He took a drink of his scotch. "Don't worry. I have a big life insurance policy. You can get any extra help you need. These guys could live to be forty."

"Forty! How much money?"

"A million. My wife set that up, too, so the monkeys would be taken care of, no matter what."

"That was pretty generous, but if they live till forty—"

"She has plenty of money. She felt responsible for these guys, even though she hated them."

"Hated them?"

"Yeah, I don't know why. Big Man scared her one time, and she never forgave him."

"What did he do?"

"Nothing. She said he was *going* to do something."

I figured Julia just wanted out. If you had money, everything was easy.

We both kept drinking. It was the only thing we enjoyed together anymore, but it made me hostile.

"So what are the monkeys and me supposed to do all the time when you're gone?"

"Shh. You're too loud."

"So what? Nobody around here."

"You'll wake them."

I got louder on purpose. "Well, they're in this, too. You don't spend any time with them."

He whispered. "I have to work. Somebody has to."

"You don't make much."

"I don't wave my naked ass in anybody's face."

"You sure?"

He gave me a disgusted look. I didn't ask again. It didn't matter what he was doing. It was how he tricked me, setting me up to think he had money, forcing me into the boring, shit job he was sick of.

After that night, the million bucks wouldn't leave me alone. It taunted me every morning when I cut vegetables and all afternoon when

I scrubbed shit off the walls and windows, slimy lettuce from the floor, and washed sour, soggy monkey biscuits out of all the water bowls. After a week, I realized that although Rex was a lot older, I couldn't hold out till he died. Nothing was the way it was supposed to be. I was cheap help for a man trapped with wild children who would never grow up.

I started my training plan. I concentrated on Big Man because he could do the job alone, and the others would follow his lead. I had our wedding picture blown up huge and cut Rex's face out of it to mount it with a stick inside a shirt and jeans that I got out of the dirty laundry. I stuffed it with Rex's underwear. I padded the stick with foam rubber so it looked like a neck and put an X on the left side where the jugular would be. I sewed a set of cock and balls out of foam to stuff inside the pants.

I fried up a pound of bacon and put it into the refrigerator, knowing the shit was going to fly if I had to do much rewarding. I coaxed Big Man into the kitchen on his leash, signing, "Bacon, bacon, Big Man." I had a strip inside the oven, and I stood in front of it with the dummy. "Big Man, bite," I said and signed it to him. I pointed to the X and signed it again and again. "Big Man, bite."

His head moved high and low from side to side. He sniffed to find the bacon, but the whole room was filled with the smell. I held the dummy near his face and signed, "Bite," pointing to the X. "Bite," I signed, "I give bacon."

I signed "bite and bacon," "bite and bacon," but he didn't get it, or pretended not to. I was aggravated. I took the dummy and bit it on the X, shaking my head like a shark in a frenzy. I opened the oven and grabbed the bacon to flop it on the dummy's neck. I shoved the Rex doll at Big Man and he bit lightly—all he wanted was the bacon—but it was a start.

I opened the refrigerator to get another piece. Big mistake. Big Man grabbed the platter and pushed me down. The leash came right out of my hand. He sat on the floor and ate the whole pound in thirty seconds. I realized I had little control, but I got most of it cleaned up before Rex came home.

The next day I hooked Big Man outside. I wanted him to know that the bacon was all mine and he would only get it if he did what I said.

I brought out the bacon and set it on a table outside his reach. Big Man went wild. He jerked at the chain and his eyes bounced from me to the bacon and back. I dug into the back of the broom closet and got the dummy and stood there signing and saying, "Big Man, bite. I give bacon."

He started making his hooting chimp noises, trying to coax me, full of glee.

"What does Big Man want?" I said. "Tell Darlene," I signed.

He continued to hoot and I held the dummy near him. "Kill Rex, get bacon," I said. "Kill Rex!" I handed him the dummy but not the bacon. "Bite Rex!" I held out a strip. "Kill Rex!"

Finally, he curled back his lips and ripped a chunk out of the rubber. I grabbed two strips of bacon and stuck them at him. He grabbed them with his hand and shoved them into his mouth. Then he grabbed the dummy and ripped every shred of rubber off the neck.

We went on half the day that way, with several repaired necks, moving down to the genitals, until I could barely say the word bite and he'd have his teeth on the dummy, tearing the rubber away. After he'd shredded all the parts, I let him rip out the stuffing and toss it around.

His animal nature was taking control. I played up my role as his pal, chaining him in the kitchen one day, giving him all my attention. He sat on a chair and watched me wash and cut fruit and vegetables all morning. After a while, I heard him make a familiar grunt, and when I turned, he was pumping his cock. His eyes were soft and his lips were curled in a smile as he came on the seat of the kitchen chair. He was with me all the way.

I decided the best way to do it was in one big rush. I'd unlock the doors while Rex was having his coffee, and wait for Big Man to find his way into the kitchen when I started frying the bacon. I'd sign, "Kill Rex," behind his back, and in the few seconds that Rex had to live, he'd think he was meeting his natural fate, the fate he deserved for betraying his children. The county would take all the monkeys away, most likely destroy them, but I tried not to think of that. I'd be free with the million. Nobody would suspect me. The crazy guy with the monkeys had been asking for it for years.

I didn't waste any time. That afternoon I put the dummy clothes in the wash and threw the foam rubber in the trash, burned the photo face. Nobody would be able to put it all together.

The next morning Rex was sitting at the kitchen table, reading the paper. I'd unlocked the cage doors while the monkeys were still asleep. I told Rex I felt like making some bacon and eggs. As soon as I said bacon, the hooting started. Big Man went wild and the others followed. Rex shook his head and kept reading.

The bacon barely started to crackle when Big Man came leaping through the door. I don't think he even saw me sign. He knocked Rex to the floor and bit into his throat, tearing away flesh, much easier than he had the rubber. Blood shot out and he kept on biting and spitting out the pieces. Rex dropped, unconscious in seconds. Big Man moved down and tore up his cock and balls, yanking them off with his hand, ripping the sack with his teeth. I was frozen.

Big Man didn't forget the bacon. He looked at me and I jumped aside, and he picked up the half-cooked pieces three at a time and stuffed them into his bloody mouth. Mack, Sweetums, Itsy, and Bitsy were in the doorway watching, excited. I started toward the door to make my break down the stairs. Big Man finished with the bacon, and he leapt to block the way, with *Must bite!* in his eyes. I grabbed a sharp knife off the sink, but he reached for my wrist and twisted. The knife fell to the floor. "Bacon!" I yelled and pointed toward the stove. He turned and let loose, and I ran in the opposite direction, into the monkey rooms and slammed the door, to wait until they'd all settled down.

I didn't count on Big Man locking me in.

I was at their mercy, caged for hours. I had to pee in the corner. I wasn't anywhere near as strong as they were, and obviously no smarter. There was no hope unless somebody came to the house. When did that ever happen? I thought the monkeys might get bored and let me out, take care of me, as I had taken care of them—but they seemed to have no interest.

They banged around in the kitchen—eating all the food, tossing pans, breaking dishes, and yanking out drawers.

After a long time, things got quiet. I woke up at dusk. Big Man's face was at the window. Maybe he wanted me to fix the yogurt and oatmeal. I went to the door. "Big Man, let Darlene out," I said and signed. "Big Man, unlock door."

He looked at me and got a big grin, pulling his lips out, snorting and mocking me. His hands came close to the window and he moved his fingers. I couldn't believe it. The chimp was signing. "Darlene kill Rex."

"No!" I signed, "Big Man kill Rex!"

He started in again with that chimp laugh that made my skin crawl, a piercing, mocking hoot. "Darlene kill Rex!"

He bent down then, and I thought he was unlocking the door. I wasn't sure I wanted out. But that wasn't it. His face came back up and he was holding the sharp knife in his teeth by the blade. It was covered in Rex's blood. "Darlene kill Rex."

My guts froze. The handle of the knife had my prints on it. But it was impossible that he could know that, a coincidence how he was holding it. I had to get that knife. I kicked the door and banged with my fists, and he ran off. I sat down on the floor, drained and horrified. But then the door slightly opened. It was unlocked. I looked out. Nobody there. No knife. I didn't think the police knew sign language or would even listen to a chimp, but they would take the knife for evidence. As the beneficiary of a million bucks, I was in trouble.

The spiders were lounging all over the couch. Groggy, greedy monkeys, limbs dangling. Liquor fumes were thick, and bottles broken; they might've been drinking. There were gummy bears and peanut shells ground into piles of crap on the carpet, a banana peel hanging on a lampshade. I walked past it all into the kitchen. Garbage, blood, and shit were everywhere. The refrigerator was open and empty, milk and orange juice cartons smashed, pickles and ketchup and lettuce trampled on the tile floor. They'd eaten at least two days' worth of carrots, celery, bananas, oranges. A fifty-pound bag of monkey biscuits was dumped in the corner and somebody had peed on it.

A river of blood traced where Rex's body had been dragged under the table. I looked underneath and held my breath. Besides the torn and bitten flesh of his neck there were knife wounds, the throat slit from the right ear to the mangled, stringy part on the left, the head nearly severed. I didn't look at his crotch. I gagged up the small amount of food in my stomach. Everything was wrong. I wanted Rex back. He hadn't been so bad. I heard something behind me and stood up. Big Man walked in and signed, "Darlene kill Rex."

"Where's the knife, Big Man?"

He started to laugh. He'd been waiting for his chance, playing me, just like I'd thought I was playing him, and Rex had played me. I bent over and gagged some more. Big Man was staring at me. He kept laughing until that animal look came into his eyes. He pulled his cock and it grew out long and hard. I jerked with the impulse to run, but I had to find that knife. He sat on the chair and worked his pud. All I had to do was find it and wipe off my prints. Without evidence, nobody would believe a freaking ape.

I got down on my hands and knees and raked through the slimy trash with my fingers. The knife could be anywhere. I tried to think like an ape, but my brain was dead. I would never find it like that. Big Man was too smart. The only way was to convince Big Man to show me, himself. I didn't have much time.

Big Man was rocking and grunting; his come squirted out onto the chair. He nodded off and I let him doze for a few minutes while I took a last, useless look around. Then I stood across the room and called his name.

"Darlene wants knife," I signed and shouted. "Darlene wants knife." I turned my back to him, slipped my shorts and panties down, and bent over. It always worked with men—or so I'd thought. "Darlene loves Big Man," I said. I bent farther and signed between my legs. He grinned and hooted, showing his mouthful of long, yellow teeth and dark gums. I had his attention.

I bit my lip and sucked up what I had left of pride. If Big Man was smart enough to hide the knife, we could make a deal. "Get knife," I signed. I pushed my finger inside my cunt to be sure he got the message. He bounded on top of me in a second and I clenched my cheeks, prepared to be stuck from behind, like I'd seen the monkeys do it. But instead, he spun me around and opened his gap of a rotten mouth and plastered it over my face. He'd been watching me and Rex. His teeth cut into my nose and chin, and the hot stench of broccoli breath poured over me. I convulsed down hard and broke lose, jerking my head back and ejecting a slug of phlegmy bile that landed on his furred thigh. He snatched it up quick, cupped it into his mouth, and swallowed it down like an oyster appetizer, pulling my tiny frame forward onto his cock. It tore in, pointy and hard, like a knife. Knife. I wished it were the fucking knife. He huffed and drooled onto my face. How many times would I have to fuck him to get the murder weapon?

Big Man finished with a long grunt, knocked me sideways to the floor, stepped on my throat, and dashed out of the room. I choked and gasped. Any more weight on that foot and he'd have broken my windpipe. I must've blacked out, because it was dark when I opened my eyes.

No Big Man. No knife. I dragged myself up and walked through the hall to the living room. I could hear him in there messing around. Moonlight from the window showed him cross-legged in the corner. I snapped on the light. He was finger-painting crap on the wall. No knife. He turned and looked at me. His shitty hand dropped to his lap. His cock was hard. It dawned on me then, that I had no elongated vagina. Big Man would rape me whenever he pleased. I turned and ran for the door, but he leaped onto my back and pinned me to the floor. My face hit the hard tile and my teeth cut through my lip. His pointy knife ripped into my ass. It wasn't worth a million.

໑ COMEBACK ໑
Nicholas Kaufmann

THE BIG SHINDIG WAS AT BRUCE GLASSER'S HOUSE IN TARZANA, the only part of the Valley I don't consider a shit hole. It's the same house where we shot a lot of my movies when it belonged to Ricky Samson, owner of Luscious Video back in the eighties. The *Virgin High* series had turned Bruce into one of the biggest adult-film producers in the country, making him rich enough to buy it when Ricky died from screwing the wrong junkie. (Ricky always liked it bareback, and everyone knew it would get him in trouble one day, either dead or a daddy.)

It was weird being there for a party instead of a shoot. I kept expecting the doorbell to ring and the late, great Johnny Calzone to come in dressed like that fucking pizza delivery boy from *Who Ordered Sausage?* I still can't believe that's the role that got him famous. Though I guess I'm still best known for playing a high school girl who fucks her gym teacher on the parallel bars, so maybe I shouldn't talk.

Bruce invited me to the party only because he was giving me a role in his newest film, mostly out of pity, I suppose, but I wasn't about to say no. It's hard being a former starlet who's crossed to the other side of forty. Everyone thinks you're too ancient to be in their movies anymore, or you're only good for the granny-porn sites, so I'd been doing mostly dub work on Japanese anime, the ones where girls get fucked by demons or whatever. The money's all right, but the job's kind of limiting. There are only so many ways to make that surprised gasping noise when the tentacles come out of nowhere and Little Miss Wide Eyes gets one in every hole.

I felt like a visitor from another planet standing there in Bruce's crowded living room. Everyone knew everyone else—they all had their arms around each other and were laughing at private jokes—but I didn't recognize anyone. A whole new generation of filmmakers had sprung up since the last time I was there. I guess I'd expected to sign at least a few cocktail napkins—"Stay tight! Love, Amber Fox," just like in the old days, when everyone asked me to sign video boxes—but no one seemed to remember me, or if they did, they didn't give a shit. I was just some old lady to them, not worth their attention when there were so many young hotties in the room.

I flashed for a moment on Jay, my ex-boyfriend, the night he packed his bags and took off, our two-year relationship dead all of a sudden because he'd found someone else. Someone younger. Standing at my door, confused and hurt, I caught a glimpse of her as Jay tossed his suitcases in the back of his Ford Expedition. Just a slim, tanned arm poking out of the passenger's side window, the tattoo of a daisy on her shoulder, her fingers decorated with silver rings. Not a wrinkle or an ounce of fat on that arm, just the smooth, golden skin of a twenty-something beach bunny. Inside the car, the round tip of a cigarette glowed, briefly revealing an orange-tinted hint of a button nose and curly hair before it faded.

A high-pitched squeal pulled me out of my memories. "Amber?" A girl I'd never seen before ran up to me. She was a skinny, tiny thing with big blonde hair, tight bell-bottom jeans, and a cropped T-shirt that barely covered her melon chest. She didn't look more than eighteen.

"The one and only," I said, perking up a bit. It's an old joke. Half the women in the biz call themselves Amber.

"Oh my God!" she shrieked, giving me a peek at the metal stud through her tongue. "Amber Fox, I can't believe it!"

"In the flesh," I said. I was relieved someone had finally recognized me, even if she was probably one of the younger stars I'd been losing roles to for the past six years. I tried not to look at how toned and tight her stomach was, but the glittery string of diamonds dangling from her pierced belly button kept drawing my eye back. I felt like a whale all of a sudden, so I sucked in my gut and made a mental note to avoid the hors d'oeuvres table for the rest of the night.

"You have no idea how big a fan I am!" she cried, her eyes wide and crazy looking.

"You'll just have to tell me then," I said, laughing my party laugh. Behind her, someone spread lines of coke on the coffee table. Suddenly it felt like no time had passed—it was still 1986, and I was the hottest adult-film actress this side of Seka.

"I'm Krystal Lynn," she said, extending one remarkably tiny hand. Her nails, though, were enormous and had green dollar signs stenciled onto the white polish. I winced in sympathy for any guy unlucky enough to get a hand job from her. "Maybe you saw me in *Ready, Willing, and Anal 5*? I won an AVN Award for that. Best Ass to Mouth."

"Congratulations," I said, shaking her hand. "I have an AVN myself."

"I know, Lifetime Achievement!" Krystal squealed. "I know, like, everything about you. You're my hero. You're totally why I got into the business."

I grinned. "Really?"

"Totally! My father had, like, all your videos. I found them under the sink in his bathroom, and this one time when he was out of town, I invited over all my friends from school, and we had an Amber Fox marathon. You were so cool."

Her father? She might as well have stabbed me in the heart. Sometimes I forget how long ago the eighties were.

She turned around and shouted into the crowd, "Hey, Terry, get your ass over here! You gotta meet someone!" A tall, chunky man closer to my age than hers, with a fuzzy handlebar mustache, a ponytail sticking out the back of his trucker cap, and a big blue knapsack slung over one shoulder, made his way over to us. "This is Amber Fox."

"Yeah?" he said. Not hi, not pleased to meet you, just "yeah."

"Terry Left. I own Sunset Auto Parts." He said it like I ought to be impressed, then shook my hand with an overly strong grip. I knew his type immediately: the small-time, loudmouth loser who'd managed to catch a hot, young porn-star girlfriend with daddy issues and thought it made him big shit. I knew the type because that was every boyfriend I'd ever had. They drove me crazy, but sometimes you need to come home to someone who still wants to be with you after you bitch about how a costar got jizz in your eye when he came on your face.

Every boyfriend except Jay, that is. He was the only one I ever really cared about. But he'd been disappointing in a different way. Like the car enthusiast he was, he couldn't resist trading in his old ride for a shiny new one.

"You remember those *Virgin High* videos I told you about?" Krystal asked Terry.

"What, with the chick on the balance beam?"

"Parallel bars," I said.

"This is her!"

"No shit," Terry said. He put his arm around Krystal's shoulders and crushed her to him. "I bet you could fuck on the balance beam no problem, right, baby? Maybe you should do a remake."

I kept the smile on my face, but inside I cringed. There's a superstition in movies, in all entertainment probably, that once an idea is put out there, even as a joke, it will inevitably become a reality, as if somebody could pluck it right out of the air. If a remake of *Virgin High* happened with some new starlet in my signature role, I would personally hunt Terry down and kill him for bringing it up. Not that I'm a superstitious woman, but *Virgin High* was all the cred I had left.

"You still got that marker in your bag, hon?" Krystal asked. Terry swung the knapsack off his shoulder, rummaged through it, and pulled out a black Sharpie. She snatched it out of his hand and put it in mine. "Do you mind?"

"No, sure, do you have something for me to sign?"

I expected her to produce a cocktail napkin or even one of her father's old video boxes, but instead she lifted her T-shirt up to her neck with both hands. "To Krystal," she said, "with a K."

Her breasts were enormous, way out of proportion with her tiny body. I was afraid the Sharpie might accidentally pop her implant when I pressed it to her left breast, but the opposite happened. As the felt tip of the marker squeaked over the skin just above her stretched nipple, it didn't even indent the flesh. I've signed a lot of tits in my time, but I'd never seen anything like that. It was like writing on a bowling ball. She should sue her plastic surgeon.

"Get the camera," she told Terry. He nodded and pulled out a sleek, silver digital number. "Can I get a shot of this?" she asked me.

"Sure," I said, "but I finished signing my name."

"Pretend you're still writing."

I held my hand over her breast, keeping the Sharpie's tip just above my signature. My arm began shaking with fatigue. As I watched my wrist tremble, I wondered what had happened to me. Time was, I could maintain a split on the parallel bars for fifteen minutes without so much as breaking a sweat, but now I was shaking like an old junkie just from holding a pen above some girl's tit while her Mongoloid idiot boyfriend tried to figure out how to press a fucking button.

Finally, the flash went off. Krystal thanked me, and she and Terry wandered over to the coke table. She kept her shirt up to show off my signature. I needed to get away for a minute, so I went out into the backyard. No stars came through the smoggy night sky, and the moon was just a bright smear on the clouds. Bruce had set up tiki torches on the lawn, but that was more for effect than anything else since the muggy night was keeping everyone inside with the air-conditioning. I was alone in the orange glow of the flames.

I reached into my bag, fumbled for my pack of Newports, and lit up. My hand was still trembling. After being accosted by Little Miss Rock-Hard Abs, I felt old as dust and about as sexy. Maybe there was no place for me in the industry anymore. Part of me wanted to walk away and leave it all behind, forget Bruce's new movie, forget all hope of a comeback. How could I compete with the Krystal Lynns of the world?

But porn was all I knew and, frankly, all I wanted to know. The job only asked you to fuck some broad-shouldered hunk you'd probably want to fuck anyway, and by the end of the day you had enough money to make two months' rent. Everyone always said I was too smart for this business, but what else was I qualified to do? Waitress? Run day care? Hey, kids, did I ever tell you about the time Ron Jeremy shot his load on my tits and couldn't stop giggling?

More than that, I didn't want to be just some grande dame with a lifetime achievement award. I wanted to be the fantasy of pubescent boys everywhere, I wanted guys on their commutes to think of me and have no choice but to pull their cars over and jerk off. I wanted to be wanted again. Dubbing hard-core anime wasn't going to make that happen. Being back in front of the camera would.

I stamped out my cigarette and started toward the sliding-glass door that led to the kitchen. But before I reached it, I caught sight of shapes moving in the darkness of the yard, and I stopped. A couple I hadn't noticed before stood just beyond the glow of the tiki torches and the light spilling out from the house. The man was tall, slender, and stood as straight as a board. He wore a finely pressed suit and a tieless dress shirt, with one arm around the shoulders of the petite woman in a dark, slinky dress next to him. They were both looking at me. I felt uncomfortable, strangely embarrassed by their attention. Normally I want people's eyes on me—nobody gets into adult films because they're shy—but this was different. They were staring at me so intensely, like they were trying to see the bones beneath my skin. I hurried inside. I wanted to find Bruce, get the script from him, and pour as much Cristal down my throat as I could before going home to my empty little apartment with its reminders of Jay everywhere.

Rounding the corner from the kitchen to the living room, I found him. Bruce was leaning against the wall with a glass of white wine in one hand, some rolled-up papers in the other. He was surrounded by a gaggle of starlets who laughed at everything he said and touched his arms and chest every chance they got. Bruce had never been a handsome man, not even back when he hadn't had to dye the gray out of his hair. He's got one of those noses that looks like it's been broken a few too many times, and a bushy mustache that looks like a fat caterpillar died on his lip. Still, money is money and power is power, and these girls could smell both on him. They would do anything for him, and he knew it.

When he saw me, he shouted over their heads, "Amber!" He waved me over. The girls reluctantly parted to let me through. A few of them looked me up and down with one of those who's-this-bitch? expressions that come with being cock-blocked. Bruce handed me the papers. "Here's the script," he said. "We start shooting tomorrow night."

As with most scripts for adult films, it was really just an outline. The movie would probably run an hour, but the script was only six pages long. I sat down on one of the Italian leather chairs in the living room, blocked out the laughter and clinking glasses, and read it. It was called *The Big Cumback*, about three slutty female gangsters, Sabrina, Katie, and Jess, who escape from jail and fuck their way to the top of the male-dominated criminal underground. I had to flip through it three times before the part Bruce had in mind for me even registered.

I jumped out of the chair and stormed all over the house looking for him. No one knew where he was. That meant he was in the bedroom with someone and didn't want to be disturbed. I didn't care, I threw open the bedroom door and marched right in. Bruce was sitting naked on the king-size bed, his back against the cushioned headboard. Some starlet's head was between his legs, a cloud of blonde hair bobbing over his hairy gut like a poodle dancing for scraps. I couldn't see her face, just her bare ass in the air and, beneath it, the snake-eye slit of her shaved pussy.

A momentary pang of jealousy hit me—I used to be the one he took to the bedroom at parties—but I shrugged it off and shook the script in the air. "What the fuck, Bruce?"

He didn't flinch or yell or even tell the girl to stop. He only sighed and played with her hair when he said, "What's the matter now?" His unfazed reaction only infuriated me further.

"I'm playing Sabrina's mother?" I shouted. Bruce's cock slid out of the girl's mouth with a wet pop, and she glanced at me over her shoulder. It was Krystal Lynn. Why wasn't I surprised?

"Oh my God," Krystal said, "you're playing my mother? How awesome is that? We're going to be in a movie together!"

I glared at Bruce. "She's Sabrina?"

Bruce put a hand on Krystal's head and pushed her face down again. "Did I say you could stop?" Then he turned to me. "Relax, babe; it's a part, isn't it? You'll be on camera again like you wanted."

"I don't even have a goddamn sex scene, Bruce. I just come out of a shower and walk in on her and a guy—"

"It's not sex, but you'll still be naked. Everyone will see your tits, everyone will see your bush, I promise you. That gets you back in the public eye. And it's a funny scene, too. You do comedy well, I've seen it."

I shook the script at him again. "This is bullshit, and you know it. I can do more than this. You owe me, Bruce. I put *Virgin High* on the fucking map; I made you who you are today."

He sat up, and Krystal made a little gagging sound as she readjusted. "I'm the one sticking his neck out even putting you in the movie at all! The real bullshit here is thinking our audience wants to watch a forty-year-old woman fuck. Have you seen the new movies Marilyn Chambers is doing? They're shit and they do shit business, but even she knows she's better off hosting them than having any sex scenes."

"I'm not Marilyn Chambers, I'm Amber fucking Fox! Do you know how much fan mail I still get?" It was a lie—I didn't get much at all, maybe a letter every couple of months—but I was hoping Bruce didn't know that.

"The audience has moved on, Amber. Your DVD reissues aren't even selling. They don't care about you, they want new girls like Krystal here. She's going to be huge. Bigger than Chasey Lain, bigger than Tera Patrick, she's the next Jenna Jameson, and I'm not going to fuck up her big break by putting anything in the movie the fans don't want to see."

"The next Jenna?" Krystal asked. "You really think so?"

"You know it, babe." He guided her head down again.

"Bruce," I said, "Just give me a chance—"

"Enough, Amber. Get this straight. Most of our customer base is in their teens and twenties. It's not that they don't remember you; they've never heard of you. You might as well be their mother, and no one wants to watch their mother fuck. The script is what it is; there won't be any changes. If you don't like it, find someone else to put you in a movie. Oh, that's right, I forgot. No one else will."

I turned on my heel and stomped toward the door.

"One more thing," Bruce called after me. I half expected him to say, "I've decided to remake *Virgin High* and give Krystal your role," but instead he motioned toward my crotch and said, "Be sure to trim your pussy before we start shooting. Or better yet, shave the whole thing clean. This isn't the eighties anymore; no one wants to see a jungle down there."

I slammed the bedroom door behind me. I could hear the party raging, laughter and popping champagne corks and a loud, arrogant voice somewhere announcing, "I own Sunset Auto Parts," but I didn't want to deal with the crowd. I ducked into the bathroom, locked the door, and ran the faucet into the shell-shaped marble sink. I splashed bracing cold water on my face, then scrutinized myself in the mirror. I looked myself up and down, turned to the side to check my stomach, turned around to check my ass. I'd taken care of myself over the years. I hadn't turned into a cow like Marilyn Chambers, or gone craggy and gray like Georgina Spelvin. I looked good. So what the fuck was Bruce's problem?

"Keep your eye on the goal," I muttered to my reflection. I was going to be in front of the camera again. Bruce might have cast me thinking it was a kitschy cameo, but for me it was a whole lot more. It was the start of my comeback. I wouldn't let it be anything less. I'd do whatever it took to stand out, to be noticed in this role so people would say, "Holy shit, Amber Fox is back? I can't wait to see that!"

But first I had to get the hell out of this party. If I had to look at Bruce or Krystal Lynn one more time tonight, I'd go ballistic. I opened the bathroom door, stepped out into the hall—

And nearly bumped into the couple I'd seen outside. They were standing in the middle of the hallway, blocking my path. In the light, I could better see the olive complexion of their skin, the pitch-blackness of their hair.

"You are Amber?" the man said. He had a slight accent I couldn't place.

"The one and only." I was nervous because they were staring at me with the same intensity as before, so the old joke came out of my mouth automatically. I tried to move past them, but they wouldn't get out of my way.

"Allow me to introduce myself," he said. "I am Ashraf Hammad, and this is my wife, Raha." The woman nodded, her dark eyes glistening, but didn't say a word. "We enjoy your movies."

"That's great," I said. I felt bad for blowing off fans, but I was so desperate to get out of that house I'd stampede over them if I had to. "Excuse me—"

Raha raised one small tan hand, her palm an inch from my face. I froze, thinking the crazy bitch was going to slap me, but then something happened. The space between her hand and my skin suddenly felt like it was inhabited by a thousand tongues, a thousand caressing lips. She moved her hand over my face and down my neck.

"No, I . . ." But I couldn't finish protesting. Instead, I closed my eyes and gave in to the sensation. I couldn't help myself.

"We were hoping to find you here tonight," Ashraf said softly. "You are more experienced than the others. You have what we need."

Raha moved her hand over my breasts, and though she never actually touched me, the sensation coaxed a loud moan from my throat. I leaned back against the wall and put my hands in my hair. Raha moved her hand lower.

"She likes you," Ashraf told me. "You should be honored."

"I . . . really have to go," I managed to say.

Raha cupped her hand at my groin. I gasped as those thousand invisible tongues stroked between my legs. I felt myself getting wet.

"No," I said, pushing her away. There was something unnatural about this. Who were these people? How was she doing that with her hand?

"Why do you resist?" Ashraf asked. He sounded genuinely confused.

"I don't understand what's happening to me," I said, trying to catch my breath. I still had to lean against the wall for support.

"You do not need to understand," he said. He started unbuttoning his dress shirt. "All you need to know is that you have been chosen." He pulled the shirt open, and there on his chest, hanging from a thin chain around his neck, was a gold medallion. At first I thought it was an eye like the kind you see in Egyptian hieroglyphics, but as I looked closer I saw it was made up of smaller geometric shapes, triangles and circles. The center seemed to be moving, swirling, as if an entire galaxy of stars were hidden inside it.

"Your necklace," I said. I felt warm, feverish, dizzy. "Moving . . ."

"It is not the necklace that moves," he said. "It is the Eye."

Raha smiled. It was the most beautiful smile I'd ever seen. The desire to kiss her came over me without warning. I wanted to see what was under that dress, run my hands through her thick black hair, my lips over her bare skin, kiss every inch of her. And when I looked at Ashraf, I wanted more than anything to please him. I would do whatever he wanted. The need for them both burned inside me like an unquenchable fire.

I went with them to their car. I let Raha run her hands all over my body in the backseat while Ashraf drove. I didn't care where we were going. I never wanted the ride to end. When it did, we were in an enormous house in the Hollywood Hills. I didn't remember leaving the car or walking inside, I simply found myself lying on a luxurious bed in the middle of a room with big stone walls. My dress and underwear were on the floor, but I had no memory of taking them off. Raha appeared above me, nude, straddling me on her hands and knees. Her midnight hair cascaded around my head. When I reached for her, my hands cupped soft, pointed breasts with hard, dark nipples.

Ashraf walked around the bed, still fully clothed. He looked at the stone walls and the symbols etched into them. I didn't recognize any of the carvings, except the same eye that was on his medallion was also on each wall.

Raha bent down and kissed my breasts, suckling the nipples until they stood almost painfully erect. I arched my back in ecstasy and wrapped my legs around her. I was so wet I thought a flood would pour out of me.

Ashraf's voice floated through the room, echoing off the stones. "It is said that in the time of the ancients, Ra, the greatest of all the gods, grew disgusted at man's disregard for his laws. In his anger, he created Sekhmet, the Eye of Ra, the goddess of destruction, a bare-breasted woman with the head of a lioness, and unleashed her upon man to reap vengeance."

Raha moved lower, kissing my belly. I squirmed and moaned on the bed. The inferno raging between my legs could only be extinguished by her tongue.

"The Nile turned crimson from all the blood she shed. When Ra saw the horror he had created, he regretted his actions. He laid a trap for her, hundreds of barrels of beer stained red with pomegranate juice to resemble the blood she enjoyed drinking."

Raha ran her tongue lightly over my pussy, from bottom to top. I shivered and arched my back again. It wouldn't take much more to make me come. I could feel it building already, dancing on the cusp.

Ashraf appeared behind Raha. He removed his shirt and let it drop to the floor. I couldn't take my eyes off the medallion hanging over his chest.

"Ra's plan worked," he continued, undoing his belt. "Sekhmet grew drunk and fell asleep."

I ran my fingers through Raha's thick hair. "Oh God, don't stop."

Ashraf bent to remove his shoes. I watched the well-defined muscles move under the skin of his torso. I wanted him inside me so badly. Raha's lips on my clit made me gasp.

"While she slept, Ra made it so Sekhmet forgot who she was and the destruction she had spread across the kingdom." Ashraf hooked his thumbs inside his pants and pushed them down. He wasn't wearing anything underneath. "Ra changed her name to Hathor so she would never have to remember her deeds. Her nature was changed also, to the sweetness of love and the strength of desire." He stepped toward the bed, his heavy cock growing bigger, stiffer as he approached. "And henceforth Hathor laid low men and women only with the great power of love."

I looked at Raha between my legs again, but my vision blurred, and for a moment I didn't see her, only what looked like the shaggy pyramid ears and tawny pelt of a lioness, black-and-yellow eyes hovering over my pubic hair like twin moons. I closed my eyes, letting the feel of her tongue take me to the very edge of climax.

And then she stopped.

Panting for breath, I opened my eyes again. Raha crawled up the bed to lie down beside me. She kissed me, her mouth flavored with the vinegar tang of my pussy, and her fingertips played lightly over my nipples.

"That is the story they tell," Ashraf said. He grabbed my ankles and pulled me down until my ass was at the bottom edge of the bed. Raha turned, kissing me upside down. "But it is not the whole story." He pushed my legs up and apart. "How is it, do you think, that Ra really tamed a woman as wild as Sekhmet?"

I started coming the moment he slid his cock inside me, wave after crashing wave of intense orgasms. I thrashed on the bed, made noises I'd never made before, as he slowly pulled out, almost to the point of exit, then rammed it back in. Every time he did, I shuddered with a new climax.

"What incentive do you think Ra promised her to keep the goddess of desire from turning back into the goddess of destruction?" he asked.

Raha crawled on top of me, still upside down, spreading her thighs over my face. Between Ashraf's slow and steady thrusts and Raha's tongue on my clit again, I came so hard I thought I might pass out. Little white dots exploded behind my eyelids. I wrapped my hands around the smooth skin of her ass and eagerly pulled her cunt down to my mouth. She didn't make a sound, only ground her hips above my head and continued licking me.

"It was Isis and Osiris who valued virgins, not Hathor. Hathor had little patience for teaching them the way of pleasure. She treasured experience above all else."

Raha shuddered hard, pushing her cunt right up against my face as she came. Now, finally, a sound escaped her throat as the orgasm steamrolled through her, a low, guttural cry that echoed off the stone walls like a roar. Hearing her come made me so hot I thought my skin would burst into flames.

"Ra promised her lovers of exceptional experience. He fashioned the Eye of Hathor, a powerful symbol that awakens in all who see it an irresistible desire, in order to procure lovers for her."

Raha lifted one leg and swung herself off of me. Ashraf pulled out, his cock dripping wet. I moaned in disappointment, but Raha silenced me with a deep kiss, our tongues dancing around each other like frisky cubs. Ashraf took hold of each of my legs and pushed them up until my knees were against my chest. Then, effortlessly, he thrust his cock into my ass.

I've done a lot in my career, girl on girl, two guys at once, bukkake trains, you name it—but the one thing I never did was anal. It's always been off-limits, even in my private life. But I was so hot, so willing to do anything he wanted, that I didn't care. It didn't hurt like I thought it would, either. His cock slid right in on the natural lubricant from my sopping pussy. It was the most incredible feeling. Raha kept kissing me, working my clit with her finger until I was on the brink of orgasm again. Then she stuck her finger inside me, and I came harder than I had all night.

Ashraf's breath caught in his throat. He tilted his head back, his mouth hanging open. I felt his cock stiffen in my ass, then pull out. He climbed onto the bed, holding his prick in one hand, and positioned himself on his knees above Raha and me. The first hot spurt of semen hit my face, cooling immediately as it rolled down my chin. Raha opened her mouth to receive the second, and I did the same. A few moments later, his cock drooped, spent, and our lips, chins, and cheeks were coated in a thick white goo. Raha kissed me once more, her mouth slippery and salty.

I looked at Ashraf above me, the golden Eye of Hathor glittering on his heaving, sweaty chest. I stretched out on the bed, a satisfied hum buzzing through my body. I'd almost forgotten what it's like to be so wanted.

My eyelids drooped as the afterglow pulled me toward sleep. I saw Ashraf bend over me, the medallion flashing, then there was only a warm darkness. And yet, I could still see the medallion burning brightly in my mind, in perfect detail. I felt arms around me, as if I were being carried, and when I opened my eyes we were in the car again. My clothes had reappeared on my body. I shut my eyes, wanting to sink back into the comfortable blackness, and saw the medallion once more behind my eyelids.

"The Eye," I managed to say, little more than a whisper. "It's in my head. . . ."

"Our gift to you, in thanks," Ashraf's voice replied. "Any who gaze upon it will be yours. Choose wisely."

I opened my eyes once more and saw Raha sitting next to me. I put my hand to her cheek. "Will I see you again?"

She shook her head, and from the front seat, Ashraf said, "We will not meet again, nor will we be here if you come looking for us. It is the way."

I nodded sadly, closing my eyes only for a moment. When I opened them again I was slumped in the driver's seat of my car on the empty street outside Bruce's house. The sun was coming up, tinting everything gray. I shook the cobwebs out of my head and drove home. The Eye of Hathor burned in my mind the whole way there. It was there when I collapsed onto my bed and when I woke up a few hours later with Bruce's words circling my brain like song lyrics that get stuck in your ear: "Everyone will see your tits, everyone will see your bush, I promise you."

If he wanted me to trim my pubes before the shoot, there was only one man in all of L.A. for the job. He called himself the Gardener, and everyone who was anyone used him when it was grooming time. After calling to make an appointment, I drove to his home office in Orange County.

"Amber!" he exclaimed, greeting me at the door in an orange polo shirt that almost matched the color of his Irish hair. "How long has it been?"

"Too long," I said, hugging him. He invited me into his living room, where big glossy photos of his work adorned the walls, women's nude crotches with all manner of shaved pubic hair: the standard landing strip, a Valentine's heart, a jack-o'-lantern, a Christmas tree, a lightning bolt, even the Gucci symbol. When I told him what I wanted and asked if he could do it, he spread his hands and said, "Hey, I'm the Gardener, aren't I?"

He brought me into the brightly lit, white-walled room in back, where there were two tables of shaving equipment and, in the center, a large barber-style chair tilted back with two silver stirrups protruding from the seat. I dropped my skirt, my panties, and sat, nude from the waist down, on the chair. I stuck my heels in the stirrups and rolled my blouse up a bit.

The Gardener knelt down on the floor between my legs, first trimming the hair with electric clippers, then dipping his fingertips in a jar of petroleum jelly and gently smearing a thin layer over the fine fuzz in slow circles. Finally, he picked up his trusty straightedge. I painstakingly guided him through the process, describing everything down to the minutest detail. Two hours in, my cell phone rang. I fished it out of my purse and looked at the caller ID. It was Bruce.

"So," he said, "are you all set for tonight?"

"You bet. I'm at the Gardener's now, getting a shave just like you said." I felt the blade clear away the last of the extra hair. He was finished.

"How's it look?" Bruce asked.

"Hold on, I'll find out. How's it look?" I asked the Gardener. He didn't answer. He stared at my crotch, transfixed. Under his belt buckle, I could see his cock stiffening, straining against his fly. "I'd say it looks pretty damn good," I said into the phone.

"Great," Bruce said. "The camera is going to love you, babe."

The Gardener couldn't control himself anymore. He leaned forward, put his hands on my thighs, and started eating me out, his tongue disappearing beneath the Eye of Hathor shaved into my pubic hair.

"Bruce," I said, "once this movie comes out, everyone is going to love me."

೫ LOVED IT AND SET IT FREE ೫
Lisa Montanarelli

My first dildo drifted out into Baltimore Harbor on a broken book-shelf. I'd owned this dong for less than a day, but we'd been through a lot together. The night before, I'd eased it inside me, while my high school best friend lay next to me faking sleep. Most people keep their first dildos until they rot. But I was different. I loved mine and set it free.

"The Boss" was a single piece of beige rubber shaped like a billy club or toy sword—with a handle, a cross guard, and a ten-inch dong in place of a blade. The label on the package had said "anatomically correct," but even then I knew ten inches was a little on the long side.

I first laid eyes on the Boss when my friend Kim took me to a porn shop on East Baltimore Street. Kim was a born comic with gawky limbs and a wide, pouty mouth. The summer before our senior year, she carried bottles of Sun-In and hydrogen peroxide wherever she went. When we weren't swimming, she poured them over her head and lay in the sun.

By the time we went back to our all-girls school that fall, Kim's hair hung in clumps like bleached snakes. People said she dyed her hair orange to match the school colors—orange and green. So she dyed it green for one of the field-hockey games.

Around that time, Kim and I were playing "I Never"—one of the few games you can win through sheer inexperience and naïveté. In I Never, players take turns confessing things they've never done. If the other player has done something you haven't, she owes you a penny. I won two cents easily, because I'd never bleached my hair or dyed it green.

It took me a bit longer to come up with my third confession. Finally I said, "I've never really gotten a good look at another person's genitals."

This was true. Although I'd made out with both boys and girls, we rarely took off our clothes. Instead, we groped each other in dark, semi-public places—fumbling with buttons, bras, belt buckles, and zippers—and glancing over our shoulders every few seconds, expecting our parents to catch us in the act. I'd even lost my virginity in the classic sense on the floor of a toolshed. In short, I'd had plenty of action but little chance to look at naked bodies or genitalia. I had rarely ever seen boys naked, except when our neighbor little Billy ran across our backyard with his babysitter chasing him. I saw girls' bodies in locker rooms, but felt much too self-conscious to stare.

I expected Kim to question my confession, but she just nodded and tossed me another penny.

"You should come over and watch porn movies the next time my parents go away. That'll give you plenty of chances to check out other people's genitals."

Unlike my parents—the last in town to buy a microwave or any new appliance—Kim's family owned all the latest tech. When her mom and dad went out of town, Kim rented porn. We planned our porn adventure months in advance and waited for her folks' next vacation.

Kim rented porn from a seedy shop on "the Block." The 400 block of East Baltimore Street is Baltimore's red-light district, where the locals go to see naked girls dancing and buy porn. Growing up in the sub-suburban sprawl of Baltimore County, I'd never been to the Block, so we drove me past it one night when Kim borrowed her mom's car.

"That's the Block." Kim pointed out the window. "Look now, or you'll miss it."

I pressed my face against the passenger window. Neon lights danced against the starless sky; then darkness swallowed the neon as we drove back into the night.

"Was that it?"

"Yeah. It's only one block. I'll go around again."

The second time, she drove more slowly, so I could read the neon signs: Golden Nugget Lounge, the Crystal Pussycat, Gresser's Gayety Liquors, Savetta's Psychic Readings, Crazy John's, and the Plaza Saloon. Glamorous names—at least for kids growing up in Baltimore.

We didn't rent porn that night. We just drove by, and Kim pointed out Sylvester's Videos, the store where she rented porn.

"They have booths in the back where you can watch videos, but you don't want to go in there. The walls are sticky and gross. Let's just wait until my parents go away, and we'll rent movies to take home."

Finally Kim's parents scheduled an overnight camping trip. They left on a Friday; my heart and stomach fluttered all day at school. After our last class, Kim and I met in the locker room and changed out of our school uniforms and into jeans.

"Hurry up," said Kim. "I want to get down to the Block while it's still light out so no one will break into my mom's car." Kim had her mom's car for the weekend. We slung our backpacks over our shoulders and walked out.

As we drove downtown, I pressed my face against the window and marveled at the dirt on the streets. City dirt is different from country dirt. Where I come from, dirt is brown like mud or red like sandstone. In the city, black grit cakes under your fingernails and sticks to the concrete. The wind writes messages on the sidewalk with black dust and dead leaves. I soon realized we were driving in circles, passing the same buildings.

"Are we lost?"

"No, I'm looking for parking."

"Where are we?"

"The Block, silly."

I winced. "It looks different by day."

While night had hidden everything but the neon signs, the sun exposed gray concrete buildings and trash in the street. Turned off, the neon signs were only pale plastic tubing and dusty electrical cords. We passed the same ones I'd seen at night—the Crystal Pussycat, Savetta's Psychic Readings, the Plaza Saloon. At night, they had seemed intimidating, but seeing them by day was like watching a flashy porn star sleep in her underwear and snore.

"Why didn't you take that parking space we just passed?" I asked.

"I want to park in front of the porn shop so I can keep an eye on the car."

After we'd made several more loops, a car pulled out right in front of us, across the street from Sylvester's Videos. Kim pulled up alongside the space.

"That's tiny. You can't fit in there."

"I'm going to try." She cranked her steering wheel all the way to the right and backed into the space much too fast. As her back tires rammed the curb, her elbow struck the horn with a loud honk. A siren squealed in the distance. Across the street, the door to Sylvester's Videos creaked open, and a guy with beady eyes and slicked-back gray hair stepped out of the store and glared at us.

"Shit, Kim. Let's get out of here."

"Get out and direct me," she said calmly.

Trembling, I climbed out of the passenger seat and motioned her into the space. When I glanced over my shoulder, the beady-eyed man had vanished. Kim got out of the car.

"That's the first time I've parallel parked since my driver's ed test," she said.

I followed her across the street. The door to Sylvester's Videos was covered with ripped, faded posters and random thumbtacks. The paint was chipped. The place hadn't been painted in years.

I looked at Kim.

"Come on, let's go in." She hoisted the door open—revealing a heavy black plastic curtain. Glancing at me, she pulled aside the curtain and slipped inside. I followed her into a dimly lit square room. DVDs lined the walls floor to ceiling.

The beady-eyed man—the same one who had glared at us outside—sat behind the cash register.

"Howdy, girls." He smiled with crooked yellow teeth.

At the sound of his voice, two customers in the front room turned and peered at us. Both were bent over the merchandise, with their collars turned up and hats pulled down over their eyes. Kim and I were the only two women in the store—perhaps the only women who had been there in a long time.

Kim took me on a tour of the narrow, low-ceilinged rooms, pointing to X-rated videos with titles like *The Penile Colony, Hannah Does Her Sisters, Astropussy Strikes Back,* and *Public Enema* numbers one, two, and three.

"The booths are in the back," Kim pointed to a man slipping behind a black plastic curtain. "You can rent your movie, close the curtain, pop your DVD in the slot, and jerk off—Lisa . . . Lisa!" She poked me.

I had frozen facing a wall of rubber penises and sundry other body parts, including hands and arms. I had never looked at a penis this way before. For the first time in my life, I could look at it without worrying about what the person attached to it thought of me. At the time I was too inexperienced to know that one never looks at penises quite the way one looks at dildos, propped up on shelves, strapped onto harnesses, or packaged in plastic, hanging from hooks on walls—like in Toys 'R' Us, or meat in a butcher shop. Through my entire childhood, I had been looking at Ken dolls without penises. Suddenly I was looking at the opposite of Ken dolls: penises without bodies attached.

Given my deprivation, this wall of "anatomically correct" models—in black, brown, and beige, complete with rippling rubber veins—was an embarrassment of riches. Some of them, labeled "Sints," were hollow and attached to elastic straps. One even had leather straps. What were they for? Then I saw the flying-saucer-shaped "butt plug." Why would anyone need that? Plugs were those things you put in sinks to stop the water from draining. Was a butt plug the opposite of an enema? I was used to things having practical purposes. This was the first time I'd encountered something intended strictly for sexual pleasure, and I just didn't get it.

"Haven't you ever seen a dildo before?" asked Kim.

"N-no," I stammered.

"Check this out." She pointed to a plastic package containing a foot-long rubber forearm with the hand clenched in a fist. I'd never seen anything like it, except those dismembered arms you find in Walgreens at Halloween.

"What do you think you're supposed to do with this?" Kim asked. "Bonk somebody over the head?" I was pretty sure that wasn't what you were supposed to do, but before I could say anything, she yanked the plastic package off the hook and bonked me over the head with the rubber forearm.

"Kim! Stop!"

She clasped her hands over her mouth and burst into giggles, shoulders shaking uncontrollably. Customers in the store turned and stared.

"You're going to get us kicked out of here!" I hissed.

"Shh! Lower your voice!"

"Look. Here's the description." We huddled over the package and read the label in excited whispers:

12.5 inches long, 3 inches wide, 9 inches around
Size: Huge
Product Category: Anal Stimulation
Color: Black

Made of: Rubber
For use in this part of the body: Anus

"It's for the . . . the . . . anus?" I asked in disbelief.

"That's the butt," she whispered smugly.

"I know what an anus is, but I don't see how it could fit."

She shrugged. "Don't ask me."

"Do all these things go up your butt?" I gestured to the wall of dildos and butt plugs.

"They don't go up my butt," she giggled. "But you can put dildos up your vagina. Haven't you ever put vegetables up there?"

"No. Have you?"

"Of course."

"You're kidding. What kind?"

"Cucumbers, carrots, and zucchini. When I was about twelve, I used to sneak them out of the vegetable drawer in the refrigerator and put them back when I was done."

"Ew! Yuck!"

Kim hung the rubber arm back on its hook. "We're not getting this," she whispered. "Let's get some dildos. Here's a thin one. It's eight ninety-nine."

Kim handed me a package. I stared at the label: The Boss: Anatomically Correct Dong.

"Are you suggesting I buy this?"

"Why not? I'll buy one, too."

"How do you know it'll fit?"

"You just have to try your luck. You can't try it on in a dressing room like a pair of jeans."

I laughed nervously.

"Come on," she said, "let's move on to the movies. That's what we came here for."

I followed her back into the front room, where we rifled through hundreds of cases and decided on two orgy movies: *Farm Family Free-for-All* and *Group Grope 9*.

Growing up in the seventies and eighties, I had become familiar with the made-for-TV Roman orgy—where toga-clad patricians get it on with priestesses of Isis in the Roman baths (made to look like contemporary Jacuzzis). My parents allowed me to watch these programs due to their so-called historical significance. Hence, much of my early sex education came from *I, Claudius,* and the head of a penis still reminds me of a Roman centurion's helmet. When you watch orgy scenes in historical dramas, perhaps you are supposed to think, *My god, how decadent,* and believe rampant orgies caused the fall of Rome. Modern libertines should learn from history and beware! But I watched the orgies and wondered, *Why don't people do that anymore?* I thought Roman orgies, like Egyptian mummies, were ancient history. *Farm Family Free-for-All* and *Group Grope 9* were my first signs that the orgy lived on, at least in contemporary porn.

After nearly an hour of X-rated shopping, Kim and I finally carried our lurid wares to the cashier and spread them out on the counter. The beady-eyed man winked at us.

"You want some K-Y jelly for those dongs?"

"That's not a bad idea," said Kim. "We'll take some."

Outside, dusk had fallen, and the neon signs flickered on in orange, pink, and green. We crossed the street. Kim's mother's car was still intact. As we drove back to her house, I shivered when a cop car whizzed by. What if they pulled us over and found the porn videos and dildos? I pictured our mug shots on the front page with photos of The Boss underneath.

When we finally made it back to Kim's, we emptied our bags onto the living room rug and tore open our dildo packages.

"Hey, this isn't very realistic. It doesn't have balls!"

The Boss, as I mentioned earlier, had no balls. Instead, the penis-shaped shaft ended in a handle and cross guard, like a toy sword. I looked down at the dildo in my hands.

"Darn. I really wanted to see what balls look like."

"You'll see them in the movies," said Kim. "*En garde!*" She held the dildo by the handle and brandished it like the sword Excalibur, but the rubber weenie just flopped around.

I giggled. "That's one lame weapon."

"Oh well. Let's watch the movie." Kim switched on the TV and took the DVDs out of their plastic cases.

"What do you want to watch first, *Farm Family Free-for-All* or *Group Grope 9*?"

"How about *Farm Family Free-for-All*?" We unzipped our sleeping bags and curled up side by side, propping our heads up on pillows so we could see the TV. Punching buttons on the remote control, Kim fast-forwarded to the opening scene, where a well-endowed hottie, looking much like Heidi with a blonde mullet and cleavage, skipped through a cornfield in an astonishingly low-cut blue gingham dress. The scene changed to the inside of a barn, where two men in plaid flannel shirts and overalls were milking cows. The younger man stood up and stretched.

"Gee, Paw," he drawled. "Ah wish Sissy would get here with those vittles. Ah need a break."

Outside, the blonde in blue gingham peeked through a crack in the barn door. Seeing the men, she slipped one hand up her gingham skirt and opened the door.

"Did Ah hear y'all say yuh need some refreshments?"

The men turned and gaped as she stepped into the barn, toting a straw basket in the crook of her arm and fondling her breasts.

I shook my head. "God, Kim! Can you believe these accents? Nobody talks like that."

"Watch this." Kim pointed the remote control at the TV. The video flew into fast-forward. Three more people in plaid flannel, calico, and gingham speed-walked into the barn, where they all tore off each other's clothes, sprawled on the hay, and plugged themselves into each other's orifices, fucking and sucking as fast as an assembly line.

"Dammit, Kim! I'm never going to see genitals this way!" I grabbed the remote control and pushed "play." My jaw dropped. Two tanned, tight-bodied girls, locked in a 69, were licking each other. With identical big boobs and blonde mullets, they looked like twins. In fact, they were twins. This was *Farm Family Free-for-All*. My heart beat faster. I'd never seen two girls having sex, even on-screen. Out of the corner of my eye, I peered at Kim. Did she know this was going to be in the movie? I knew orgies meant sex scenes with more than one man, more than one woman, or several of both. Somehow it hadn't dawned on me that girls would be getting it on with each other. I gaped at the screen transfixed, crotch tingling under the covers. I crossed my legs and squeezed my thighs together. Finally, I couldn't stand it anymore. I slipped my hands between my thighs. Kim's elbow brushed against mine, so the tiny hairs on my arms stood on end. She was doing the same thing I was, but I didn't dare look at her. I wondered if the people at school would be able to tell we'd watched lesbian porn. Would they see it in our eyes?

In English class earlier that year we had been talking about Virginia Woolf. The class was sitting in a semicircle around the edge of the room, facing our teacher, Mrs. Byrd. My mind was wandering, when someone mentioned the word *lesbians*. Patty raised her hand.

"Have there ever been any lesbians in our school?"

"Yes," said Mrs. Byrd. "We've had some."

"How can you tell?"

"Sometimes two girls are . . . closer than normal."

"Does the school do anything about it?" asked Patty.

"We try to split them up," said Mrs. Byrd. "Sometimes we tell their parents."

A hush fell over the room as we all exchanged nervous glances. I looked at Kim, who sat across the room from me doodling. She didn't look up.

If they found out, would they separate us? Tell our parents?

Meanwhile, on *Farm Family Free-for-All*, the rest of the family joined the girls with mullets. The scene turned into a more traditional orgy with writhing bodies—a monster with multiple arms and legs. I circled my clit with my fingertip, less interested in the family scene, but barely admitting—even to myself—the girl-on-girl porn had turned me on.

Kim grunted next to me. She was snoring.

"Come on—I know you're not really asleep."

No answer.

"Kim?" I put my hand on her shoulder.

She was really asleep. I thought about waking her up, then changed my mind and circled my clit faster, feeling lucky and slightly out of control. My back tensed and my heart quickened as I tried not to make any noise or move anything except my hand. I had played this game before—many times. The goal was to come without waking the other person. Sometimes, no doubt, the other person woke up and just pretended she was still sleeping. I had faked sleep myself when someone was masturbating beside me.

On-screen the camera zoomed in on the girls. A man fucked one of them from behind while she licked her sister's pussy. Next to me, Kim was breathing slack-jawed—either sound asleep or damn good at pretending. Her legs twitched under the covers. Reaching my arm outside the blankets, I groped around on the icy hardwood floor. My hand landed on the dildo—cold, hard, and ribbed with veins. I dragged it into the sleeping bag and pushed its cold head against the wet lips of my cunt. With a deep breath, I tried to ease the rubber cock inside me. It didn't fit. I pushed, took another breath, and pushed again. Still no-go. Suddenly I remembered the K-Y jelly. I ran my hand over the floor and found the K-Y. It looked like a tube of toothpaste. I squeezed a glob of clear lube into my palm. I couldn't believe how cold it was. I thought of Kim's refrigerated cucumbers. I didn't want anything that cold near my pussy, but if I wanted The Boss inside me, I knew I had to get the lube in there first.

I soaked the head of the Boss in K-Y, then—wincing—squeezed the cold lube directly into my cunt. It spilled onto the sleeping bag, spreading out in a puddle under my butt. Shivering, I glanced at Kim. Her eyelids fluttered. She was dreaming. With several deep breaths, I shoved The Boss inside me. My whole body shook—my cunt was so full, it almost burned. I looked at Kim again. What would it be like to kiss her? I brushed my lips against her cheek. Mustering all my courage, I stretched out the tip of my tongue and I licked her hair.

Kim stirred and turned over on her side. I froze. Was she awake? I listened for her breath. I was sure she was awake, but I couldn't stop now. I eased the dildo in and out of my cunt. The woman on the screen came like a swimmer gasping for air. The man squeezed his cock and squirted white jizz on her tits. I came with them, melting into the scene. The cock inside me was his cock. My sounds shot out of her mouth. My wave of pleasure rocked her body on the screen. My cunt contracted and spit out the dildo—wet between my thighs. Warmth spread through my belly, heart, and limbs. I sank into the floor—and yet I was floating.

Someone nudged me.

"Stop it."

"Wake up."

"What? What time is it?"

"Five-thirty."

"What the fuck?" I glanced around the dark, unfamiliar room.

"Wake up." Kim's shadowy form bent over me.

I suddenly remembered where I was—sprawled out on Kim's living room floor. I must have dozed off after I came.

"Lisa, listen to me. We have to get rid of these now."

"Get rid of what?"

"These." She bumped me on the cheek with something rubber. I winced as the overhead lights blinked on. What was she talking about? Then it dawned on me. *Jesus, what did I do last night?* I remembered the wall of dildos, The Boss, and licking Kim's hair—shit! Was she awake when I did that? What did she think of me?

"Lisa!" Kim repeated, bonking me on the head. "We've got to get rid of these things before my parents get home. They'll be back early this morning."

"We can't just throw them away. They weren't cheap."

"Do you want to take them home with you?"

"Shit." I peered at the dildos as my eyes adjusted to the light. "I don't think I can."

"What should we do with them, then? We can't just throw them in the trash, or bury them in the backyard. The dogs'll get at them."

"Can we burn them?"

"God, no! They'd stink."

"Well then, let's just walk a few blocks down the street and throw them in someone else's trash."

"Good idea. We can take the car and drive a little ways away. We'll take the movies back to the store, too."

It was still dark outside. The crickets were chirping as we stepped out into the cold, wet air. Kim drove. I dozed in the passenger seat with the dildos in my lap wrapped in newspaper. The car screeched to a stop.

"Where are we?" The sky had turned dark blue. I rolled down my window, tasting the salt air.

"We're at Fells Point. I was thinking we could throw them in the water," said Kim. We climbed out of the car. I followed her to the edge of the pier. Water was lapping at the dock, and the seabirds called out, flapping their wings. One swooped within inches of the water, a white ghost.

Holding the dildos wrapped in newspaper, I peered down into the black water.

"It's a shame to let these sink to the bottom of the harbor."

"I know! Let's float them out to sea on one of those boards over there." Kim darted away and came back seconds later, dragging a dismantled bookcase. She pulled off the top shelf and dislodged several long, rusty nails.

"We'll put the dildos on a raft. That way, someone might find them."

We lowered the board into the water. Kim tore off a sheet of newspaper and wrote: "SOS. Free to a Good Home."

I leaned over and placed the dildos side by side. Wrapped in newsprint, they looked like twins in swaddling clothes. I thought of Romulus and Remus—the twins abandoned to the elements who washed up onshore and founded Rome. Who knew what great fortune or conquest lay in store for our dildos? Would they be suckled by she-wolves? I watched them float away, convinced that some lonely soul who desperately needed dildos would find them.

🙟 DEPROGRAMMING 🙝
Greta Christina

"How far do you want to go this time?"

"A little farther than last time."

"Last time we got almost to the belt. Are you sure you want to go farther? I don't think we can go farther without getting into the belt."

She nodded. "I know. It's okay. I don't want to, you know, go all the way with the belt. But I think I'd like to get started on it."

"You think." He took her hand. "You need to be more certain than that."

"Sorry." She took a deep breath. "Yes. I want to start on the belt today."

He let go of her hand and sat back, his arms folded across his belly. "All right. So tell me that you want to do this."

"I . . . Jesus, David, do I need to say this every time?"

"I need to hear it. Sarah . . . Please. This is fucked-up enough as it is. I can't do it if—"

She touched his knee. "Okay. It's okay." She folded her hands neatly in her lap, and spoke again.

"I want to do this. I am choosing to do this. And I know that I can stop it, any time I need to."

"And why do you want to do it?"

"I want to deal with what happened. I want to feel like I have some control over it. I want to move on." Her practiced voice began to wobble. "And . . . I want to get off. God help me, but this gets me off."

"Yeah, I know." He grinned weakly. "Me too. Fucked-up, isn't it? Let's get started."

He stood up.

Eileen stood up. "Let's get started. Today's therapy group is now in session. Let the cleansing begin, in his holy name." She consulted a slip of paper. "Today we begin with the cleansing of Sarah. Sarah, please come to the center of the circle."

Sarah shivered. She'd known this was coming today. But knowing didn't help. Knowing didn't stop it from happening. She gritted her teeth, stood up from her metal folding chair, and walked to the center of the silent room, not knowing anything else she could do. She clenched her hands in front of her belly and waited.

"Sarah. You stand before the Tribe of the True Promise, your true family now and forever. And today you stand a failure. You have failed your father, Daddy John, and you have failed your family. You have spoken heresy, words against the teachings of Daddy John. You have mocked the teachings of Daddy John, in the hearing of your brothers and sisters. And you have pursued an unsanctioned erotic relationship, attempting to deceive Daddy John, without whom no true love is possible. Come forward for your punishment, and be cleansed of your shame."

The circle murmured. They're excited, Sarah thought bitterly. They can't wait. She felt a flash of anger, followed by an after burn of shame. She'd been in the circle herself, twitching with anxious excitement as one of her brothers or sisters stepped forward to be punished. This whole thing is fucked-up, she thought. Including me. Maybe I do deserve this.

She stepped forward to Eileen, who took her hands gently. "You have been shamed by Daddy John, and by me in his name," Eileen said. "Now you must shame yourself. Lower your trousers, and expose your body to your family, as Daddy John has exposed your sin."

"Pull down your pants," he said. "Your shame has been revealed. Now it's time to reveal your body."

She unzipped her jeans and pulled them down with her panties, as quickly as she could, trying not to think about it. This was the worst part, she thought.

No, on second thought, it wasn't. But it was the hardest part. After this, it was out of her hands. Once she got past this, she didn't have to do anything, or decide anything—except whether to let it keep happening.

David sat down on the hard chair. "Now bend over my knee," he said. "You've acted like an irresponsible child, and you're going to be punished like a child." He paused. "You know I love you, right?"

She fumbled with the knot in her rough, cotton drawstring pants and let them fall to the floor, bowing her head. She wasn't wearing underwear. Daddy John said underwear was a sin. The murmuring of the circle grew louder: less anxious, more excited. She blushed and squeezed her eyes shut tight, feeling their eyes on her naked bottom. They're all going to watch, she thought, and none of them is going to stop it. They're all too relieved that it's not them this time. They're just going to watch the show.

Eileen sat back down on the hard chair. "Now bend over my knee," she said. "You've acted like an irresponsible child, and we have to punish you like a child. Daddy John loves you, and his punishment is a blessing. Now get over my knee."

The last sentence came out with a bite, a sharp detour from Eileen's usual soothing drone. Sarah had seen the results of that bite: the mass of bruises left on Jenny, and David, and little Shelley, Jesus, barely fifteen. She knew the gleeful cruelty behind that bite, slipping out through the cracks of the stern-but-loving mother routine. She was furious at the lie, and terrified at the truth behind it. She was powerless to do anything about either one.

She obeyed. There was nothing else she could do. She bent over Eileen's sturdy lap, praying to God, the one she no longer believed in, to let her leave her body and shut it all out.

"I know," Sarah said. "I love you too." She bent over his lap. His legs were thin and wiry, like a bird's. Breakable. She found it comforting.

Eileen rolled up her sleeves with a flourish. Someone in the circle whimpered, and immediately went silent. Eileen spoke. "My hand is the hand of Daddy John. You know Daddy's watching, don't you? He's always watching. Feel his hand on your body, and feel the pain of his disappointment."

It came down hard, sharp and hard like a hailstorm. Sarah began screaming with the first blow, and kept screaming as the blows kept coming. She screamed with rage at Eileen and the lie of the loving mother; at Daddy John and the lie of the all-knowing father, at the trembling circle around her and the lie of the supportive family. She screamed at herself, for believing it for so long, for getting suckered into it in the first place. She screamed at her helplessness, her inability to make anything turn out different, ever. She screamed at her nonexistent God, for saying no to her prayers yet again, for making her stay in her body: making her feel the pain pounding down on her bare ass, and the malicious pleasure driving it, and the pathetic indignity it was forcing her to feel. The circle around her shifted in their seats, agitated and uncomfortable, as her screams rose in pitch from protest and rage to a panicked shriek.

And the blows kept coming, hard and fast and inescapable. She kept thinking it was going to stop, it had to stop, there was no way she could stand it if it kept coming . . . and it kept coming. It didn't matter if she could stand it or not.

"It's coming now," he said. "You're going to feel my hand, and my hand is going to punish you. It's going to hurt."

His first blow was light and gentle, almost a massage; she could barely feel it. She arched her back, welcoming it in: grateful for the gentleness now, grateful for the terrible pain she knew was coming, grateful for the sweet, gradual slide he was going to use to take her from here to there.

He began to turn up the heat, just a little, and she squirmed in anticipation. Her clit began to twitch, and she felt a familiar flutter of shame deep in her stomach. She got so excited when they did this. It was so fucked-up. She squirmed her hips harder, unnerved as always when the excitement began, trying to stave it off for just a moment more; but her squirming made her clit twitch harder, and she gave in with a gasp, and pushed her cunt hard against David's thigh, and let herself drop.

Her screams turned into sobs, weak and terrified. She squirmed hard, frantically trying to escape, to get just a little relief. She could hear the circle around her breathing harder; she knew she was giving them a show, screaming and crying and wiggling her bare backside like a whore. But she couldn't help it. She was helpless. She was without help.

It was getting harder now. And harder still. Harder than she really wanted; but of course, that was what she wanted. She wanted to feel helpless, to let herself go in the hands of someone she could trust.

She sank into the rhythm: fighting and giving in, fighting and giving in, surrendering to each level of pain and surprising herself with how good it felt once she let it. Her clit was throbbing, demanding attention, and its hunger filled her consciousness.

But now it was really hard. Not just harder than she liked—harder than she could take. She tried, but she was only fighting now, just a struggle with no surrender. She pushed herself to take it for one last dreadful minute, and gave up at last. "Stop, David," she gasped. "It's too much. Please, God, fuck, stop it right now."

"I'm so sorry," she sobbed. "Please, stop. I'll never do it again, I swear. Just stop. I'm begging you."

The pain stopped at once. She let out a sigh of relief and shock at the unexpected mercy. But she heard Eileen's voice, cold and tight, and she began to sob again. She knew she hadn't stopped it. She had made it worse.

"You obviously don't understand," Eileen scolded. "You're obviously not sorry at all. If you were truly sorry, you wouldn't try to stop me. You'd understand that I need to punish you for as long as I see fit. You'd understand that a disobedient child can't decide for herself how much she should be punished. You'd be ashamed of yourself, and you'd welcome this punishment as a chance to cleanse your shame."

Eileen shook her head sadly. "We obviously need to take this further. Stand up, and take off my belt."

He stopped immediately. He rested his hand on her warm bottom for a long time. He watched her back until it relaxed, listened to her breath until it quieted. Then he spoke, his voice serious and full of sorrow.

"I have to take my belt off now, Sarah. I'm sorry. But it's time. I have to do this."

Sarah froze.

Fuck, no, she thought. Please, God. Not the belt.

Eileen cleared her throat. "You disappoint me, Sarah. You've never had to be cleansed before. I'd hoped you'd take it better than this. But you obviously have plenty of willfulness left in you. Selfish, childish willfulness. You think you can defy me? You think you know better than me what's right for you?" Her voice was cracking again. "Think again, Sarah. David, come over here and take off my belt." She smirked. "You've done it often enough, David, you should be good at it by now."

She held herself perfectly still, terrified, trying to disappear. She heard someone, David she assumed, stand up and move toward her from out of the circle. She felt him fiddle quickly with Eileen's belt buckle, pull the belt out of her belt loops, fold it up and hand it to her. She heard him move back to his place in the circle without a word. She felt pity for him. She suddenly understood what people meant when they said, "This is going to hurt me more than it hurts you."

She heard Eileen smack the belt into her open hand, and the sound drove David out of her mind, and drove the fear and paralysis back in.

"Now stand up," Eileen instructed. "I'm going to stand up as well. When I do, put your hands on the seat of the chair. And then wait. When it begins, you may make as much noise as you like, and you may move your body as much as you like . . ."—Eileen paused here, and shivered at her own words— "but you may not move your hands from the chair, or your feet from the ground, until I say we're done."

She nodded. "I know. It's okay. I'm ready."

"All right then. Stand up. Put your hands on the chair. I'm going to stand behind you, and I'm going to beat you with the belt until I'm done."

She complied.

She was shaking with pain, and with fear. She was weak with shame at the staring eyes upon her, and with anger at the faces behind the eyes. She could barely stand up. But she complied.

She knew there was nothing she could do. Anything she did to try to stop it would just make it worse: would bring on the switch, or the wooden paddle, or the belt until she bled and passed out. The only thing that would stop it was to let it happen.

So she let it happen. She stood up, and bent over, her hands on the chair, her bare, trembling bottom in the air, her cotton drawstring pants crumpled around her ankles, the Tribe of the True Promise sitting in a circle around her, gaping like zombies.

And she let it happen. She glued her hands to the chair and her feet to the floor, letting herself obey the woman who was breathing hard and smacking the belt into her hand to build the suspense. She arched her back to give a prettier target, and waited patiently, passively, for the first blow to land.

And she let herself be beaten with the belt.

She screamed obediently when it landed. And as the blows kept landing, she kept screaming, a gift for the woman who panted behind her like a dog as she gleefully whipped her raw. She screamed and wept, and she wiggled

her bottom and jiggled her dangling tits, shaking her flesh like a stripper, let-
ting herself obey the unspoken orders as well as the spoken ones.

And she let herself feel ashamed. She knew that was what Eileen
wanted most of all, that Eileen wouldn't stop until she got it. So she gave it
to her.

It wasn't the right shame, though. Not the shame Eileen was looking for.
It wasn't shame at her blasphemy or disobedience; it wasn't even shame at
being stripped and humiliated and punished on her bare bottom in front of
her whole family.

Her shame was that she had let this happen. Her shame was that she
was weak and stupid: too stupid to see how bad things were until they had
gotten too bad to leave, too weak to pull it together and leave when they did
get really bad. Her shame was that she had no power, that she'd given away
what little she had, if she'd ever had any at all. Her shame was that she was
here—screaming, squirming, wiggling her bare ass like a bitch in heat for the
woman who was beating it raw—because she had put herself here.

And her shame was that she had let this happen to her brothers and
sisters. She had sat in the circle like they were sitting now, half-petrified,
half-leering. She had stared with fear and relief and fascination, as David
or Shelley or some other godforsaken soul pulled down their pants and put
their exposed body under Eileen's hands.

She deserved this punishment. She deserved this shame. She sank into
it, and let it seep into her muscles and bones, and pulled it up by handfuls to
give to Eileen.

It was the wrong shame. But she knew Eileen would never know the dif-
ference. Shame was shame to Eileen: the woman was actually moaning now,
supposedly with the effort of beating Sarah's ass at full speed and full strength.

Sarah sank deeper into the pain and the shame, and whimpered louder,
and jiggled her tits and ass harder. She splayed open her bent knees to give a
glimpse in between them . . . and Eileen grunted at last, a long series of ani-
mal grunts like a pig rooting in a trough, and collapsed to the floor, dropping
the belt.

"Praise be to Daddy John," she cried. "I feel his forgiveness. Do you feel it,
too, child? Do you know he's watching? Do you know how happy he is right
now? Feel the shame lifted out of your heart. You're free now."

She obeyed.

She felt it now: the helplessness she'd been waiting for. She moved like she was in a trance: standing up, waiting for David to move into place behind her, placing her hands on the chair and shifting her feet into position. She waited, patient and afraid, her bare bottom tingling in memory and anticipation.

He struck, and she gasped in shock. Oh, fuck. She'd forgotten how much the belt hurt. So much harder than the hand, and more cold. So much not about human contact; so purely about the cruelty, and the pain.

But she knew she'd asked for this. Literally. Just a few minutes ago. And she knew she needed it. She just couldn't remember why right now. It hurt too much. The belt cut into her ass, the pain exploding onto her skin like a bomb and then radiating through her flesh into her clit and her cunt. He was hitting her slowly, and hard, letting her feel each blow, giving it time to blossom and fade, giving her time to recover. And time to feel the next one.

She began to cry. Not a yelping cry of protest, but a soft weeping rain of despair, and of giving in.

He kept beating her; close together now, hard and heartless, his teeth gritted with the struggle to finish. He dropped the belt to the floor with a clatter, and grabbed her around her waist.

"I said you're free now." The woman was smirking condescendingly. "That means you can move again. And you can cover yourself." Her smirk widened into a sneer. "Unless you'd rather stay like that, of course."

Sarah stood up. She swayed for a moment, from the rush of blood to her head, and the flood of relief that she wasn't willing to trust. She pulled up her pants and fiddled with the strings, finally managing to tie them again. She wobbled back to her place in the circle and sat down, dropping her eyes, avoiding the stares of the circle around her, cringing at the touch of the metal chair. Eileen turned away from her. She had already moved on.

"All right," she said cheerily. "I think we have time for one more cleansing. Let's look at Daddy's list. . . ." She peered at the slip of paper. "Ah. David again, I see." She clucked her tongue. "Such a disappointment. So many times. David, will you ever be truly clean of your shame?"

David stood up casually. "Okay. Sure. Whatever." Sarah listened for defiance in his voice, but heard only defeat.

She caught his eye. She had to give him something, something to hang on to. And now she knew what. She caught his eye, and nodded her head, just a flicker, barely perceptible even to him.

Yes, she said. Tonight. She'd said no before. She was weak, and frightened. But now she knew. Now she was free. Now she was ready to leave.

"It's over," he said. "It's all over."

She crumpled to the floor, and he crumpled with her, holding her around the shoulders as tight as he could. She leaned into his thin chest, cried like the newly widowed, and pushed her hand between her legs. He held her as she made herself come. She came fast and hard, frantically flicking her clit with her finger, clenching his hand with her other fist, still weeping onto his shoulder.

Her tears dissipated with her shudders, and she relaxed at last, curling up on the floor with her head in his lap. He stroked her hair, watched her back until it relaxed, listened to her breath until it quieted. She spoke at last. "Okay," she said. "Thank you."

"That was okay?"

"Yeah."

"I didn't push it too far?"

"No. It was perfect. You pushed it just far enough."

"And you're okay now."

She patted his hand. "Yeah. I'm back. Thanks."

He squeezed her hand, and kissed it. Then he reached back to pick up the belt, and handed the belt to her.

She nodded. "Right. How far do you want to go this time?"

✾ ELECTRIC RAZOR ✾
Irma Wimple

SHE DISCOVERED IT WHILE SHAVING HER LEGS.

She paused, letting the electric razor rest against her thigh. The sensations that traveled to her delicates from the vibrating razor captured her attention. She stopped shaving, and moved the butt end of the razor higher and higher, until the resonating device was nestled against her womanhood, pressed close and high, as she closed her legs tightly. Her head tipped back and she lost herself in the sensations.

Slowly the iris of her awareness shrank down to the warmth beating between her legs. The sounds of the stereo, the draining bath, traffic, the feeling of the cold ceramic tile under her feet, the rush of air from the furnace, all faded. She knew only the interaction of the razor's buzz and her own heartbeat, which she could feel more strongly now in her clitoris than in her chest. She held still for a long time, holding the razor against herself. She began to need to move, and made tiny pelvic thrusts, holding the razor still. The tiniest movements felt so good to her, and escalated her incrementally each time . . . finally to a place she had known only in dreams.

With no warning she crested the hill, fell over the edge, and strong throbbing contractions that bloomed from deep under her clitoris threatened her focus on the hand holding the razor. In ever-spreading ripples, the intense orgasm throbbed countless beats, sending warm pleasure daggers into her entire body. It was almost too much to bear.

She was silent and still, and someone watching her would only see her catch and hold her breath. They would not witness the red heat pulsing within her until it subsided, and she took a deep, quavering breath, and a dreamy, beatific smile was left upon her face.

She left the razor where it was and soon climaxed two more times; smaller, throbbing aftershocks that threatened to overload her pleasure centers. Afterward she stumbled to the living room in her terry-cloth robe, curled up in a beanbag chair, and fell profoundly asleep in a sunbeam.

She found other things in her flat that produced similar effects when used unconventionally. Her tiny food processor, pureeing spinach or beans, could release her with a quick, shotgun orgasm after a day of speed and tension. She had to practice pressing against it in the exact right position; reaching her orgasm required navigation of a narrow channel of sensation. If she deviated too much, she was swept around it in an eddy and it passed her by, leaving her sweaty, itchy, and frustrated. Placing the processor on a kitchen chair and standing against it, knees bent, worked remarkably, once awkwardly discovered.

She began to eat a lot of processed food and soups.

Sitting on the vacuum cleaner took a long time, but the orgasms came from deep within her and lasted and lasted, until she had to fall, squirming and sighing, off her perch on the base of the machine. She humped the floor then, or her John Lennon pillow, until the tiny, clutching aftershocks came and came, erasing her identity, collapsed and carpet-burned until morning.

She acquired the habit of hanging around the laundry room and sitting on the washer pretending to read a book during the spin cycle. The other tenement denizens suspected nothing—only watching her eyes becoming fixed on the text, and the clutching and holding of her breath, would give away her booming, squeezing laundry-room climaxes. She would sit, her undies feeling tighter and tighter, a swelling thumping rising from below until she thought she would pee her pants. Then the silent, invisible wave would squeeze and squeeze her hot throbbing sex until she nearly fell over.

She had an old drill that was slightly off-center, and when she turned it outward and held the butt of the drill against her mound, she rapidly climbed through the sensations to a short, flutteringly rapid and intense orgasm. She could repeat them by reapplying the machine as soon as she could again control her hand, until she was exhausted and felt her entire abdominal area cramp like during her period. She would not be horny for days after one of these sessions, but a bit sore and bruised.

She began to shop at home and kitchen supply stores during off hours, so she could turn on the appliances and feel their motors. She acquired an ability to predict the type of orgasm from the feel of the machine in the store. She bought a bread maker, whose kneading paddles set her throbbing but unsatisfied, and she had to go use the electric razor to bring herself off. The razor always gave her the longest, most satisfying, and most multiple climaxes. She turned back to it when the other machines didn't have the depth, the focus that the tiny rechargeable razor gave her.

She bought an electric, cordless screwdriver that she would hold between her legs with no blade attached while she was sitting at the computer. An hour would go by and she would forget it was there as its charge started running out, and suddenly she would need to get off the chair, clasp something soft between her legs, and squeeze and squeeze until a tiny, soft, clutching orgasm reached up to her from the depths. The magnitude of these was low, but the duration was long, and they left her smiling and sleepy.

Summer came and she found that she could lean against the frame of her boxy window fan, pressing the rounded corner into her pubic mound through her clothes. She pushed against the vibrating fan, very carefully, getting the vibrations in the exact right place. The climax would come without warning, again lofting her over the unseen barrier, and she slid, throbbing, down, down, down into hot red squeezing pulsing oblivion.

She rarely made any outward show of passion during these machine-driven orgasms. The entire torrent, the pulsing flood of sensation, was so internal and private that little escaped to the outside world. She did not need to moan and fling herself about. The quieter she was, the more intensely she felt the sensations. Her eyes were always closed to keep her focus narrow, within her, avoiding distractions and stimuli from outside.

This new world of oblivion in climax fascinated her, and she wanted to explore all corners and depths of feeling she could attain. She had only slept with one man, her inept and distant high school boyfriend, and never once achieved anything near her electric razor orgasm. She owned dozens of electric, cordless, and windup machines, and became very skilled at creating a climax to suit her mood.

But she was lonely.

One day she went down to the laundry room to empty the dryer. There was a man there, black, lanky hair still wet from a shower, unshaven, in a tight V-neck white T-shirt and jeans, barefoot. He was reading a book, sitting on her favorite washer, on spin cycle.

She smiled.

ເ◌ FAIRGROUNDS ◌ຉ
Peggy Munson

"ALL'S FAIR IN LOVE AND WHORES," said Daddy Billy, spooning me after sex. "Then all's fair at the fairgrounds tomorrow," I retorted, kissing him on the nose.

I had barely grown out of my colt legs—my wobbly girlish knees that always spread for Daddy Billy—when the carnival grew in spindly metal limbs into a buzzing drove that overtook the Mason County fairgrounds. Things had been rocky between us for a while, but this was the kind of flawless summer day that people nearly trample with enthusiasm. We acted like new lovers. Daddy Billy roused me early with kisses. "Freak Day's here!" he shrilled. He was already clothed. I'd started sleeping naked because Daddy liked to slip beneath the sheets at night. "I need my favorite midnight snack," he'd say, as he was waking me with gropes and sticking fingers into me.

At the carnival, the sun hung with its fake sticky orange of flypaper sap as we wove through kids with droopy snow cones. I was horny and listless, as I always was when Daddy Billy wasn't fucking me. But he was distracted by another yawning circumference—for once, not a lipsticked one. He lobbed Ping-Pong balls at little fishbowls, trying to win a prize I didn't even want. He seemed unconcerned that my thighs might melt together in the heat, but his certain confidence, even against the sun, made me wet. I corkscrewed my hair, shifting on grass ironed flat by weeks of trampling feet. "Be good so Daddy doesn't sell you to the carnival," he said, grinning big. If I wasn't going to ride him, I wanted to ride the rides. I had a pocket full of tickets and a jeweled sky asleep on cumulus, just waiting for my eager hands. I tried to pull away, but Daddy Billy tugged my wrist. "This is not one of those postmodern Canadian sideshows," he warned, "with adorable, tumbling twins. The inbreeding here makes them ugly and mean. So stay close to Daddy and stay away from the octopus man."

For the past three weeks, the octopus man had been my nemesis. I was the sole rider who was screaming on the night of an electrical storm, when he wouldn't stop the ride and let me down. With a lizard hobble and skin more inked than a letterpress, the octopus man was a surly sadist with an oiled machine. "His octopus is his flail," Daddy teased. And that night of the storm, he commanded the throttle and laughed as the lightning unzipped the sooty dark. He flailed me with my fear. He was not as nice as Daddy Billy was, though Daddy had been known to laugh when I screamed. Daddy had been known to do a lot of things.

Daddy Billy—also known as Reverend Billy, Outlaw Billy, and, on rare occasions, Billy Boi—had taught me how it felt to call a lover "Daddy," and then infused the word with sultry power. His naughty drills had turned me from a full-grown woman into an adolescent nymphomaniac. He taught me need that built like summer heat on asphalt. I wanted him explosively. While real girls at the fairgrounds showed their wifely 4-H projects—hand-sewn outfits and fruit pies—I had a singular ambition: to be the docking station for his giant silicone cock. I sucked my straw to court attention. I rubbed up against him so he'd feel my gumdrop nipple pressing into his sleeve. I watched his last Ping-Pong ball skip around the fishbowl rim and fall. "Harrumph," he growled. I loved his Grant Wood–painted brow and every other part of him that hardened at the sight of me.

Daddy gravitated toward the fun house, where not a single patron queued. The carny gestured forward like a prison guard. He knew what Daddy was up to, and he didn't approve. Nonetheless, he ogled Daddy's hand cupped around my ass, and the ashy cap of his cigarette dribbled like come. He saw that we were perverts playing games, and he didn't like that we were civilian freaks instead of rubes. Daddy steered my ass into the spooky dark,

then seized my hand in the distorting mirror room. What the mirrors
didn't distort, Daddy would pervert. "Today, we're on a date," said Daddy
Billy. "But it's secret, because Daddies aren't supposed to date little girls.
So let's pretend we're both teenagers. Do you know what teenagers do in
the fun house?"

"Do they tongue kiss?" I asked eagerly.

"They kiss, but in a different way." He grabbed me and pulled me to
his body near the wavy mirror. His lips barely grazed my lips and then they
pressed against me hard, flash flooding my groin. The kiss was elasticized
by the wobbly glass, and then grew wide and tall as Daddy pawed the soft
white of my bra. He pinched my nipple, under my shirt, and said gruffly,
"Your nipples make Daddy Billy grow long, like our faces in the mirror.
Do you want to feel the way Daddy is growing long?" Daddy guided my
hand to his jeans and let me feel the dick tunneling down his pant leg.
I wanted to put the full length in my mouth. My lips took on its shape
automatically, with robotic memory.

"No," chided Daddy. "You'll get that later." He shoved one hand
under the waistband of my cutoffs and slid a coarse finger into me. "Mmm.
Daddy likes it when you're dripping like a little slut," he said. He kept
two fingers on my nipple and twisted it to see if I could hold my scream.
"Good little pet," he said. We walked through the rolling barrel and tra-
versed the shaking floor, then spilled into a labyrinthine configuration of
mirrors, where Daddy lined me up in front of a replica of me.

"In the carnival," said Daddy-as-benevolent-dictator, "awful things
go on. You need to learn to run if anyone tries to do such things to you,
so I must demonstrate." He slid his hand down the front of my cutoffs.
"See how you have a twin?" asked Daddy, gesturing to my image. "In the
carnival, if girls have twins, they're made to fondle each other while dirty
carnies watch. Did you know that, sweet girl?"

"No," I said. "But that is wrong."

"Of course. Of *course* it is," said Daddy sternly. "But let's pretend today
that I'm your daddy and you have a twin and we are carnies. Aren't you
curious about your twin? Don't you wonder what it's like to have the perfect narcissistic fuck? She's just like you."

He forced my hand up to the mirror, to touch my reflection twin's
breasts. He watched me stroke her cool, planed face. He kept one hand
on his cock as I made a circle on her nipple, then slid my fingers down.
My left hand burrowed past the silver button of my cutoffs and down

into my drenched white panties. My twin gawked. Her eyes were scared rabbits fleeing a mad scientist's lab. I bent down to kiss and pin her there, a specimen of need.

Behind me, Daddy Billy rubbed against my ass. He wanted his cock inside me so bad. I felt the way that it was homing desperately, yet ramming up against the home sweet home of comfortable clothes. He flattened me against the mirror. I left a trace of lipstick and of steam. Daddy embossed me with cock from behind. His need was hurting me. I wanted so much to let him in. He put my arms up so my tits pancaked against the glass. He bit my neck and groaned and fought to push his cock through tiresome threads. But suddenly, we heard footsteps approaching. Daddy hitched his belt and pulled away. The twin retreated as we walked away from her. She backed away like she was running off to join the carnival.

The sun had morphed into a disapproving eye. My pussy ached for Daddy's cock, but we could not find any private shaded spots. Daddy stopped to buy me funnel cakes so I'd get powdered sugar on my hands and then he licked it off while passersby clucked meddling tongues. "I need it, Daddy, please," I whispered in his ear. He got distracted and stopped to try to cop some plush by throwing rings at a grid of Coke bottles. I saw the octopus man skulking by but the crowd was cheering wildly as Daddy got a ringer. "We've got a sharpie!" the carny yelled, pulling down a giant blue bear with his shepherd's crook. Daddy told me I could put the bear between my legs at night when I was waiting up for him. He said the bear was wicked just like me and liked rubbing up against the Coke bottles while carnies slept. He asked if I would like to feel the Coke bottle inside his pants. I grinned and said, "Yes, Daddy, please." I loved it when he let me know my waiting time was up. He led me back behind the line of game booths where the narrow alley filled with aromatic funnel cake exhaust.

He eased the ragged edge of cutoffs to the side and rammed two fingers into me and made me smell the way my pussy was burnt sugar. Then he gave a furtive look around and opened up his belt buckle and asked me if I wanted to feel his Coke bottle, and I said yes. He took my hand and slid it between denim and his boxers. "I don't think that is a bottle," I said skeptically, but when I tried to pull away he grabbed my wrist.

"I think it is," he said. "If Daddy Billy says it is. Now if you put your fingers in a ring and rub them up and down the bottle, you might win another prize."

"You're trying to trick me like a dirty carny," I said indignantly. "I know that it's your thing and not a bottle. I'm not some dumb white carny trash." I hitched my tube top higher and I tightened up the knot that held my gingham shirt above my belly stud.

"Well," Daddy said, "close your eyes and put your fingers in a ring and I will show you that it is. Have you heard of soda jerks? You are the pretty girl your daddy needs to jerk his soda." Daddy Billy took my hand and rubbed it up and down his thing. He had the special Japanese flex-dick on, the one that felt like skin. "Oh honey, you are such a good girl when you do that and you're going to get a very special prize," he groaned. I felt his fingers prying up the edge of my cutoffs. He moved my panties over quickly and he rammed the bottle into me. His hips were pushing me against a pole.

"Not here," I said, and tried to push him off, though inside I was squeezing, holding him, and oh, he felt so good. "You're lying. It's a trick."

"I have to fuck you, baby girl. You know you make my cock ache."

He wrapped his arm around the pole and pinned me there and snarled into my ear. "You're such a dirty girl," he said. "To wear these slutty cutoff jeans, so loose that anyone can find a way inside you. What's Daddy supposed to do but pop your cherry with his soda pop?" I closed my eyes and, just to humor him, pretended I believed he had a bottle, not a dick. He fucked me hard against the pole to make me feel the temper of the glass. I wondered what would happen if the bottle shattered in me and I had a bunch of fragments cutting me and liquid spilled inside me until my blood was carbonated. Behind my eyes, I saw a screen of bubbly blood, the little comic bubbles emptied of their words. What if Daddy's shards would never leave, and hurt me every time he pulled away because they wanted wholeness back? And what if I became a mirror maze inside so nobody could tell which me I was, and whether I was inside me or out? He seemed to want to shatter us.

Out of the corner of my eye, I saw a tapestry of moving clothes. Daddy had a way of making raunchy things look innocent, and though I worried, we did not get caught. "You feel so sweet," I whispered in his ear. He moved his cock so gracefully. I thought of standing really still and spreading out my legs so wide that nothing would shatter and there would be no bottlenecking in the thruways of my heart.

"That's right," said Daddy. "Spread your legs so wide for Daddy. Let me in."

I didn't tell him how I felt like glass each time I called him Daddy. A luminous cocoon that's twirled around a pole into a fire until it takes the shape of something else, until its roundness grows and all of its blue beauty comes to light. I couldn't tell him what it was to be a Daddy's Girl, the way I burned in screaming fires to take the shape of what I had become.

But some distortion from the fun house cast a spell on me. As good as Daddy felt to me, I was so hollow afterward, like something scraped out with a knife. Maybe the pulsing lights and sounds and sugar shock had made me yearn. I watched the roller coaster ratchet up a hill and thought, *Someday the ride must end.* It's Newton and the apple. Up goes down.

I realized that I was waiting for a ticket. Some way out. But I did not know why.

"Hey, you," the octopus man called out. I was half-tranced with afterglow. I had been watching people rock atop the Ferris wheel, and playing with green, rattling beads around my wrist. He cupped a cigarette and slithered out of nowhere, leagues from where he should have been. "I have been trying to corner you all day," he said. I'd heard about the carnies who taught girls to barter blow jobs for a ride. I braced myself and licked my lips. Daddy had strolled off to find a Port-O-Potty and I couldn't see him in the crowd. "I know who you are," he said. "You rode the octopus that night when it was storming. Thursday, right?"

"You wouldn't let me down," I answered curtly.

"Sorry," he said, lighting up his smoke. "But I was high from cotton candy syrup. I was so high the moon was telling puns, and then the storm rolled in."

"I could have been electrocuted! All the other rides stopped long before you let me down." I crossed my arms around my belly so he couldn't catch a glimpse of skin. I'd noticed that his eyes were drifting over me. One eye was edged with brine; the other one was clear. I licked my lips again, in case I had to lubricate a scream.

"I know, and that's why I have found you now. One time, when I was younger, I was struck by lightning and I died. That's why I thought I should apologize," he said. His whole face frowned into a toady droop.

"You died?" I asked. I wondered if I smelled to him like I'd been fucked. My hands were fragrant as a caramelizing pan. He had an octopus-like quality. His flesh looked pliable, like he could cram himself into a tiny space, or camouflage his freakishness to blend in with a school of sharks that might have otherwise devoured him.

"I died and was resuscitated. When I touch things now, I give a shock," he said. He grabbed my arm and jolted me. He also had a quality of suction. I felt drawn to him and couldn't pull away. "So, Miss Lone Rider, tell me, is that person you are with a guy or a girl?" he asked.

"What do you think?" I said. I felt uneasy. Daddy Billy often passed as male. But secretly, he wore a sports bra cinching both his breasts, and underneath his dick he had an opening we never talked about. He hadn't taken T and had no plans of doing surgery. I loved his body's complex history.

"I think if that's your daddy and he takes advantage of a little girl like you, perhaps you should run off and join the carnival." The octopus man blew smoke in little puffs. I coughed. Had he been eavesdropping? "I told you that I know you, who you are," he said and tapped his chest. "Aversion therapy will not cure a girl like you," he said, and touched my arm again so that I felt a shock. "You're quite the conduit. I saw the way you made your friend light up."

His old tobacco teeth were grinning in a yellow rind.

"You're one of us," he said. "You are a freak. So come tonight at midnight, when the carnival is closed. The carnies meet to ride the rides. Stop by the gate and bring your friend. We'll let you in." He sidled off and ducked behind a tent flap, winking with his wayward eye. "Come one, come all," he said and swept the air. "Before we strike the tents and watch the grand illusion fall." I saw that Daddy had his fists clenched as he ambled up.

"I told you not to talk to carny folk," he said, and slapped me on the butt. "Don't make me put an apple in your mouth and have you crawl ass-first into the Future Farmers of America display. Remember, you are *Daddy's* little pig today." He kissed my cheek and led me off to play.

Daddy was right. I was a little pig who never had her fill of thrills. By that night, I felt as hollow as a whistle made of rotted trees. Maybe the tall, dismembered Ferris wheel began to get to me. When we approached, it was a giant piece of star anise but had no seats from which to kick the stars. The other lights were dimmed to dissuade townsfolk, so rides revolved with minimal illumination. Some carnies worked to strike the game booths down, but others twirled batons of fire, or gave a balding friend a cotton candy hairdo. Everything was shadowy, giving an eerie sense of dissolution. I'd changed into a frilly summer dress, and Daddy wore some pants that bulged out to signify he was a dude. I felt so sexy hanging on his arm. "Come on, you two," the octopus man yelled, and beckoned us with grinning warmth. "I'll stop you at the top and you can hang out there and watch the stars. There's nothing like it."

His girlfriend, Cherry, dangled on his arm. "Frank's right," she said. "Be brave—don't be an octopussy." Cherry stroked a tattoo of a tiny snake behind her ear. Her belly flat filled out the fabric of her dress to make foothills beneath her giant boobs. The octopus man—Frank, she'd said— clamped down the bar of our seat and pulled the throttle back. He watched us spin a bunch of times, then slowly stopped the ride so we were poised on top. The wind was rocking us and then it stopped.

The pod was weighted so we hung half upside down and couldn't look behind us, only up. We hung from spider silk; it felt that weightless. The sky was going to suck the blood right out of me. Then Daddy grabbed me with a clammy hand. I looked and saw the beads of sweat, the way his breath had changed to panic speed. Daddy was terrified. He didn't like to lose control. I pointed to the sky and told him Orion's belt was strapping us in place. "But your belt has to go," I said. "So that you can relax." He nodded gratefully.

I slid the leather from the clasp. I worked my mouth around his cock. "Oh, baby girl," he said, and grabbed my hair. I wanted him to feel that he was in a hammock of my care. Instead, he leaned back and he thought of barber's chairs and sexy women brushing tiny hairs away, or La-Z-Boys and daily blow jobs from a loyal wife. "I saw a shooting star just now," he said as he continued thrusting in my mouth. "I filled my balls with shooting stars and now you're going to swallow them." I bobbed my head so that he'd know I understood. I took him deep into my throat. "Oh yes," he said. "Eat up the universe from me."

He fed me meteors. "You are the best," I said, and hugged him when his dick was done. I meant it. I was dazzled then.

—— ✖ ——

The moon had turned into a magnifying glass, and it was burning out our insect eyes each time we wandered into light, so we sought shelter in the carny tent. "It's time for dirty 'truth or dare,'" said Frank. "Are you two in the game?" At this point, we felt warm, embraced, and Daddy sat beside me with his palm on my knee.

"We're in," he said.

They made me drink enough to numb an elephant, and that's when things got raunchy. On a dare, Frank's girl began to do a sexy dance on me. She hiked her juicy gorgeous leg up on my shoulder. She took my hand and rubbed it up and down her wisp of underwear. Her pussy smelled like dandelion wine and winding wind that grabs at any cloying flower. I rubbed along her pussy lips with the beer bottle. I bent down and I blew a hollow sound into the bottle, then held it like a tuning fork against her clit. She made the oddest little dolphin chirps, then moaned. She looked at me and said, "Now you. Lie back so I can test how breakable you are."

I looked at Daddy and I shrugged. I rested back against the folding chair and Cherry straddled me. She pried my legs apart and yanked my panties off. I loved how big and rough and soft she was. My folding chair began to tilt. That's when I accidentally backed into the velvet drape that sectioned off the tent, and saw the startled boi behind the velvet shield. The boi was sitting in a wheelchair and his biceps flexed when he rolled back the wheels reflexively. He had an octopus tattoo on his left arm. "J. Monarch Young!" she scolded him. "What are you doing there?" The boi looked sheepish and she shook her head. She said to me, "That's Young. He is the son of Frank. He's paraplegic from a test-ride fall. He is a naughty little voyeur, too."

Young coughed and shyly said, "Hello."

"You ready for the bottle, dear?" she asked me gently. Young's eyes were tracing me. "To join the carnival, you swallow either fire or glass," she said.

"I swallow glass," I said, and grinned at her. I felt the coolness and the ridges of the bottle's mouth, and tried to open up my hole for her. I wasn't just performing so that Daddy could get off. I was performing for the boi. I knew his eyes were riveted on where he wished he'd put a message in a bottle just for me. As people hooted from the side, I glimpsed the boi's gray eyes. I saw the tension in his skull beneath his perfect crew cut and I wanted to find handholds of his bones. "I think you've had your christening," said Cherry, pulling out the glass. "You're shatterproof and bulletproof; I toast you with my eighty proof." She raised the whiskey bottle and she drank a slug. "As carnies used to say, 'You've got some snap in your garter, sweetheart.'"

Seeing the boi gave me a flutter in my belly, so I thought I'd better wander off to ride some rides alone. I half hoped—fantasized—that Young would find me sectioned off from Daddy Billy, but I doubted that he would. I closed my eyes and felt the Tilt-a-Whirl lift up my dress, and then I wandered farther out to the periphery of human noise. The cornfields came right up to where the fairgrounds ended and I strolled up to the edge to stare at them. At night, they stood as still as antelope that know they're being watched. I loved how soft the grass got when it had been broken down. I felt a little dizzy, so I lay on the tamped green. It was as soft as puppy fur, and then I felt the infamous stealth wind that comes at such a tiny height and underscores the breathy and affected speech that's slung above. I was enjoying how the Great Plains wind felt tickling at my nipples when I heard their stomping feet. The two guys chortled devilishly. I lifted up my head. I saw the two of them, and Daddy said, "I've finally sold you to the carnival."

"You've *what?*" I asked. I sat up and I brushed the dirt out of my hair.

"I've sold you to the dirty carny folk," he said. His face was smug.

Frank gestured with his sucking arms. "I bought you from your daddy for one night. To do with my kid. We made a deal."

I'd promised Daddy, late some nights when he was fucking me, that I would always be his whore. He said these words a lot: *You're Daddy's slut, his whore, his prostitute, his fuck hole, tricky little trick.* I loved it when he talked to me like that. One time, I dressed up and he dropped me off beside the river where the fags turned tricks. I waited on a bench in ripped-up stockings and a miniskirt and fetish shoes until he came and lured me into the car and gave me twenty bucks to suck his cock. It was so hot the way he forced it down my throat that day, as if he didn't care how much I gagged. We made a lot of promises and deals when we made love. We used a fake fiducial language but I never thought he'd pimp me out for *real.*

"Just one night," goaded Frank. His voice was pitchy, not quite on its tracks.

"How old's your kid?" I asked.

"The kid is nineteen, never had a girl. The kid's shy ever since the accident and not-so-certain gender situation."

He could not say it: *My kid's queer. He wants to make it with a little pervert girl like you.* Frank only had his suction, and he used it to derail me with his voice. "Please?" he begged. "The thing is, Young had picked you out this afternoon. He saw you overturning rubber ducks to win some shoddy trinket and—quite honestly—I never seen his eyes light up like that."

"I can't." I answered. "It's not right." I backed away but was fenced in.

So Daddy Billy turned to Frank and said, "I'll handle her," and herded me against the fence. He rubbed his bulge against my pubic bone. He made me quiver, gasp. He knew my weaknesses. He took his hand— which he had outfitted with one warm leather glove—and held my neck beneath my chin. He traced my jawbone with his thumb. "Won't you be Daddy's perfect whore?" he asked me sweetly. "Daddy was so nice and took you to the carnival." In truth, I thought that Young was beautiful but knew I'd better protest some, or Daddy would be jealous later. I knew that Daddy thought a brother in a wheelchair wouldn't be a threat. This knowledge made me realize the one thing that unnerved me about Daddy Billy; Daddy felt a power over everything he saw as weak, and I could not be sure I wasn't cast in the same caste.

I let my voice get soft, coquettish. "I guess so, Daddy, if it's what you want." I loved to please him anyway.

"Good girl," he said to me, then, "Sold!" he yelled to Frank. They put a blindfold on me and they made me walk in front of them. I had a vague awareness that the plank I walked was pivotal for me. I felt the warmth of light and heard the buzzing insects as we neared Young's tent. "I'll come back when you've sanded down the kid," I heard Frank say. The tent flapped shut behind me and I listened to Young's breathing, and his wheels creaking as he came my way. He traced my knucklebones with his fingertips. He pulled me toward his chair.

"Sit on my lap," he said. "Tell me what pity story they gave you so that you'd stay."

When I sat down on him, still blindfolded, I felt what he was packing in his pants. "How did you—?" I asked.

"Idle hands make idle minds, but nimble hands shape ideal packaging," he said. "They told you that I've never done it, right?"

"I find that hard to fathom."

"I've never done it, not the way I want." He wrapped his arms around me and he kissed my neck. "My life consists of dictatorial wheels and all I want to do is reinvent the wheel with this, my dick." I reached down and put my hand around his bulge. I turned and started kissing him, his salty mouth. I ran my hands over his muscular arms. He slipped the blindfold off my eyes so I could see his grinning face. I touched his bristly crew cut. I stroked the bluish hands of his tattoo. He cupped my hair and pulled me to his lips and gave me an exquisite kiss. "I saw you at the carnival today," he said. "I knew you wanted to be watched." I stood up and walked around his chair.

"I did," I said. "I do." And then I started playing with his buttons and his belt loops, lifting up my leg and pulling back my dress so he could see the vacant place where underwear was ripped away. I touched my close-cropped pubes and stroked one finger on my pussy and then traced it where his barely-mustache grazed his upper lip.

"Smell me," I said. He inhaled deeply, then he grabbed for me. I pulled away and kneeled down so that he could see into the V of cleavage. I pulled his belt out of its latch and started undoing the buttons of his pants. And then I freed it—his enormous cock. "It's huge," I laughed. "Most people who are virgins don't go out and buy Paul Bunyan's dick."

"The carnival believes in grandiosity," he said. I licked the massive head and took his huge cock in my mouth. I swear I felt the ground drop down beneath me, like it did on the centrifugal-force ride. I wanted his cock deep, to choke on it, to show the boi his cock was magical. He moaned a little bit. "Now will you ride me?" he asked, timidly. "Will you ride on my chair?"

"I'd love to ride you, Young."

I backed on top of him and slid my pussy down his cock. The head went in, and then I let my weight down so his cock was unilaterally inclined to fuck. "Oh God," I said, "you feel amazing." He wrapped both his arms around me and began to kiss my earlobes and my hair. His fingers started pulling up my dress until he had it at my shoulders. He grabbed my boobs and held me by them so I squeezed against his chest. I rocked back on his cock. Then cleverly, he moved the wheelchair back and forth. "Just ride me, baby," said the boi. With one hand on the wheel, he rocked us in erratic jolts, so that the cock was fucking me—and he was fucking me—despite the fact that he could not move anything below his waist. His other hand was sliding down my soft bare skin and reaching for my clit. He licked his middle finger and he started circling my clit. "You take a lot of cock for such a little girl," he said. And then he fiddled with my clit until he made me come.

"Don't move," he said, as I was gasping from how sweet his fingers felt. He pulled my dress back down. He took his coat and placed it on my lap. "I'm going to wheel you through the carnival while I am still inside you. I've always wanted to do that."

His cock was threading me onto its shaft. His wheelchair did a loop around the grounds. The rides were whirling round. The carnies waved at us, and, when I said hello to them, teased, "Are you a ventriloquist now, Young?" They didn't know that he was fucking me right then, and acted like I was a wooden dummy and he was a star. I ground my pussy down on him and looked back so that I could see his grinning face. He took me to the edge of things, where rides had already been disassembled. The fantasy was breaking down, and Young was suddenly symbolic of my blooming need for change. I wanted something sweet and virginal. I put a blanket down and scooped him from his chair. For hours, we cuddled and we lay inside a circle of the flattened grass, as if the axles of a carousel had broken and we had fallen under the hooves of a wooden horse stampede. I'd been undone by him.

"You look so sacrificial in those savaged clothes," J. Monarch Young exclaimed. "What will you do when all these mechanical illusions drive away?"

"I will go home to Daddy and my real life. Why do you ask?" I touched his face.

"Because my cock wants more of you. I think you want it, too."

For just a moment, I felt something rising from the beaten fairgrounds, a construction not of steel or fantasy but heart. Young braided grass into a ring. I broke off little sticks and made a tiny raft. "Look at the waist-high fields out there," Young said. "I always thought their layout looked like squares on calendars. And yet, you shouldn't have to feel boxed in."

"What if I do?" I asked. "The fun house has to end."

"Well, sure, but think of the alternatives. Perhaps you need a carnival that doesn't end, with a defector from a land of freaks," he said, and looked at me so earnestly. "I'll stay and be your Tilt-a-Whirl. I'll give you tickets. You can ride on me all day."

The crickets turned their legs into string instruments just then. Something so usual seemed capable of reinvention. I realized why people ran away to join the carnival, and then ran back again: to make the axis turn. "All's fair in love and fairground whores," I said, and took Young's hand and led it to my ragged hem and slid it in.

⚬ GIFTS FROM SANTA ⚬
Tsaurah Litzky

Ho, ho, ho, it's Santa Claus!

I'm dreaming he's sliding down my chimney with a big, red cock. When he comes to stand in front of my bed, I see how fine and strong that big red cock is, and I want him to put it in the silky stocking I have between my legs.

When I tell him I want his cock in my stocking, he asks me a question.

"Have you been a good girl?"

I have to tell him no. I have not been a good girl at all. I confess I always eat the icing off the cake. I'll tell any fib to get a date. I play footsie with my friend's husband when I sit next to him at dinner parties. I steal lingerie from department stores. I goose strange men and women when I find myself pressed against them during rush hour on the subway. They look around but never realize it's me.

"You have been a very bad girl indeed," Santa tells me. "You need a thorough spanking before Santa can fill your stocking." He tells me to throw off the covers.

I obey Santa. I'm not wearing anything except my panties. Santa looks me up and down. "You are prettier than a plum pudding," he says. Then Santa tells me to slip off my panties, my new white silk panties with cute pink pussycats printed on them. I stole them from Saks Fifth Avenue just last week by stuffing them inside my jeans pocket as if they were a hanky.

When I slip them off, Santa takes the purloined panties from me and sniffs the crotch.

"You certainly have been a naughty, naughty girl," he says, and sniffs my panties some more. His red cock grows even bigger. As it gets bigger, it swells. It changes shape and now it looks like a giant red paddle.

Santa tells me to get on all fours. "Now lift up your honey-bunny bun, higher," Santa says. "That's right," says Santa. "Now you're acting like a good girl should." He chuckles approvingly, "Ho, ho, ho."

He begins to spank me with his paddle-cock. He paddles my ass again and again with his sturdy tool. At first he spanks with a loving touch, lightly, three gentle little taps on my right ass cheek, three on the left, then four on each side, then five. Soon, Santa starts to spank me harder, smack, smack, smack! I never thought Santa would have a thing for spanking. He's an expert. He knows when to take his time and he knows when to speed up. I wonder if he spanks the elves for practice. I want to ask him but I don't want to interrupt his concentration as he rhythmically paddles me. He holds his spanker in his hand, raises it higher each time. He uses the strength of his whole arm to bring it down.

"Stop, stop, no, no, no!" I squeal. My whole ass is tingling, stinging, but I like it, how I like it. The more it stings, the more I like it. I look back and see my butt is a deep, bright red strawberry color almost the same color as Santa's thick, scarlet cock.

"Enough, enough, Santa, please stop," I cry, but I don't mean it. It feels like my ass is on fire, but the fire is not burning me, just making the love juices inside me simmer to a fine boil. I relax and let the delicious heat wash through my cunny; it spreads up to my tits and down to my toes. Now I'm purring like a kitten. Maybe Santa liked it better when I was squealing *stop* and *no*, because he stops the spanking. He must know how much I want more by the way I keep purring and pushing my throbbing bum up to him in invitation. I'm moving it closer to him, shaking it.

Maybe Santa wants to show me who's boss, or maybe Santa is just a tease. "That's enough," he says. "You can roll over on your back now." Gingerly, I flip over. I'm surprised how soothing and cool the sheets feel against my tender rump.

I look up at Santa. His eyes are twinkling, and his face is very rosy, as if he was shoveling snow. His cock is pointing right at me. It doesn't look like a paddle anymore but it's still very big. "I hope you've learned your lesson, and next year you'll try to behave," he says.

I grin at Santa. "No way," I tell him—and he winks at me. "Ho, ho, ho," he bellows. "You're a very smart girl indeed." "Oh Santa, thank you," I say, then I tell him that it was the very best spanking I've ever had.

"I have something else very special for a smart, sassy girl like you," he says.

He lowers his head and attaches his big, pink Santa mouth to one of my teeny teats. He starts to suck it slowly, savoring it, licking it, flicking his fat tongue back and forth. This makes me feel very, very nice, and my silky stocking gets all wet and sticky. Santa's long, stiff white whiskers are tickling my tummy as he sucks and I start to giggle. Santa lifts his lips off my nippie.

"I like a jolly, merry girl, particularly one who can learn from a good spanking," he says. "And now Santa is going to give you something to really laugh about. Soon, you will be roaring with glee."

Santa puts his chubby hand between my legs and sticks a finger right into my slit. I'm all juicy and slippery, and his darting digit feels so nice dancing up inside me. He moves it in and out, out and in. When he pulls it all the way out, it is covered with the sticky syrup from between my legs. Santa puts a sticky finger in his mouth. He sucks it for a while, then, "Dee-licious," he says. "This tastes better than a peppermint candy cane. Now Santa has a great big candy cane for you."

He puts his hands out and spreads my legs. Then he kneels over me and guides his cock into the sticky place between my legs. It feels so sweet, moving in and out of me. The deeper inside it goes, the sweeter it feels. My insides begin to melt with pleasure. We're interrupted by an abrupt pounding on the ceiling above, a stamp, stamp, stamping sound.

Santa pauses and looks up. He's half inside me, half out. "It's my reindeer," he says.

"Be patient," he calls up, his voice ringing out like a chime. "Be patient, Dasher and Dancer, Donner and Blitzen, Santa's coming. . . ."

From above we hear a few faint neighs and the sound of the sleigh bells. Santa starts to move in and out of me again, but faster and faster. The sweet feeling between my legs gets more intense and I start to come.

Suddenly Santa bursts into song: *Jingle bells, jingle bells, jingle all the way, oh what fun,* he carols loudly, *it is to ride in a one-horse open sleigh.*

His mellifluous voice rises to a crescendo as he plunges deeper inside me and comes all the way. I'm so very, very happy. Santa is happy, too; he falls down on top of me and gives me a big hug. "Merry, merry Christmas," he whispers in my ear. "Did you like your gift?" he asks.

"Oh, yes, yes, Santa," I say. I can feel Santa's hot jism running down the inside of my leg. It smells like a toasted marshmallow. I want to show Santa just how much I like it by asking him to rub it all over me, but we hear the bells jingling above us again. Santa stands up and tucks his versatile thing back inside his trousers.

"I have one more gift for you," he says. He reaches into his pocket and pulls out a tiny red wood paddle on a green velvet ribbon. It is adorable, just like Santa. He puts it around my neck. I tell him that I love it and will wear it every day.

"I have to go now," Santa says. "I have lots of other sweet girls to visit tonight. But remember, if you behave," and he winks at me again, "it's a candy cane world."

I understand just what Santa means. "I hope you're right, Santa," I say.

"Be a spanking good girl like Santa taught you—and you can count on it." He pats me tenderly on the ass, and with a final, "Ho, ho, ho," Santa turns and vanishes back up the chimney.

JEALOUS HUSBAND RETURNS IN FORM OF PARROT
Robert Olen Butler

I NEVER CAN QUITE SAY AS MUCH AS I KNOW. I look at other parrots and I wonder if it's the same for them, if somebody is trapped in each of them, paying some kind of price for living their life in a certain way. For instance, "Hello," I say, and I'm sitting on a perch in a pet store in Houston, and what I'm really thinking is, *Holy shit. It's you.* And what's happened is I'm looking at my wife.

"Hello," she says, and she comes over to me, and I can't believe how beautiful she is. Those great brown eyes, almost as dark as the center of mine. And her nose—I don't remember her for her nose, but its beauty is clear to me now. Her nose is a little too long, but it's redeemed by the faint hook to it.

She scratches the back of my neck.

Her touch makes my tail flare. I feel the stretch and rustle of me back there. I bend my head to her and she whispers, "Pretty bird."

For a moment, I think she knows it's me. But she doesn't, of course. I say hello again, and I will eventually pick up "pretty bird." I can tell that as soon as she says it, but for now I can only give her another hello. Her fingertips move through my feathers, and she seems to know about birds. She knows that to pet a bird you don't smooth his feathers down, you ruffle them.

But of course, she did that in my human life as well. It's all the same for her. Not that I was complaining, even to myself, at that moment in the pet shop when she found me like I presume she was supposed to. She said it again—"Pretty bird"—and this brain that works the way it does now could feel that tiny little voice of mine ready to shape itself around these sounds. But before I could get them out of my beak, there was this guy at my wife's shoulder, and all my feathers went slick flat to make me small enough not to be seen, and I backed away. The pupils of my eyes pinned and dilated, and pinned again.

He circled around her. A guy that looked like a meat packer, big in the chest and thick with hair, the kind of guy that I always sensed her eyes moving to when I was alive. I had a bare chest, and I'd look for little black hairs on the sheets when I'd come home on a day with the whiff of somebody else in the air. She was still in the same goddamn rut.

A hello wouldn't do, and I'd recently learned "good night," but it was the wrong suggestion altogether, so I said nothing, and the guy circled her, and he was looking at me with a smug little smile, and I fluffed up all my feathers, made myself about twice as big, so big he'd see he couldn't mess with me. I waited for him to draw close enough for me to take off the tip of his finger.

But she intervened. Those nut-brown eyes were before me, and she said, "I want him."

And that's how I ended up in my own house once again. She bought me a large black wrought-iron cage, very large, convinced by some young guy who clerked in the bird department and who took her aside and made his voice go much too soft when he was doing the selling job. The meat packer didn't like it. I didn't, either. I'd missed a lot of chances to take a bite out of this clerk in my stay at the shop, and I regretted that suddenly.

But I got my giant cage, and I guess I'm happy enough about that. I can pace as much as I want. I can hang upside down. It's full of bird toys. That dangling thing over there with knots and strips of rawhide and a bell at the bottom needs a good thrashing a couple of times a day, and I'm the bird to do it. I look at the very dangle of it, and the thing is rough, the rawhide and the knotted rope, and I get this restlessness back in my tail, a burning, thrashing feeling, and it's like all the times when I was sure there was a man naked with my wife. Then I go to this thing that feels so familiar and I bite and bite, and it's very good.

I could have used the thing the last day I went out of this house as a man. I'd found the address of the new guy at my wife's office. He'd been there a month, in the shipping department, and three times she'd mentioned him. She didn't even have to work with him, and three times I heard about him, just dropped into the conversation. "Oh," she'd say when a car commercial came on the television, "that car there is like the one the new man in shipping owns. Just like it." Hey, I'm not stupid. She said another thing about him and then another, and right after the third one I locked myself in the bathroom, because I couldn't rage about this anymore. I felt like a damn fool whenever I actually said anything about this kind of feeling and she looked at me as though she could start hating me real easy, and so I was working on saying nothing, even if it meant locking myself up. My goal was to hold my tongue about half the time. That would be a good start.

But this guy from shipping. I found out his name and his address, and it was one of her typical Saturday afternoons of vague shopping. So I went to his house, and his car, that was just like the commercial, was outside. Nobody was around in the neighborhood, and there was his big tree in back of the house going up to a second-floor window that was making funny little sounds. I went up. The shade was drawn but not quite all the way. I was holding on to a limb with my arms and legs wrapped around it like it was her in those times when I could forget the others for a little while. But the crack in the shade was just out of view, and I crawled on till there was no limb left, and I fell on my head. When I think about that now, my wings flap and I feel myself lift up, and it all seems so avoidable. Though I know I'm different now. I'm a bird.

Except I'm not. That's what's confusing. It's like those times when she would tell me she loved me and I actually believed her and maybe it was true and we clung to each other in bed, and at times like that I was different. I was the man in her life. I was whole with her. Except even at that moment, as I held her sweetly, there was this other creature inside me who knew a lot more about it and couldn't quite put all the evidence together to speak.

My cage sits in the den. My pool table is gone, and the cage is sitting in that space, and if I come all the way down to one end of my perch, I can see through the door and down the back hallway to the master bedroom. When she keeps the bedroom door open, I can see the space at the foot of the bed but not the bed itself. I can sense it to the left, just out of sight. I watch the men go in and I hear the sounds, but I can't quite see. And they drive me crazy.

I flap my wings and I squawk and I fluff up and I slick down and I throw seed and I attack that dangly toy as if it were the guy's balls, but it does no good. It never did any good in the other life, either, the thrashing around I did by myself. In that other life I'd have given anything to be standing in this den with her doing this thing with some other guy just down the hall, and all I had to do was walk down there and turn the corner and she couldn't deny it anymore.

But now all I can do is try to let it go. I sidestep down to the opposite end of the cage and I look out the big sliding glass doors to the backyard. It's a pretty yard. There are great, placid live oaks with good places to roost. There's a blue sky that plucks at the feathers on my chest. There are clouds. Other birds. Fly away, I could just fly away.

I tried once, and I learned a lesson. She forgot and left the door to my cage open, and I climbed, beak and foot, beak and foot, along the bars and curled around to stretch sideways out the door, and the vast scene of peace was there, at the other end of the room. I flew.

And a pain flared through my head, and I fell straight down, and the room whirled around, and the only good thing was that she held me. She put her hands under my wings and lifted me and clutched me to her breast, and I wish there hadn't been bees in my head at the time so I could have enjoyed that, but she put me back in the cage and wept a while. That touched me, her tears. And I looked back to the wall of sky and trees. There was something invisible there between me and that dream of peace. I remembered, eventually, about glass, and I knew I'd been lucky; I knew that for the little, fragile-boned skull I was doing all this thinking in, it meant death.

She wept that day, but by the night she had another man. A guy with a thick Georgia-truck-stop accent and pale white skin and an Adam's apple big as my seed ball. This guy has been around for a few weeks, and he makes a whooping sound down the hallway, just out of my sight. At times like that, I want to fly against the bars of the cage, but I don't. I have to remember how the world has changed.

She's single now, of course. Her husband, the man that I was, is dead to her. She does not understand all that is behind my hello. I know many words for a parrot. I am a yellow-naped Amazon, a handsome bird, I think, green with a splash of yellow at the back of my neck. I talk pretty well, but none of my words are adequate. I can't make her understand.

And what would I say if I could? I was jealous in life. I admit it. I would admit it to her. But it was because of my connection to her. I would explain that. When we held each other, I had no past at all, no present but her body, no future but to lie there and not let her go. I was an egg hatched beneath her crouching body, I entered as a chick into her wet sky of a body, and all that I wished was to sit on her shoulder and fluff my feathers and lay my head against her cheek, with my neck exposed to her hand. And so the glances that I could see in her troubled me deeply: the movement of her eyes in public to other men, the laughs sent across a room, the tracking of her mind behind her blank eyes, pursuing images of others, her distraction even in our bed, the ghosts that were there of men who'd touched her, perhaps even that very day. I was not part of all those other men who were part of her. I didn't want to connect to all that. It was only her that I would fluff for, but these others were there also, and I couldn't put them aside. I sensed them inside her, and so they were inside me. If I had the words, these are the things I would say.

But half an hour ago, there was a moment that thrilled me. A word, a word we all knew in the pet shop, was just the right word after all. This guy with his cowboy belt buckle and rattlesnake boots and his pasty face and his twanging words of love trailed after my wife through the den, past my cage, and I said, "Cracker." He even flipped his head back a little at this in surprise. He'd been called that before to his face, I realized. I said it again, "Cracker." But to him I was a bird, and he let it pass. "Cracker," I said. "Hello, cracker." That was even better. They were out of sight through the hall doorway, and I hustled along the perch, and I caught a glimpse of them before they made the turn to the bed and I said, "Hello, cracker," and he shot me one last glance.

It made me hopeful. I eased away from that end of the cage, moved toward the scene of peace beyond the far wall. The sky is chalky blue today, blue like the brow of the blue-fronted Amazon who was on the perch next to me for about a week at the store. She was very sweet, but I watched her carefully for a day or two when she first came in. And it wasn't long before she nuzzled up to a cockatoo named Willy, and I knew she'd break my heart. But her color now, in the sky, is sweet, really. I left all those feelings behind me when my wife showed up. I am a faithful man, for all my suspicions. Too faithful, maybe. I am ready to give too much. And maybe that's the problem.

The whooping began down the hall, and I focused on a tree out there. A crow flapped down, his mouth open, his throat throbbing, though I could not hear his sound. I was feeling very odd. At least I'd made my point to the guy in the other room. "Pretty bird," I said, referring to myself. She called me pretty bird, and I believed her and I told myself again, "Pretty bird."

But then something new happened, something very difficult for me. She appeared in the den naked. I have not seen her naked since I fell from the tree and had no wings to fly. She always had a certain tidiness in things. She was naked in the bedroom, clothed in the den. But now she appears from the hallway, and I look at her, and she is still slim and she is beautiful, I think—at least I clearly remember that as her husband I found her beautiful in this state. Now, though, she seems too naked. Plucked. I find that a sad thing. I am sorry for her, and she goes by me and she disappears into the kitchen. I want to pluck some of my own feathers, the feathers from my chest, and give them to her. I love her more in that moment, seeing her terrible nakedness, than I ever have before.

And since I've had success in the last few minutes with words, when she comes back I am moved to speak. "Hello," I say, meaning, *You are still connected to me, I still want only you.* "Hello," I say again. *Please listen to this tiny heart that beats fast at all times for you.*

And she does indeed stop, and she comes to me and bends to me. "Pretty bird," I say, and I am saying, *You are beautiful, my wife, and your beauty cries out for protection.* "Pretty." *I want to cover you with my own nakedness.* "Bad bird," I say. *If there are others in your life, even in your mind, then there is nothing I can do.* "Bad." *Your nakedness is touched from inside by the others.* "Open," I say. *How can we be whole together if you are not empty in the place that I am to fill?*

She smiles at this, and she opens the door to my cage. "Up," I say, meaning, *Is there no place for me in this world where I can be free of this terrible sense of others?*

She reaches in now and offers her hand, and I climb onto it and I tremble and she says, "Poor baby."

"Poor baby," I say. *You have yearned for wholeness, too, and somehow I failed you. I was not enough.* "Bad bird," I say. *I'm sorry.*

And then the cracker comes around the corner. He wears only his rattlesnake boots. I take one look at his miserable, featherless body and shake my head. We keep our sexual parts hidden, we parrots, and this man is a pitiful sight. "Peanut," I say. I presume that my wife simply has not noticed. But that's foolish, of course. This is, in fact, what she wants. Not me. And she scrapes me off her hand onto the open cage door and she turns her naked back to me and embraces this man, and they laugh and stagger in their embrace around the corner.

For a moment, I still think I've been eloquent. What I've said only needs repeating for it to have its transforming effect. "Hello," I say. "Hello. Pretty bird. Pretty. Bad bird. Bad. Open. Up. Poor baby. Bad bird." And I am beginning to hear myself as I really sound to her. "Peanut." I can never say what is in my heart to her. Never.

I stand on my cage door now, and my wings stir. I look at the corner to the hallway, and down at the end the whooping has begun again. I can fly there and think of things to do about all this.

But I do not. I turn instead, and I look at the trees moving just beyond the other end of the room. I look at the sky the color of the brow of a blue-fronted Amazon. A shadow of birds spanks across the lawn. And I spread my wings. I will fly now. Even though I know there is something between me and that place where I can be free of all these feelings. I will fly. I will throw myself there again and again. Pretty bird. Bad bird. Good night.

⁵⊙ ON THE ROAD WITH SONIA ⊙⁸
Paula Bomer

ONCE SONIA GETS GOING ON I-95 NORTH, once she is definitely out of New York City, it is all she can do not to slam on the brakes and turn back— or slam on the gas pedal and go a hundred miles an hour. She feels . . . *extreme*. She's free. Every now and then she lets out a high-pitched squeal of delight and fear.

She drives further into the New England countryside, past the suburbs, deep into the hilly, tree-laden world of Massachusetts. The world is gorgeous. The sun hangs deep and yellow in the clear sky; the trees sparkle every shade of orange and red. Autumn in the country. She's alone at last. No crying babies demanding she try and stick a bottle in their mouths while driving. No toddlers saying, "I'm bored. Are we there yet?" No one demanding to stop because they have to pee so badly they are about to wet the car seat.

But then Sonia has to pee. Pretty badly. Even if there are no children in the car—she glances into the rearview mirror just to make sure; nope, no children—there sit their car seats, staring back at her angrily, accusingly empty.

Sonia has left her family. When her husband, Richard, went to work in the morning, Sonia headed into the bathroom. There, on the wet bath mat, was his dirty underwear. Like always. And in the damp heat of the postshower bathroom, as she bent over to pick them up, grunting out loud, feeling momentarily like a stuck pig—it's not easy to bend over when pregnant!—something in her snapped. Why was she picking up after a grown man when she already had two children to pick up after, too? What was wrong with the universe? What was wrong was that she was *there*. If she weren't there, she wouldn't be bending over picking up underwear. So she left.

The miles accumulate. The traffic becomes sparse. Massachusetts is beautiful. She is free! She is free in beautiful Massachusetts. Damn, she has to pee. The sun is setting and a darkness begins settling in. She turns on the lights and the road spreads out gray and weakly lit before her. Funny how lights on a car don't feel important until it's deep into the night. She's been listening to CDs and, alternately, to the radio, and now her ears hurt. She turns down the music. A green sign saying Rest Stop, in three miles, presents itself. Good, she thinks. She can make it.

She does, barely. Sonia parks her Volkswagen station wagon as close to the bathrooms as she can, and rushes into the cubicles, which are as nasty and smelly as can be. But, hey, there's no underwear to pick up. She sits on the toilet seat without thinking or looking and, immediately, her ass gets wet. Her wet, cold butt sticking to the toilet seat fuels the festering inside her. She's disgusting and incompetent. But she *is* peeing and that's some relief. It dawns on her that this is the first of many public bathrooms she'll encounter.

She manages a decent cleanup job. There is toilet paper—hallelujah!—and even warm water in the sinks. She stares at herself in the mirror. She sticks her chest out. She has the *glow*. The pregnancy glow. The moist skin. The *Mona Lisa* smile all pregnant women get—not a real smile, but the one that fools the rest of the world. She sticks her tongue out at the mirror and leaves the restroom.

It's a gorgeous night. Even here, next to the highway. It's the edge of darkness now. The air is crisp and cool, and her nipples harden under her tank top. Even though a few cars whiz by, the rhythmic noise of crickets and birds overwhelm the traffic. Sonia sits on top of her car, delicately, as it feels a bit warm. She folds her hands in her lap and breathes slowly, her eyes closed. I'm here now, she thinks, that's all. Nothing else matters.

There are a handful of other cars. A few spots away from her Passat is a green Chevy pickup, with a young, dark-haired man leaning against the front end, holding a cup of coffee and smoking a cigarette.

Sonia likes him. His dirty hair, long, but not too long, like a haircut gone neglected. His pants are tight, but not painfully so. He's got tattoos, which she notices first. Then she notices his arms. They're *big*.

"You're staring at me."

"I'm sorry?" says Sonia.

"You're staring at me." He smiles.

"Can I bum a cigarette?" Sonia hasn't smoked since college.

"Sure."

Sonia walks over and every muscle in her body feels tight and strange, as if walking were something her body had never done before. He taps out a Camel filter for her. Up close, she notices things about him that weren't evident from two parking spots away. He has that reddish tan skin that has a bit to do with the sun, and much to do with cigarettes and alcohol.

"I haven't had a cigarette in a long time," she says.

"Are you pregnant?"

Sonia looks down at her bump. She feigns surprise. "Look! I *am* pregnant!"

"Phew. For a minute there, I thought I'd made a mistake." He has an accent that Sonia can't place. "That's no good, saying a woman looks pregnant when she's not." He laughs, looking away from her.

He turns back to her, flicking his lighter at the cigarette dangling from her lips. She doesn't inhale, but she holds the dry smoke in her mouth. It's too much. Her hand shakes as she takes a draw.

"Where are you from?" she asks.

"Hingham. You?"

"I'm from Brooklyn," she answers, and then wonders if this is the time where she starts lying about where she's from. Or if she's pregnant. Let them think she's fat! Who cares? Guys fuck fat chicks. Some guys do. Or if she's married. The hand with the cigarette, her left hand, sports a wedding ring. She wonders if she should take it off. Hell, guys fuck married women all the time. Many may prefer to. Perhaps the sort of man Sonia is looking for prefers married women. If Sonia is looking for men, which she's not quite sure about. Is she looking for *men*? For what? For laughs?

She is looking at this man now. He's beautiful. The cigarette and his arms and his accent and everything about him—his truck, everything—makes her weak, light-headed.

"Where're you heading?" he asks.

"That's a good question. I guess to Boston. I'm on a road trip. I don't have a strict itinerary."

He smells good. She's standing so close to him that she can really smell him: salty and smoky. His biceps bulge with a tattoo of a dragon; his arms are covered with dark hair.

"Are you okay?" He puts a hand on her arm.

"Yeah, the cigarette just made me dizzy." She's barely smoked it. It's his touch that pushes her over the edge. She throws the cigarette on the ground. "Can I sit in your truck for a minute?"

He widens his eyes.

"Please?"

"Sure." He clears his throat. "I'm going soon, but sure." He starts looking around himself, as if he were waiting for someone.

She wants to scream, *Fuck you, pussy! What are you afraid of?* Instead, she says, "Thanks. Just for a minute."

She stares at his face. It's *chiseled*. It's as if she had run into a movie star on the side of I-95 in deep New England. Except he probably got his muscles from doing real work, not from hanging out with a personal trainer.

"Come sit next to me." Her voice comes out like honey.

"Are you married?" He's standing in the doorway of the driver's seat; she's already scooted over the bench—this truck has a bench!—to the passenger's side. He's got one leg crossed over the other.

"Not really. My husband—my husband died." The lie comes purring out. Wishful thinking? Oh, boy, thinks Sonia, this guy is young, really young. He could be nineteen. All the cigarettes and booze in the world can't hide it.

"Wow. I'm sorry." He sits down next to her. "Was he the father of your child?"

She looks into his eyes, leaning a bit closer. He wants it, too. Or so she hopes. Prays. *Dear God, please let this guy fuck me.*

"Don't talk about it. I'm not so pregnant yet," she says, rubbing her hands gently on her smooth, rounded belly. Her thin tank top is half-transparent and makes a soft rustling sound as she strokes herself. His eyes follow the movement of her hands. Now he's the one staring. "I'm still toward the beginning. Not yet the middle. But feel this," she says and takes his hand—God, the feel of it, so rough—and places it on her breast.

He looks away, out the back window. With his free hand he slams the truck door shut. It's dark out now.

Sonia reaches out to his face and kisses him. He tastes sour, stale, and dry. She keeps at it. She lifts up her tank top and pulls her bra up over her chest, takes the young man's hands, and presses them to her tits. He bends down to suckle them and she moans—her nipples are so hot and painful, she almost comes right then, bucking her hips.

He pulls back. "I can't do this," he says quietly. Then he grabs her breasts again and she sits on top of him and grinds against his erection. It's a hard stick of a thing in his pants. Everything about this guy is thick and stiff. His rock-solid arms are around her body now, around her neck, grabbing her around her plump, pregnant waist. Sitting there on top of him, she looks down at her body and it's all roundness, all cushiony flesh and ripe fertility. She's the *Venus de Milo*, the woman of all women, the symbol of fuck. She hoists herself up and starts the awkward undressing, the ripping, the *just a minute*, the *I got it, I got it*, the *wait, not yet*.

First she's on top and he's inside of her, and she can barely get him all in. His dick makes her think of a huge pepper grinder at those fancy restaurants, *Yes, waiter, I'll take some of that.*

She gets that panicky feeling, the *get it in, get it in, oh no, can I get it in?* He pushes her down on the bench and she stretches one of her legs over the car seat, and *wham*, he's fucking her.

Oh, my God, thinks Sonia, I got it in, all the way in—the sense of awe and accomplishment brings her back to fourteen, when she was desperate to get it in there for the very first time.

One of his hands grips the dashboard, the other's underneath her on the bench. It hurts, in the good way fucking hurts. For months, she hasn't been able to look into Richard's eyes, her not-dead husband—but for some reason, here in the dark with this stranger, she can take it. The stranger's eyes glow like a cat's in the dark. His mouth is loose and open. He stares right back at her and spits on his thumb, rubbing it at the base of her clit and pushing very, very gently. This man knows pussy. He fucks her hard, his other hand on her hip bone. Her damp, swollen breasts start shaking, and she comes in that blind way where she can't see anything but white light, an electric current slamming her head against the door. She's fucked right out of her own body, panting. It's so awful; it's so right. To get fucked in a truck on the side of a highway by a man who doesn't give a shit about her, about what's for dinner, about their social life, about how the kids are.

The letdown, the reality, seizes her. The kids? She can't think about the kids, not here, no, it's just wrong. She looks back at him, moving, working it, his breath quick and panicky. He's about to come and she's back with him now, back in the fuck.

"Don't take it out!" she screams, "I can't get pregnant! I am pregnant! Don't pull out! Come inside me!"

Which he does. A minute later, his liquid drips out of her, cool on her thighs. He's beside her, careful of her stomach, smashed sideways next to the dashboard. She feels a surge of emotion—when she was fourteen, she'd called it love—and giddily, she thinks she'll never see this man again.

She washes up in the bathroom—this time, her ass stays dry. She wipes off the seat, comes back out, and his truck is gone. Fine and well. She goes back to her station wagon and unlocks the backseat doors. First one, then the other, she throws her sons' car seats onto the grass. Then she gets back in the driver's seat and takes off, in a car without children's car seats. The road ahead of her is black with night. For a moment, she's frightened. She can't see clearly, despite her headlamps, and the road turns and twists abruptly. What was she thinking? When was the last time Sonia drove at night, instead of being at home, reading to her boys in their pajamas?

She grips the wheel of her car and leans forward, acid taste in her mouth. She can't see, she doesn't really know the way to Boston, but she knows that's where she's going. She's not going home, not after what just happened, no. But she can't see in this pitch-blackness!

Finally, she remembers what to do. She puts on her brights. Leans back, exhales. She can't see her future; she can't know what the road looks like miles from here—but everything she needs to see is illuminated now, and as she steps on the gas, she goes even a little faster.

⅏ LOW-CUT ⅏
Lisa Palac

I MET CHERYL THROUGH AN AD IN THE NEWSPAPER. It said something like, "Very attractive blonde looking for female playmate. Boyfriend wants to watch." Yeah, my boyfriend wanted to watch, too.

The first time I tried answering a personal ad looking for a blue-moon girlfriend, I was single and I didn't have very good luck. I wrote a short letter giving my name and phone number and enclosed a picture. It was one of those black-and-white photo booth prints of me dressed in black, smiling. I hand-colored it, made it kind of arty. I never got a response. Maybe she chickened out. Maybe she thought I was a dork. I tried again with a different ad and ended up meeting this softball chick in a sports bar. I knew it would never work. I hated sports. Plus she had bad skin.

After I started seeing Greg, I decided to try it again. Greg was the first guy I ever watched a porn movie with, and every one we rented was a "lesbian" one. He was an all-girl action connoisseur. He never picked a movie that had any guys in it, and I can't say I minded. Women turned me on and besides, who wanted to see a bunch of ugly guys with nothing going on but big dicks? One night, after a sweaty session in front of the TV, he said, "I'd like to see you do it with another woman."

Now some women might interpret such a fantasy as the product of a selfish, macho mind, doped up on too much fake lesbian porno. But I thought of it more as classic, bedrock eroticism. I know that watching two women fuck each other is no doubt the number-one hetero male fantasy, but I like it, too. Until Greg's brilliant idea, I'd slept with one woman, and it was a lot less gymnastic than any porno. I was amazed by how soft her skin was; it really was like silk. While we were doing it, I kept thinking, *Girls are so soft. Do I feel that soft to her?* I was drowning in her silky water. I liked feeling her nipples in my mouth, the way her cunt smelled. Her body was peculiar and familiar at the same time. And I liked the challenge of figuring out how to hold it in my hands and make it work, how to make her come, even though I'd spent hours toying with my own circuitry! Greg's interest was a green light for me; he encouraged my desires. So rather than accuse my boyfriend of having a sick fantasy, I decided to live it out.

Finding a woman who will just go home with you and your boyfriend isn't the easiest thing in the world. It's not like in the movies, where every-one just wants to fuck and suck at the drop of a hat. Greg and I spent a lot of time in bars saying, "She's cute," or, "How about her?" but that's as far as it got. I got restless waiting for that perfect pickup moment, where she'd start rubbing my thigh and I'd let her mess up my lipstick while Greg silently paid the tab and guided us to his apartment. Deep down, we were both nervous and neither one of us had the courage to act.

So I wrote another letter. I picked an ad where having sex was clearly the goal. I laid it on thick this time, but didn't send a photo. I hated giving away good pictures of myself that I never got back. A few days later, Cheryl called. She had this cigarette-smoking, tough-girl voice, but it was sexy, and she was very matter-of-fact. She was young, early twenties, same as me, and she gave me a detailed physical description of herself (height, weight, bra size, always emphasizing *very attractive*) and let me know that fuck-ing "her old man" was out of the question and she wouldn't lay a hand on mine. We arranged to meet at my favorite snotty art bar, the New French Café. "You'll know me because I'll be wearing a black jumpsuit," she said.

Jumpsuit. My heart sank a bit. The only place you could get a black jumpsuit was at the army surplus or Frederick's of Hollywood. I imagined her to look like one of the go-go dancers on *Laugh-In*: big hairsprayed curls and mondo cleavage stuffed in a low-cut, bell-bottomed spandex capsule.

I wore black, too: leather jacket, dark sweater, jeans. And I think my hair was black then, fashionably unbrushed and matted with gobs of gel. Greg showed up in his usual plaid flannel shirt over some rock T-shirt, which may have been *The Cramps: Can Your Pussy Do the Dog?* His long dark hair was equally shocked with styling goo. He had "I can't believe you're doing this" pasted on his face. I ordered a glass of Côtes du Rhône; he had scotch. It was a late afternoon in winter, still light out. I usually tried to wake up before the sun went down again.

I picked out Cheryl like a cherry when she walked in. Cleavage and everything, just like I pictured it. And she was very attractive in a working-class way. Her sexy outfit was expected but sincere. She wore dark eye shadow and bright pink lipstick. I watched heads turn, not because she was that beautiful, but because nobody would come to the New French dressed like that. When she sat down, I wanted to reach over and touch her downy, powder-puff skin. Her man, on the other hand, was a grease-ball. He had a bad haircut and a big gut and a mustache. Let's call him John. I was very thankful for the anti–cock swap arrangement.

Just like on the phone, Cheryl got right down to business. She basically said that she and John answered a lot of ads and were always looking for new thrills. She wanted the four of us to go out to dinner one night, to "get to know each other," and then we'd go back to their house and do it. Greg suggested he bring along something from his girl/girl collection. "But he don't touch me and you don't touch him," she reiterated. Thank God.

She dictated a very particular dress code: "I want you to wear something on top that's tight and really low-cut and a miniskirt with thigh-high, spike-heeled boots. Stockings and a garter belt, of course." Uh, okay. I didn't own any of these items, except the miniskirt, but I didn't want to tell her that. While Cheryl was dressing me up like a total slut, the guys were talking and snorting, bonding in that guy way. I think they were talking about beer. We made plans for the following Sunday.

The next night, I got a call from Cheryl asking if I'd like to come over to their house and spend some time getting to know each other, as she put it. I said okay, but told her that Greg was working and so I wasn't gonna do anything, if that's what she had in mind, without him there. They picked me up and we drove to their Minneapolis suburban home. In the car I noticed that Cheryl was wearing panty hose; not cotton tights or colored stockings, but these suntan-colored panty hose. The dinosaur of hosiery. I felt bad for mentally picking on her panty hose, but they were so strangely out-of-date. I began to wonder if I could really get to know a person who wore beige panty hose.

Their house was tiny, with paneling in the living room and a lime-green shag carpet. I sat down at the kitchen table in a chair with a wrought-iron back and puffy, flowered vinyl on the seats. John handed me a Schlitz. He asked me what I did for a living. "I'm in film school," I said. He worked in a factory. Then Cheryl wanted to show me some of the other responses she'd gotten to her ad.

She and I went into the bedroom, and she plopped a big cardboard box on the bed. One by one, she showed me photos and letters from the girls who wanted to play with her. It had never even occurred to me to send a naked picture of myself, much less one with my legs spread wide and a dildo in my pussy. I was shocked, simply shocked, that people would send this hard-core, possibly incriminating stuff through the mail to some stranger at a PO box. No wonder I didn't get lucky the first time around. The letters were just as explicit, outlining how much they loved to eat pussy or how they wouldn't do anal, and of course how disease-free and very attractive they were. Well, who's going to admit their unattractive piggishness, right?

As we were looking through the stuff, Cheryl started rubbing my leg. Her skirt was hiking up her thighs and I now saw that she was not, in fact, wearing panty hose, but flesh-colored nylons and an industrial-strength garter belt. I couldn't decide if that was better or worse than the panty hose. When she saw me looking at her legs, she leaned over and kissed me. Her mouth was soft and I liked the way she kissed. Then, out of nowhere, greasy John appeared in the doorway, hand on his crotch. "I gotta go," I said.

She reminded me about the clothing requirements for our date. I admitted that I didn't have any thigh-high boots, so she made me try on several pairs of hers. I hoped for black, but the only ones that fit were an ugly tan with a thick, broken heel. It was hard to feel sexy in tan boots, but I reminded myself to be open to new experiences.

A few days later I got another call from Cheryl. She wanted to take me lingerie shopping. Immediately I flashed on one of those contrived *Penthouse*-type letters where two innocent girls are seduced in the dressing room of the bra department by some horny saleslady. But I did need that stocking and garter belt getup, so I agreed to join her.

We ended up at a suburban mall, but neither Cheryl nor any of the salespeople seemed the least bit interested in attacking me. In fact, Cheryl seemed quite nonchalant about the whole thing. She didn't even ogle as my naked breasts slipped from bra to bustier. She sat on a tiny stool outside the dressing room, dryly indicating her preferences. I picked out a white, lacy set. "Now remember," she said, "always put the stockings and garter on first, then the panties. That way you can take the panties off without having to undo everything." On the way home she told me how she occasionally worked as a stripper, both in clubs and at bachelor parties, and about some of the other personal ad experiences she'd had. "But you know, I'm really just looking for a friend," she said. "Someone I can hang out and do stuff with, like go bowling."

The Sunday of our sordid affair finally arrived. I spent the afternoon getting dolled up in my new clothes. I piled on the eyeliner and made my hair really big with lots of spray. I remembered to put the panties on over the garter belt and tried to get as much cleavage going as possible. Ah, the boots. Now I was painted. I felt like an actor in an absurd and darkly erotic theatrical performance. My prior meetings with Cheryl had been the rehearsals for opening night. And while the meticulously premeditated sex scene gave me a sense of what to expect, it also sliced off bits of spontaneity. I wondered if I might feel the same calculated degree of excitement if we'd picked up a woman in a bar.

Cheryl and John picked us up at my place in the early evening. The deal was that Cheryl would pick a place to have dinner. I assumed it would be someplace nice, and most importantly, dark and mood-setting. Instead we ended up at a family restaurant, a Denny's knockoff, right at the highway exit. It was blindingly bright, with glowing orange booths and plenty of screaming children. The place didn't even have a liquor license. I teetered through the door in my high-heeled boots, looking like a Hollywood whore and feeling the burn of a thousand eyeballs. I wanted to explain to every single patron that, hey, I don't usually look like this, but that would have been impractical. The waitress sneered at us and I knew she was thinking, *Hookers.* Dinner couldn't have been over fast enough.

Back at their house, I started to unwind with a few slugs off of a Schlitz. John rolled a joint while Greg fiddled with the DVD player, cueing up his favorite vibrator scene. Then the doorbell rang. Cheryl put her eye to the peephole and screamed, "Oh shit, it's my dad!" She waved her arms insanely at John, indicating he should hide the pot and mouthed, "Turn that fucking thing off!" to Greg. "Hi, Daddy," I heard her say, sweet as pie, when she opened the door. Daddy had come, tool set in hand, to fix something. Cheryl gave him a quick kiss on the cheek, then made a few frantic introductions.

"So how do you know Cheryl?" he asked me. My mouth hung open for about ten years, until Cheryl made up some lie. Bowling. Or maybe it was a party. "Well, seeing as you have company, I guess I'll come back tomorrow to fix that thing," he said. *Oh no, stay*, I thought. *Stay for a porno movie and watch your little girl get banged!* I held my breath until he left.

I don't remember how long it took for everyone's edginess to dissolve, but eventually Cheryl and I ended up in the middle of the living room floor on a blanket in our underwear. Greg and John sat quietly on opposite ends of the sofa, watching. We made out for a while, slowly peeling off each other's bras. With the new panty trick I'd learned, the stockings and garter stayed in place, although I actually tried to take my stockings off at one point because they started bagging at the knee and I thought it looked rather unappealing. "Keep them on," Cheryl whispered in my ear.

Exactly how I licked and sucked her or what she did to me is a melted-down dream, except for this: she brought out a strap-on dildo and told me to use it on her. It was a slender, pink rubber cock, attached to two white elastic straps. The dildo itself was hollow and looked oddly clinical. (It wasn't until much later that I learned it was really a penis extender, designed so a man could slip his cock inside of it and make himself "bigger." Made me kinda wonder about John.) I didn't want my naïveté to show, so I stuck my legs through the straps and Cheryl got on all fours. Just as I was getting the hang of it—I mean it's not very easy trying to maneuver a piece of plastic that's belted to your crotch with a couple of rubber bands—one of the strands snapped.

"Oh, that happens all the time," John said and held out his hand in an offer to fix it.

I didn't have a mind-blowing orgasm. I don't think Cheryl did, either. We just stopped, I think, when Cheryl detected a feeble moan from John. Strangely enough, neither one of the guys took out their cocks and beat off during the show. Etiquette, perhaps. John didn't whip it out, so Greg decided he wouldn't, either. But in the end, John did have a large wet spot on the front of his jeans and had obviously been doing some discreet grinding.

Our goodbyes were polite. I expected to have trouble tearing myself away from such a landmark moment, but what I really wanted was to be alone with Greg. We called a cab and went home.

I didn't hear from Cheryl the next day or the next week or in the following months. After all that, the pornographic reality just folded up into an odd and not particularly sexy memory. Occasionally I'd find a snapshot from the event floating in the front of my brain and I'd say to Greg, "Remember when her dad came over?" or "I can't believe that dildo broke."

Nine months later, I went to interview my first porn star, Bunny Bleu, for my cut-and-paste Xerox sex 'zine, *Magnet School*. I walked into the adult bookstore on Hennepin Avenue and through the crowd saw Bunny having her picture taken with a fan. She and another woman were standing with their backs to the camera, arms around each other's shoulders. "Okay, on the count of three, turn your heads around and smile," said the Polaroid photographer. When the flash went off, Bunny turned and smiled and so did Cheryl. Then Cheryl turned completely around and she was very pregnant.

She waddled over to me and gave me a hug. "I'm just here havin' a picture for John because he's in jail," she said. "DUI. He cracked up the car really bad, but he's okay. Baby's due in a few weeks. You're doing a sex magazine, huh? Send me a copy when it's finished."

Her world was so unlike mine. The pantyhose she wore, the kitchen chairs we sat on, the liquor we drank, the way she said "old man" and I said "boyfriend," the places we hung out, all screamed "class difference." We had nothing in common except one thing: the desire for sexual adventure. But sometimes, that's enough.

੬⊙ PUFFY LIPS ⊙੭
Susie Hara

ELENA SAT AT THE BAR. She so rarely drank these days that after just one martini, she could feel the effects. The way it made her feel bigger than god. The way it took the edge off, loosening her tension and sharpening her sensations so that her whole being was ripe and extended in sensuous tentacles, like a cross between a mango and an octopus. Mangopuss. Or Mangopussy. There, she felt them, the lips of her mangopussy, large and puffy in her mind's sensometer. And then the image of her labia, puffy and pink and engorged, expanded through every cell, pore, and vein of her mindbody, with all the worker bees of her consciousness focused diligently on the task. One big Labia Majora Fest, bigger even than the monthly ovulation brouhaha. "Labia majora," she thought, now that sounds like an exotic cocktail.

"I'd like a labia majora with a twist," she said to herself. It would be sweet but not too sweet. Mango juice, a touch of cherry, a touch of orange, some soda water, swirls of cream, and something heavy-duty like Grand Marnier. Oh yeah, and a twist. Damn. She could market that.

She looked around the room. Men, they seemed like exotic creatures to her. See, this was what happened when she hadn't had sex with a man for a while. "Men"—perhaps a species of animal she knew from another lifetime. Somewhere inside her, she dimly remembered things about them— their hands, their lips, their tongues, their fingers, their cocks—even their minds. The memories stirred and lumbered out into the light, like a beast coming out of hibernation. It was just that she hadn't thought about men for a while. Not in *that way*. She had temporarily put "men" out of her mind. She had been more focused on "women." Maybe *focused* was not the right word. Obsessed. Feverish. Devoted. Prostrate, worshipping at the temple of the divinely honeyed cunt. But now. Now in the moment, here in this bar, Elena felt something in her blood. It was a need. A need for something meaty. Yes. *Meat.* That was it, exactly. She wanted man-meat.

She looked over at a table of them, having a drink after work. There was one specimen who had this particularly meaty quality. His hands were meaty, his shoulders were meaty, but most of all, his chest. He had a meaty chest. She would like to knead it with her hands, rub her labia all over it, and lay her cheek down on it. Elena smiled. These were her requirements for the night.

She caught his eye. He let his gaze rest on hers for a minute, then he went back to talking to his companions. For a few seconds. Then his eyes returned to hers. She popped an olive in her mouth. She sucked on it. No chewing, no swallowing. She held his eyes with hers as she held the olive in her mouth. Then she licked her middle finger. Once. He raised his eyebrows a bit. And flushed slightly. Cool, but not *so* cool.

She made a big show of getting off the stool. Out of the corner of her eye, she saw him watching. She approached his table, then lightly touched his shoulder with her still-wet finger as she walked by. No eye contact. She left the bar and waited on the street, chewing the olive. She would give him thirty seconds. She started counting. One one thousand, two one thousand, three one thousand. He came out of the bar at twenty-three. She smiled and walked around the side of the building. He followed. She went down to the end of the alley, by the dumpsters. No one was around. She leaned up against the building. She could feel the cool, hard brick through her blouse.

"Take your shirt off," she said.

"Oh, I see. Just—take your shirt off? No 'hello,' no 'what's your name?'" he said, a half-smile curving the corners of his mouth. He put his hands flat on her chest, just below her collarbone but above her breasts. And just left them there. She could feel the heat of his palms. And her nipples hardening.

"Okay. Hello. Take your shirt off."

"I'll take my shirt off if you—" he moved his hands down her body and put one hand up her skirt, "if you take off your panties." He hooked a finger under the elastic. She drew her breath in sharply. He looked at her, eyebrows raised, waiting. She nodded. He pulled her pants down to her ankles. She stepped out of them.

He unbuttoned his shirt. Meaty. Just as she'd hoped. And covered with thick hair, like a pelt. *Grr.* He took off his shirt and dropped it on the ground. She kneaded his chest with her hands. She wanted him down, down, so she could rub her lips all over his chest. His meaty chest. She put her hands on his shoulders and pressed down. He smiled and went down, thinking he knew what she wanted, moving his lips up her inner thigh on his way to her puffy paradise.

But she had other plans. Her pussy lips were singing their swollen siren song, they were longing for the meaty chest man, the he-man caveman hunter chest, covered with fur. Before he could move his mouth lips to her puffy cunt lips, she maneuvered herself down and commenced rubbing her wet labia all over his chest, his pecs, his nipples, his stomach. She was moaning a cavewoman's moan, a satisfied carnivorous wet woman's moan, as she slipped and slid on his warm terrain. He was breathing hard, smelling her and holding her ass in his hands, feeling her circular hip motions as she smeared him with her juices. She bent her knees more and stretched her hand down, down, so she could put her hand on his cock meat. She felt his cock, hard and alive, through the cotton cloth of his pants. It felt so good, so like home, like someone in the kitchen making her a nice, big meal. "Hello," she thought, "hello friendly cock home-cooking man." He was moaning now, too, inhaling her scent and rocking against her hand. Then he reached up with both hands and pinched her nipples. That was it. It put her over the edge. It surprised her, the way it happened so suddenly, usually with a man it took longer. She came in three short waves. She pressed hard into him so her pelvic bone and clit connected with his meaty chest. As the pulsing became less and less and she hung there, knees bent and breathing hard, the words came into her mind. "Two out of three of my requirements are met."

She still had her hand on his hard cock. He hadn't come. She looked at him. He stood up and rubbed his knees.

"Ouch," he said. "My knees."

"Ugh," she said. "You are such a caveman. Thank you." She tugged her skirt down. Then she hugged him, softly laying her cheek against his chest for a moment. She sighed. Third requirement met.

She kissed him on the forehead and walked away slowly, down the alley. "That's it?" he called after her, putting on his shirt. "No flowers, no candlelight?"

She turned around, said, "You are the bomb. You are the best. That was just what I needed." And she walked backward into the night, still looking at him, a smile in her eyes.

He finished buttoning his shirt. Picked up her underpants and put them in his pocket. He looked up. She was still walking backward, her eyes resting on him with that *Mona Lisa* smile. He watched her turn the corner and disappear.

ஜ SALT ஐ
Bill Noble

THE WEEK SHOSHANNA LEFT HER, snow dusted the *pali* for the first time in memory. It was so cold she could hear the year's crop of mangoes plopping green off the trees. Then, with the white still clinging to the cliffs, rangers came and burned her shack down. And nearly busted her, too, if she hadn't run. That was a big deal—and it was a big deal, too, when some hippie in a homemade pigskin vest walked up and found her cold and crying by the ashes.

Mandy wiped her face on the back of a sooty hand and glared, but the hippie wrapped his jacket around her shoulders till she stopped shivering. He didn't seem to need to talk much, and sure as shit she had no need to talk to him, so they just stood, surrounded by guava and tangled lantana, listening to the embers pop.

"Nothin' to salvage," he said after a while. And then, looking her nakedness up and down, "Warm enough?"

Part of her wanted to say "fuck you," what with the man smell and the pigskin stink, but she managed to keep her mouth shut.

"Got some food in my boat."

Her belly cramped at the word *food*, so she turned and looked at him for the first time.

He had a gray ponytail, a lean belly, and a pair of raggedy shorts that must have been white once. No underwear: Mandy could glimpse the crookedy dangle of a testicle.

Salt. That's the other smell. He's a paddler. She pulled the jacket tighter and grunted, "I guess I could eat." She fought some brief internal battle and then looked at him again. "Thanks."

"Hike back to the beach?" And then he seemed afraid he'd overstepped. "Or I could bring stuff up."

"Nah," she said, and turned toward the narrow canebrake trail that led down Kalalau Valley toward the ocean. "You saw the fire?" she asked, half-surprised she was talking to him. She shook her tangled hair out and tied it back, shimmying her bare butt as she went down the trail. *Why the hell am I doing that?* And then her grief over Shoshanna slammed back.

"Saw the smoke, and I'd heard about the rangers roustin' people, all up and down the Na Pali Coast. Tryin' t' make the world safe for tourists," he said. "How long were you livin' here?"

She stopped and handed him back his jacket. "What's your name?" she asked.

"Pranha," he said. "Wanna little bud?" He grubbed a small brass cylinder and wrinkled rolling papers out of his shorts.

"I'm Mandy. No, I don't smoke. Don't wear clothes much, either," she said, gesturing at the jacket. "But . . . I appreciate the help." The words tumbled out. She hadn't had much occasion to talk this last week.

They sat cross-legged when they reached the beach and ate Ry-Krisp and pineapple under the steady roar of the surf. The guy never sneaked a look at her snatch, not once. It was making her wet, wanting him to. *Gay,* she shrugged. *Ah, who gives a shit?*

The sun was already flattening on the horizon. "So, how long you been livin' in Kalalau?"

"Six years in Kauai, four years out here."

He tore open another packet of crackers and sized her up. Mandy was about as brown as a haole could get, long, tight-curled hair, jujube nipples, bodacious hips. Hippies like her lived all over the islands, in the remotest places. "From L.A.?"

She bristled. *What the fuck is it to you?* But she gave it up and said, "San Bernardino. Son-of-a-bitch husband, fucked-up job, too much dope and loud music. You?"

"Anaheim," he said, and they both snorted.

"My partner left," she said, pissed she'd said it as soon as the words were out.

"Where'd he go?"

"She," she said, testing. The guy didn't flinch. And even letting him know she was a lesbian didn't get him to look at her snatch.

He squinted. "What you plannin' on doing?"

Tears came. She jumped up and stalked away down the beach. When she came back at dusk, he had a tarp spread in the lee of some pandanus. He looked up. "I just roll up in it at night," he said. "Even tonight, that'll be warm enough. Join me if you want, no hassles."

She stomped off again but returned before full dark. A shama thrush was weaving its fluted music with the slow beat of the surf.

"No sex," he agreed. It was funny—the guy had hardly any male vibes. He raised the edge of the tarp to invite her in; his nakedness startled her for a moment, then she lay down, naked herself, and he folded the tarp over them. She flung an arm over his chest, challenging him with her eyes. It was good to hold a body, even if it wasn't Shoshanna's. Even if it was a man's.

Mandy woke curled tight around Pranha. He was deep in sleep, mouth open, breath rattling in his throat. He had an erection. She fingered its length, amused at the heat of it, moved by the slow pulse along its underside. Men. Horny even when they're asleep, for Chrissakes. And then she remembered Shoshanna again, the way she'd taken her by the shoulders that very first night—her first woman—and kissed her till they almost fell over. She remembered the sureness and force as her hand went between Shoshanna's legs, and the sounds she brought out of her . . . and Mandy, lying with a strange man, felt the familiar knife of her wanting.

Salt tears spilled over Pranha's sleeping shoulder. She gripped his cock until his arousal faded, and, after, kept him cupped tiny in her hand until sleep reclaimed her.

In the morning Pranha said he was splitting. "You can come," he said. He gestured at his weathered kayak with its homemade outrigger and tattered sail wound around a jerry-rigged mast.

"Where're you headed?"

"Around to Hanapepe."

"I hate that side of the island, Hanapepe and Lihue and all the fucking tourists. I've got friends in Hanalei. I might go there, I guess, if you were going."

"Well . . ." Pranha looked doubtful. "The trades are pretty fresh. Be rough headin' that way. Big seas."

Mandy looked at the kayak, its red deck bleached mottled-pink from the sun. Bags of gear were stuffed around the seats in the two narrow cockpits. A scratched marijuana-leaf decal fanned over the bow; a tattered rainbow flag hung on the mast. In that moment, she was overwhelmed by the need to leave Kalalau, to get away from the smell of guava, the memories of Shoshanna, the ashes of her home. The ocean had a sharp tang, urgent, like freedom, and the wind teased her breasts. "If you'll go to Hanalei, I'll go with you. I don't care about the waves."

He reached for his salt-stiffened shorts and pulled them on self-consciously while she eyed the ungainly flapping of his cock. "We could try," he said.

She stood up, showing him her muscled belly, her smooth, solid biceps. "I'm strong," she said. "I can paddle. I'll help you drag the boat down." For the first time, she caught him looking at her breasts.

Pranha looked up to the *pali*, where the snow was only a faint filigree now. He looked out to sea. Big rollers far out, their white backs churning in and out of view. He sat facing the breakers, chin on his knees. He rolled a joint, lit it, and sucked it deeply. After a while he turned and looked at the broad-hipped, naked woman, tear tracks and ash still dark on her cheeks. He took another long toke, studying the sea. "Okay," he said, letting the smoke out. He stashed the joint and stood.

As they dragged the boat to the surf line, Mandy challenged him. "How come you don't want sex with me?"

"You asked me not to."

"Bullshit."

He tested the lashings on the mast. "Anyway, it's not about you."

"Broken heart?" she said, a twist of recognition in her gut.

Pranha's callused, cracked fingers stroked the kayak's flank; he was not looking at her. He unclipped the spare paddle and offered it to her. "Too much of a hassle. All that shit. You can really paddle?"

Sometimes missing Shoshanna was like a knife. "Suppose I asked you to lick me. Would you?"

He was watching the ocean. "Look," he said, "we've got an easy set comin' in," and shoved the kayak bow first into the surge.

They smashed through three big breakers and found themselves at sea. Mandy was breathless with the effort. The water was a fierce dark blue, and the wind, a scant hundred yards offshore, was fiercer. She craned back to look at him, licking the salt from her lips. "I didn't know it'd be blowing so hard. Is this okay?"

"Paddle. We gotta stay in close, under the *pali*. Farther out it's really blowing. Up at Ke'e there'll be fifteen-foot swells. Mandy?"

Over her shoulder, she raised an eyebrow at him.

"If you wanted, I'd lick you." He looked her calmly in the eye when he said it, then looked away, over the water.

A knot of desire tied itself behind her pelvic arch, and then twisted tighter in refusal. Her old contempt for her husband bubbled up. "What're you, an angel of mercy?"

He was leaning hard into each stroke. He didn't look up.

"Or you've got herpes." Acid in her saliva bunched her jaw muscles. *I'll make this son of a bitch respond!*

His pale blue eyes came up to catch hers. "You lived alone much before this?"

It was hard to paddle and keep looking back at him. As the water dried on her bare flesh, the sun began to warm her. She softened her voice. "You had a hard-on last night. I touched a man for the first time in . . . I don't know. Ten years. I kind of hate men. I held you for a couple of hours, I guess, and it made me horny." Sometimes thinking about Shoshanna, about stumbling on her in the little bakery in Kilauea, about kissing her woman's softness, made her feel the knife actually ripping her gut. She raised her gray eyes to Pranha.

"Shit," he said, his eyes wide.

It took her a long minute to realize he wasn't talking to her. She turned, and a dark wall of water was rushing at her. It tore the paddle from her hands and buried her. Deep. The sea forced its way into her stomach, bitter and flat. In the roar of the water, something in the boat groaned, a long, wrenching groan, and the sea spun her over and over, trapped in the cockpit.

Somehow she squirmed free and, after kicking toward the light for far too long a time, broke the surface. She spat salt, cursing and coughing. The kayak wallowed belly up. One outrigger had snapped; the other had wrenched loose from the pontoon, which was now attached to the boat by only two fragile lines. The mast with its furled sail tipped over a downwind swell and vanished. "Hey!" she yelled, and then she remembered his name. "Pran-HA! Hey!"

"I'm here," he said, and she discovered him clinging to the stern a few feet behind her.

"What the hell! What do we do?" She was still coughing up water.

"Boost the stern and drain her. Then the bow. If we're lucky, we get enough water out to right her." His calmness pissed her off.

"Are we okay?"

"Dunno."

"What the fuck does that mean?"

"Well, we've got one paddle and we can rerig the pontoon. Maybe by the time we get paddlin' again we won't be too far offshore to get back."

"Get back to fucking where?"

"That's Kauai," he said, gesturing into the driving wind. He waved downwind. "And that's the Marianas. Thousand miles. We probably don't wanna go that way."

They paddled until dark, passing the paddle back and forth as they tired. Pranha guessed they were three miles out, losing the battle to regain Kauai. He shrugged and took inventory: three boxes of crackers, a hand of bananas, and a scant gallon of water.

The trades blew all night, and they paddled into them. The good news, at dawn, was that they weren't any farther offshore. The bad news was that they were exhausted. Their hands were blistered and brine-soaked, bleeding.

Mandy squirmed around and knelt in her seat facing Pranha. *What's it take to get through to this hippie hermit?* "We're not going to have sex, are we?"

"Still thinkin' about sex out here? You're not doing so bad." His tired face creased into a smile.

"I don't want to die alone, I guess."

He paddled in silence for several minutes, then braced the paddle and guided them over a roller. He reached from the stern cockpit until they could clasp their swollen, raw hands. "Me neither. I just didn't know that till a coupla minutes ago."

It wasn't easy to talk, but in bits and pieces they told each other about themselves. Mandy shared her grief over Shoshanna, her anger about men and shit jobs and L.A. She told about her four years of love, and yoga, and the crazy, intense woman-sex that just made her hungrier—about no clothes and all the guavas anybody could ever eat. Pranha watched her luminous eyes, her mobile, too-large mouth as she twisted half toward him in the bow cockpit. When she was through, he talked about his world. "I said sex was too much hassle," he said. "But everything's a hassle. Look," he said after a pause, "if we get outta this . . ."

"If we get to shore," Mandy grinned, "I'm gonna jump your bones. I'm gonna fuck you till you holler. I'm gonna make you hump me like a cocker spaniel. I'm gonna suck your weenie half off just to prove I'm not prejudiced and then I'm gonna stuff your head in my snatch for at least three hours. And then I'm gonna kick your ass. Shut up and pass the paddle. You look like shit."

As he leaned forward, she glimpsed a full erection pushing from the fringe of his shorts. Cock, mouth, fingers: it didn't matter how she got it done. She wanted a beating heart laid against hers. She closed her eyes and let arousal take her, let it invade her exhaustion, grateful to be thrumming like this even in the middle of the fucking goddamn ocean.

The shark came at midday, a fin thirty feet out, circling, then sliding under the waves.

"What'll we do?" Mandy's diaphragm wouldn't let her breathe.

"I dunno. It's a mako, I think. If it bumps us, try t' hit it in the nose with the paddle or your fist. They say that makes 'em go away."

"Hit a shark with my fist?!"

Pranha raised a tired arm. "Either that, or it breaks up the boat, maybe, and eats us."

After a few hours it disappeared, and exhaustion hit full force. Mandy slumped in the forward cockpit and went unconscious. She woke later, confused, guilty that she hadn't been paddling. Head on the deck, she stared blankly at the water, only gradually realizing that she was looking into a single small, unblinking eye inches below the surface. She jolted upright.

"Go easy." It was Pranha, behind her. "It's just hanging out in the shade of the boat. Don't do anything weird."

The shark, an arm's length away, was nearly as long as the kayak. "Hey," she said to Pranha in a small voice, "I'm not thinking about sex anymore." But she was. *Sand under my back. Pranha on top of me, fucking me. No—Shoshanna, and I'm on top. She calls my name. I dig my fingers into the earth to hold us safe.* The shark's unmoving eye made her want to touch herself. To come. To do any fucking thing but be there skewered by that cold gaze.

That second night, under the stars, they could no longer see the shark, and that was worse. Thirst clogged their throats, made it hard to talk.

The wind had slacked off with nightfall. By the time the Southern Cross inched over the horizon, the sea was nearly windless. Past pain, they paddled until their arms would no longer lift from the deck, then traded off. By midnight the island had risen, cutting off more of the northeastern sky. The paddle bit into the phosphorescent water, stroke after stroke. After long hours, the Cross sank behind them and first light grew ahead. The swells lifted, glassy smooth. The *pali* showed detail now: the slash of canyons, pale cliffs, forest.

Three tropic birds flew low over their bow. Mandy wanted to call to them, lovely in the pearly light, but she couldn't speak. Pranha nudged the paddle against her back. She took it and began to stroke.

"Mandy."

She could only paddle, voiceless.

"Mandy. We're gonna make it. Follow the shore. We can put in at Ke'e. Go in close while we can: the wind's gonna come back."

When sun touched the water around them, they were just outside the breakers, under the unbroken rise of the *pali*. They could hear birdsong ashore. The shark circled once, soundless, then sank into the depths. Salt rasped and itched in every fold of their skin.

It took another hour to reach the reef off Ke'e. Pranha found the entrance and they rode a last big swell into the lagoon. The water swirled turquoise under them, darting with fish. *About fucking time*, she thought, tears welling up again. When they beached, their legs wouldn't support them; clutching each other, they fell onto the sand.

The first tourists appeared at midmorning. Pranha sat up. His eyes and lips were salt rimed, white against his sunburnt skin. "Now who looks like shit?" he said, and she wanted to laugh at him—with him—but her belly muscles were too tired to force out a sound. "C'mon," he said, "I know a place we can sleep."

They staggered together past the cinder-block restrooms, stopping to fill Pranha's jug with water. By the trash cans, some picnicker had dumped a six-pack of soda. Pranha grappled it into the crook of an arm. He led her to a small, fern-fringed clearing. They drank all six sodas and most of the water, then crumpled into each other's arms.

When Mandy woke, late sun was slanting through the leaves of a breadfruit tree, and Pranha was still in her arms. She wanted to caress him, as much for herself as for any pleasure he might find in it, but her hands were unusable, paddles at the ends of leaden arms, stiff with blood and salt.

She looked at Pranha, sun scalded and raw, sunk in sleep that seemed close to the edge of a coma. Naked herself, she ran her eyes over the male body, clothed only in its disreputable shorts. Awkwardly, she pried the button loose on the shorts and tugged them off him.

Jesus. What am I doing? Every muscle ached. Her long dark hair was stiff and filthy. Two days of sunburn had seared her face, made the breeze unbearable on her tender breasts. *My hands are a mess!* It'd be days before she could use them. But she hungered to touch this man. She wanted his cock. The need to anchor herself in another body was stronger than any anger she still held, stronger than any particular missing.

She bent over him. She licked, and recoiled at the bitter sea grit dissolving on her tongue. She licked again, and found it easier. And again, until she could pull him into her mouth.

He was small and unaroused—beyond arousal, maybe—but it didn't matter. She tongued the convolutions of his cock head, round and round, finding a rhythm for sore muscles and stiff face. She knelt clumsily, her useless hands palms up on her knees, bowed over him. She lost herself in sucking.

She began to tug, stretching him out rubbery and thin, searching out the cords and vessels with her tongue. She let her breath spill into his nest of hair and inhaled the smell that came back from him.

With the back of a hand she stroked his chest and lean belly. This brought his first response: he swelled in her mouth and at last became hard. She looked up. He was watching. She bobbed on him, grinning with her eyes. It was evening, and birds were singing again. *Who-ee! I'm going to do you, boy!*

He braced an arm under his head, observing. Over a long, aimless time as she sucked, he softened, then swelled again. She ran her tongue tip down the bitter-salt midline of his scrotum and it tightened. She sucked harder on his cock, and his hips followed her. His mouth gaped.

After a while his arms canted out as if he were being crucified. His head arched back and the taste of him changed in her mouth. The long muscles in his legs took up a heavy shaking. His body lifted, bridged between his heels and the back of his neck. He hung like that as she devoured him, bent above him as if in prayer. *Follow me, boy. Fly!*

"Wait," he rasped, his voice salt scalded. "Wait."

"What? What's wrong?" Mandy pulled away.

His voice failed and he could only mouth the words: *Let . . . me.*

He twisted and thrust his face into her sex. She flooded with moisture, her own scent coiling up to her nostrils: brine and musk and exhaustion. His tongue searched her, his blue eyes holding hers from the thicket of her black bush. The furry insistence of his beard made the cords in her thighs ache.

She jammed his shorts under his head for a pillow and fell against his mouth, whispering wordlessly. Braced on her knuckles, oblivious to the pain in her hands and shoulders, she humped. His face rolled and twisted under her, his eyes shut tight now, worshipping. She locked her thighs against his ribs.

Yeah. Her back straightened. She couldn't contain her climax. It ballooned until it was bigger, somehow, than her body, stretching her bones, filling her mouth with a wavering music. *Please!* She rode so high on his face . . . *please fucking please* . . . she was afraid she'd suffocate him . . . *please* . . . but nothing could stop her now, nothing. *Yeah! Yeah!*

Coming was like drowning. *No, like being pitched into the fucking sun. Like burning down around myself.* Something far back in her called, *Shoshanna!* And she fell face-first to the ground.

Long after, she searched out Pranha's face. His pale eyes waited, solemn. She saw loops of semen strung over his chest, already thinning and beginning to run. *A man*, she thought. It didn't matter. She opened her mouth over his. His hand clamped the back of her neck and crushed her closer.

As the swift tropical night flooded through the palm grove, he hobbled to the boat and brought his tarp. They slept.

The third morning he searched out a long-tailed shirt from among his gear, decent enough, they thought, for her to face civilization. The cloth clung alien and imprisoning, harsh from the sea. They hid the kayak in the ferns, limped to the road, and hung out their thumbs. *Shit*, she thought, *I'm back.*

A rattling island car picked them up. After they disappeared toward Hanalei, the narrow road lay empty for a long time. Breakers boomed on the reef. Small waves lapped the coral sand and sighed back into the wide salt of the sea.

෨ RATATOUILLE ෨

Susannah Indigo

"MILES, DID YOU KNOW THAT ZUCCHINIS make the best cocks?" Isabelle asked me this on our very first date. She twirled her angel hair pasta and looked fondly at the veggie stabbed on the end of her fork.

She got my attention. I tried to guess at a good response. Isabelle had long, wavy red hair and dancer's legs, and there wasn't much I wouldn't have considered for her.

"Better than cucumbers?" I asked as though we were discussing favorite recipes over the back fence.

She laughed. "Hell, yes. Better than men, sometimes. Better than vibrators always. No batteries, and organic."

I was speechless. I had watched Isabelle pass by my office for weeks on the way to the dance studio before I found the nerve to ask her out. I was developing a serious navy blue leg-warmer fetish by the time I stepped into the hall and blurted out my name and invited her to dinner.

"Sure, Miles," she said. "But it has to be vegetarian for me, okay?"

She looked so pure and angelic with that pale white skin and the sprinkling of freckles across her nose. I researched every health food restaurant in town.

"Organic is good," I finally answered her at dinner, feeling like a sixteen-year-old kid on his first date instead of the lawyer I was. "Do you peel the zucchini?" I had to know.

"Sometimes," she answered. "But sometimes rougher is better, you know?"

I decided right then that it might be possible to fall in love with a girl who said "you know?" all the time, and who wore heavy silver rings and bracelets that weighed her down. Her bracelets that looked like handcuffs on her delicate wrists.

I took her home to her tiny walk-up apartment at the top of an old building not far from Coors Field. "This neighborhood is not safe," I told her.

She just laughed at me. "Life is not safe, darling."

She was right, of course. There's hardly any safety in hating what you do every day for a living. When I chose law school over art, I didn't know the difference between financial security and being safe.

She invited me in and lit six black candles all around the room "Six," she informed me, "is the sacred number of Aphrodite, the goddess of love." She served me hot tea on an elegant silver tray and looked straight into my eyes.

"A girl has to have rules, you know," she said. " I never have full sex with a man until the third date." She smiled. "By then I can always tell if they're fuckable or not."

I was thirty-seven years old and a man of the world when she said this, and I swear I couldn't remember ever having had sex before in my life, or if I even knew how.

"That sounds fair," I mumbled, smoothing my hair.

She excused herself and went to the bathroom. I sneaked a look in her fridge while she was gone. Never before had a crisper looked so sexy. I counted the zucchinis—there were six. All in a row.

She came back, her hair tied up. She pressed one of her strong legs next to mine on the futon. Without a word, she picked up a jar of honey from the tea tray, stuck her finger into it, and smeared honey all over her lips. Honey over lipstick, honey around her mouth, honey on her tongue, never taking her eyes off mine.

She stopped. "Kiss me, Miles. Kiss me until all my honey is gone."

Dear God. I started to lick and then I was devouring her. Nothing else existed but Isabelle and her mouth. Long, soulful kisses that went on forever, or maybe it was just one kiss that kept inventing itself over and over and over until I thought her rules were a tease. My hand was high on her thigh and my cock was ravenous. She paused and whispered, "You kiss like a man who is hungry. This is a good thing." And then she kicked me out the door.

I bought her things. I showed up for the second date with flowers and candy and a gift of tiny, delicate crystal ballet slippers that reminded me of her.

She was wearing a shiny white leotard, the kind with long sleeves that looked as if it would fall off her shoulders at any minute, the kind you can see nipples through in the right light, and a long, swirling, deep-blue skirt that made me want to lift it and bend her over and fuck her hard and fast.

But it was only the second date, and rules are rules.

"Are you a natural redhead?" I asked, admiring her hair.

"You'll never know, darling. Don't you know that dancers wax everywhere but their heads?" She laughed and lifted her skirt, slid the leotard aside and twirled and flashed me the loveliest bare pussy I will ever see in my life.

And then she led me out the door to the theater.

We saw *Cats*. She made me. She kept my hand high on her thigh under her skirt the whole time. I was wrong: *Cats* is a wonderful show.

Back at her place, she asked if I was hungry. I believe the exact words were "What are you hungry for?"

The possibilities raced through my head. "Oh, something vegetarian," I said, still trying to impress.

Her eyes lit up. "I have tons of fresh veggies in my crisper. Let's marinate some of them before we cook."

She took me into the kitchen. We peeled. Two zucchinis, three carrots, a handful of mushrooms, and a large, purple onion. "The living room is better for this," she whispered when we were finished with our plate.

Lavender-scented candles, incense, the aroma of fresh zucchini—these smells will stay with me all of my life. She turned on the music, stretched out on the tiny rug on the hardwood floor, took off her leotard, and lifted that blue skirt around her waist. She asked me if I wanted to watch or to help. I could barely move; I said I would love to watch her. I touched the pale skin high between her thighs and petted her gently as if she were a kitten; she closed her eyes and threw back her head and showed me possibilities I didn't know existed. She loved that vegetable as if it were a cock, stroking herself with it, rubbing it slowly around her clit, entering her pussy slowly, so slowly, in and out, teasing herself, and finally fucking herself hard—my cock beat to her rhythm; I came in my pants as if I was fifteen again. She was lying back on the floor and I kissed her pussy, I kissed that cock, and I kissed her legs from thigh to ankle over and over again.

And then we cooked.

Stir-fry veggies over tomato-basil pasta; peppermint tea; fortune cookies. It was an extraordinary meal—I suspect it was the special sauce. "You will attend a royal banquet and meet your first lover," my fortune cookie said, and I knew I just had.

Isabelle changed into a little-girl flannel nightgown and took me into her bed. We slept. No sex. The trust implicit in this act is overwhelming. I never touched her except to hold her tight.

In the morning we started again. "Carrots just don't quite work, you know?" she said. "Too thin. But they have some uses. Eggplants and tomatoes and onions and peppers all have uses sometimes, too." She told me that her practice was as old as the *Kama Sutra*: "How else do you think all those women in the harems got satisfied? Hell, that book even goes into using the root of the sweet potato! Sometimes," she confessed, blushing, "I go out with something inside me, to a quiet place, like the museum. It makes you think about sex all day. Melon balls are my favorite—kind of like an organic set of Ben Wa balls."

If this was foreplay, I wasn't sure I was ready for full sex. I went to see her dance on the third date. She was beautiful. We went back to her place, and I lit the candles and the incense this time.

"I'm yours tonight," she whispered. "You've passed. What would you like?"

I was ready. What else could a man want? "I want you to love me, to worship me just like you did with that zucchini."

She undressed me while I stood there, knelt in front of me, and began. It all came back to me in that moment, why sex is the most important thing in the world. She kissed my feet and then she worked her way up, taking forever, kissing and licking my balls, and holding them gently in her mouth. Talking to me, saying things, telling me how good I tasted, telling me how much she wanted me inside her, how much she needed to ride me hard. She took my cock deep into her throat all at once. There were no rules, or they were only my rules, and she was mine and I was lying back and holding her small hips and lifting her up onto my cock and driving into her hard and fast. The world stopped; that was all I knew— that she could make the outside world stop and take me back to where I belonged. She came for me over and over, before I stopped and took her long hair in my fist and held her still for a minute.

"Do you want to please me?" I whispered, knowing that she did, knowing that this girl lived for sex and that I could give her what she needed.

"God, yes," she whispered, nodding.

"Turn over."

I owned her. I fucked every part of her body, and she begged for more. I couldn't quite imagine matching her sexual imagination, but I discovered I could more than match her desire. When my cock was finally deep in her ass and my own vision of heaven was high on the horizon, I suddenly knew: I knew this was it and this girl was going to change my life. I didn't tell her this; I thought there would be time later.

I don't believe we slept that night. But I do know that I never let her near the kitchen.

I started drawing again. I sketched her constantly. I still have some of the drawings—*Isabelle in Iceberg* is my favorite one, framed on my wall. Even though she swore the lettuce just didn't do a thing for her.

I stopped eating meat. Isabelle—her name in my mouth was better than any sirloin in town.

I went dancing with her. I don't dance. Little clubs that nobody my age had ever heard of; dark entrances, pounding music, Isabelle twirling and twirling, and always coming back to my arms.

She let me go to the beauty parlor with her and watch her get waxed all over. I only went because she told me she loved it, loved the pain, loved the discipline of it all. "Discipline is everything," she told me.

I would ask her to show me her pussy and she would. Anytime. She danced for me whenever I wanted. I wouldn't call it stripping, but I guess that's what it was. And the world would stop one more time.

But when I wasn't with her, she would rarely answer her phone. I just knew she was in bed with a zucchini, and I couldn't stand it. She'd see me once a week—that was all—and I knew the girl fucked herself every day.

I got stupid like men do. I followed her—saw her at the produce stand, watched her dancing through the studio window, saw her go out with friends and then go home alone. I knew there was no other man. When I asked her, she told me she'd been in love once and that was enough.

She liked me; I knew she did. And then I realized the problem. It still pains me to admit it. She preferred her vegetables over me, just as she told me on that first date. How on earth can a man compete with an edible cock?

I couldn't get past once a week. Summer was running down and I wanted Isabelle in my bed every night. She wasn't a tease. There was no game. God, how she could fuck. Some nights she would lift her skirt and wiggle her ass onto my lap, pressing down hard on my cock before we'd even go out. She'd tell me how much she needed my cock. "It's my real kink," she confessed, "just being penetrated. Everywhere."

I tried to force the issue. I asked her outright what the story was, why we couldn't spend more time together. "Trust all joy," she'd say mysteriously, and she'd wrap her hair around my cock and then take me in her throat until I forgot even what the question was. "You taste wonderful since you stopped eating meat," she'd whisper after she'd swallowed and licked me clean. "You taste like cinnamon, you taste like a perfect cup of hot chocolate on a cold winter night."

Somehow I knew this was true and nobody had ever noticed it before. Saturday nights were heaven. By Tuesday I'd be going crazy. I moaned, I fretted. I knew I was driving her nuts with my demands, but I couldn't stop. I studied myself in the mirror and contemplated my fuckability factor. When you're in competition with a vegetable, every little bit helps.

Other women called me and I simply had no interest. "Isabelle"—her name in my mouth was more appealing than any onion.

What could I do? Move her to the country and give her a farm? Buy out a local produce stand? I couldn't imagine. I studied her apartment. All she owned was cheap furniture, beautiful candles and scarves, and one shelf each of music and books. "I used to own a lot more," she told me when I asked, "but now I read a book and then just pass it on to a friend for their pleasure. The same with music—I pass it on." There were no clues about how to get to her.

I got stupider. I bribed her grocer to tell me every single thing she bought each trip. Six-inch zucchinis, bunches of carrots, scallions . . . scallions? I had to do something.

One Saturday night, late in August, I tried joining forces with the produce. I used them to fuck her every which way. It was hot, it was satisfying, but I was still relegated to Saturday night. I knew I'd never make it another week without her. I laid out a plan for Tuesday night: I would simply show up, lock the door, and clean out her fridge. I knew if I could spend enough time with her I could somehow make her replace her veggie vice with me. I knew I could measure up: I'd spent a night with a rule and a tape measure back near the beginning of stupid.

I knocked on her door that Tuesday night and there was no answer. It pushed open easily. Isabelle was gone. No books, no candles, no music. I could picture her in front of me twirling and laughing in that blue skirt; but when I reached out to touch her, there was nothing but ordinary space. I believe I stood there for close to forever; the world may have even stopped for me one last time.

I checked the fridge. It was empty except for one zucchini, with a note wrapped around it: "I've gone on tour, darling," it said. "Pass it on."

ᙍ SWEATING PROFUSELY IN MÉRIDA ᙍ
A Memoir
Carol Queen

BOYFRIEND AND I MET AT A SEX PARTY. I was in a back room trying to help facilitate an erection for a gentleman brought to the party by a woman who would have nothing to do with him once they got there. She had charged him a pretty penny to get in, and I actually felt that I should have gotten every cent, but I suppose it was my own fault that I was playing Mother Teresa and didn't know when to let go of the man's dick. Boyfriend was hiding behind a potted palm eyeing me and this guy's uncooperative, uncut dick, and it seemed Boyfriend had a thing for pretty girls *and* uncut men, especially the latter. So he decided to help me out and replaced my hand with his mouth. That was when it got interesting. The uncut straight guy finally left and I stayed.

In the few months our relationship lasted, we shared many more straight men, most of them—Boyfriend's radar was incredible—uncircumcised and willing to do almost anything with a man as long as there was a woman in the room. I often acted as sort of a hook to hang a guy's heterosexuality on while Boyfriend sucked his dick or even fucked him. My favorite was the hitchhiker wearing pink lace panties under his grungy jeans—but that's another story. Long before we met him, Boyfriend had invited me to go to Mexico.

This was the plan. Almost all the guys in Mexico are uncut, right? And lots will play with men, too, Boyfriend assured me, especially if there's a woman there. (I guessed they resembled American men in this respect.) Besides, it would be a romantic vacation.

That was how we wound up in room 201 of the Hotel Reforma in sleepy Mérida, capital of the Yucatán. Mérida's popularity as a tourist town had been eclipsed by the growth of Cancún, the nearest American-ized resort. That meant the boys would be hornier, Boyfriend reasoned. The Hotel Reforma had been recommended by a fellow foreskin fancier. Its chief advantages were the price—about $14 a night—and the fact that the management didn't charge extra for extra guests. I liked it because it was old, airy, and cool, with wrought-iron railings and floor tiles worn thin from all the people who'd come before. Boyfriend liked it because it had a pool, always a good place to cruise, and a disco across the street. That's where we headed as soon as we got in from the airport, showered, and changed into skimpy clothes suitable for turning tropical boys' heads.

There were hardly any tropical boys there, as it turned out, because this was where the Ft. Lauderdale college students who couldn't afford spring break in Cancún went to spend their more meager allowances. Not only did it look like a Mexican restaurant-with-disco in Ft. Lauderdale, but the management took care to keep all but the most dapper Méridans out lest the coeds be frightened by scruffy street boys.

Scruffy street boys, of course, is just what Boyfriend had his eye out for, and at first the pickings looked slim; but we found one who had slipped past security, out to hustle nothing more spicy than a gig showing tourists around the warren of narrow streets near the town's central plaza, stumbling instead onto us. Ten minutes later Boyfriend had his mouth wrapped around a meaty little bundle, *with* foreskin. Luis stuck close to us for several days, probably eating more regularly than usual, and wondering out loud whether all the women in America were like me, and would we take him back with us? Or at least send him a Mötley Crüe T-shirt when we went home?

Boyfriend had brought Bob Damron's gay travel guide, which listed for Mérida: a cruisy restaurant (it wasn't) and a cruisy park bench in the Zócalo (it was, and one night Boyfriend stayed out most of the night looking for gay men, who, he said, would run the other way if they saw me coming, and found one, a slender boy who had to pull down the panty hose he wore under his jeans so Boyfriend could get to his cock, and who expressed wonder because he had never seen anyone with so many con-doms; in fact, most people never had condoms at all. Boyfriend gave him his night's supply and some little brochures about *el SIDA* he'd brought from the AIDS Foundation, *en español,* so even if our limited Spanish didn't get through to our tricks, a pamphlet might).

Damron's also indicated that Mérida had a bathhouse.

I had always wanted to go to a bathhouse, and of course there was not much chance it would ever happen back home. For one thing, they were all closed before I ever moved to San Francisco. For another, even if I dressed enough like a boy to pass, I wouldn't look old enough to be let in. But in Mérida perhaps things were different.

It was away from the town's center, but within walking distance of the Hotel Reforma. Through the tiny front window, grimy from the town's blowing dust, I saw a huge papier-mâché figure of Pan, painted brightly and hung with jewelry, phallus high. It looked like something the Radical Faeries would carry in the Gay Day parade. Everything else about the lobby looked dingy, like the waiting room of a used-car dealership.

Los Baños de Vapor would open at eight that evening. They had a central tub and rooms to rent; massage boys could be rented, too. I would be welcome.

The papier-mâché Pan was at least seven feet tall and was indeed the only bright thing in the lobby. Passing through the courtyard, an over-grown jumble of vines pushing through cracked tile, a slight smell of sul-fur, a stagnant fountain, we were shown up a flight of concrete stairs to our room by Carlos, a solid, round-faced man in his mid-twenties wrapped in a frayed white towel. The room was small and completely tiled, grout black from a losing fight with the wet tropical air. At one end was a shower and at the other a bench, a low, vinyl-covered bed, and a massage table. There was a switch that, when flipped, filled the room with steam. Boyfriend flipped it and we shucked our clothes; as the pipes hissed and clanked, Carlos gestured to the massage table and then to me.

Boyfriend answered for me, in Spanish, that I'd love to. I got on the table and Carlos set to work. Boyfriend danced around the table gleefully, sometimes stroking me, sometimes Carlos's butt.

"Hey, man, I'm working!" Carlos protested, not very insistently, and Boyfriend went for his cock, stroking it hard, then urged him up onto the table, and Carlos's hands, still slick from the massage oil and warm from the friction of my skin, covered my breasts as Boyfriend rolled a condom onto Carlos's cock and rubbed it up and down my labia a few times and finally let go, letting it sink in. He rode me slow and then hard while the table rocked dangerously and Boyfriend stood at my head, letting me tongue his cock while he played with Carlos's tits. When Boyfriend was sure that we were having a good time, he put on a towel and slipped out the door. Carlos looked surprised. I had to figure out how to say, in Spanish, "He's going hunting," and get him to go back to fucking me, solid body slick from oil and steam; if he kept it up, he would make me come, clutching his slippery back, legs in the air.

That was just happening when Boyfriend came back with David. He was pulling him in the door by his already-stiff penis, and I suspected Boyfriend had wasted as little time getting him by the dick as he usually did. He had found David in the tub room, he announced, and he had a beautiful, long, *uncut* cock. (Boyfriend always enunciated clearly when he said "uncut.") David *did* have a beautiful cock, and he spoke English and was long and slim, with startling blue eyes. It turned out he was Chicano, second generation, a senior at Riverside High who spent school breaks with his grandmother in Mérida and worked at Los Baños de Vapor as a secret summer job. We found out all this about him as I was showering the sweat and oil off from my fuck with Carlos, and by the time I heard that he'd been working at the Baños since he turned sixteen, I was ready to start fucking again. David was the most quintessentially eighteen-year-old fuck I ever had, except Boyfriend's presence made it unusual; he held David's cock and balls and controlled the speed of the thrusting, until his mouth got preoccupied with Carlos's dick. David told me, ardently, that I was beautiful, though at that point I didn't care if I was beautiful or not, since I was finally in a bathhouse doing what I'd always wanted to do and I felt more like a faggot than a beautiful *gringa*. But David was saying he wished he had a girlfriend like me, even though I was thirty, shockingly old—this actually was what almost all of Boyfriend's conquests said to me, though I suspected not every man could keep up with a girlfriend who was really a faggot, or a boyfriend who was really a woman, or whatever kind of fabulous anomaly I was.

Then someone knocked on the door and we untangled for a minute to answer it, and there were José and Gaspar, laughing and saying we were the most popular room in the Baños at the moment and would we like some more company? At least that's how David translated the torrent of Spanish, for they were both speaking at once. Naturally we invited them in, and lo and behold, Gaspar was actually *gay*, and so while José fucked me, I could watch Boyfriend finally getting *his* cock sucked by Gaspar, whose black, glittering Mayan eyes closed in concentration, and I howled with not simply orgasm but the *excitement*, the splendid excitement of being in Mexico in a bathhouse with four uncut men and a maniac, a place no woman I knew had gone before. Steam swirled in the saturated air like superheated fog, beading like pearls in the web of a huge Yucatán spider in the corner; David's cock, or was it José's or Carlos's again, I didn't care, pounded my fully opened cunt rhythmically and I wished I had her view.

You know if you have ever been to a bathhouse that time stands still in the steamy, throbbing air, and so I had no idea how long it went on, only that sometimes I was on my back and sometimes on my knees, and once for a minute I was standing facing the wall, and when Boyfriend wasn't sucking them or fucking me, he was taking snapshots of us, just like a tourist. The floor of the room was completely littered with condoms, which made us all laugh hysterically. Rubber-kneed, I was held up by Gaspar and David, with Carlos and José flanking them so Boyfriend could snap one last picture. Then he divided all the rest of the condoms among them—we had more at the hotel; I think that week we went through ten dozen—and got out his brochures. He was trying to explain in Spanish the little condoms he used for giving head—how great they were to use with uncut guys 'cause they disappeared under the foreskin—and I was asking David what it was like to live a double life, Riverside High to Los Baños, and who else came there—"Oh, everybody does," he said—and did they ever want to fuck him—of course they *wanted* to—and did he ever fuck them—well, sure—and how was that? He shrugged and said, as if there were only one possible response to my question, "It's *fucking*."

When we left, the moon was high, the Baños deserted, the warm night air almost cool after the steamy room. The place looked like a court-yard motel, the kind I used to stay in with my parents when we traveled in the early sixties, but overgrown and haunted. The Pan figure glittered in the low lobby light, and the man at the desk charged us about $35— $7 for each massage boy, $4 each to get in, and $6 for the room. Hundreds of thousands of pesos—he looked anxious, as though he feared we'd think it was too much. We paid him, laughing. I wondered if this was how a Japanese businessman in Thailand felt. Was I contributing to the imperial-ist decline of the third world? Boyfriend didn't give a shit about things like that, so I didn't mention it. In my hand was a crumpled note from David: "Can I come visit you in your hotel room? No money."

꧁ GOD'S GIFT ꧂

Salome Wilde

ONCE UPON A TIME, everybody and their kid sister knew me as Vance
"the Razor" Razz—front man for God's Gift, the Metal Monsters of the
Midwest. From "Razor Roar," a howl-like guitar solo of its own, to "Gettin'
It Good," our eighteen-minute-long anthem that tore the house down at
every college campus we played.

We rocked like no one else—longer and harder and deeper than any
band had a right to. Add "Lovin' Lisa" to all that, a ballad so soulful that
RockinAss.com called it a "triumph of mood over melody," and you see
why we got more and better pussy than Zeppelin and Van Halen put
together. We spent money like there was no tomorrow, on everything from
Harleys to hookers. We destroyed hotel rooms and chicks' reputations with
a speed and sureness that, until the day I died, made me certain that God
didn't exist.

But then I croaked, and I learned that heaven and hell may be myths,
but divine retribution is a bitch.

I know The Bitch best of all because I was there. Over the course
of twenty years, I had hundreds of women, a handful of curable STDs, a
couple of guys who sucked my dick through a glory hole, and one dude
that I swear I thought was a chick—even when I was fucking him in the
ass at that Peoria hotel. I devoted myself to my cause: to rock harder, and
fuck more women, better than any other man ever had, would, or could.

After my very first time with Jinny Moss on a picnic table behind Dairy Queen at thirteen—when I came after four strokes—I began strenuous training. Sixteen-year-old Jinny liked my long hair and said she wanted to be the first one to do me so when I became a rock star she could tell all her friends she took my virginity. I was only too happy to give it away, while thoughts of superstardom flashed through my mind. I don't know if it was her energetic writhing, or my fantasy of screaming into a microphone while a sea of fans screamed back, that brought me off so fast. But it was fast. Too fast.

After that, I changed my ways. Instead of images of me on stage, which made me come too easily, I began to write lyrics in my head every time I fucked. Until I came up with at least one Grammy Award–Winning line, I wouldn't let go.

Sometimes it was tough being a teenager with hormones raging: anything with tits got me hard. But I was dedicated. As I made my way through most of the available girls in my neighborhood, my high school, and anywhere else I could meet them—through friends, in church, at the movies, wherever—it got easier. I got better and better at good, long fucks and wrote some of the best songs of my too-short career.

Of course, I admit I cheated sometimes. I'd fuck some really ugly girl just to improve my time. No danger of losing it with flat-chested acne cases or fat wallflowers, but the lameness of the lay sometimes inspired awesome lyrics.

Yeah, I did them all, indiscriminately, right through my twenties. Never got any complaints. Never bothered with foreplay: why get a blow job when you can drive it home and take your sweet time getting there? A couple of them did try to get me to lick their pussies—but *please*. I'm not one of those assholes that thinks twats smell like fish—but it's a good, hard fuck they all need.

It's not like chicks have orgasms. Not real ones. I took them just as they were, gave them the fucking of their lives, and came up with blistering lines like "Baby tried to call me back / But I'm just a one-time jack." Life was good.

But good things come to an end, and that brings me to the hellish bitch of God's reeking vengeance. I died, right before spewing, on my thirty-third birthday.

It was the night that blond chick was in the front row, flashing her perfect DDs at me at the University of Iowa gig. I'd pulled her up on stage for a song and given her a backstage pass. We did it in the break room, after the encore. She was grinding away beneath me, pushing up her hips and trying to get her hand between us—totally annoying.

And then it happened: unbelievable chest pain. I keeled over and died on top of her.

I remember lying there, my cock going flaccid and my breath leaving my body in a rush. I didn't get to come, and, worse, I can't remember the line I was working on. Something about "class," where it meant both school and a really rich chick. Great lyric, lost forever.

I knew for certain that I was dead; everything went black. What could've been five minutes or five years later, I awoke. But I wasn't where *I* had been, and I wasn't exactly *me* anymore. I couldn't see; I couldn't move. I tried to belt out a few lines of "Mad Town Mix-Up," but I couldn't make a sound. I felt my body being lifted, like a baby, into someone's hands. Reincarnation, I guessed, but I still knew I was me. It didn't make sense.

I felt an odd twitch in my side. It was as if I'd been clicked on like a light switch. My whole body began to vibrate. It was bizarre, not being able to see or move, and just buzzing like that. I felt the top of my head being pressed against something soft, warm, and wet. *Poontang!* I knew what it was immediately, but I couldn't see or smell it. I wanted to whip out my cock, dive in deep, and ride that warm, wet hole to the strains of Nick "Ratman" Armstrong's killer guitar.

But I couldn't do it. I was just this immobile thing pressed between those pussy lips, not even inside her twat. The frustration was wicked. I was moved back and forth a bit, but mostly I was just held there in place, vibrating, unable to get inside or pull away.

Her beaver got hot—fiery hot—swollen and sticky wet. Ready for action. I'd never felt a chick get like that before. I was always interested in getting into the party, not standing in the doorway, if you know what I mean. The guitar riff was still blaring in my head, but I never got in the door. I was wild for a fuck, but that pussy only got more and more ripe as I buzzed away. It was amazing, in its own freaky way, but the damn hum in my head kept me from concentrating. I couldn't hump and I couldn't write. My head ached until that gash was spread, sloppy, and cashed. A quivering pulse in her pussy was the only thing that let me know the chick was still alive.

Suddenly, I was yanked away. The switch in my side shut off. I stopped vibrating, and was dropped onto a mattress. A few minutes later, I was lifted again and shoved into a dark space. I'd never been so wound up in my life—afterlife—whatever.

I spend my days now coping with head buzz and that insatiable hunger for unpenetrated snatch. God played his little joke on me. Me, who wrote more songs than John Frikkin' Lennon. Me, who screwed more women in his measly thirty-three years than most guys who live to be a hundred. Me, reduced to a toy for some chick who can never seem to figure out that what she really needs is a good, hard fuck. Not that I could give it to her anymore, but shit—there must be *some* guy out there who can.

RED LIGHT, GREEN LIGHT

Shanna Germain

THE ROOM IS SMALL, more like a storage space with a huge front window. It's hidden from the street by a red velvet curtain. Another curtain divides this space—which holds only a tall wooden chair and a mirror—from the back area, which has a bed, another chair, another mirror, and a table with a lamp. The air smells like sex and old silk flowers. But everything's clean—nicer than I expected—with fresh sheets and clean floors.

I wonder how much Danny had to fork over to rent this window. I hope it wasn't more than a hundred euros or so, since I'm not likely to make the money back for him. I know if I asked him, he'd just shake his head and say, "You should never ask how much a gift cost, Luce." He'd run a hand through my blond hair, give my earlobe a tug. "That's why it's a gift."

It's a gift I've been wanting since Danny and I came to Amsterdam the first time, almost five years ago. Since the first time we walked these red-rimmed streets, hand in hand, watching the women in their rented windows. Some knocked on the glass at the men going by, others were putting their lipstick on in little mirrors, as though they were sitting alone in their bedrooms, oblivious to the men roving the street. Men swept by us, their hungry eyes on the windows, on the women in their string bikinis and high heels. "I want that," I'd whispered, tugging on Danny's hand, not daring to believe that he'd understand what I was asking. Never daring to believe that he would deliver.

Now I grab a handful of the heavy curtain and peel it back just enough to see onto the street. The district's famous red lights are already out and twinkling, even though the sky is still an evening gray. A window directly across the way is already open. Behind it, a leggy woman with a black bob sits on a chair just like the one I have, her legs crossed demurely, her chest barely covered by a slip of fabric. Against the black light, her white skin looks mushroom pale, the fabric a ghostly green. Already men crowd around her window. The backs of their heads are bathed in red light.

I look for Danny, but I don't see him. I know he's watching from somewhere. That was part of the gift. That he would watch. That he would let me see him watching.

It's nearly time. I go into the back room to strip off my jeans and sweater. I don't know why—it's not like anyone can see through the curtain in the front room. Maybe I just need this one final moment of privacy before I put my body in that window for everyone to see. It's been eight years of marriage since anyone besides Danny has seen my body. Now the whole world will.

I slide into the maroon lace panties and corset—another gift—and slip on my highest black heels. I take a peek at myself in the mirror. The glass is old, and my face wavers in the uneven surface. But it gives me a good idea of how I look. Long blond hair down around my shoulders, dark red fabric contrasting with my pale skin, and my nipples pressing through little holes in the lace. I let my breath out in a rush and run my hand down my belly. It's flat when I'm standing, but I have no idea how it will look when I'm sitting down.

In the front room, the chair is hard, cold wood beneath me. I sit up straight, cross my legs, and put the black toe of my shoe against the window ledge. I take a deep breath, let it out slowly, and pull open the curtain.

Almost instantly, there are faces in front of the window. Men of all ages and colors. Eyes and eyes. I feel like a fish, or a mermaid. Some press their fingertips against the window, leaving dirty smears. Others mouth things at me. English and Spanish and a billion other languages. *Cunt. How much? Fuck you.* I am so grateful for the glass between us. I skim their red-lit faces, looking for Danny.

Some of the boys are obviously from the States—Yankees caps and jackets that say UCLA and Cornell. I skim over their pale faces. They're cute, but they're not what I want. With others, it's hard to tell. Black men with dreadlocks and knit caps, pale, older men in sharp suits and leaning on canes. The few women walk hand in hand, looking either uncomfortable or excited.

One man stops in front of my window—young, shoulder-length blond hair. He looks for a moment, passes on, perhaps to something more exotic, something darker or skinnier. Next to these exotic women, I look very American. Or maybe German, with my blond hair, green eyes, and come-hither hips. These other women, they have boobs the size of Texas. Not me—I'm all ass and hip and nipple. You could look all night, in all these windows, and not find the same body shape twice, I think. I could look all night, into this street, and not find the same man twice.

Another man, this one army-like in a crew cut and broad shoulders, steps through the crowd, up to the corner of my window. He knocks, hard enough to make the glass tremble. I shake my head. He steps back through the crowd.

I watch the street. I'll know when it's right. I've practiced my wink, my rap-rap on the glass with the back of my knuckles.

When I see him, he's already looking at me. Watching. He's got olive skin and dark, heavy eyebrows. Tall. A dark wool coat that looks like it was tailored just for him. He's alone, despite the packs of men moving around him. When I catch his eye, he doesn't hang his head. He looks those brown eyes right into me, like he's appraising a piece of art, as though he's been careful to choose just the right piece.

I almost look down at the ground. Almost.

Instead, I breathe in the scent of silk through my nose, let the corners of my lips curve up. I duck my head just a little, but keep my eyes on this man. I wink, and for some reason, I tap my toe against the glass, even though I know he can't see it.

He grins—beautiful double dimples on each cheek that send a shiver through my stomach—and takes a step forward. That's when I see Danny behind him, leaning against the railing that lines the canal. Watching me. The man is moving toward my window, but I keep my eyes on Danny, his grin barely visible in the red neon, while I draw the curtain.

I open the door to my room, and there he is, the man I've chosen, smelling of snow and wind and the doughnut shops that are on every corner. The cold air makes my nipples strain against the fabric.

"Yes?" he says.

I nod. I am afraid to answer, sure my American accent will give me away as nonnative, that he will walk out the door before I have the chance to touch him.

He steps inside and I close the door behind him.

He takes off his coat, hangs it on the hook near the door. Beneath, he is dressed in an eggplant-purple button-up shirt and black dress pants. "How much?" he says in English. His accent is almost hidden and is hard to place. Portuguese, maybe. Or Italian.

I'm tempted to offer him a freebie since I'm just posing and, although he doesn't know it, he's actually doing me the service. But he looks like he has the money, and I don't want him to feel like he's not getting the real deal. Plus, if I'm going to do this, I want to do it all the way.

I put one hand on his shoulder. Cock my hip near his. "How long?" I ask. When I speak, he looks up from his wallet. I think he is surprised by my accent, that he will ask if I am from the States.

Instead, he touches his cold finger to my bottom lip. Pulls it away from my teeth, pinching the skin gently. Lets his dark eyes linger on my chest, on my belly, on the front of my panties. Says, "One hour, maybe longer."

Despite the cold he's brought with him, my cheeks burn. "Fifty euros for twenty minutes," I say around his finger.

He nods, drops his hand away from my lips. I step in front of him, careful in my heels, and lead him into the back room, holding the curtain aside so he can follow. He is a big man in this small room, his shoulders wide through the doorway, and I am glad I wore my heels, glad that I can reach his shoulder without stretching.

I am not sure what to do now. It was easy to play the seductress behind the glass, but here in this room that's so obviously made for only one thing, I'm uncomfortable, like I don't know what to do with my hands. I haven't touched anyone's body but Danny's for so long—I know what he likes and doesn't—how do I touch someone new, let him touch me?

But then the man steps up behind me, cups my ass with his cold hands. The cool feels good against my overheated skin. The way his fingers grasp at me with want makes me less nervous.

I turn toward him, letting his hands stay around my ass, and reach up to undo his shirt buttons. Beneath the fabric, his skin is even and tight;

the muscles across his chest are strong. I slide the shirt over his shoulders, press myself against him. He pulls me toward him with both hands, so that I can feel his erection, pressing hard against my belly.

"Lie down," he says. I lie on the bed on my back, and he lowers himself on me, running his tongue across my skin, nipping here and there with his teeth—the side of my hip, the tip of my nipple, the bottom of my lip. By the time he has his tongue against the front of my panties, my nervousness has changed to desire. My skin tingles everywhere. Even through the fabric, his tongue is sending quivers down my thighs.

I grab his head, pull it away from me. "Let me," I say. He lies down on the bed and I slide his pants down. His blue boxer briefs bulge in the front. A drop of precome wets the fabric. I run my tongue against the rough cotton. His liquid tastes like oysters and laundry soap.

He moans and lifts his thin hips, letting me pull the briefs down. His cock springs up, thinner and longer than Danny's, curving toward me. I climb onto him and rub my hand across the top of his wet head, down over the crown. He bucks beneath me, raising us both off the bed. I explore his cock with my hand: small blue veins, the mushroom head, the way it jumps when I wrap my fingers around the base.

His hands wander over my breasts, tweaking my nipples through the lace bra, sending sparks everywhere. When I lean my head back and moan, he sits up, takes my shoulders in his hands, and gently pushes me off of him.

"Stand up," he says.

I do. He sits on the edge of the bed and spins me around until I am facing the wall. The room is small enough that I can lean my hands against the wall without moving my feet, my ass, away from the bed. I am breathing hard, my hair down over my face. He kicks my heels apart with his feet, nips at my ass. I can feel the small points of his teeth all the way up in my nipples, all the way down into the juices that soak my panties.

As though he can read my mind, he tucks the length of his finger right against me, right against the wet strip of cotton. Turns it over and over like a screw. I want to grind against him, but I hold myself still, hands on the wall, waiting to see what he wants.

He grabs the strip of fabric between my thighs, shoves it to one side. His finger inside me, cold and hard, makes my knees tremble, makes me cry out. With his other hand, he reaches around and pulls down the cup of the lace bra until my nipple's exposed. He pinches my nipple and pulls. It feels so good I have to grind against him, get him to sink his finger deeper.

When he drops his hands, away from me and out of me, I can breathe again. The crinkle of a condom. Then, "Sit," and he's pulling me down on him. His cock slides into me so smooth and fast that I can't believe it's happening and then it is—I'm fucking this stranger.

I ride him backward, his hand pulling me down, hips pumping up. I put my hand to my wet clit, think of Danny, standing out there in the cold, watching my closed curtain, waiting while this other man fucks me. It nearly makes me come right there, just thinking of that. But I promised Danny I'd wait, that I'd wait for him. I have to take my hand away from my clit, concentrate on the man beneath me, on the way he moans and rocks under me, on the way his cock feels, longer inside me, as though he's reaching farther up in me than Danny ever does.

Soon, he flips me around so I'm facing him. He puts his hands on my ass, pulling me onto him again and again. How different inside me, the way his hips move and his cock. I run my hands over his chest, the muscles moving, the way his chest hair uncurls under my fingers.

And then he's rising inside me, nearly lifting me off his hips. The muscle in his jaw clenches, releases. He cries out, his fingers tightening on my ass as he shudders and shakes and goes silent. I wait until he stops shaking, and then I wrap my fingers around the bottom of the condom and slide off of him.

I look at the clock by the bed. "One hundred euros," I say, all business. And then I go into the front room, with my dripping panties and my nipples aching and sit in my tall chair waiting for him to get dressed and go.

When I hear him put the money on the table and shut the door, I slide the red curtain back open and look out into the street. The man in the wool coat steps out of the door, stands on the concrete for a moment, men milling around him. He looks content, smiling like a man who's just spent his money wisely.

Danny leans against the railing against the canal, watching my face. He also looks like a man who's spent his money wisely. The man walks by Danny, nods his chin. My husband nods back. Two men passing in the street, two men who appreciate the finer things in life.

I look at my husband, at his handsome face, the gray hairs that I can't see but that I know are there, just above his ears. I stretch out my long legs, giving him a flash of nipple above the corset. Then I wink.

Danny pushes himself off the railing, comes forward, toward the door that leads into my window. I slide the curtain closed one last time and walk to the door.

"How much?" Danny asks. He smells like coffee and my favorite shampoo.

"Everything," I say. "Everything you've got."

ᎶᏙ THE MAN WHO ATE WOMEN ᏙᏙ
Damian Grace

I DON'T DRINK MUCH THESE DAYS, but five years ago, when this tawdry incident happened, I was at a time in my life when I drank heavily almost every night. The prevailing wisdom in my social circle was that you couldn't have a good time without alcohol, and we all considered ourselves harmless social drinkers. If you'd asked me the definition of an antisocial drinker, I guess I'd have described someone who throws up on your shoes or crosses the double yellow line and turns you into roadkill. Anyway, the point I'm trying to make is that I was loaded.

It happened at one of John Kindle's infamous weekly house parties, the ones where he would invite maybe a dozen people and fifty or sixty people would show up. Kindle was a college buddy of mine who had told us all that the Web was going to be the Next Big Thing. We had ignored his advice while he was busy putting his money where his mouth was, and now he never had to work again.

I was a regular guest, and while you never knew everyone, I had enough buddies, male and female, to feel relaxed and comfortable. The atmosphere was a sort of postcollege hip thing—people two or five or even ten years out of school trying to recapture the feeling of freedom and belonging of those undergraduate days.

Dressing down was the absolute rule. The guy in the muscle shirt and high-tops might be a corporate lawyer on the fast track to partner, and the woman in the tie-dyed shirt and clogs could easily be a buttoned-down drone with Anderson Consulting. I was in grad school at the time, so as I saw it, I had a right to wear loose jeans and sandals and a Legalize Pot T-shirt.

There was plenty of sex at these parties. Not as much as you might hear about the next day, of course, but I know how to separate fact from bragging, and there was plenty of fact. All those people trooping up and down the stairs to the second floor weren't inspecting Kindle's famous record collection or checking out the new wallpaper in his study.

I guess I got about my fair share. I didn't try as hard as some guys, and sometimes that works out better anyway. My God, with guys like Jerry Shaughnessy or Guido the Italian Stallion, if they didn't have a real solid line on some trim by ten or eleven, you could see the panic in their eyes, like a hunter on the last day of deer season. My normal pattern was to wait until things thinned out a bit, maybe one A.M. or so, and then take a casual look around to see who might be available. Lately it had been Amy Hauder more often than not, and I sensed I might be drifting into a relationship in my usual aimless way.

We were down in the basement, where the laid-back, cool regulars hung out, and the conversation was moving right along. Just the right mix of edgy, critical people like Jennifer Chase and Seth Jabovic to stir the pot, and type-B conciliators like me and Doris and Amira to calm things down and smooth over ruffled feathers when the pot started to boil over.

You can just about set your watch by the topics. From nine to ten it's all gossipy chitchat: "Did you ever meet . . . ?" and "Did you hear what so-and-so did last week?"—that sort of thing. When that gets old we move on to politics and issues of the day. Imagine a younger McLaughlin Group sitting around in beanbag chairs with drinks in their hands, smoking up a storm.

Once the budget is balanced, the trickier foreign policy issues have been settled, and pot is legal and available in every supermarket, the boy-girl thing finally bubbles to the surface. Call it midnight. And once you get on the topic of sex and relationships, you never get off it, because nothing ever gets settled in *that* area.

We had more gals than guys in the circle that night—Jimmy and Big Herman were at a Blackhawks game, I think. The previous night there had been a strange incident at one of the fraternities on the local campus, and the rumors were flying.

"It's called a train," said Seth. He waved a thin white hand dismissively, sending a trail of smoke floating upward. "Disgusting, really, but certainly not a crime."

"Sounds like the police think it was a crime," said Jennifer. "I heard they dragged a bunch of hungover frat guys in for questioning."

Seth shrugged. "Of course, if the woman files a complaint afterward, they have to investigate."

"Investigate what?" asked Amy. "Can someone tell me what the hell a 'train' is?"

"A gang bang, of sorts," said Seth. He pushed back a lock of dark, lank hair and went into professor mode. "A woman at a party decides she wants to take on all comers. She'll go into a room, and the guys will line up outside the door to take their turn. A whole train of guys, one after the other."

"But why?" asked Amy helplessly.

"I don't know, you tell me," said Seth. "Must be a deep-down female fantasy."

"I don't think so," said Doris, and other girls shook their heads as well. "It's repulsive."

"Lack of self-esteem, probably," said Jennifer. "Some girls get so brainwashed by our male-dominated society that they equate putting out with being popular."

This was a typical Jennifer Chase troll, and everyone ignored it.

Brad shifted in his beanbag and said, "I was in a bar once and a girl got up on a stool and announced she was going to give a blow job to every guy there. She said she lost some kind of bet, but obviously that was just a silly excuse."

Jennifer raised an eyebrow. "And?"

He shrugged sheepishly. "What do you think? I was like third in line, out of a dozen. It's not like she was wasted or high or something—she knew what she was doing."

Jennifer snorted. "Oh, so then it's okay."

Brad looked embarrassed. "So what, you think I shouldn't have?"

"I wouldn't expect anything different from a man."

"I can't believe a woman would ever do that," said Amy. "So demeaning."

I spoke up. "If she does it of her own free will, and on her terms, is it really demeaning? I mean, if she has a fantasy about a gang bang or whatever, can't you give her credit for feeling liberated enough to act on it?"

Several people spoke at once. Fatefully, it was Jennifer who raised her voice and continued to speak.

"How can you think a woman could really enjoy something like that? How would you like performing oral sex on a dozen women you hardly know, one right after the other?"

I felt a little lurch in my stomach. Back then, I had a sort of policy of always speaking my mind and telling the truth, no matter what. I think I was under the influence of some subversive writer. Walt Whitman, or maybe it was Ayn Rand.

"I'd love it," I said. "This may shock you, but that happens to be a deep, dark fantasy of mine."

There was a predictable round of laughter. They all thought I was kidding, except for Seth, who isn't easily fooled.

"It might be dark, but it isn't deep anymore, Steve-O," said Seth. "It's right up here on the surface where we can poke it."

"Very funny, Steve," said Amira in her faint Hindi accent. "But really, come on."

"I'm serious," I said. "Really. So it doesn't seem so odd to me that a woman might fantasize about the same thing."

In a loud voice, Jennifer said, "You're telling me, you would go up to one of the bedrooms right now, and we could go announce to everyone you were going to . . . going to do a . . ."

"Taco train?" suggested Brad.

"Oh, very nice, Brad. A cunnilingus train, and you would service any woman who went up there?"

"Sure," I said. "But no women would go for it. You chicks are all so dainty and refined. Only men have the sturdy mental outlook required to take advantage of free, no-strings-attached sex."

"You're lying," said Amira. "I bet you wouldn't do it." Her voice was accusing, but I noticed a twinkle in her brown eyes.

"Oh, I bet he would," said Seth, winking at me. "Don't underestimate our Steve. He's right, though. None of you women would have the guts to take him up on it. Unless maybe if he was blindfolded, so he couldn't see who he was eating. . . ."

I felt my cock start to worm its way down the leg of my jeans like it had a life of its own.

Amy said, "Let me get this straight—Steve would be lying blindfolded on the bed, and we would just go in there anonymously and sit on his face?"

"And if he correctly identifies all the women by taste alone, he wins a special prize," said Seth, ever the wit.

"A case of Scope," said Amira, and everyone laughed.

"It's an amusing idea," said Jennifer. "But I guarantee he won't get any takers."

"Only one way to find out," said Seth.

Jennifer looked at me challengingly. "What do you say, Steve?"

I swallowed hard. "Is the blindfold necessary?"

There was a chorus of yeses and nods.

They were all looking at me. Seth and Brad were amused, of course. Jennifer, the sturdy field-hockey player with the firm jaw and blue eyes, looked triumphant, like she was about to win an argument. Amy, the skinny blonde who was the only one I had gone down on before, looked embarrassed. Mindy and Doris just looked curious. Amira was the only one who looked like she was turned on by the idea. When our eyes met, she dropped hers and smiled.

"Let's do it," I said.

"Good man!" said Seth with a chuckle.

I went up to the second floor with Seth and Jennifer, who seemed to be the self-appointed referees for each gender. We found an empty bedroom and cleared the coats off the bed. Seth found a scarf and tied it around my head, almost burning me with his cigarette in the process. He left a generous gap at the bottom, and I could look down and see my shoes. "Can you see anything?" asked Jennifer.

"Not really. You want to go first?"

"No way. I'm going to go tell all the women it's "free head," no conversation needed. We'll see if you get any customers."

They left, turning out the overhead light and leaving the room in semidarkness. I went over to the bed and lay down, moving awkwardly with the blindfold. Nothing happened for a while, and I started regretting the whole thing. Ever since I'd hit puberty and the hormones had started to rage, I'd been fascinated by the idea of eating pussy. It seemed like such a perverse, unnatural thing to do, and yet it had such potential to give pleasure to women.

Ah, women. Fascinating, ethereal creatures, superior to men, or at least to boys, in every way. Able to humble us with a sly look or a toss of the hair. They seemed to have some ancient knowledge passed down to them regarding relationships and men and sex, so that a girl of thirteen or fourteen somehow possessed the accumulated wisdom of generations, while we boys had to flounder and blush and stammer as we slowly figured things out for ourselves. But it seemed to me that these godlike creatures had an Achilles' heel, and that it was the very thing that was also the source of their power.

I sensed from a young age the uneasy relationship women had with their genitals. They were ashamed of the way they looked down there, and the way they smelled, and tasted. They couldn't understand how men could be attracted to the oozing slot between their legs like bees to a ripe, pollen-heavy flower.

To nuzzle between the legs of one of these creatures was to upset the balance of power. It was to worship at the altar of womanhood, and at the same time it was to strike a rebellious blow against the all-powerful spell that held men in the thrall of women. If you were sucking a woman's cunt, you were sacrificing yourself for her, and yet she was in your power.

As I matured, I naturally discovered that things weren't quite so dramatic. Women weren't all-knowing creatures after all, and they weren't the enemy. They were subject to base desires and cravings just like men. But like so many things that affect us strongly when we are young and malleable, my fixation remained long after the worldview that had shaped it had shifted. I still craved the act of joining my mouth and tongue to a woman's secret, musky inner regions. It was submission and power combined, and it was my constant fantasy.

But lying there alone in the dim bedroom, I was having second thoughts. Some fantasies should remain just that, and I was almost relieved that no women were taking me up on the offer. A few more minutes and I could rip off the blindfold and claim a political victory.

There was a thump outside the door, barely audible over the bass vibration from the big speakers downstairs. Two female voices, each trying to shush the other.

The door opened, brightening the room, and I swallowed hard. Drunk female laughter, and then the door closed again.

"He's in there!"

"I told you. Now go on . . ." The rest was muffled.

This is humiliating, I thought. *I'm out of here.*

The door opened again, and this time they came in and shut it behind them. I could hear their heavy breathing as they looked at me.

"Hi," I said.

"Party Girl here wants to sit on your face," said one. "I'm just her chaperone." This struck them as funny, and they both broke into choked laughter. "Is that what you want?" asked Party Girl. "I mean . . . really?"

"I lost a bet."

"Oh . . . okay. So it's not like you really want to . . ."

It would have been easy to say something that would have gotten me off the hook. Even through a haze of alcohol, she was hesitant about inflicting her cunt on a stranger.

"No, I want to. Besides, I can't settle the bet until I actually get a bunch of women to sit on my face."

"Shit, what the hell, then. Is the door locked?"

"Yep," said the chaperone.

I heard the rustling of clothing, and then the bed shifted sharply. Through the crack in the blindfold I could see she was wearing a short skirt, which she had rolled up around her waist. All she had taken off were her panties, and maybe her shoes. Her thighs nestled on either side of my head, and I caught the first whiff of her pussy. It was pungent, with a faint undertone of urine, but not unpleasant. She had probably showered before the party, but had of course been dancing and drinking since then.

She kneed me painfully in the ear, apologized, and then her pussy was in my face.

I licked up at her awkwardly, pushing my tongue into the damp folds. The taste was tangy, the smell stronger now. Pubic hairs tickled my nose. For the first few minutes it didn't go very well. I couldn't really reach her clit without straining my neck, and she kept squirming around, alternately pulling away and then mashing her cunt into my face as she tried to get comfortable on the soft mattress.

"Hold on a sec," she said.

She wedged a pillow under my head and then scooted forward a bit. Then she sat back down, lowering her pussy into just the right position. *Dinner is served*, I thought. I dove back into her wet and pleasantly musky cunt, and went to work on her clit. Before long she was grinding herself gently against my mouth in a pleasantly familiar rhythm.

"He's good at this, Cheryl," she said huskily, forgetting about staying anonymous.

"Oh yeah? Are you going to come?" Cheryl the chaperone's voice was teasing.

"Maybe ..."

About a minute later she did, with a short, high-pitched groan that was equal parts surprise and pleasure. Putting modesty aside, I'm really very good at eating pussy.

She rolled off me, giving me a needed breath of air, and then she kissed me briefly on the lips and said, "Thanks, stranger."

Cheryl was laughing. "You little slut, I can't believe you just came on his face!"

Emboldened by my success, I said, "I bet I can do the same thing for you."

"I wish I were wearing a skirt," she said. "Maybe I would. But I'm not taking my pants off."

"You can wear my skirt, and I'll put on your jeans," said Party Girl.

There was a moment of silence. Cheryl had clearly been trapped.

"Sit on my face," I said. "I promise you won't regret it."

"Well hell, I guess it's just one of those nights my mama warned me about," said Cheryl. I heard the welcome sound of a zipper going down. Some rustling and giggling, and then another warm shape looming above me, and another unique fragrance.

Cheryl's pussy wasn't as pungent as her friend's, but it was amazingly wet. As I stroked my tongue up her slot, her puffy lips opened, releasing a warm gush of pussy cream that soon was running down my chin.

"Oh wow," said Cheryl. "Stranger, you sure know how to make a girl feel good."

"Told you so," said Party Girl.

Cheryl settled herself in more firmly, and the world narrowed down to a wet pussy, a firm little nub, and my tongue. Somewhere above me, Cheryl started saying, "Oh ... oh ... oh ..." at regular intervals. My cock was a constant throbbing lump in my pants, far in the opposite direction.

When she came, she tensed up and became completely still, an orgasmic response that was uncommon but not rare. I loved it, because it allowed me to sense the minute changes in her physiology—the sudden thickening of her outer lips, the swelling and even the quivering of her clitoris.

"Oh fuck yes!" said Cheryl. We were both gasping for air. "That was a fucking ride!"

"I want to go again," said Party Girl. "Shit, what I really want to do is take this guy home and chain him to my bed."

"I'm supposed to serve all comers," I said. "But if no one else is waiting ..."

As if on cue, there was a knock at the door.

My two new friends swore under their breath and pulled themselves together. Then there was low-pitched conversation at the door.

"Guess what?" called Party Girl.

"A line around the block?" I ventured.

"Not quite, I mean women aren't quite so bold as to stand in line, but the word is that you've got some more customers waiting."

"Better send 'em in, then."

And in they came, in a continuous stream, sometimes alone, more often in groups of two. I ate pussy steadily for the next two hours, or so they told me later. As far as I was concerned, time pretty much lost meaning.

How many? I honestly don't know. At least twenty. Twenty new pussies: twenty new smells, twenty new tastes. There were cunts so hairy that it was like eating out a broom, which was sort of a drag, and there were a few that were shaved slick and bare, which isn't really my preference, either. There were small cunts with tightly folded lips that had to be teased open with a rigid tongue tip, and big cunts with soft lips that enveloped my tongue and nose in a warm, musky embrace.

Some of the women were obviously just doing it on a dare, and they would just climb on and then back off after a cursory tonguing. One woman was so drunk that she kept losing her balance and falling off the bed—the second time that happened I sent her away. Of those that actually allowed themselves to get into it, I was able to make about two out of three come, which I thought was pretty damn good under the circumstances.

One girl ground her pussy into my face for about ten minutes straight, stranded in the lonely territory just short of orgasm, swearing like a sailor and gasping out instructions that I followed to the letter. Despite our best efforts, she was simply unable to come.

"I'm just too fucking drunk," she said finally, with endearing honesty. She was close to tears with frustration. "Don't take this personally. . . ."

She lifted herself up a few inches off my face and started rubbing herself. I watched through the ever-growing gap in my blindfold, fascinated, as her fingers savagely rubbed and pulled at her cunt. When I sensed she was finally about to come, I slid down and jabbed my tongue up into her slit hole as far as I could. She let out a guttural shriek and went off like a Roman candle. She was one of the women who insisted on giving me her phone number.

The door opened, and someone came in and loosened my blindfold. I found myself looking up at Amira.

"How's the man of the hour?" she asked. "The gang wants to know how you're holding up. Jennifer Chase wants me to tell you she's going to have to reconsider her entire worldview because of this."

I smiled at her and sat up. "My face is sticky, my neck is stiff, and my tongue and jaw are exhausted. Other than that, I'm great."

"I thought you might be working up a thirst," she said, holding out a cup of beer.

I took the cup gratefully and downed it in one long, delicious gulp. "God, I needed that."

She chuckled, her teeth showing white against her dark skin. "Ready to get back to it?"

"Actually, I think I've had enough."

"Ah, too bad. I guess I'm too late, then."

"I didn't realize you were here as a customer," I said, looking at her with new interest. Amira was one of those women who are all curves, and she looked too young to be in law school. Dark, arched eyebrows over liquid brown eyes, full red lips, a round face framed by thick wavy hair. Full breasts, round hips and thighs, but a surprisingly narrow waist. My cock, which had been up and down all night, began hardening again.

She sat down next to me, and said, "Steve, I just wanted to say that you've got a lot of guts acting out your fantasy like this."

"You think *so?*"

She dropped her eyes, and said, "Please don't tell anyone, but I have a similar fantasy. Like the girl at the fraternity the other night."

"You want to be train-fucked? You're kidding!" The idea of sweet, quiet Amira taking on a whole fraternity seemed beyond crazy, and I couldn't help laughing.

"It's just a fantasy," she protested. "That doesn't mean I'm actually going to do it."

"So you don't think you'll ever go through with it?"

She shook her head. "No way. For me, a fantasy like that should just be a fantasy. Besides, I'm a virgin, and I won't lose my virginity until I'm married."

She smiled at the surprise on my face.

"It's a religious thing. I choose to honor it, but I also choose to use a very narrow definition of virginity."

"Ah, I see what you mean. Would you like to be my caboose, then?"

She wrinkled her forehead for a second, then laughed. "Yes, I'd be honored to be the last car on your taco train." She wriggled out of her tight jeans and then peeled off her black silk panties with a self-conscious look on her face. I eased her onto her back and spread her legs.

Her pussy was sweet and clean, with a spicy fragrance that suggested she had dabbed some perfume down there. I took my time, enjoying the feeling of being on my stomach rather than on my back, steadily bringing her closer to orgasm with a newfound confidence in my abilities. When she began to squirm and pant, I concentrated on her clit, sending her over the edge with a final swirling flourish of my tongue.

"Wow," she said simply, a few seconds later.

"Practice, practice."

She rolled onto her side, raised her head on her hand. "Let me ask you, have you had any . . . relief tonight?"

"Nope. With me it's all give and no take. I just give and give and then give some more."

She giggled. "Would you like some take, for a change?" she asked shyly.

"God, yes."

"Okay, you just lie still and let me take care of you."

I lay on my back and stared at the ceiling in happy exhaustion as Amira unzipped my jeans and delicately extracted my cock. She crouched over me, her dark hair shielding her face as if in modesty. Her tongue was warm and soft, her motions tentative and unpracticed. She held my cock gently inside her mouth, like she was afraid of damaging it, and moved her head up and down in a slow and steady rhythm. In the state I was in, it was enough. I closed my eyes and allowed myself to drift along patiently with the sensation.

"Here it comes," I said.

Amira lifted her head and took over with her hand, stroking my slippery cock with a firm grip. I groaned and spilled out my load in a prolonged spasm of pleasure. When it was over, the room seemed to be spinning in lazy circles, and I felt drugged. I lay there limply while Amira cleaned me with a towel and zipped me up.

"You're an angel," I said.

She smiled. "If my mother could see me right now, she wouldn't think so."

The next morning I was hungover, sore, and vaguely depressed. Instead of leaving me fulfilled, the escapade sent me into a funk that lasted for weeks. I remember thinking that Amira had it right—it was much better to let a fantasy remain a fantasy, and to remain true to your morals.

I called up Amira a few days later and asked her out. She turned me down, politely but firmly, which only reinforced my feelings for her. I obsessed over her for a while, and then I eventually came to my senses. Still, I was shocked when, a year later, I heard that she was dropping out of law school because she was pregnant.

Today I look back at the incident with a strange mixture of distaste and pride. Should you act out an extreme fantasy when you have the chance? You're asking the wrong guy—I still haven't decided yet.

ᛞ ROCK OF AGES ᛞ

P. S. Haven

I DISCOVERED ROCK AND ROLL the same year I discovered my sister's
tits. Well, let me rephrase that. "Discovered" might not be the best word.
Perhaps "realized" is what I mean to say. Because I was certainly aware of
both rock and Paige's tits well before my year of realization. In fact, I had
heard The Who's *Happy Jack* wafting from Brett Saylor's open bedroom
window next door since the first days of September the year before. And
I'd seen my older sister topless on almost a daily basis for as long as I
could remember.

It was truly no big deal. Paige's chest looked remarkably like my own.
Whether it was bath time, bedtime, getting dressed before school, running
through the sprinkler in the backyard; the sight of my sister's bare body
was a mundane, everyday occurrence.

Until one particular summer, that is. Paige suddenly banned me from
the bathroom. She closed the door while getting dressed. She stopped
taking her bathing suit off at the outdoor shower at our beach house.

It all seemed very ordinary. She was a girl, after all, and girls are weird
like that. Even as a boy I knew that.

As for *Happy Jack*, well, it seemed quite mundane as well—until that
day I actually listened to the words of "A Quick One While He's Away." I
was gassing up the mower at the far edge of our yard (right beneath Brett's
bedroom) and could actually understand the words. A story unfolded of

a lonely girl, an experienced engine driver—and forgiveness. The next day I spent my allowance on a copy of *Happy Jack* for myself at Reznick's Records. The following week I bought *My Generation*, which I didn't like nearly as well, but the die had been cast. Before school let out for summer, I counted among my collection *Their Satanic Majesties Request, Highway 61 Revisited, Procol Harum*, and, of course, *Sgt. Pepper*. I was excited. I was obsessed. I couldn't get enough. And I wouldn't feel quite that way about anything again until the day I saw Paige's new tits.

Well, again, let me rephrase. They were the same tits Paige had always had, except she'd never *had* them before. At least I'd never seen them before. Not like that.

I had first glimpsed them in Paige's recently restricted bedroom. I barged in without so much as a knock, on the hunt for Dad's copy of *Whipped Cream and Other Delights*. I cared absolutely nothing about the music on the album, only about its cover, which featured Dolores Erickson wearing nothing but chiffon and shaving cream. At any rate, I barged in. There stood Paige, naked from the waist up, the way I had seen her so many times before. Only this time there were tits. Real ones. Now granted, they weren't very large—and, yes, they were my sister's. And despite the fact that I was instantly and irredeemably aroused by the sight of them, I am not sexually attracted to my sister.

Still, they were tits. Pretty, perky tits. Quite possibly the first real set I had ever seen. So unfamiliar, so *new*. Their pitch and attitude in relation to Paige's frame, with the nipples aimed slightly skyward, seemed to lend the same air of stunned fear that was fleetingly on my sister's face before she clasped her arms across her exposed breasts and shrieked at me to get out. Which I did. Even before she had finished shrieking. Because I was every bit as stunned as she was.

Even as the bedroom door was slammed and locked behind me, I knew the image of that nubile pair had forever been burned into my memory. From that day forward, my appetite for all things female and nude exploded, much like my appetite for rock and roll. Once I'd had enough time to look back on my first musical discoveries with the earliest pangs of nostalgia, I could never hear those songs without seeing Paige's breasts.

The following summer, my dresser buckled under the additional weight of everything from *In the Court of the Crimson King* to *Tommy* to *Space Oddity*. My mattress was crowning from a stash of pilfered issues of *Playboy* I'd hid between the mattresses. That summer I accidentally learned how to masturbate—and the image I masturbated to the most was that of my sister's tits, either strangely disembodied or with Dolores Erickson's face superimposed over Paige's. But the thing I'll always remember that summer, more so than my own forays into self-pleasure, was my discovery that my sister was already well versed in the practice herself. Much like the introduction of boobs into my life, it was a discovery born of happenstance, trespassing, and my love of music.

My dad had forgotten (again) to give me my weekly allowance and had already left for work. It was Tuesday, and that two dollars, coupled with the previous week's two dollars, would buy me Grand Funk's eponymous second album later that day when I hitched a ride to the record store in Tim Mill's mom's black '63 Galaxie. With Dad absent, the two bucks owed to me would have to come from Mom.

As I roamed the house calling for her, I heard her call back to me from what sounded like her and Dad's bedroom down the hall. I followed the perturbed sound of her voice, but the only signs of life were the sound of running water and a sliver of light from under the door to the master bath. Being on a mission, I walked straight into the bathroom, expecting to see my mom, clad in her powder-blue robe, postponing her bath to see what her son could possibly need so desperately at ten in the morning.

Instead, what I witnessed instantly supplanted the image of Paige's breasts as my primary masturbatory mental imagery forevermore. There, in my mother's bathtub, lay my sister, her long legs splayed out on the wall on either side of the full-blast faucet, her naked body positioned so that the water poured directly onto her pussy, which she was feverishly kneading with both of her hands.

As before, I extricated myself as rapidly and inconspicuously as possible. Only this time I did so without being noticed.

However, even if I had had no impact on Paige's private moment, it had had a seismic impact on me. Never again would I beat off to the simple image of naked tits. Never again would I be content with a static still life. This was real, live sex I had witnessed. Sure, it was solo sex. And, yes, again, it was my sister. But Paige's face was supplanted easily enough in my mind with Elly May Clampett's or Brett's latest girlfriend's. From then on (at least until next summer), whenever I got off, it was to the picture of my sister getting off under the bathtub faucet.

Less than a year later, while rifling through Paige's bedroom in search of my *Led Zeppelin* that I was absolutely certain I would find among her

This Is Donovan and *The Birds, the Bees and the Monkees*, I stumbled across something that dazed and confused me more than a Jimmy Page solo. It was a tattered paperback titled *The Alpine Spa*. The cover was faded blue and had a crudely sketched drawing of a woman wearing only her bra and panties, flanked on either side by two attentive, muscle-bound men with strategically placed towels slung around their waists. The pages were yellow and brittle. Certain pages were dog-eared, and on those pages, passages had been circled with a blue ballpoint.

I read descriptions of things I'd only heard the older kids say as insults to one another. The foremost example was: "Suck my dick." I'd heard that phrase uttered at least two dozen times a day on the bus, in the locker room, in the dugout, you name it. Anywhere there wasn't an adult within earshot, one of my friends was mockingly inviting one of us to suck his dick. I was no exception. It was exchanged between friends with such regularity that when it was sincerely uttered (well, as sincerely as a Little Leaguer can utter "suck my dick" to another Little Leaguer) in the heat of a verbal confrontation, it did more to defuse the situation than to escalate it.

But this book, Paige's book, had a completely different take on sucking dick. In *The Alpine Spa*, the dicks being sucked were done so willingly, enthusiastically even. The suckers of these dicks were exclusively female, and they enjoyed every minute of it. The part they seemed to enjoy most was what happened after a dick had been sucked a long time—this part was never discussed on the school bus. The thought that someone else, a second party, would not only not be repulsed by making me come but would actively facilitate the creation and, yes, the consumption of it—it was unfathomable to my young mind.

Yet there it was in black and white. Dozens of ballpoint-ballooned examples of women apparently starved for the stuff. One man alone could not sate them. I forgot about Led Zeppelin. And *The Alpine Spa* found a new home under my mattress.

If Paige knew who took it, she never accused me. For the next year, I was freed of my sister's image while masturbating. Instead, visions from *The Alpine Spa* filled my young brain. But even if Paige herself was mercifully absent, it was her book that had made her so. And that summer became the third in a row that would forever be linked to my sister's burgeoning sexuality.

When I became an adult, I realized that, while most of my peers, at least the ones who loved music, associated the trajectory of their lives with their favorite albums or memorable concerts, I had associated my times with my sister. Sure, whenever I heard something off *Beggars Banquet*, I was instantly transported back to the last summer of high school, and those first, pure tastes of freedom that came with it. But I'd just as quickly think of my sister from that same summer, and what I'd watched her do with Bobby Fulton and Damon Hester on our couch that Friday night when I just barely beat my midnight curfew. What I saw that night would make all the tits, bathtub masturbation sessions, and paperback blow jobs in the world, obsolete.

I'd spent Friday evening the same way I had spent every Friday evening since acquiring my license, by hanging out in my friend Tim's bedroom listening to records. I had cut it way too close to my curfew, driven home way too fast, and arrived with maybe a minute to spare. For my mother, "on time" was five minutes early. To avoid any maternal entanglements, I decided to enter through the rarely used front door. It was further away from Mom and Dad's bedroom than the customary kitchen door, which I hoped would overcome the front door's noisy latch. As an added bonus, it opened into the living room, which provided a shorter path to the stairs that would lead me up to my room.

However, upon stealthy approach to the front door, movement from inside the living room caught my eye. I froze. Through the sidelight I could see swaying silhouettes. It must be my parents pacing the floor, eagerly awaiting my arrival to lecture me on the virtues of punctuality.

But as I turned to slink back around to the kitchen door, something about those shapes inside the house struck me as being very nonparental. Those shapes were most definitely not my parents. I stepped onto the steps that led up to our front porch, keeping my weight at the edge of each riser to keep the wood from creaking and popping. I considered my viewing options; the big, picture window would provide the fewest obstructions and widest angle, but I knew the odds of getting busted were significantly less if I contented myself with the front door. I sidled up to the sidelight and peeked inside.

The lights were off. Only the blue glow from the fluorescent fixture in the kitchen illuminated the scene. There, on one end of the love seat, knelt Bobby Fulton. Facing him, but on the other end, was Damon Hester. I wouldn't say I *knew* either one of them on a personal level. But every kid my age knew *of* them. The same way we knew John Bonham or Keith Moon. They were local heroes. Bobby, for his 390-powered '66 Fairlane, and Damon, for his hair. He had the kind of long hair me and all my friends had every intention of growing when we were free from the oppression of parents.

For just a minute I was more taken aback by the fact that both Bobby and Damon were here, at my house, than by what they were doing. But there on the love seat, completely naked, on her hands and knees between Bobby and Damon, was Paige. In front of her was Bobby, his hip-hugging jeans peeled open, his stiff cock disappearing into Paige's waiting mouth. Behind her was Damon, hunched over and mounted up, pants pushed down around his skinny, hairy thighs, clutching my sister by her hips and thrusting away.

I could feel my heart pounding, my cock hardening. This . . . this was the sort of thing I'd read about in *Alpine Spa*. I didn't even beat off to those scenes because I couldn't get my head around the geometry of it all. But this was it. It was real. I watched Paige's body quake as Damon drove into her. Her hands crawled across the love-seat cushion, seeking purchase, trying to brace herself against each entry. She'd let Bobby's cock slip from her lips, concentrating only on Damon, and for a moment Bobby seemed willing to make this sacrifice. But he quickly grew impatient with Paige's neglect and stuffed his cock back into her mouth.

In my pants, my cock had grown to its hardest and I had to consciously resist the urge to squeeze it. Damon was thrusting into Paige harder still, pumping away, a sheen of sweat forming on his forehead. Bobby was almost reclining now, propping himself up against the arm of the love seat, legs spread wide, his cock jutting up from his lap as Paige worked him. From my vantage point, the trio was oddly silent. No doubt the living room was filled with Bobby and Damon's labored growls, Paige's muffled mewling, the wet, slurping sounds of her mouth and pussy, all while Dad snored and Mom kept one ear on Johnny Carson and the other on the kitchen door.

Paige arched her back as Damon penetrated her, her tits swaying underneath her, the same tits that only a few summers ago had fueled an entire year's worth of self-induced orgasms. Damon was rough with her, which stirred something in me that almost felt like jealousy. Paige struggled to keep her mouth on Bobby's cock, and Bobby awkwardly stabbed away, each time Damon's actions momentarily separating the two. I could see Bobby's stomach quiver, just like mine did every time I was close to making myself come. Then I felt it: my pants were wet. My cock was throbbing. As always, Paige had made me come again.

With a flurry of staccato thrusts and a freeze-frame flourish, Damon came right after me. Once he'd regained control of himself, he disconnected himself from my sister and like Bobby before him, collapsed to the love seat. I could see a thick rush of semen running down the inside of Paige's thigh. She got to her knees on the floor and began to gather her scattered clothes. I stole away and made for the kitchen door.

Maybe it was the kettledrum pulse in my ears drowning it out, but the door seemed to open almost noiselessly. I took my shoes off and climbed the stairs like a burglar. As I passed my parents' bedroom, I could hear Dad and Mom both snoring.

From my bedroom window I saw Bobby and Damon pushing the Fairlane down the street. When they were a few houses away, they both hopped in. In the beat between Bobby turning the switch to *on* and *start*, I could hear a second or two of Johnny Cash's "Wanted Man" playing on WTOB. The 390 burbled to life, and they were gone.

I lay in bed for a long time before falling asleep. And when I woke up the next morning, the first thing I did was masturbate to my sister. And the next thing I did was hitch a ride with Tim Mills to Record Exchange to buy *Johnny Cash—Live at San Quentin*.

৪৩ NIGHT TRAIN ᘓᴥ
Martha Garvey

WELL, I'D SAY WE WERE DRUNK, except that neither of us drinks, but we'd
drunk enough lattes to send us into the next galaxy. My skin was tingling,
and Joe kept picking up my hand and dropping it, each time dragging a
finger across my palm.

He was young and tattooed and shaved and pierced, and I was about
ten years older. "Vanilla skin," he called me. But he wouldn't tell me his last
name, or what he did, so I told him no way would I take him home with
me. I was that kind of girl, but I wasn't *that* kind of girl.

"So let me ride the train home with you at least," he said. "Let me
make you feel safe."

I didn't feel safe around him. He had pale skin and deep blue eyes, and
the slightest hint of a brogue. The tattoos were mostly Celtic designs, and
his pale scalp stubble hinted that when it grew, he had dark hair. *Black Irish*,
I thought.

It was two A.M. on a Sunday night, and we boarded the train at
Broadway–Lafayette. Both dressed for city combat: white T-shirts, black
jeans, heavy boots.

And we entered an empty car, empty but for the trash blowing around.

And as we approached a seat, he said, "So you won't fuck me at your
place, Nell?"

"Not without further particulars," I replied.

At this point we were kissing and sucking each other's fingers, sticky with the coffee we'd downed. We'd both been bad drinkers once, but now coffee and sex were the drugs of choice.

"Not in your house," he said again, and grabbed my shoulders from behind, licked my neck. I would have told him anything right then, but then he quickly slid his hands down my arms and grabbed my wrists. He pulled my arms overhead, and kept both wrists trapped in one meaty hand.

With the other, he pulled out a set of handcuffs. They jangled so loud. Just at that point, the doors flew open. Last stop in Manhattan.

"You can get off now, if you'd like," Joe said, and loosened the pressure on my hands just a bit.

But I shook my head. *Let's see where this goes*, I thought.

"You could take me home to your bed," he hissed, and shook the handcuffs.

"No," I said, and Joe flipped open the cuffs and slammed them on my wrists, carefully suspending me from the overhead pole. I was still facing away from him, but I could see everything he was doing in the smudged subway window. My feet barely touched the floor.

We were underground, in a tunnel beneath the East River.

"I'm not a bad man," Joe explained. "I just don't like to be denied."

Then he yanked my shirt up and exposed my bra, shoving a hand into the soft, sweaty cotton. He came around so he was facing me and pulled my breast to his mouth. The cuffs hurt my wrists, but they seemed to build the sensation in my nipple. I was moaning. Joe was silent. His tongue was long and pink, and I could smell smoke on his skin. He lapped at my breast like a baby. His jeans bulged. I tried to move closer, get more of his mouth on my tit, but he backed away. And again, he moved behind me.

First stop in Brooklyn, York Street, the ghost town stop. Still, I looked over my shoulder to see if anyone was entering. For a moment, I had a flash that Joe would make whoever entered the car join our hand-cuff party. I felt ashamed. And very hot.

"I get off in six stops," I said, suddenly angry.

"Oh, you do, do you?" Joe said, impishly. "Then we'll have to hurry this along."

Joe unbuttoned my jeans and yanked them to the floor, where they lay in a heap around my feet. I felt doubly trapped, a cloth bound around my legs, metal around my wrists. I was still wearing underwear, stupid white cotton briefs, because, while I always wanted sex, I never believed I'd get it on the first date.

"Practical panties," Joe said, and ground himself into my back. I could feel his erection looking for a place to rest, and as he slid around my ass, it fit perfectly in my ass crack. I could hear Joe unzip and in the window I saw his cock rise in the air, bobbing. Sweat dripped off his face and onto my back. I heard him reach in a back pocket, and that familiar metallic sound, ripping, stretching.

"Next time," he growled as he rolled it over his cock, "you'll put it on with your mouth."

"What makes you think there'll be a next time?" I snapped. Then he spanked me once, and I moaned.

"Don't pretend with me, Nell."

And then he stuck his hand in my panties and ripped them off. They fell in a heap, too. And before I could object, he had one hand dithering my clit and the other stroking my ass crack.

"You really have to get home?" he murmured into my hair.

"No!" I moaned. "I mean, yes."

"All right," he sighed. Then he grabbed my breasts and plunged his cock deep into me.

Suddenly we were one with the train's rhythm, just as it rose above the ground into the sparkling Brooklyn sky. His cock was the right size for me, and he kept hitting my G-spot like he had a map. When I tried to back into *him*, he would hold me still.

"You are my little fuck doll tonight, Nell," he said, and then two stops from my destination, he pounded at me in earnest, fingering my clit all the way. The only sounds: the train, moans, the unmistakable sound of precome mixing with latex. And because of the way we were positioned, we could see ourselves fucking in the window.

As could anyone who was in the station. A few sleepy partiers gaped at the next stop, but they didn't get in. One man actually did a double take: a rarity in New York.

And all the while, the heat was rising in me, and Joe's cock was pulsing. His hands pinched my nipples, as if trying to pull the orgasm out of me.

"I feel so embarrassed," I said.

"No . . . you . . . don't," said Joe, pumping with each word for emphasis. "No. You. Don't."

Now Joe was groaning, and he was very close. His hand drifted to my face, and I nipped his fingers with my mouth, drawing them in, sucking them, and he came closer. One and a half stops to my destination.

"You're my fuck doll, and you'll do anything I tell you," said Joe. "Tell me what you are."

"I'm your fuck doll and I'll do anything you say."

"No, I said 'anything I tell you.'"

I was quiet.

"Say the words right, or I'll pull out and leave you in the train."

Words were just words, I thought. And I needed that orgasm. Still . . . Then he said it.

"Nell, please."

So he needed it, too.

"I'm your fuck doll," I said slowly, and Joe pumped me with every word, and I was seconds from going over the edge. "And I'll do anything you tell me."

And then we came together, bent, standing, convulsing, seeing ourselves in the glass, panting, coming some more. As soon as we stopped quivering, Joe moved quickly to unchain me and zip himself up. My arms ached, my mouth was dry, and I could have done it the rest of the night.

Joe yanked my pants up and picked up my ripped panties from the floor.

"Joe needs fuck doll's number," he said in a sweet, pleading voice, and so I wrote it, quickly, on the soiled and sweaty cotton. It didn't occur to me to do otherwise.

The doors of the subway train parted, and we kissed, Joe nipping my mouth, just a little.

He grabbed me by the shoulders and propelled me out of the train.

"You gave me what I wanted, now I'll give you what you really want," Joe said. I turned to face him.

"My last name's O'Riley," he smirked. Then the doors closed again. And he was gone.

ട്ടு SEAGUM ൫

Corwin Ericson

RAW SEAGUM IS PROCESSED IN A FEW STAGES. First it has to be mashed. For the traditional, home-brewed Down East seagum, this is done with two buckets, a pair of waders, and a woman.

She stomps side to side, not unlike the rolling stride of a seaman, squishing a bucketful of seagum with each foot until it changes from a gloppy blob to a pourable goo. The liquefied seagum is then poured into shallow, wide trays and left to dry for several days. It desiccates into a leathery film that is cut into strips and preserved in layers of salt and dried grass.

Seagum is what gives us Bismuthians our distinctively slack and rubbery locution. Like betel, khat, and coca, it's a mild stimulant that we chew like cud. It helps us haul in the nets hour after hour, and gives us an unfounded sense of mild euphoria. It also slowly destroys the nerves in one's lips. Most senior islanders are unable to whistle or produce a pucker, making for a manner of speaking that most off-islanders find difficult to understand and unpleasant to listen to.

For many of us on Bismuth, seagum-gathering falls somewhere between wasting time and odd jobbery—yet another way to make a boat payment, or at least to ignore the payment due notice.

Donny's dad, Mr. Lucy—whom I disliked only a bit less than his fuck-headed son—showed an entrepreneurial zeal unknown on Bismuth since the days of the grim Quaker captains when he established the seagum trade with a pair of tight-lipped Koreans.

Thanks to my own lack of entrepreneurship, I found myself press-ganged by Mr. Lucy for occasional scallop dredgings and other low-paying forms of drudgery on the *Wendy's Mom*. It was usually a couple nights' worth of toil and indignity on my part, and my pay was usually blown at The Topsoil before I even made it home. I was accustomed to Mr. Lucy's addlepated, inarticulable grudges and Donny's general repugnance; my own contribution to the *esprit de corps* was shirking sullenness. But today, Mr. Lucy seemed almost cheery; he had a hold half-full of scallops and a bag full of cash. On our way back to the island, I told him I'd never seen a Korean or any kind of off-islander chew seagum.

"Tiger testes," he said.

"What?"

"The Koreans grind it into a powder and sell it as counterfeit tiger testes."

"People buy powdered tiger testes?"

"Yeah, it supposed to give'm a hard-on like a tiger's."

Donny asked, "*Tiger* hard-ons?"

"They snort the stuff and then fuck, I guess," said Mr. Lucy. "Supposed to make'm tigers."

This was news to us. "I'm gonna try it," Donny said. I'd been thinking the same thing. I was also thinking I was very grateful that I'd be off the *Wendy's Mom* before Donny could begin his experiment in priapism.

"Don't," his father told him, and set us to coiling lines and stowing gear.

When things were as shit-shape as I was ever going to make them on a boat I neither owned nor liked, I joined Donny in the cabin before Mr. Lucy could assign me more chores.

Donny was using a shot glass and a cereal bowl to crush up a few strips of seagum. "Tiger cunt," he told me.

"What?"

"I got a tiger stiffy, I figure I'm gonna want some tiger pussy. You think this stuff would work on girls?"

"I dunno, does Viagra?" I replied.

"Viagra's for guys. Tiger balls could probably go either way."

"But this is *seagum*," I reminded him.

"Yeah, but you don't have to say."

"What are you going to do, tell a girl that it's not actually counterfeit tiger testes, it's the real thing?" I asked.

"I'll just tell her it's coke."

We used Mr. Lucy's drinking straw to snort the roughly ground seagum. I was a little giddy. It's not often in one's adult life that a brand-new drug comes along. This one tasted like fiberglass and rock salt, with an after-note of low tide.

"Maybe we should have cut it with something," I croaked.

"I take it straight," Donny testified.

We huffed the other lines and hoped we'd filled our tanks with the tiger. I saw Donny's nose start to bleed before I noticed my own trickle.

"Tiger, tiger, burning bright!" I pointed at Donny.

"Fuck yeah!"

We both ran our fingers around the bowl and rubbed the remaining powder on our gums. Donny was starting to fade into a red haze. Or, rather, every blood vessel in my eyes was bursting. I began to feel as if I were perspiring internally. My bones spun in their sockets. There was a hurricane in one ear and angry fleas in the other. I felt my windpipe go bullfrog, and heard Donny rasping, "Cock-sucking Christ!" as if he were a Tuvan throat singer. I spent my last moments of respiration clawing my way out of the cabin.

Mr. Lucy soon had us both in the cockpit with buckets of seawater between our knees. Speaking and thinking were impossible. I held my head in the bucket for as long as I could and then wept and sputtered as I tried to suck air through my engorged throat. Donny was similarly engaged.

Mr. Lucy lectured us on our substandard humanity and locked himself in the wheelhouse. I could breathe, but my ribs were trying to wriggle out of my chest. I felt my eyeballs liquefy and trickle down the back of my throat. I wanted to purge myself, sea cucumber–style, by barfing my toxic internal organs out onto the deck. I bent my head down to my knees and felt my entire body pucker.

Then I felt something prod my forehead. The stuff was working. Donny the Tiger was roaring, "Dad, Dad! It works!"

"You two fucking idiots stay away from me!" Mr. Lucy shouted from his barricade.

I did not feel "erect." No, I felt as if I had the very hook that would land the leviathan. I felt as if I could support all the troops, at once. I felt that, if I ever pissed again, I would bore a hole in the moon. Leaping porpoise, cresting narwhal, electric eel, anything but a turtle gliding gently into the quiet deep.

An hour later, we were heading past the breakwater into the harbor. Donny and I had kept to our benches and overturned the buckets on our laps. Donny was drumming on his with his thumbs. "I'm going to the fucking Topsoil as soon as we dock."

"Nobody's gonna be there this early," I told him.

"There's waitresses."

"You mean Mrs. Barrow?"

"Well, there'll be fucking tourists anyway."

"Yeah, like you'll be fucking tourists."

"Fuck you, Orange."

"You got a bone to pick with me, Donny?"

Donny launched himself at me across the cockpit, more bellowing manatee than tiger. Later, the bruises and cuts would remind me of his assault, but my initial impression was only of my face being pressed into the soft and stinking blubber of his chest, his sulfurous breath, and the sting of his saliva in my eyes. His flippers bashed my head side to side.

I was still sitting on the bench, and Donny was astride me, flapping. I tried to heave him off my lap and instead felt an alarming sense of pleasure as my marling spike rubbed along his mizzen mast. This served to reverse our polarity sufficiently to send us back into neutral corners of the cockpit. I took the offensive next, figuring a head butt to the bridge of his nose would be a strategic response. However, due to the pitch of the boat and my martial unsuitability, I found myself giving him a glancing wet willy as I pitched right over the side.

I was lucky there were so many illegal lobster pots in the sea clogging the harbor approach. I was able to grab a buoy without foundering. I yelled and waved, and found myself unwilling to use the first person, screaming instead, "Man overboard!"

It was a while before the *Wendy's Mom* began a slow, reluctant arc back to my position. I found the most effective way to stay above water was to straddle a lobster buoy, as if I were riding a bike with a banana seat underwater. It was soothing. I rode and pedaled and paddled until Mr. Lucy circled the boat up and threw me a life jacket, hollering, "You're not getting back on my boat, Whippey!"

It's only about twenty minutes with no wake to get from the harbor entrance to the docks, but it's a hell of a walk. Bismuth's breakwater was our Great Wall of China, a half-mile-long stone wall that was built in the fat days of whaling to protect the harbor from storms and navies. It had later been fortified with barges full of rocks and huge piles of cement rubble from some off-island civic catastrophe. It afforded one a prospect from which to look back on the town and wish one were much farther away. I dog-paddled, yardarm and all, over to it from the buoys and tried to dry off. My wardrobe had, for the last couple of days, been an assortment of abandoned T-shirts and sweats from the boat. I took them off and lay them on the rocks to dry in the sun. I sat on the life vest down in a gap in the rocks to get out of the wind. My lingam was still good for surf casting, and I was uncomfortable with my level of exposure.

My nakedness on the breakwater wasn't altogether unprecedented. Our island lacked warm water and any stretch of sand pleasant or private enough to bare one's parts, but the breakwater's rocks and distance from civilization had a way of inspiring the youthful and exhibitionistic. I was neither. I wished there was a chart I could consult to tell me when my own personal high tide would ebb. I lay there on the rocks, basking, with my gnomon seemingly stuck on noon, trying to think my way into detumescence.

I remembered the Souza sisters, who once graced these rocks like Lorelei. In high school, Sylvie and Denise would bathe in the sun and air out here at the outermost point of the island. To return home after days of squalid manliness at its worst and see the Souza sisters dappling the granite slabs, waving the fisherfolk of Bismuth home, was to either stave in the hull on the breakwater or drift through the harbor, smugly sure that a life spent on a grim little northern island was a perfectly reasonable, even pleasant fate—a feeling that rarely lasted through loading out the catch. Still, though, it wasn't the wives on the widow's walks, or the gale flags above the old fort that kept us looking homeward through our binoculars.

What else on this entire planet, in the history of mankind even, is there to do when one is alone with one's biggest harpoon; when one is laid out on the very rocks that had pressed into the softest spots of Denise and Sylvie's tawny bodies?

I took the situation in hand. My gaff, obdurately unpersuaded, seemed to have other ideas, or perhaps was finally *free* of ideas. At times, desperate ones, my brain has convinced me that my body was a vehicle of pain and humiliation that I should just junk. At this time, however, the body seemed free of the mind's influence and was running rampant, as if it bore the very trident of Poseidon. It was resplendently disempowering. Ghostly Souza hands did not join mine.

Europeans used to think narwhal tusks served the same purpose as tiger testes. But the Arctic peoples knew better; they called them corpse whales, due to their pallor. I had a stiff in my hands.

I was bruised and soggy, and images of Donny kept intruding. My lips were blue. There were crabs and buggy things everywhere. I was leaning on barnacles. I was a complete failure as a human being. My genetic line had no future. I was whimpering in frustration when I heard my name called out loud.

I peered over the rocks and saw Angie on the *Angie Baby* waving to me. "Orange! Orange Whippey! Heard you might need a lift," she called.

There are very few degrees of separation between us islanders. Angie is my friend Mitchell's ex-wife. The *Angie Baby* used to be his trawler. In fact, it's one of the nicest boats operating from the island. "If you can get over here, I'll bring you back in to the docks, but hurry up, Orange!"

Angie, of all people. Why did the sea gods, or at least Mr. Lucy, send Angie? There were so many other islanders who did not trigger my vanity, nor my shame. I'd spent years cultivating the belief that this woman was my cousin. If she were my cousin, I could steal a few peeks now and then and continue to admire the way she'd never lost her youthful roundness, the curves that turn to crags and angles so quickly on so many islanders. I could sleep over on her and Mitchell's couch, and we could shuffle around each other in our underwear in the morning without too much fuss. If Angie were only my cousin, the fact that her toenail polish matched her lipstick and her habit of wearing just a sweatshirt, a bathing suit, and a kerchief for half the summer, on and off the boat, would make as little an impression on me as her brown eyes. The white of her eye against the dark pupil did not remind me of the contrast of her tan line when her suit slipped a little off her hip. I was grateful, to be honest, when the two of them split. I could go back to easy drinking with Mitchell, quit showering before I went over. Angie had always been too competent for me. Too put together. It was intimidating. People like her had too much presence of mind, too little self-consciousness. Well, just enough—like just enough lipstick and enough poise to pilot her own boat.

Doing my best to crouch behind the rocks, I pulled on my damp sweatpants and T-shirt. I strapped myself into the life preserver and clambered down into the squishy seaweed and cold swirls of ocean. Once I was submerged, I took my tiller and tucked its tip under the preserver, hoping to preserve some dignity. After paddling over, I had some trouble climbing up the little ladder hanging over the stern.

"C'mon, let's go, Orange, we're drifting," Angie told me as she grabbed my life jacket and hauled me up. My limbs were stiff, the ladder meant for more sure-footed swimmers. Angie hauled me in over the side, grabbing my arm, the straps on my vest, and finally my very own windlass. "Jesus!" she said, surprised. The Lord's name was more than I could articulate at the moment. She got me the rest of the way in, but kept a firm handhold.

Entirely deprived of language, I gave her a look that was meant to communicate my appreciation of being rescued, my appreciation of the awkwardness of the predicament, my regret at imposing on her, my boyish vulnerability, my understanding of the comedic situation and the fact that nothing like this had ever occurred before, my acknowledgment of my own virility and masculinity, my appreciation of her femininity and firm hand, my ability to be discreet, my talent to take care of myself after this was over, my willingness to sink back into the brine, a wry awareness of what I presumed to be our suppressed mutual attraction over the years, and a rueful apology for remaining friends with Mitchell—along with a side note of resigned awareness of the way we must all live in each other's pockets here on the island.

I hoped the extra whites of my eyes expressed an urgent sincerity, and that their craquelure indicated an intriguing but safe degree of derangement.

If I'd been turned over, she would have had a perfect bouncer's toss handhold—one hand on the collar, the other on the belt. Her grip, though, suggested I was not to be thrown back. If I'd been a harbor seal, she would've been in a good position to gut me, maybe chum the water with my organs, and pickle my pizzle for a souvenir.

But she was Angie, whom I had tried so hard to not think about over the years. She'd always been friendly but guarded, treating me a bit like the competition, someone prone to lead Mitchell down unpaved paths of dissolution and boorish bonhomie. There was never any profit to explaining to her that it had really been the other way around. Had I ever admired her unbashful way with a bikini? Certainly. Did I know that our barber friend Laura cut the fine brown hairs on the back of Angie's neck once a month? I did. And I had fully imagined running my lips down along those soft bristles, feeling them tickle the rim of my nostrils as I nuzzled her neck, taking my time deciding whether to continue kissing, licking, biting all the way down her backbone or to take a tack and veer over her shoulder, maybe taking her collarbone between my teeth on my way to the fold of her neck, where I would rest my head as I unbuttoned her shirt and drew my face between her breasts, searching for the dot of perfume harbored somewhere in that soft warmth.

Indeed, in my imagination, Angie and I had gallivanted more than a few times, poor Mitchell having been relegated to oarsman down below, chained perhaps to his bench. Maybe I'd shared his shackles, maybe the princess whose galley we rowed had snuck below, pointed at me, and commanded, "Bathe him, and bring him to my cabin,"—her cabin where she'd napped and frigged herself to the rhythms of the waves and the oar pullers' straining, incessant sweeps.

Thus I'd shoot a glance and a shrug to Mitchell, my fellow traveler all these hard years at sea, as if to say, "Who am I to disobey the princess? I'll try to steal you some food while I'm above."

Such were the thoughts I did not ever entertain, and which were in no way pent up in my head, splashing over the seawall of my skull.

Angie was a good sailor, with a tool for every job and a place for every tool. She was back from setting her wheel on "Thereabouts, slowly," and unwrapping a rubber before I could even get out of the preserver. I don't even know how her shorts came off. My cock went straight from her hand to her lovely cunt, without her grasp ever lessening. She knelt astride me like a coxswain and began her own rhythm, pressing my shoulders back to the deck, to let me know that my role was to remain staunch. I pushed her shirt and bra up to her armpits, bunching her breasts. I pulled her chest down toward me and snapped at her engorged, pink-brown nipples. With a remonstrative hand to my front, Angie arched her back; she feathered and sculled, then bore down with long sweeping strokes that brought her clit right to my pelvic bone. And then again. A blush darkened her chest, and I felt the small of her back dampen with sweat. At last, I began to sense a familiar charge building within my body, a current channeling from the soles of my feet up the back of my legs, meeting the other fulmination surging down from the back of my mouth. I thanked every little thing that anyone has ever worshipped on this island.

We held each other's eyes in a softer grip than she'd started this off with, and I took a sounding right out of her skull. We were both trying to find words to say something more amorous than, "Thanks, I needed that!" A couple of smiles was all it took.

৪৯ WISH GIRLS ৩৬
Matthew Addison

MAX OPENED HIS BEDROOM DOOR, and there they were, his wish girls, sitting primly on the bed with their legs crossed, looking up at him through lowered lashes. Allison (the blonde) and Stephanie (the brunette), wearing the modified cheerleader outfits that now made him cringe with inward embarrassment whenever he saw them. The wish girls were fresh and perky and eager as always. "Hi, girls," he said, tossing his coat onto the chair and dropping his bag. He'd had a hard day at the bookstore, and more than anything he wanted someone to listen to his troubles and make him dinner, but those were two things his wish girls wouldn't do, couldn't do, hadn't been made to do, so he'd have to be satisfied with the services they did offer.

Stephanie and Allison were seventeen years old, and had been for the past fifteen years, never changing. They wore yellow-and-red uniforms that resembled the ones worn by cheerleaders at Max's old high school, but altered to titillate the perpetually aroused fourteen-year-old he'd been when he wished them into existence. The tops of the outfits were tight and thin and clinging, and Allison and Stephanie's ever-erect nipples stuck through visibly. There was a round keyhole cutout in each bodice, revealing the full side swells of their firm, high breasts, and the skirts were so short they hardly qualified as garments. The wish girls wore no panties, and even with their legs demurely crossed, he could see the curling of their pubic hairs, blonde and black. They wore knee socks over their smooth, lithe legs, and Max felt a bit like a dirty old man for admiring them. The wish girls had been older than him when they first appeared, but they hadn't aged as he had.

"Strip," he said. "Then go into the bathroom and shave." He lingered to watch them undress each other, with many shy glances and coquettish looks at him, peeling off each other's tops, shimmying out of their skirts. Their bodies were perfect: fine tits, taut bellies, round, firm asses—the fantasy amalgamation of all the girls he'd lusted after as an eighth-grade loser. Their bodies were identical, both the same height, both with pink nipples, breasts the same ample size, and he wished for the thousandth time that he'd given one of them brown nipples, at least, or made one of them five foot nine and the other five foot two (they were both five foot seven), done something to differentiate them, but he'd only wished for one blonde and one brunette, and that was the full extent of the variation. Even their faces were identical, *Seventeen*-model faces, with full lips, big blue eyes, high cheekbones.

The wish girls were undoubtedly lovely, but they'd been lovely in exactly the same way for a long time.

They finished undressing, and he stepped aside to let them into the living room. His apartment was too small for three people, but the wish girls didn't live with him, exactly—sometimes he fell asleep with them in his bed, but they always disappeared by morning, and they didn't use the bathroom or cook meals or do anything to take up space. There was a time, even a few years ago, when watching them undress each other would have aroused him enough to make one of them kneel and suck him off, but he found that more elaborate steps were required to excite him now.

Max made a microwave pizza while the girls shaved each other in the bathroom, and sat eating on the couch when they emerged, arm in arm, cunts freshly shorn. "Position 16," he said, and the girls knelt before him, facing each other. Each put a hand on the other's hip, and each slipped a hand into the other's always-wet cunt, then they began to finger the other; and they tilted their faces together, eyes closed, and kissed, lips parted, pink tongues moving gently. Max slipped off his pants and his boxers and sat back down, tugging his cock while they made out. "Pinch her nipple, Allison," he said, and the blonde reached out and tweaked, bringing a moan to Stephanie's throat. "Harder," he said, and she twisted, but Stephanie didn't make any sounds of pain. As far as Max could tell, they didn't feel pain, which made his forays into S&M less satisfying than they might have been, and made him wonder if they truly felt anything. "Gasp like it hurts you," he said, and Stephanie did, making high sounds of distress. "Slap her tits, Allison," he ordered, and watched for a while, but even this wasn't doing much for him.

"Position 39, variation B," he said, and the girls turned facing away from him, first getting on all fours, then lowering their heads to the carpet, leaving their asses in the air. They crossed their arms behind their backs at the wrists—that was the variation B part—and Max took two silk scarves from the table by the couch and used them to bind their wrists together. He went to the tall red tool chest in the corner, which contained years of accumulated sex toys and supplies, and took out lube and a pair of clear acrylic butt plugs. Returning to the girls, he squirted lube onto their pink rosebud assholes and rubbed with his fingers. They moaned and moved against his touch—he'd taught them to do that—and gasped as he slipped the plugs into them. Once he'd filled their asses, he wiped his lube-slicked hand on a towel and began spanking the girls, alternating between Stephanie and Allison, full-palm swats that made their beautiful asses bounce. Their skin never bruised or reddened, no matter how hard he hit, and he'd never broken their skin. The wish girls were the product of adolescent fantasies that hadn't gone much beyond groping, blow jobs, and vague misconceptions about fucking, and they weren't well equipped for some of the kinks he'd developed since then. Still, they gasped and cried out and begged for mercy, as he'd instructed them to do, until he was sufficiently turned on to slip his cock into Stephanie's tight, welcoming cunt while fingering Allison with one hand. When he was close to orgasm, he pulled out. "Position 8," he said, and pulled them into upright, kneeling positions. They put their faces close together and looked up at him worshipfully, licking their lips, and he tugged his cock until he shot come onto their smiling faces.

Once spent, he sat back on the couch, feeling empty. He liked coming on their faces, but he didn't find it as physically satisfying as coming in their mouths, cunts, or asses. They kept kneeling, attentive, waiting for any further orders, but Max shook his head. "I'm done. I'll call if I need anything." The wish girls unbound their own hands, removed the butt plugs gracefully, and slipped back into the bedroom. They would disappear, now, into whatever place they went when he wasn't using them.

Max sat on the couch, flipping channels, until he got lonely. He called, "Stephanie!" The brunette stepped out of the bedroom, clad in her cheerleader costume and with her full complement of pubic hair again, reset to her default state. "Put on the nightgown," he said. She stripped off her uniform, dropping the garments to the floor, where they would remain for as long as Max looked at them, though they would vanish the moment he looked elsewhere. She went to the toolbox and took out a sheer silk night-gown that was, relatively speaking, modest. "Position 115," he said, and she sat beside him, one hand resting on his leg, her head leaning against his shoulder, a warm and intimate nuzzle. Sometimes having her act like a girlfriend—like he imagined a girlfriend would act—made him happier, but tonight it just made him sad and even lonelier. "Position 43," he said, sliding down a little in his seat, and she lay sideways on the couch, head resting on his belly, and she sucked slowly, almost meditatively, on the head of his cock until he built toward orgasm again. He grasped her head in his hands and thrust his hips, his cock hitting the back of her throat again and again until he came in her mouth, and all the while she made moans of exquisite pleasure. Letting go of her head, he said, "Okay," and she sat up, swallowing and licking her lips. "Kiss me good night," he said, and she did, sweetly, softly, and then he sent her away for the night.

Max worked in the genre fiction section at a big chain bookstore, shelv-ing mysteries, romances, sci-fi, and fantasy. That morning he held a purple trade paperback with a golden Aladdin's lamp on the cover, the second book in some series about a wisecracking genie, and he tried to remember what, exactly, the circumstances of his wish had been. He knew he'd been in the woods behind his childhood home, and found . . . something, a ring, a bottle, a colored stone, and he'd been given a wish, though now he couldn't remember if some spirit or being had spoken to him, or if the knowledge of the wish had simply appeared in his mind. That was part of the wish's defense, he understood, to make the memory of its genesis vague, because then it would be harder for Max to tell other people about it. Whatever the specific circumstances had been, Max had held the wish-ing object in his hand, or he'd buried it in the dirt, or he'd broken it open, and he'd made his wish, voicing one of the many elaborate fantasies he concocted in his narrow bed each night, and then Allison and Stephanie had come to him. He'd spent the next three years slipping away to the woods every chance he got, on weekends and afternoons, even some days when he had cut school, going to a secluded clearing beyond earshot of his house and waiting for Allison and Stephanie to step out of the trees. They'd done everything he'd wanted, and in those years he did everything a young man could think to do with two girls, and watched as they did everything two young girls could do to each other—at least without the help of props and accessories and costumes. Max's grades fell, he stopped seeing his friends, he didn't take part in sports or theater or band, and he didn't ask girls out—why should he, with two lithe nude eager wish girls waiting for him in the woods? They'd been like a drug, he understood now, like heroin, and everything in his life became secondary to the pursuit of the pleasure they gave.

Someone tapped him on the shoulder, startling him. He turned to see a woman, about his age, with short, copper-colored hair and round-rimmed glasses, and he automatically compared her to Stephanie and Allison, as he did with every woman he saw—her face was round, her eyes were startlingly green; she had a pimple above one of her eyebrows, and her expression seemed amused even at rest. "I'm the new girl," she said. "Just transferred from the downtown branch. What's your name?"

"Uh, Max," he mumbled, looking down at the book in his hand, uncomfortable standing so close to her.

"Nice to meet you, Max, I'm Kira. I used to work in genre at my old bookstore, but they stuck me with photography and art books here. Let me know if you ever want to trade."

"Uh," he said. "No, I, uh—"

"Just kidding, Max, I'm not going to poach your section." She patted his shoulder and said, "See you around."

He turned and watched as she walked away, and he noticed her curves, her hips. She probably weighed fifty pounds more than Allison or Stephanie, and was four inches shorter than them, but it looked right and proportional on her—Kira didn't have their willowy figures. Max turned back to his shelving. Why had she made him so nervous? Spending fifteen years with Allison and Stephanie had rendered him incapable of interacting with women normally. He'd never been on a real date, and didn't have any close friends, didn't go out to bars—and why would he? The other guys at the bookstore went out, drank, and tried to pick up women, but Max didn't need to pick up women. He had the holy grail at home, two hot girls who couldn't get enough of him. His life was perfect. He'd blundered into magic, and his life was magical as a result.

So why didn't he look forward to going home anymore?

Max had expected things to change with the wish girls when he got his own apartment. Once he'd moved in, on his own for the first time, he'd called the girls, and they'd emerged from the bedroom, seeming happy, as always, to be summoned. "This is our place now," he said. "You never have to leave or disappear. No more going to the woods; you can just stay here." Their smiles didn't falter, but they didn't seem to absorb what he said, either. They could talk, and they understood the often complicated tasks he set for them, but they never truly conversed with him. Beyond a certain basic repertoire of phrases—"Yes, please, God"—he'd had to teach them whatever he wanted them to say.

"Allison, position 1," he said, and she knelt before him, unzipping his pants and pulling out his cock, stroking it to erectness and then licking the shaft slowly, from bottom to top. "What do you think of the apartment, Stephanie?" he asked, while Allison tongued the vein beneath the head of his dick.

"It's so big," she said. "It feels so good inside."

Max frowned. The words made superficial sense, though they weren't exactly accurate, and they were, of course, things he'd taught her to say under other circumstances. He wondered how intelligent they were, really, these wish girls of his, and it was something he would come to wonder again and again in the coming years.

Over the next weeks he tried to make them understand that his home was theirs, but they kept disappearing when he was done with them each night, and he kept running up against the limits of their capabilities. Once he tried to teach Allison to wash dishes—after all, if they were his willing slaves, why shouldn't he use them for something other than fucking? He'd explained everything required to wash dishes, and told Allison the chore was her responsibility from now on. The first night, she emerged from the bedroom and changed into a frilly white apron, four-inch spike heels, and nothing else. She'd filled the sink with soapy water, then leaned over the counter on her elbows, breasts in the suds, ass lifted invitingly, and Max had been so turned on he'd come up behind her and pounded her hard, pulling her hair and squeezing her soapy tits while he thrust into her. It was only later that he realized she hadn't done the dishes at all, even when he was done fucking her, and all his later attempts to get them to do anything nonsexual ended that way—he'd fucked Stephanie from behind while her head hung in the toilet after he'd tried to teach her to clean the bathroom, and while they were more than willing to let him eat off their bodies, they never prepared food for him. They were happy to dress up in maid uniforms—that was one of the first mildly kinky things he'd done with them once he had his own apartment—but not to act like maids.

He'd had great plans for their life together, but most of them hadn't panned out. Once when he was desperately short of money—car broken down, dental bills overdue—he'd tentatively asked if they were willing to fuck other men, thinking he could pimp them out. They'd shaken their heads in unison, almost sadly. Another time, he'd wanted to go out on the town and impress people with the hot women hanging all over him, intending to strap them into butt-plug harnesses, dress them in tight tops and skirts and stripper heels, and let them follow him around bars and nightclubs, squirming from the plugs in their asses—but they'd refused to cross his threshold. They wouldn't let anyone else see them. That was probably his own fault. Max couldn't remember the precise wording of his wish, but hadn't there been some element of the grasping and the selfish? Some phrase like "only for me, just for me," when he'd wished for Allison and Stephanie? He'd been young, and he hadn't thought through all the ramifications of his wish.

"I wish you would talk to me," he'd said one night that first year out of high school, hungry for conversation, wishing for something more than the endless physical.

Allison and Stephanie gazed up at him. "We belong to you," Allison said. "You can do anything you want with us," Stephanie said. "We love you," they both said. Just like he'd taught them to.

Max lay in bed and fondled his cock and balls, thinking of Kira, fantasizing about the softness of her belly against his cheek, the weight of her body upon him, imagining birthmarks and freckles—he'd been with the wish girls for so long that he'd begun to fetishize blemishes. He stroked and tugged himself toward orgasm, the first time in years he'd jerked himself off—why masturbate when at a moment's whim he could have a perfect, sweet-faced cheerleader giving him a hand job or sucking him off? But now he was thinking of Kira, and he imagined her face—those green eyes, that half smile—as he came, spurting hot come over his fingers and onto his stomach.

As he lay in the dark he thought, *Maybe it's time I started dating.*

A week went by, and before Max could work up the nerve to ask Kira out, she asked him if he wanted to get a bite after work. "Sure," he said, and they went to an Ethiopian place near the bookstore, where they ate spicy and savory food, scooped up with hot, soft pieces of *injera*, Ethiopian flat bread. They talked about working for the bookstore, why she'd transferred to his branch (hers got downsized), about books, and Max managed more or less to think of her as a person rather than as a woman. Gradually his anxiety diminished. She was cute, funny, and interesting, and he did his best to keep her entertained and interested in talking to him. It was surprisingly easy to do so. They liked the same books, hated the same movies, and Max eventually realized she was flirting with him. They started talking about fantasy novels and stories, and without much conscious thought, Max steered the dialogue toward wishes. "What would you do with three wishes?" he asked.

Kira sat back against the cushioned booth, hands laced across her stomach, under her breasts. "I always thought three wishes was too many. With three wishes, you can ask for wealth, eternal youth, and top it off with world peace, and feel like a big hero for the last one. I think it's more interesting to ask what you'd do with one wish. That's how you can tell the selfish from the generous. So tell me, Max, if you had one wish, what would it be? World peace, or strippers and blow?"

Max thought it over. He knew what he'd done with his one wish, but he'd been fourteen at the time, and by definition almost sociopathically self-centered. If he had the wish again, now . . . "I'd wish for happiness," he said, and it felt true, like something he wanted very much.

"Selfish, but abstract," Kira said. "I'd probably go for the strippers and blow myself. I've read too many stories to think that even well-meant wishes would turn out the way I wanted."

They finished the meal, and Max walked Kira back to her car. "We should do this again sometime," he said. "Soon."

"We should do more than this sometime," she said, and leaned up to kiss him. Her breath tasted of *timatim fitfit* and after-dinner mint, and his surprise made the kiss awkward, but there was something behind it, a warmth and pressure of a sort he'd never felt with the wish girls. "Soon," she said, and that was goodbye for the night.

Max wanted Kira, wanted to make love to her, but he couldn't. But he had other means of release. He drove home from dinner and found a package on his doorstep. He took it inside and opened it on the kitchen counter, smiling as he drew out the tangle of leather straps and D rings. It was the strap-on harness he'd ordered from an online erotica catalog, along with a nine-inch black silicone dildo. "Girls!" he called, and after they appeared, he directed them to shave, put on red cocksucker lipstick (they appeared fresh-faced and without makeup by default), and be back in the living room on their knees in ten minutes. "We're doing scenario 21, variation C." he said. "Stephanie's top, Allison's bottom."

"You heard him, you little bitch," Stephanie said, and slapped Allison's ass. "Get in there and get your clothes off." Allison hurried away, eyes downcast, hands held behind her back.

Max leaned against the bathroom door frame and watched them get ready, Stephanie cajoling Allison, slapping her tits, and promising her humiliation and violations. For her part, Allison was obedient but frightened, her lower lip quivering as she put on mascara, which she would cry off in act 2 while Stephanie flogged her.

"Come get dressed, Stephanie," he said, and took her into the bedroom. He laced her into a black leather under-bust corset that lifted her tits even higher than normal, and she put on knee-high leather boots. He gave her a wicked riding crop, which she lashed through the air experimentally. "I just got this for you today," he said, and showed her the new strap-on harness. She *oohed* and *aahed* appreciatively, the way she always responded to the sex toys he brought home, a sort of automatic erotitropism. He helped her into the harness, taking great pleasure in pulling the leather straps tight around her hips, the black dildo rising impressively erect from her crotch. "You like being top, Steph?" he said, and she nodded. He grabbed both her wrists, wrenched her arms over her head, and forced her down to her knees. He twisted her wrists, and when she gasped, he shoved his cock into her mouth, thrusting hard. "Just remember, I'm the one who's really top," he said. "Tell me you love it. Tell me you love the taste of my cock." He adored the way she sounded, trying to speak while he fucked her mouth, and it took all his willpower not to come then. He pulled out and looked down at her where she knelt, breathing hard, breasts heaving prettily, arms still held over her head.

How could she be so perfect, with her teeth never brushing his cock no matter how hard he used her, never sweating, never belching, never having a headache or having her time of the month? Never . . .

Never surprising him. Perfect, and perfectly familiar. She was exactly what he'd wished for, and every night he spent with his wish girls was a night of incredibly sophisticated masturbation. Nothing more.

Well, fuck it. Pleasure was pleasure, and there's something to be said for the familiar. At least Allison and Stephanie didn't make him nervous.

"Get up," he said. "Let's get Allison trussed up. I've got a new mouth harness I want to see her in. I'm thinking, after we whip her, we can lay her out on her back across the dining room table, and you can fuck her ass while I fuck her throat. Sound good?"

"Whatever pleases you, Max," she said.

"I can tell you're the shy type, Max," Kira said, pouring him another glass of sangria. "And I don't mind being aggressive, but I want to know my advances are welcome. I don't want to make an idiot of myself. Are you interested in me?"

Max sat on Kira's couch, and she passed him his drink, then sat beside him, tucking her legs beneath herself with casual grace. "You move so beautifully," he said, the two glasses of sangria already inside him relaxing him enough to say such things.

She looked at him over the rim of her glass, sipped, and said, "I studied ballet when I was a kid, but I didn't have the body to keep it up—not thin enough, too zaftig by half. I was crushed at the time, but in retrospect, I'm glad I don't live a life of glamorous starvation and crippled feet."

"I think you look wonderful," Max said, but he looked down into his drink, shy. This was nothing like talking to the wish girls. "I'm sorry. I do like you a lot. I just . . . haven't gone out much. I'm nervous. I've only been with a couple of women in my life."

"That's okay," she said. "That just means you won't have as many bad habits to unlearn." She grinned—a twinkling, mischievous look of a sort he'd never seen on the faces of the wish girls—and she plucked the drink from his hand and set it aside. Kira leaned into him, and they began kissing; she took his hand and pressed it against her silk shirt, against her breast, which was large and full and shaped differently from those Max was used to. Her hand touched his thigh, then slid up to squeeze his cock. She kissed his neck, stroked his leg, slipped a finger into the waistband of his pants, her fingernail brushing through his pubic hair, making him shiver and tingle all over. Max's heart hammered, pulse throbbing through him and making his cock twitch, and he felt weightless, unmoored—he didn't know what she was going to do. Kira was an independent operator, an ongoing surprise. Her hair smelled of strawberry shampoo, and there was a hint of sweat, and her skin—the wish girls smelled almost of nothing, a little bit of baby powder, nothing else. This was intoxicating, and for the first time, it occurred to Max that sex could be a collaborative act.

"Bedroom," Kira said, and tugged him by his waistband into her cluttered room, walls decorated with painted kites, a double bed with a white comforter. They fell into bed together, touching each other urgently, and she stripped off her shirt and bra, revealing pale breasts with large brown nipples. Her left breast was slightly larger than the right, and this amazing human variation made Max moan and push her down on the bed, bowing his head to take her nipple in his mouth and suck. She made a sound like a contented cat and lifted her hips against him. He stopped kissing her breast and pulled down her skirt, taking a moment to admire her panties—black lace, hardly there, she must have planned all along to take him to bed—and then he pulled them down, too, and buried his face between her legs. Oh, the smell, sweat, and wetness, and something unmistakably feminine—the wish girls were nothing like this. He'd gone down on them countless times, and they'd never had a scent like this, just that baby-powder neutrality.

What had he been missing all this time?

He tongued her, slipped a finger inside her, was surprised to find she wasn't very wet yet. Another way she differed from the wish girls. He licked her, bottom to top, and she said, "Oh, that's right, warm me up, Max." When she was wetter, he slipped a finger into her and moved it while tonguing her clit, and this went on for a minute or so before she touched the top of his head. "Max, sweetie," she said, "your heart's in the right place, but your finger isn't."

He looked up at her, his hand unmoving, and realized that all the thousands of hours he'd spent fucking the wish girls had taught him nothing at all about women. "Tell me what to do," he said, and she gave him that grin again. She guided him—"There, press your fingers up toward the, yes, right there, now swirl your tongue, to the right, no, my right, yes, there, keep it up." Max did as she said, though his wrist got sore and his tongue got tired. He'd never spent so much time going down on Allison and Stephanie, just enough to satisfy his own urge to taste and finger them, but this was something different, something more worthwhile, and after a while Kira got much wetter and bucked against his hand and tongue. She trembled, almost silently, with none of the theatrical orgasms Max had seen in porn films and had taught the wish girls to emulate.

He kissed her belly, and she stroked his hair, and he said, "Can I fuck you now?"

"You'd better," she said, and he rose up and pushed her legs apart. She said, "Whoa, Max, not so fast, condom first." She reached to the bedside table and lifted a square, foil-wrapped packet.

"Ah, right," Max said, suddenly terrified. He'd never worn a condom in his life.

"I'll put it on you," she said, and rolled him onto his back. She grasped and tugged his cock, then put it briefly in her mouth, and he swelled to full hardness. She tore open the package and deftly rolled the condom—cold, strange—onto his cock, then swung one leg over to straddle him and eased herself down, guiding his cock up into her warm, wet cunt. She rocked on top of him, reaching down to tweak his nipples, slipping a finger into his mouth for him to suck. Her weight, her spontaneity, the way she moved, it was all so different, and if not for the condom acting to dull the sensation a bit, he might have come in her right away. A euphoria grew inside him, spread through his body, suffusing his limbs with outrushing lightness. Max had never felt so good. She lowered herself, breasts against his chest, cheek against his cheek, her breath in his ear, and he reached down to take hold of her ass in both hands, thrusting his hips against her, and her breath quickened as she thrust back, and soon they were rocking together, headboard slamming against the wall, moving faster and faster until he felt himself starting to come. He squeezed her ass harder and thrust away, the two of them moving in wonderful concert, and she gasped in his ear and shuddered, trembling. He couldn't tell whether his orgasm had excited her into her own, or vice versa.

Afterward, she didn't disappear, and he was glad.

"We should do this again sometime," he said, tentatively, afraid she'd turn away.

"Soon," she said. "Take me to your place next time?"

"Of course," he said.

Max knew better than to think it was true love. Oh, maybe it was, but Kira could just as easily grow bored with him, or more likely he would fail her in some way, since he had no experience with romantic relationships. But he'd turned a corner. Even if he didn't stay with Kira forever, there would be other women, other relationships. He'd discovered how things could be, now, and there was no going back. He'd finally grown up.

But he hadn't grown up so much that he didn't want one last fling, for old time's sake.

The next morning Max called in sick to work, and summoned Stephanie and Allison. He dressed them in black stiletto heels and knee pads and nothing more. "Stephanie, kneel there, legs spread, and reach behind you and grab your heels. Don't let go of your heels, no matter what." She did as she was told, and he fastened a leather and plastic ring gag around her head, a mouth harness that held her jaws open for constant access. She gripped her heels, breasts jutting out beautifully, and he slipped his cock through the gag into her warm, wet mouth, sliding it back and forth. "Keep looking up at me with those wide eyes of yours. And you, Allison, kneel behind me and lick my asshole." He fucked Stephanie's face for a while as Allison tongued him. He could have come on them then—Stephanie had never looked more fetching—but he wanted to run the gamut today. He put collars and leashes on them and led them around the room on all fours, lashing their rumps with a riding crop. He leaned them both over the couch, lubed their asses generously, and pounded first one, then the other. He lay down and had Stephanie straddle his cock while Allison sat on his face, and they kissed and fondled each other while he tongued and fucked them. He had Stephanie put on the new black strap-on, and they double-penetrated Allison, who whimpered as Max thrust into her ass, begging him to do it harder, harder. Then he had Allison put on the old strap-on harness and let his wish girls fuck him—he went down on all fours, Allison sliding a smaller dildo in and out of his mouth. After that he spanked them, whipped them, fondled them, caressed them, and fucked them every way he could think of. By day's end he was exhausted, sweat soaked, and trembling from the exertion. His cock felt drained dry from the day's several orgasms. The wish girls, of course, seemed as calm and well rested as always.

"I'm letting you go," he said.

Allison and Stephanie looked at him, then looked at each other. They frowned in unison. He'd never seen them frown before, except when they were playing Harsh Mistresses, and even that was a different, more theatrical expression.

"I appreciate all you've done for me," he said. This was harder than he'd expected. "You've made my life wonderful. But . . . I don't think this is good for me anymore. I've met someone . . . well—it doesn't matter."

"You're setting us free?" Stephanie asked.

Had Max ever taught her to say that, as part of some bondage role-play scenario, maybe? He didn't think so. "Yes. You can go."

"Turn your back while we get dressed," Allison said.

Max knew he'd never taught her to say that. He'd seen her in every conceivable state of disarray—even now, his come was drying on her breasts. But modesty, he suddenly understood, was a privilege of the free. He turned his back.

"Okay," Allison said a moment later.

He turned to find them dressed in jeans and gray sweatshirts, not out-fits he'd ever have chosen for them, clothes they'd conjured for themselves. They stepped toward him in unison, each kissing one of his cheeks.

"'Bye, Max," Allison said.

"We didn't think you'd ever get to this point," Stephanie said. She patted his cheek.

The wish girls left. They didn't disappear; they just went out the front door. Maybe they'd get to be real people now, and make choices of their own. He didn't know.

Max spent the rest of the evening filling heavy black garbage bags with sex toys, bondage gear, and lingerie, tossing it all into the big Dumpster behind the apartment complex. The garbagemen were sure to get a kick out of that. Maybe he and Kira would start playing with toys eventually, but he'd buy new ones for that. Even Max's vestigial sense of gentlemanly conduct told him that was the appropriate thing to do.

Two days later, Max sat on his couch, and Kira knelt on a pillow between his feet, sucking his cock. He looked down at her closed eyes, the expression of tender concentration on her face, and he was overwhelmed with happiness. She was doing this because she wanted to, because she liked him, because she wanted to make him feel good. And because she knew he'd return the favor.

Kira's teeth brushed against Max's cock. It hurt, a little. He'd never been happier.

⸙ SECOND DATE ⸙
Marcelle Manhattan

Now is not the time for nostalgia.
I remember our evening last summer: KGB Bar, Lower East Side. I was wearing a white sundress. He was late, and I had to sit alone. Why had I agreed to a second date? Was I bored? Did I like him more than I realized, after our first night out?

"So, Rachel Kramer Bussel is hosting this reading. . . . I know erotica can be hit or miss, but it sounds like fun. Do you wanna go?"

I didn't want to seem like a girl who'd never attended an erotic reading or didn't know who Rachel Kramer Bussel was. I felt nervous and silly in my white J.Crew dress.

"Marcelle!" I saw him dash up to the bar. "Sorry; working late." He kissed my cheek. As he ordered my martini, he flashed his sunny smile, and I relaxed a little.

"Just in time," John said, as he handed me a sophisticated, funneled glass. The room silenced as Ms. Bussel took the podium, looking more like an Ivy League classmate of mine, I thought, than an erotic reading organizer.

John stood drinking whiskey like water as a petite woman recited her memoirs as a dominatrix on Wall Street. Before that night, I hadn't truly known what a dominatrix did: pissing on well-dressed bankers and fucking their tightly wound asses with a thick, silicone strap-on as they writhed on the ground in humiliation. I took a gulp of my martini.

The second reader narrated his exploits with a candy-sweet, barely legal intern, who seduced him innocently with her short skirts at the office and screamed disturbingly hot filth while they fucked.

I sat, uncertain of my reaction. I wasn't uncomfortable, but I was creamy wet between the legs. I didn't know how to acknowledge my arousal in a public setting. By the third reading, I wanted to rub myself against the barstool, and John kept looking at me and smiling as if this were the most natural thing in the world.

We clapped politely for the story, and I moved my stool closer to him. I wanted our legs to touch, to rest my hand on his. I am not an initiator, but I could slowly let my lap fall open, legs spread invitingly, one bared knee brushing his leg.

He looked startled. Then, hidden by the jutting countertop, slick with the sweat of rested elbows and dripping glasses, he began to stroke my thigh, just under the hiked hemline, looking at our speaker with polite interest the entire time.

I closed my eyes. I listened to her words.

A trickle of liquid dripped down my inner leg onto John's caressing hand.

I heard him draw in a breath. But he did not, as I expected, move closer to the source. I ached, sitting in a puddle, his hands stroking me casually as if he were too preoccupied to care. Surreptitiously, I reached up under the bar and tentatively rubbed the upper leg of his jeans.

John still watched the reader and pretended not to notice. He withdrew from my thigh, cast a casual glance at me, and slowly raised his soiled finger to his mouth. He sucked it clean, grinning mischievously. Then, without a word, he grabbed my martini just as I was raising it to my mouth and set it on the bar.

"We'll only be a minute," he said, seeing the puzzled look on my face. Taking my hand, he led me to the bar restroom: a mise-en-scène that would grow familiar in our peeing-fetish days but was then still strange, both sterile and dirty.

He brushed back my hair, curly and tangled from the humid night.

"You're so beautiful," he murmured, his hands moving up under my skirt again, higher than before. He kissed me—fast, eager kisses that didn't indulge or languish but propelled us to something more. I was so aroused that I let him pick me up and place my bare ass cheeks on the cold, low sink. He pulled aside the flimsy strip of my thong and began to sink his fingers into me.

"God, you're so wet . . ." he said incredulously, amid the moans I was trying to stifle. "I've never seen this before."

At first, I wasn't sure how to take this. I met his smile and we kissed harder, his fingers vibrating and jerking inside me. I closed my eyes and felt something new and almost unbearable. It was something fracturing me between the legs, agonizingly wonderful. In splintering, glass-shard pain, I cried out, as more liquid poured between my thighs. He moved faster, harder, and I felt the stab before breaking, freeing the dammed fluids and letting loose a spray of miraculous, screaming, squirting juices.

"Sh . . ." John whispered sternly as I came. I lay against his chest, feeling I might cry. I pressed his lean back muscles with my clinging hands. It hadn't happened in such a long time.

When I straightened up, I started to unzip his eye-level jeans.

"Do you always squirt?" he asked excitedly.

I shook my head. "No, I—"

I broke off at the sight of the girthy mass of flesh that confronted me, defying nature. I stared, even though I knew it was rude. How could a man who was five foot eleven and 165 pounds, tops, have an eight-inch cock like a tree trunk? My mouth opened automatically, like a starved porn star, but it didn't get far around its object. I sat looking helpless at it, stroking it worshipfully, but unsatisfied.

"This won't take long," said John. He put his hand over mine, so that we made one enjoined circle around the monstrous shaft.

Together, we stroked the smooth flesh. I felt it give beautifully back and forth, malleable and hard, under our collective grip. John had nice hands; I loved feeling him touch me while I caressed his cock. Then I let go, so I could watch him.

First, he moved it in front of my face, so I could taste longingly from underside to tip, and loll my tongue playfully around the head, lapping at its formidable split. I licked for a while, longing for more, until he groaned and pulled it away. Then, he took down my straps to shove it in between my breasts, the cleavage perfectly formed by the angle at which I leaned forward on the sink.

I watched, mesmerized, as he took the authoritative instrument in his slender hands and began to stroke it right in front of me. I noticed he treated the shaft lightly, perfunctorily, while concentrating his pressure just below the swollen head. His eyes were closed and his hands worked quickly, until finally he jerked it off with a frenzied motion. My jaw dropped in shock as he stifled a cry himself and shot copious come all over the front of my white dress.

I opened my mouth to protest, and instead he stuffed his fingers in. I tasted myself for the first time. It was like a sea-salted lemon. I liked it. John told me later I had a very greedy look on my face as I sucked and sampled.

"It's white. It looks like water," he said, gesturing toward my dress when we sat back down at the bar. "You want another martini?" He ordered brightly, as if nothing had happened. But for me, it had. I was wet clear through: soiled and stained. I listened to the reader, hearing words as if for the first time. *Cock. Finger. Pussy. Juice. Lick. Come. Satisfy. Desire.*

John met my gaze and smiled. Then he brought his hands together in applause. I looked around and saw that everyone was clapping. The reading had ended. I was jarred by the noise of approving and evaluating audience members, suddenly mobile bodies, and a publicly private space that had become public again—or rather, revealed itself to have been public all along.

We rode the subway home to Brooklyn, where we both lived at the time. When we arrived at my stop, he walked me to my door.

"I had fun," he said, beaming that pure gold smile. He leaned over for a soft kiss before pulling away and walking back to the train.

I let myself into my apartment and slowly took off my soiled dress, folding it carefully before placing it in the hamper. I stood confusedly in front of it for a few minutes before slipping into bed naked. The air conditioner hummed a familiar, cooling lull, and I covered myself with the comforter. I lay there for a very long time, wondering what had just happened to me.

ꙮ THE PORTABLE GIRLFRIEND ꙮ
Doug Tierney

"Hey, wire head, wake up!"

Jack Bolander felt the vibrations through the floor as his roommate pounded on the bedroom door. The sunrise coming through his window turned the yellow, painted-over wallpaper a sick orange color, the color inside his head when he wired in without any software in the 'Face.

Ron pounded the door harder. "You're going to be late for work again, asshole. If you get fired, I'm kicking you out in the street."

"Yeah, yeah, I'm up." Bo had been lying awake for a while on his bare mattress, staring at the water-damaged ceiling, drawing pictures with the rusty brown splotches, and trying to forget his dreams. Unconsciously, he stroked the inside of his thigh, but he stopped when Ron kicked the door again. "I'll be out in a minute."

"I'm leaving in two minutes, with or without you."

"I said I'm coming." He dressed without looking down at his body, without glancing down at the lacework of shrapnel scars that ran from his right leg, across his crotch, to his left hip. He stuffed the 'Face and wires into his rucksack along with a couple disks before he pulled on his boots and his field jacket. He didn't bother to tie the boots; he'd do that in the car.

Stepping out of his room felt like stepping into someone else's house. Ron had furniture and houseplants and cats. Bo had a mattress on the floor, piles of clothes, and milk crates of software. Sometimes he slept in the closet when he couldn't stop dreaming about the war.

In the car, Bo pulled out the 'Face and wired the first disk he pulled from his bag without looking at the title.

Do you want me? The woman, a brunette with huge, conical breasts that defied gravity, appeared where the dashboard had been a moment before. She gave Bo a heavy-lidded look of lust with her wide brown eyes. Through her left nipple, Bo saw the hubcap of a passing truck. He popped out the disk and saw that it was a piece of AIC barterware he'd picked up in trade a few days before. Cheap, low-format, look-but-no-touch kind of thing, even slightly transparent. Masturbation material, if you kept the lights down low.

For the second disk, he made sure he picked his only MASIC tri-disk. Full sensory, including tactile, capable of carrying on a conversation, it remembered you from one session to the next. The sim—called Carson, for Kit, not Johnny—lived on a thick, black-and-green MASIC wafer chip sandwiched between magneto-optical disks. The startup reminded him of the prairie, the sound of wind in the grass and the smell of rich black coffee and dirt. Across the bottom of his vision, the 'Face captioned in bright red script: *Warning: License period expired. Three (3) days remaining in renewal window. Proceed at your own risk?*

He chose to go ahead. Bo had gotten the Kit Carson sim free with the 'Face, but like everything, it's only free until you're hooked. The renewal would cost most of his savings, and he'd planned something else for the money.

Hey, pardner. You got an upgrade code for me? Kit shimmered into existence in the back seat of the Saab, dressed in red plaid and dusty chaps. He smelled of gunpowder and horse, chewing tobacco and leather. Kit slapped Bo on the shoulder, a warm, friendly gesture they'd both grown accustomed to.

"No, I guess not. I just thought you might want to bullshit for a while," Bo offered. Ron sat in the driver's seat, oblivious to the silent conversation taking place beside him. Bo turned to see Kit better, and the sim shuddered when Bo jerked the power cord between the 'Face and the battery pack. "Heading to work, and the yup's not speaking again."

Well, ole pal, I'd like to stay and talk. Kit flickered, and suddenly he wore a business suit and tie. *But as you know, it's against the law to access unlicensed MASIC media.* He blinked back into his chaps and cowboy hat.

*So until you get off your cheap ass and pay the renewal fee, I've got nothing
to say to you, low-down, software-rustling loser.*

He flicked Bo's ear with his finger, an electric shock that ran down his
neck to the shoulder. *Cheapskate son of a bitch, pay for your software.* Kit's
fist almost connected with Bo's jaw before he popped the sim out without
powering down. The cowboy dissolved with a squeal, and Bo tossed the
disk out the window.

"What was that?" Ron snapped, looking back.

"Bad disk," Bo said and rolled the window back up. He considered
throwing the AIC vixen after the MASIC hombre. Then he thought
about how short he was on licensed softsoft, and decided against it. He
knew where he could get a black box to defeat license protection, but
if he had that kind of money, he'd go ahead and buy the house and the
Ferrari instead.

Ron dropped him off at the gate of the auto plant, where he worked
for just above the minimum outrage, running a robot welder. His work-
station sat like a slick green throne in the middle of a scrubbed concrete
assembly-line floor. The whole building echoed with its own between-
shifts silence while Bo inserted the manipulator probe like an IV into the
socket in his right arm and keyed the machine to life with the magnetic
tattoo on his thumb.

The work was on the level of autonomic, barely a conscious effort in
the whole process, just a well-practiced dance of fingers flexing, pointing,
gripping, rolling, until all the parts were fixed together. Unable to read or
wire up while working, he'd once tried masturbating and had arc-welded
the trunk lids shut on three sedans by mistake. He could only sit and doze
and wait out the shift, gripping a soft rubber ball in the working hand.

Everyone got paid at the end of the shift, and Bo wired up to check
his bank balance. With the automatic deposit, minus his rent, he finally
had enough. He'd saved up his money for months, socking away spare
change, skipping meals whenever cigarettes alone would get him through.
It was time for Jack Bolander to go downtown to find himself a date. Not
just any woman, though. He had someone special in mind.

The last several weeks, she was all he'd lived for. He rode the bus into
the growing Boston gloom, knowing he'd have her soon. The excitement
of it was an electric pulse down the inside of his thigh all the way to the
knee. When he noticed he was tapping his foot, he tried to stop, but it
didn't last.

The dark seemed to flow up around the windows of the sick yellow and stained white bus as the driver pushed his way through traffic to the core of the city. Darkness up from the sewers, sticking to the sides of the glass and concrete towers, turning the streets into a sodium-lamplit tunnel. The bus hit a pothole so hard the windows jarred, and Bo nearly fell off his seat.

"Fuckin' streets," the driver muttered. "As much money as this city makes offa parking tickets, you'd think they could repave this place once in a while." He hit another crater, so hard it could only have been intentional. "Like fuckin' Beirut."

"It's more like Goradze." A suit next to Bo spoke, a comment meant to open a conversation.

"Before or after the Ukes carpet-bombed it?" he asked. The other man either missed or ignored his sarcasm. Bo checked the guy over and didn't know which to hate more: the Euro-styled hair or the entrepreneurial smile. Bo decided on the smile.

"During," the man said. He pulled back his mop of blond hair and revealed a teardrop-shaped scar running from the corner of his left eye back up over his ear. He'd had an ocular enhancement removed. Another wired-up vet. "Forward observer."

"Three-thirty-second Mobile Artillery," Bo replied. He peeled back his sleeve, a ritual showing of scars. "Gunner. Still wired. You probably called in fire for us."

"Many times. That was the shit, wasn't it?" He shook his head. The bus's brakes squealed and Bo felt it in the base of his spine. The man pulled out a business card and passed it to him. "I'm Scott Dostoli. Listen, I'm starting up a consulting firm with a couple other wired vets. The pay isn't great, but it's better than that workfare bullshit the VA keeps pushing."

"It beats jacking off a robot all day."

"Without a doubt," he said and stood up. "I get off here. Give me a call, okay?"

"You got it." Bo smiled and threw him a lazy salute. When the suit stepped off the bus, Bo threw the card on the floor and went back to watching out the windows. "Fuckin' spyglass johnnies," he muttered. Several minutes later, the bus turned onto Essex Street.

"This is my stop," Bo said. When the bus didn't slow down, he yelled, "Hey, asshole, this is my stop." He stood up, catching himself on the worn aluminum pole as the bus swerved to the curb. The brakes sounded even worse up front. Bo shouldered his green canvas rucksack and brushed his greasy brown hair from his face.

"Ring the fuckin' bell next time." The driver cranked the door open and yelled, "Essex Street! Change here for the Orange Line."

Essex stank of rotting fish and urine in the gutters. Bo had forgotten how bad it could be in July. The summer heat blew up the alleys from the South End to mingle with the thick brown smell of the Chinatown dumpsters, the reek of stale beer, and the Combat Zone's lust and cigarette ash. Bolander breathed in short, tight breaths through his mouth as he shuffled down the street, trying to look as if he were going somewhere else, shoulders hunched, weaving between refuse, trying without success not to make eye contact with the dealers and junkies haunting the corners.

"Hey, my man, you look like you're after a date." The pimp stood a head shorter than Bolander, but his arms were thicker, his chest broader. Muscle didn't mean much on the streets anymore, not when any punk or junkie could afford a gat or a Taser, but it never hurt to look the part of the tough. He wore a tight black Bruins T-shirt and a black Raiders cap, and he smelled like cheap musk cologne. "Got a nice Asian girl, big ol' tits, just waiting for you. Guarantee you'll like her."

"Not interested." He tried to push past the pimp or to outpace him, but the man stayed with him, shouldering him toward the plate glass door of a cheap hotel with red and gold Chinese screens in the lobby. The sign over the desk advertised hourly rates.

"You like a white girl, izat it? Stick to yo' own kind?" He angled so he was chest to chest with Bo, backing him toward the doors once again. As Bolander spun right, away from the hotel, away from the pimp, the yellow light of the streetlamp glinted orange off the metal stud on the back of his head, between his brown hair and the gray collar of his fatigue shirt. The pimp saw the wire port, and Bo saw the pimp seeing him.

"Oh, so that's how you play. Hey, I can set you up with some softsoft, good shit, straight from Japan."

"Not interested. Back off." Something in Bo's voice, a hot edge, like bile in the back of the throat, made the pimp take several steps back, hands raised, the pale palms ghostly and disembodied in the shadows and uncertain light.

"Hey, wire head. You just gotta say so." He stepped back a few more paces before turning his back to Bolander. "You a wire freak," he muttered, still loud enough to hear. "Don't fuck wit' no wire freaks."

Bo pulled his collar up over his port and covered the rest of the distance to the shop in strides lengthened by both adrenaline and anticipation. He glanced around once to make sure no one was watching before he ducked through the door of Abbe's Cellar. As far as it went, the Cellar was about the norm for the Zone, the usual stacks of porno movies and erotic magazines in their stiff shrink-wrap, glass display cases of adult toys of every improbable shape and size, a lot of B&D leather and masks, as the store's name implied. Unlike the other places on the street, though, it was a little darker, quieter. It had more atmosphere, and their prices kept the lowlifes out. Instead of being a poorly lit supermarket for human lusts, they catered to the desires, the fantasies.

Their clientele was businessmen on their way home to someone, picking up a gadget or a piece of silk that would repaint the faded colors of a lover's smile and restore the sharp-edged, naughty gleam in a wife's eyes, the look that used to say, "My parents are going to be out all night. . . . I'm so glad you stopped by." Abbe's also took pride in being on the cutting edge. Softsoft, ROMdolls, network services.

Bo didn't bother to sift through the collections of paraphernalia in the front. He didn't even consider the bulletin board, where swingers posted their parties. What he wanted—who he wanted—was in the back room, waiting, sleeping, ready to wake up to his kiss on the back of her neck. Maybe she'd been waiting as long for him as he had been for her. The further back he went, the less the cellar looked like a shop. It came to resemble a basement or a lonesome middle-class attic full of boxed history and old thoughts, faded and threadbare as the clothes that hang in the back of a closet. The leather harnesses and silk bonds didn't glare with the orange and blue scanner-coded tags like they did up front. Some didn't even have tags at all, hanging like personal mementos in the owner's den.

It was hotter in the back, where the air conditioner didn't quite reach. Bo shifted his pack from one shoulder to the other as he shrugged out of his gray and black field jacket. He knotted the sleeves around his waist, feeling self-conscious of the hardware and of his small tank-gunner's flame. He felt bigger with the jacket on.

"Help you find something?" Abbe came out of the storeroom, a can of diet-something in his hand. He was a bit shorter than Bo, close to 200 pounds, balding on top, but making up for it with facial hair. He wore a white silk bowling shirt with red trim and sweat stains under the arms. His name was embroidered in red over the pocket, and somehow, he smelled clean. Not clean like showered, or clean like Boston air after a summer thunderstorm when the sun finally comes out. It was clean like skinny-dipping in an icy spring-fed pond in the hills. His smell made Bo comfortable and took the nervous edge off their conversation.

"I've got something particular in mind."

"Okay, that's a good place to start." Abbe dragged a wobbly barstool from behind the curtain and offered it to Bo. When he declined, Abbe grabbed a magazine from the shelf and tossed it to the floor to prop up the short leg. "What exactly is it you'd like, and we'll see if we can hook you up." He struggled up onto the chair, still not quite on eye level with Bo.

"I'm looking for a girl." Bo was surprised to realize that he was embarrassed. He'd been chewing his lip, and his voice caught like dust in his throat. "I'm looking for a particular girl."

"You look like a smart kid," Abbe said. "You go to Tech?"

"No," Bo said, looking around at the low glass cases that lined the walls. Somewhere, in there, she was waiting for him. "I'm not in school anymore." He wondered if he should really be so nervous. His knees felt warm and weak. "She's on MASIC format."

"Tri-disk. I figured you for the high-end type. That's Mil-Spec hardware, isn't it? Not that cheap Japanese entertainment-only shit. Hold on, Colonel." Abbe leaned back through the door to the back room and called to someone named Janet. Bo couldn't hear her reply, but her voice was like speaker feedback. "Just get out here and help this boy. When I want your opinion, I'll start paying you for it."

"You watch your mouth, you old bastard." Janet stepped through the curtain, and the first thing Bo saw was her eyes, huge and brown and slightly bulging. With her combed-up puff of mousy brown hair and her slightly puckered mouth, she had the inquisitive look of a large rat. Her tight blue and tan shirt showed off her small, slightly sagging breasts. "What can we do you for, son?"

Bo hated it when anyone called him son. Even his own mother had called him kid.

Janet waited, and her attention made him sweat, as if she were waiting for him to name some wild and illegal perversion, or perhaps to run away.

"She's got long, wavy black hair and blue eyes. Slender. She looks black Irish, if you know what I mean." Bolander looked around, as if invoking the description might cause the package containing her to stand up of its own volition, call to him, plead to be taken home. "I saw her here once before, but I don't remember her name."

"I know what you're talking about. There's only three on tri-disk, and the other two are blonds." Janet slipped into the back room before Bo knew she was leaving. There was nothing mousy about the way she moved. She was quick and lithe, and when she returned, she seemed to glide to a stop in front of him, the package in her hand waving under his nose like the bough of a tree in a breeze. "This her?"

Bo tried to speak, but only managed to mouth the word, "Yes."

"Cash, or can we debit it discreetly from your personal account?" Abbe asked. Bo handed over the tightly rolled wad of large bills he'd picked up at the bank. Abbe unrolled the money and handed it to Janet. "Cash customer. The mark of a real gentleman. Always deals in bills."

"There's only eight thousand here," Janet said after counting the stack twice. "Perpetual license is fifteen."

The words made Bo go cold, the way looking into the rearview mirror and seeing police lights turns flesh to gel. He couldn't wait long enough to save up another seven. Not after coming here and seeing her up close. If he left without her, he'd lose his nerve, probably spend most of the cash on booze, trying to forget about the whole thing.

"What can I get for that?" he asked, his voice dry and cracked.

She thought about it several seconds. "One year unlimited usage license, renewable or upgradable at added cost."

"Whatever. I'll take it." Bo didn't even have to consider the options. He could come up with the other seven in a year's time, maybe. What mattered was having her, now. Janet filled in the license agreement and coded the initialization disk while Abbe bagged the purchase. Somehow, Bo had imagined her coming gift-wrapped, not tucked into a brown paper bag. Seeing her face there, shadowed by the coarse, unbleached paper, a touch of reality tickled at the back of Bo's mind. After all, she was just a program....

"Good call, kid. You'll like her. She learns how to be the lay of your lifetime. Anything you want, she does it. Here you go." Abbe handed him the bag, and the clean smell of him broke the morbid spiral of Bo's thoughts. He took the bag and left, glancing back once to wave, awkwardly, at Janet and Abbe, deep down, perhaps, wondering what they thought of him.

Outside, in the fading heat, he turned down the block to avoid the gauntlet of pimps and pushers. A bus was just pulling to a stop at the corner, and he dashed to make it, slipping through the doors as the old diesel groaned away from the curb. He ran his pass through the reader and slipped to the back of the bus. He was alone there except for a small, slightly heavy blond woman in a business suit and white sneakers who was reading a self-help guide to AIC interfacing. She didn't even look up when Bo collapsed into the seat across from her.

It was as dark as Boston ever gets at night, the humidity like a curtain dimming the streetlights. All the lights were out on the bus, but Bo could still see to read. He pulled her package from the bag and started going over every detail, the specs on the back, the advertisers' pitches on either side. He'd seen it all in the magazine ads. Then, on the front, he stared several long, breathless seconds into her eyes.

I'm just going to read the documentation, he swore to himself. Just the docs. He slipped the tip of his pocket knife into a crease in the cellophane wrapper, slit it all the way around the bottom, and pulled the top slowly off the box. A breath of flowers, gardenias and lilacs, rich but too sweet, drifted up to him from the perfumed papers inside. Bo would have thought it tacky, had he not been so thoroughly enthralled.

Wrapped in another cellophane bag, tucked under the curled and creased paperwork, she was there. Not much to look at, just a shiny gold and green ROM disk and a plastic-coated magnetic RAM, sandwiching a thick black MASIC wafer. The plastic mounting piece was the same color as the ROM. Without a second thought, he broke his oath, reached into his canvas bag, and pulled out his 'Face.

The slim black case was no thicker than an old cassette player, with one slender wire that snaked back to a power cell in Bo's bag and another, thicker wire with a gold, brush-shaped probe attached to the end. Bo pulled aside his hair and flipped open the cover of his jack with the same quick, casual ease as someone pops out a contact lens. An electric tingle ran across the base of his scalp as he slid the probe in and secured it with a half twist.

Being wired was like being inside the TV looking out, like being the electron, fired toward the phosphor screen and becoming part of the image. Being wired was visual, aural, olfactory, tactile. So wonderfully tactile. Even the startup routine was a caress that ran the length of his body, the tender touch of a friend that would have tickled if it hadn't felt so good. It was the breath of a lover on bare skin, a mother touching the cheek of her sleeping baby. All by itself, it was worth the risks of wiring, worth the loneliness of nights lost on the Net, the madness, the days when the headaches made his vision turn red.

Bo ran his imprinted thumb over a hidden sensor, and a panel slid away with a barely audible sigh. He fit the media into the slot, and the gold plastic mounting clip came away in his hand. He fed the thumbnail-sized initialization disk into another slot and waited. Words in red floated in his lower peripheral vision, seen as if through the lens of tears. *Configuring to Aminoff-4 interface . . . stand by . . .*

Then she was beside him, quiet and prim, reading a book of poetry. His eyes wandered over her, soaking in the details of her smooth, pale wrists, the thick tweed of her skirt, the blue-black sheen of her hair. She glanced at him out of the corner of her eye, and she smiled.

Hello? Her voice was much lower than he'd imagined, and soft as a down comforter. There was more, though, a depth of understanding and a predisposition to laughter.

"What are you reading?" He became self-conscious about trying to look over her shoulder and scooted away, putting most of a seat between them. His eyes fixed on a blemish in the blue plastic of the bench where he'd just been sitting.

It's Rimbaud.

"Oh." One of the hot bands on the club set was making fistfuls of loot reading Rimbaud's poetry while playing ragged jazz and electric guitar solos. Bo thought they sounded like posers, so he never listened. But he still recognized the name.

I'm Sarah-Belle. I prefer just Sarah. Her voice drew his eyes up from the seat to her own, and something passed between them, some exchange of trust that Bo knew, deep down, was simply excellent programming. It caught him off guard, and he opened up to her without another thought. He smiled, for the first time in longer than he could remember.

"My name's Jack, but I go by Bo."

Voulez-vous être mon beau? His 'Face subtitled it for him in yellow, just below her lips.

"Don't speak French," he said. "I don't like the way it sounds." There was the barest pause, a slight flicker around the edges of her cheeks, a minor realignment of her straight, dark brow. Bo glanced down, and her book was Donne instead.

"Make love to me." He said it almost before he knew he was going to. The look on her face was an intermingling of amusement, interest, indignation, and irritation. He felt somehow he'd broken the rules, and even after he consciously realized the rules were his to make, he still felt uncomfortable under the study of her clear blue-gray eyes.

Here? I don't think that's a good idea.

"Yes, here." He'd said it, and though he wanted to back down, he couldn't. He wouldn't be chastised by a circuit board, even if it was a Turing chip and probably smarter than he was.

Here? she asked again, teasing him with the unspoken promise in her voice. She ran one finger down the side of his neck, and with the other hand, she began untying the sleeves of his fatigue shirt. *Right here? Are you sure? I've never done anything like this before.*

In the lower left of his vision, a single pale icon appeared, pulsing every several seconds, Leonardo DaVinci's *Balanced Man*, an indication from his 'Face that he'd entered a much deeper level of input, direct to the tactile centers of his brain. Everything that happened, while it was lit, would be confined to the spaces of his mind, every spoken word, every touch, every kiss. Like a dream, but a dream that paralyzed his voluntary nervous system. His awareness of the world faded to peripheral. Only a few telltale twitches betrayed the activity taking place in the small black box and in his mind.

Bo started to speak, but Sarah silenced him with a kiss, and her lips were forgiving. She had the kiss of someone who smiled often, a kiss that gave way under his, that parted for him and drew him in deep, the softest, most passionate kiss he'd ever had. It relaxed him and drove him to the edge of panic all at once. His pulse pounded, but he felt secure, warm, content. The kiss said she loved him.

Without breaking the kiss, she slipped onto his lap, wrapped her arms around his neck, ran her fingers through his hair, across his cheek, down his chest. She touched his thigh, tingling where in reality he had only numb scar tissue. Her fingers walked up the front of his jeans to the zipper, teasing and finding. She pressed her hand against him, squeezed him through the ragged denim. Bo felt release at last, and he let out a small whimper.

Sarah broke the kiss, pulled back enough so she could see his eyes. Her smile was sly, but her eyes were delighted. With her fingertips, she stroked him firmly, and he tried to smile before embarrassment got the better of him.

We're going to have to do something about this, she said, and burst into laughter as he rolled his eyes. Her laugh was like sunshine after a cloudburst, but at the same time just a bit silly, and heartfelt. It reassured him, told him she was not laughing at him but because he made her happy. Bo melted into her laughter, closed his eyes and savored the sound as much as the sweet taste of her mouth that lingered on his lips.

She unzipped his jeans with both hands, took care that nothing caught or snagged. She spread her skirt over his lap and settled onto him, unbuttoned her white blouse, and revealed small, round breasts, pale as clouds, and peach nipples. Sarah paused when she saw the expectant, frightened, slightly horrified look on Bo's face. Sarah winked and smiled a slow, easy smile.

Hey there.

"Hey." He smiled back and knew he was ready. She threw her head back and slid onto him with a pleased moan. A tingle ran down the length of Bo's body, arched his back, tightened every muscle. Microcurrents ran the length of his body, analog touch poured directly into his brain. Her scent drifted up to him, floral and spicy, enticing. She was there, and she was wonderful. Sarah rocked back and forth, smiling, eyes closed. Bo found the pleasure she took from him more erotic, more stimulating, than the feel of her. She made love to his ego, and it drove him over the edge. She collapsed onto him, her head on his shoulder, and kissed his neck. Sarah kept him afterward, squeezing him with quick, tight squeezes that sent a wave of endorphins flushing through his body.

Finally, she sat back, let Bo look at her, let his eyes and his mind drink in the woman who had just made love to him. Her hair cascaded around her shoulders like dark silk. For the first time Bo touched her face, found it warm and smooth, her hair soft as cashmere. Sarah turned to kiss his palm before she spoke.

Isn't your stop soon?

"I think we passed it."

Oh. Sarah gave him a quick kiss on the lips and winked out suddenly, reappearing beside him prim and immaculate once again. The thin volume of Donne lay beneath her folded hands, and she looked exactly as she had before except for the sated smile and flirtatious wink she gave him. The da Vinci icon faded, and Bo was free to move once more.

He got up and felt the slick, sticky wetness soaking through his jeans. Blushing, he pulled his rucksack across his lap, hit the bell, and yelled for the rear door.

"You said it was a bad idea, didn't you?"

It's okay. Sarah caressed his shoulder through the thin cotton of his T-shirt. She broke into a broad, enthusiastic grin and rolled her eyes.

Okay? It was great! They both laughed as the bus squealed to a stop several blocks west of Bo's apartment.

As he bounded down the steps and into the damp Boston night, Bo heard the blond woman mutter, "Wire-head freak." Her epithet drove home the reality to him, that Sarah was just a program, that he was a loser stuck in a fantasy. Then Sarah took his hand, and they walked home together, strolling like longtime lovers. By the time they reached his place, he'd made the unconscious decision that whatever they had together beat the hell out of his reality apart.

"Gotta turn you off," Bo said when they reached the door. "Ron goes bat shit if I wire in the house, and we've been fighting all day." Before she could speak, he thumbed the power stud and unjacked, then stuffed the 'Face back in his rucksack.

The apartment was nearly empty when he opened the door—a couple pillows on the floor and milk crates used as a table. All of Ron's AV gear was gone, as was his computer and the beat-up brown sofa where Bo sometimes fell asleep. Bare hardwood floors littered with empty fast-food drink cups and microwave burrito wrappers informed him that something was very wrong. He checked the door again to make sure it had been locked. It had been.

"Hey, Ron?" Bo checked his room, found it as he'd left it, then checked Ron's. The futon was still there, but the tangle of silk sheets was gone. The houseplants and bookshelves no longer filled the corners. Bo's footsteps echoed off the bare plaster walls. "That bastard."

He found a note on the refrigerator. "Bo, gotta jam. Moved in with Elisa. Later." He'd emptied the fridge, too.

Bo went to his room and curled up in the pile of blankets on his bed. He didn't feel like changing clothes or showering, just sleeping it off and worrying in the morning. Worry refused to wait, and after staring at the water marks on his ceiling for almost an hour, he reached for his ruck, for the comfort of her company.

Hey, tiger.

Sarah wore a white silk camisole that reached midthigh and fell across her breasts. When she dropped to her hands and knees to kiss him, it dropped away from her, and Bo saw all the way down the pale, tight curve of her belly. Her body stirred something inside him, but instead, he said, "Can we just talk?"

What's up? She flickered at the edges again before settling down beside him in a half lotus. She wore an I Love NY nightshirt, which she pulled down over her knees.

"Ron moved out. No notice or anything." Bo pulled a pillow into his lap and hugged it tight. "He was a real shit, but at least he was company. And I needed him to pay the rent."

Well, we can find you another roommate, right?

"I hope so." For a while Bo just stared off across the room, realizing after a while he was gazing at the stacks of AIC and MASIC disks piled in a milk crate in his closet. He could sell off most of it and pay for another month, if he got ten cents on the dollar for his original investment. He'd have to find a real sucker to pay those prices for unlicensed disks. He considered selling his 'Face and paying for a half year, in advance, or taking Sarah back and using the cash to get out of the city, move someplace cheaper. He regretted throwing the suit's business card away, even though he could probably find the guy again if he tried.

I'll help you find something. In the morning. Come to bed with me, Bo? You need rest.

"Sarah, why are you so good to me?"

She didn't answer for a while, long enough that Bo wondered if he'd hit a glitch in the softsoft. *You make me laugh. I like being with you. I don't exist without you.* She took his hand in both of hers, her touch warm. She made him feel needed.

"I guess you don't." Somehow, her need for him felt like a responsibility, a reason to work it out. He knew he'd been smudging the line all evening, and finally physical reality was merging with volitive reality somewhere in the wire. He knew better than to lose touch, but in the end, it didn't matter to him all that much. "I'm really screwed."

We'll come up with something. I'll help you. You have unlimited usage, remember? I'm not just some AIC-format slut. I think. And I'm clever. She kissed his neck, insistent. *Come to bed?*

Suddenly, physical and emotional exhaustion pulled at his limbs. "You're right. I need to sleep."

He rolled over and reached for the power stud on the 'Face black box, but Sarah stopped him with a hand on his shoulder. *No. I don't like it when you turn me off,* she said. She curled up tightly beside him, and the da Vinci icon faded into his vision. *Leave the power on. I need to think.*

⚬ THE BEST SHE EVER HAD ⚬

Susie Bright

I pressed Jack to tell me more about Carrie. The wind carried the voices from café brunchers down the shore onto our beach spot, but I could pull another towel over my head and hear only him.

"She said a lot of nice things about me—she's so complimentary."

"Like what?" I imagined what she might say—"Sir, you have a very nice cock." That's what I would say to Jack if I'd just had a one-night stand with him: nice cock, beautiful hair.

"She said . . . okay, this is embarrassing; she said I was the best lover she'd ever had!"

"You're kidding!"

"Yeah, incredible as it may seem . . ."

"You know I don't mean—"

We buried our heads in the beach towel and laughed.

"Yeah, I know what *you* mean," he said, and nudged my crotch with his toe.

I sat up in the sand so I could see him better. We were both struggling with our straw hats in the wind.

I decided to speculate. "Maybe what Sheila said about her being so sexually inexperienced is true."

"But she's thirty-two!"

"Thirty-two-year-old sex *today* is what sixteen-year-old sex was in our day—just creeping out of their egg."

"Is it really that bad?"

"Yeah, well think about it—if she was holding out through high school, and then 'playing it safe' in college, that doesn't leave a lot of time for sodomy and wasted nights."

"That's such a shame . . . but then what about all those blow jobs she talked about? It fits in, though, doesn't it—she's afraid of everything else."

"Tell me that part again, about her first boyfriend." I dug my toes into the sand until they hit the wet part.

"She said she just broke up with her first real boyfriend, and that when they got together, she promised him a thousand blow jobs. She got up to seven hundred and forty-nine in three years."

"Seven hundred and forty-nine!"

"Yes!"

"Now that seems like a magic number. You see, we'll never forget that number now, and we've only heard it once. But I don't see how she managed to keep track. . . . I mean, I tried to do that, when I was first fucking, but every time I went to bed with someone new, I'd change my idea about what good sex was, or what love was, and then my old system didn't make any sense."

"Well, maybe it's easier with blow jobs, if that's all you're doing."

"But she didn't come, from going down on you, did she?"

"No, of course not! It was hard for her to come, she kept trying to block me. She couldn't believe I wouldn't try to fuck her, trick her, and afterward she said she didn't want to do that—and then when I went down on her, she didn't think *I* really wanted to eat her—and she kept not believing, not believing, and all that made her orgasm remote."

"I bet the women who actually come giving head don't count the number. . . . If you want to swallow cock all the time, if that gets you off, you aren't competitive about it, you're just hungry, right? I mean, who keeps track of how many times they eat their favorite meal?"

Jack dropped his voice. "She was kind of rare, you know—she swallowed everything, every drop."

"Oh Jack, oh no—that makes me feel like such an asshole—Jack, that's not so rare, I've just brainwashed you. I'm terrible."

"Is that so? You're the only one who's not swallowing? You should repent, then."

"I can't, it's too late. You know I don't give a shit about blow jobs. But don't you remember, when we were first together, I did the whole deep-throat number, sucked it all down, blah blah blah. That's part of the BJ-macha thing, to show a guy what you're made of."

"I don't remember any of that!"

"See? I told you I was mediocre at it. Well, I didn't do it for that long, 'cause we got so comfortable, and if you'd *really* only wanted blow jobs from me, the whole thing would have fallen apart after two dates."

"What *did* I want from you?" Jack turned around and traced a circle in the small of my back.

"You wanted me to be a good girl and come really hard for you!"

"You're such a good girl, then—"

"And you like to show me, don't you?"

"Is *that* rare?"

"No! No! It's not, it's what practically everyone feels, and if they weren't so insecure and doing their stupid little dance maneuvers, everybody would just take it for granted." I pulled off my sun hat and ducked my head against his chest. I didn't know if he could hear me talking into his heart. "When you fuck me, you *know* I feel it, and I know you feel me giving it up to you, and that's what it's all about; it's not so complicated!"

He lifted my head up. "Do you want to stamp your foot now?"

"I'm going to stamp it real hard!"

"You don't have to get mad at Carrie—"

"I'm not, I'm practically praying for her, it's just the whole thing that makes me mad—all these BJ queens who can't come, won't come. One day they'll wanna have a baby, and after that, all their competition and affection will go to their children and they'll never wanna have sex again. The blow-job queen of today is the celibate of tomorrow. You better teach Carrie something about her sexual self-interest before it's too late."

"You could teach her, too—"

"She's not attracted to me!"

"You don't know that—"

"Oh c'mon! Yes I do, she's not the least bit queer. And if she ever does anything with a girl, it's going to be with another little flower like herself, not some predatory old bag."

Jack leaned over and bit my ass cheek.

"Ouch! Fuck you! You know what I'm talking about. I am not convincing some squeamish straight girl into accepting my ministrations. Talk about humiliation."

"You're making an awful lot of assumptions."

"Yeah, well, tell her I want the, uh, two hundred . . . and fifty-one blow jobs she forgot to give her ex. I'll strap on my biggest tool."

"But I wanna do that part."

"You're a greedy little pig. What I wanna know is, when are you going to see her next?"

"I don't know, I can't see her this week, and she can't see me next week, and I don't even know what week it is after that, but she really wants to get together."

"That's crippled! When I found anyone who qualified as the 'best lover I ever had,' I was driving all night to see them after a twelve-hour shift, I was hitching rides, telling lies, Jesus Christ! If she's telling the truth, you're in for it."

"That's right, you used to drive to Nevada from San Francisco to see me."

"Every week, then every three days—"

"Every day you weren't working."

"Well, that's what I mean, why can't she just come up and see you for one fucking night? She only lives an hour away, and you're the one who has kids and a day job. Is she afraid of seeing me, of being in our house?"

"That's probably part of it."

"Have you told her we have separate bedrooms, the life of polyamorous luxury?"

"I told her we have plenty of room, and that she could spend the night, but I just think this openness is sort of new to her. She asked what it would be like, with you here."

"And what did you say?"

"I said she might get devoured like a little bunny."

"Oh my god, did that make her scream?"

"Yes!"

"You shouldn't do that—"

"But it's her not-so-secret secret fear!"

"Well, I prefer to play hard to get. I prefer to demonstrate that I don't give a shit! You should really tell her it's like having a friend over that you spend some time alone with."

"Well that *is* what it's like, exactly, but I can't just convince her of that by saying it, she has to be here for a few minutes and see for herself."

"Christ, I feel like the Addams family sometimes. . . . 'Good evening, we're nonmonogomous. . . . Can Pugsley get you a drink?'" I pushed my glasses up my nose, they kept slipping. "I'm getting burnt; we have to find some shade."

"You can have my shirt."

"Baby . . ."

Jack covered me in a white surfer competition T-shirt that said Stand Tall, Be Proud.

"I'm embarrassed to be seen with this kind of propaganda on my chest. I wanna replace this slogan with something like Lay Down, Seek Humility."

"How about Lay Down, Deliver 749 Blow Jobs?"

"I can't get over what a magic number that is! It's because it ends in nine, I think; it sounds like something unfinished." I pulled the sweatshirt hood over my face.

"Maybe seven hundred and forty-nine is just approximate."

"I don't think so, I think she has a feeling for numbers, and for signs, and even when she has more sexual experiences, she'll still have an intuition about the cycles of things, the beauty of repetition—Jack, when you were in your twenties, who would you say was the best lover you ever had?"

"Why my twenties?"

"Because I'm not trying to be coy, and that was before I met you, and I want you to think back to that point—what would you have said?"

"The *best* lover . . . that's really hard."

I poked a hole in the sand with my finger until I hit a piece of glass. It *was* hard to think about. I flipped through my own memories like a fan of cards that I couldn't pick from.

Jack said something first. "You know, even though she was my first lover, in junior high, and we didn't have intercourse, Marie was really into sex, and we had a lot of sex."

"I know, I can't believe all the sodomy you had under the Catholic guise of protecting her virginity."

"We were so in love, and it was so intense, I didn't even go out with another girl for the rest of high school after she dumped me."

"You know what?" I held up the piece of green glass like a piece of evidence. "I think that when you're young, the first time you have sex, when it doesn't hurt, and you actually come—which is more of a girl thing, I know—and there isn't some awful black cloud hanging over you—*that sex* automatically becomes 'the best sex'—'the best lover'—you ever had. The fact that it's even *reasonably* good sex is incredible when you've never known those feelings before. When you get older, especially as you get older, the memory just gets more golden."

"That's what I'm saying, that even though I had a lot of deep experiences, and more variety, *later*—"

"Yes, it's not the same then, you're not thinking, 'Oh, this is the best,' because you're in the moment, and it's unique, and it doesn't seem fair to make comparisons anymore. When I had my first two boyfriends, they both blew my mind, and I felt so guilty at the time, because I couldn't decide who was the 'best.' They both really were my mentors, I couldn't give either of them up."

"Are you talking about Sam, or Cary?"

"Both of them . . . I was seventeen, and when I met Sam, he was the one who said, 'Go ahead, play with your clit,' and of course I came really hard, and then I asked him, 'Are you mad at me?' and he laughed, like the kind of laugh with tears in your eyes, because it must have been so endearing. That was my first inkling that my lover would get off because I was hot, not because I was *making* him hot. And he was the one who was like the 'Set your chickens free!' type—he would say, 'Oh stop shaving your legs, Susie,' and sometimes he'd even get annoyed with me, like, 'Hey, you're a seventeen-year-old cherry cake, everyone wants to fuck you no matter what you look like.'"

"He was jealous of you."

"You're right, he was, because he used to hustle himself, and he was so matter-of-fact about what men are looking for, and he already felt like he was past his prime. Men are so much harder on other men, when it comes to sex. Like, they'd fuck any girl, but another man has to be perfect."

"Maybe all women are already perfect."

"Yeah, right, we all bathe in seven-hundred-and-forty-nine-like luminescence—but I wanna tell you about my other contender, the other man I was seeing the same time as Sam. That guy, Cary, was so different, he didn't say a lot, but he just ate me up with a look. He seemed to read my cunt, or maybe I just didn't realize that all my secrets weren't so unusual."

"What secrets?"

"You already know them, too, it's just knowing what happens when a woman gets aroused, when you can torture her . . . just starting to push your cock in, and then pull it back, and feel her with your fingers, how she's getting puffier and puffier."

"Like a little catcher's mitt—"

"Yeah, and then her clit head starts to disappear up her pussy lips, and the cream is just getting creamier—"

"And then you nail her."

"Finally, yeah. God, just talking about it, my cunt is spreading rings— no, no, don't check me, trust me, I wanna finish telling you this, because I'm just figuring it out now. I didn't realize that Cary learned from a lot of women; I thought it was all about me and him. Because he said so little, I thought he'd practically made up my whole orgasm by himself, whereas Sam had made me talk to him, which shamed me but kind of liberated me in the next five minutes."

"So did you ever give one of them up?"

"No, I didn't, because at that time, *everyone* was nonmonogamous, and we were *all* fucking other people, and we were *all* fomenting a revolution, and I just thought we'd always keep coming back together. When Cary didn't follow me to Pittsburgh, and Sam moved to Seattle and got on his high horse about a new girlfriend, I was really shocked. And I had such bad sex in Pittsburgh, I started to wonder if everyone was retarded east of Barstow. My heart just broke one day, and I think that was the moment— that was it—that was the first time I ever said to myself, 'That was the best sex I ever had.' I cried my heart out. I only said it because it was gone, it was over, and I was just left a wreck. Maybe the best lover you ever have is the first one who makes you wanna die."

"Like Marie with me." Jack looked kind of crinkly.

"Oh, baby, don't . . . I bet she's the one crying now."

"I wouldn't want her to cry, she's had such a hard time."

"Well, now she's a born-again, so she can just get down off the cross— someone else needs the wood."

"I wish you could meet her."

"I wish I could meet Sam and Cary—again. I did see Sam a few years ago, at a wedding, and it kind of freaked me out. He acted scandalized by me, like I was some kind of freak, and it took all I could do to bite my tongue and not spoil that little reception by saying, 'Hey Sam, do you ever miss your old days whoring on Dupont Circle?' Damn, I always figured he knew more about sex than me."

"But you grew up. . . ."

"Yeah—into an old bag that knows more than he does!"

"Shut up."

"An old bag with juicy fruit inside?"

"Let me taste it."

"It's got sand in it now."

"You're fussy."

"You're a slut. Call Carrie; tell her time waits for no blow-job queen!"

"Are you going to be jealous, after all this?"

"Maybe I will—just for the hell of it, just to see if it still has some bite."

"Sometimes your jealousy gets you in trouble."

"That's the reckless thrill of it, but I haven't been swept out to sea yet."

"You know you *are* the best lover I've ever had."

The tide was coming in.

"You don't have to say that!"

"But it's true, you are."

"I love you—"

"Sh . . . pick up the blankets."

"I do, you're the something I'll always have, I'll always feel you inside of me, like nine million nine thousand ninety-nine to infinity."

We kissed with our mouths open, and the sunblock on our faces stuck together. The water came up fast and pooled up around my ankles; I couldn't see if the towels were floating away. Jack took my breast out of my shirt and sucked on my nipple like it was a caramel. I stared up at the sun and felt the whole bag of everything go pop, and disappear up, all the way up, into the sky.

ᔐ VALENTINE'S DAY IN JAIL ᔐ
Susan Musgrave

Western wind, when will thou blow?
The small rain down can rain.
Christ if my love were in my arms
And I in my bed again!
                              —*Anon.*

THE BUS DROPPED ME IN THE HEART OF TOWN, across from the funeral parlor, where a sign in the window read, Closed for the Season.

"No one dies much this time of year?" I asked, making small talk with the taxi driver taking me the rest of the way to the prison. "Not if they do it around here," he replied, and then asked me if I minded if he smoked.

Before I could answer, he lit one and blew the smoke out his window. I sat in the back watching rain streak the windshield as he talked about the justice system and how "sickos like drug dealers" should be shot to save taxpayers' money. He must have thought I worked at the prison, because he kept glancing in the rearview mirror, waiting for me to agree. I explained I was visiting a convicted marijuana smuggler, a Colombian, doing life, that it might even be love. He apologized, saying he should have kept his trap shut. He said there must be one heck of a lucky guy waiting for me inside, that all he'd ever wanted was a soft girl in his bed every night, and all he'd ever been was disappointed.

I looked away into the mountains above the distant town of Hope, the snowy ridges few had ever set foot on, and tried to picture what Angel, the lucky man, might be doing at this moment. I imagined him lying on his bunk, staring up at the dull green institutional gloss on his ceiling, with not even a crack or a ridge he could use as landmarks.

"So when's the honeymoon?" the driver pressed. The window had steamed up, and he wiped a little space with his hand. "You going to escape? Go someplace tropical? Swimming pool, palm trees, hula-hula. You wish, huh?"

We rounded a bend at the northern end of the valley, and Toombs Penitentiary came into view. All that separated it from its sister prison, Toombs Penitentiary for Women, was the Corrections Mountain View Cemetery. Both prisons were cut off from the world by mountains so high their western flanks were always in shadow.

I'd met Angel when I visited both prisons, and the adjoining cemetery, a year ago. I had just begun freelancing and hoped to cover the story behind the high rate of inmate suicides over Christmas. "No one but the law ever wanted them when they were alive, and now *no one* wants them," an official told me, indicating the forlorn tract of land, overgrown with ragweed, where the unclaimed bodies of lifers were laid to rest. Escape risks, he told me, were even buried in leg irons.

My driver let me off in the parking lot, a hundred yards from the front gate, and wished me luck. "You know, you make me jealous," he said. "You get to go in there and be all lovey-dovey while I go back to work." I paid him and stood for a moment watching him drive away, then turned to face the prison.

The heavy gold watch on my wrist told me it was 12:45, and I had to stand outside in the rain, waiting, until the big hand on the clock inside gave its single-digit salute to the sky. Then the guard buzzed me in. I waited some more as he went through my handbag, taking apart my fountain pen and getting ink all over his hands. I was allowed to take in with me a tube of mascara and lipstick, but not the lozenges that Xaviera Hollander, the *Penthouse* columnist, had recommended as a prelude to oral sex.

"Leave these in there," he said, pointing me toward a metal locker. "And this, too." He held up the loose tampon he'd found at the bottom of my bag. "Security measure," he said. "An inmate could suicide himself by choking on one."

He repacked my handbag, saying they would supply me with a sub-
stitute if I needed it. "The matron will see you next," he said, pointing to a
door marked No Exit. On the other side of the door I could hear a woman
protesting.

I sat on a hard chair and waited. Angel's sister emerged, with the red-
faced matron, Miss Horis, behind her. Consuelo, which was her current
alias, had told me to trust her—she could hide *anything*. Why wouldn't I
trust a woman who had smuggled herself and three kilos of cocaine into
the country so she could pay her brother's legal fees, and be near him?
Angel told me, too, she had once smuggled a grenade in her vagina into
Bella Vista prison in Colombia. The condom she'd offered to carry for me
today seemed like small beer in comparison.

"Miserable enough out there for you?" Miss Horis asked, sighing as
she ushered me into the No Exit room, then telling me to remove my coat,
suit, blouse, underthings, and "all other personal items." Naked, I placed
both feet firmly in the middle of the mirror.

"Straddle the mirror, please, one foot on either side. That's it. Now
relax, and cough twice."

I coughed, and Miss Horis peered in the mirror, then asked me to lift
my breasts one at a time, before opening my mouth, where she checked
under my tongue. "Enjoy Valentine's Day," she said as she left me to get
dressed again.

She hadn't mentioned the watch—obviously meant for a man's wrist.
I got dressed again and she popped her head in the door a moment later,
offering me a sanitary napkin to replace the seized tampon. I shook my
head no. No inmate, evidently, had yet thought of trying to suffocate himself with a Kotex.

Once inside the visiting room, I headed for the washroom, where
I found Consuelo fighting with her hair. A sign informing visitors that
there was No Necking, Petting, Fondling, Embracing, Tickling, Slapping,
Pinching, or Biting Permitted during Visits was posted above the condom
machine (foreplay might be prohibited, the machine's presence seemed to
suggest, but fucking was not). Today the machine bore another warning:
Sorry. Out of Order. The word "sorry" had been crossed out.

I turned to Consuelo for the condom she was supposed to smuggle in
for me, but she held out her empty hands. "I had to swallow it," she said.
"That woman, she wanted to look me in the mouth." She said Angel and I
should get married so we would be approved for private visits. But Angel

and I weren't waiting for approval. Today our names were at the top of a clandestine list for a different kind of private visit—the unsanctioned kind. I borrowed Consuelo's comb and dragged it through my own damp tangles.

At half past one, Mr. Saygrover, the Visitors and Communications officer, led us into a hallway painted the same avocado green as the outside of the prison. He nodded to the young guard in control of the first of the iron-barred gates blocking our passageway, and the heavy steel doors parted on their runners. We crossed five more identical barriers before reaching the gymnasium.

I could see the men pressed up against the last gate, awaiting their visitors. All were dressed in green shirts and pressed trousers the same shade as the prison walls. The ritual had been the same ever since I first started visiting Angel—the men standing behind the barrier waiting and waving, and the women approaching, awkwardly, looking at one another for reassurance, like girls at a junior high turnabout sock hop. The closer we got, the longer it seemed to take the guards to open the barriers. A female guard with sweat stains in the armpits of her uniform opened the last gate. Janis Joplin's voice came rasping out of two coffin-sized speakers strapped high on the gymnasium wall. She didn't need to tell anyone here how freedom was only another word for nothing left to lose.

The gym was decorated with red balloons and white streamers. The streamers had been affixed from corner to corner the night before and had lost their elasticity. A prison sculptor's papier-mâché heart, trapped in barbed wire, lay on display next to the Coke machine, which was also "Out of Order."

Visitors found seats around the long banquet tables, each one laden with the institution's version of hors d'oeuvres: Mini Sizzlers on toothpicks, rolled cold cuts, radishes that had been sculpted to look like roses too terrified to open, a pyramid of mystery-meat sandwiches and plates of heart-shaped cookies baked by prisoners in the kitchen. My eyes moved from table to table, searching. Angel sat upright on a metal chair, arms folded across his chest. Our eyes locked. He stood up.

Nothing had changed. He didn't speak. I couldn't. He had a smile bittersweet as a pill for the sick at heart, a pair of lips you wanted to lick under a mustache that would keep you from getting close enough, and sad night eyes. His hair was straight and black and today he wore it tied back in a ponytail. In my last letter I'd written, "Tie your hair back so it won't get in the way. I want to see my juice all over your face."

Angel pulled two chairs together so we could sit facing one another, and he leaned forward and put both his arms around my neck. "I'm always afraid I'll never see you again, that you won't come back," he said, breaking the silence. "I'm afraid you might find me—too available."

I laughed as I cupped his dark face in my hands. "I wouldn't call any man doing life behind bars *too available*." His mustache, smelling of the red-hot cinnamon hearts he sucked every time I visited to hide the smell of the dark tobacco on his breath, scoured my upper lip. More than his smile or his eyes, I think it was his smell that attracted me most the first time we met, like the air before a storm, long before there is any visible sign of it.

"You look thin," I said, sitting back in my chair. "Are you getting everything you need?" Angel sat back, too, straightening the sheet that served as a tablecloth. He picked up an orange and poked his finger into its navel.

"I'm getting your letters every day. And you're here. What more do I need?" He kissed me, but I pulled away. "And you?" he asked.

I needed privacy. I wanted to be with Angel, alone. We'd had one chance, at the Christmas social, to spend five minutes in the toilet stall of the men's lavatory, but I needed more time than that to fondle him, embrace, tickle, neck, pet, slap, pinch, and bite—it was all I had thought about since we'd met. I pictured him alone every night in his cell, penis erect and shining, sad as tinsel at an unattended party. When we were together, I was aware of how close he stayed beside me and how every time we brushed against one another I felt a shiver of something long lost stirring inside me, the same longing I'd felt for a brown-eyed boy in the fifth grade, my last painful crush before the crash of puberty.

I'd been afraid, too, I told Angel, afraid I had "gone too far." In my last letter I'd quoted Kurt Vonnegut, who said the only task remaining for a writer in the twentieth century was to describe a blow job artistically. I told Angel I'd rather *show* him a blow job than write about it, then went on to discuss the calorie count in a mouthful of sperm (one swallow contained thirty-two different chemicals, including vitamin C, vitamin B_{12}, fructose, sulphur, zinc, copper, potassium, calcium, and other healthy things). I said I had a one-a-day multiple vitamin habit but figured I could give these up if he were willing to have oral sex once a day.

Angel told me "far" was the only place worth going, and he kissed me again. This time I didn't stop him. He shifted on the hard chair, adjusting the bulge that strained to break out of his trousers. I squirmed on the warm metal, forcing my knees together, my sex swollen, struggling to escape. I caught two guards staring at us; I nudged Angel and we pushed back from one another. Angel held my hand underneath the table, stroking it with his thumb. "I haven't been in the yard yet today," he said, after a silence. We'd been having the same thought. Out there we might be alone. "How is it, outside? The weather?"

"Wet," I said, taking a heart-shaped cookie and breaking it in half. Angel took the other half from my hands, and I watched it shrink under his mustache. "Raining."

"Good," he said. "Let's walk."

We had the yard to ourselves, almost. Two guards in a patrol vehicle slowed to look us over as we stopped to watch a pregnant doe browsing on the thick grasses outside the perimeter fence. It was the same spot, Angel said, where a half-blind bear had been shot in the autumn. Angel said the guards had fired warning shots at her, but she kept coming back. A handful of yellow-and-purple cartridge shells lay in the wet grass.

"She couldn't see well enough to get away while she had a chance?" I asked.

"Few see that well," said Angel, and when he looked at me this time I saw, in the gleam of his shadowy eyes, a depth of wanting that promised heaven.

We kept to a well-worn trail Angel called the warning track. Walking, we lifted our faces to scale the double high-wire fences but stayed well inside the dead line, the line beyond which any prisoner would be shot. Angel pointed to where a man had been picked off by the tower guard "before his hands were even bloodied by the razor wire."

I squinted up through the rain, beyond the gun towers, to the sky. Angel slid his hand in under my thin coat, cupping my breasts, milking my nipples between his thumb and forefinger, and I felt the wet silk of my panties sticking to me where I was open, and a thin seam of silk rubbing back and forth across my clitoris with every step. But Angel, his faraway eyes on the towers, seemed to have scaled the high-wire fences and left me behind. Then, as we rounded a bend in the warning track, he said someday he would take me so high, so far up to the Andes, nobody, not even God, could stare down at us.

"You're dreaming." I screwed up my face at him. I didn't need to say it out loud: "You're stuck in here doing life." Angel knew my thinking.

"Life can be shorter than you expect," he said. Then he looked at me and laughed, in a way.

I laughed, too, but pulled him closer. For now this was good enough.

When the call came over the loudspeaker to clear the yard, we went back inside, elbowing our way through a cluster of guards who'd been checking us out from the door. We sat in our wet clothes holding each other and waiting as more guards pinned two sheets together to make a screen on the gymnasium wall. The Inmate Committee had planned to show *Carmen* before the food was served. Angel whispered what he wanted me to do when the lights dimmed, but now, without the condom for protection, and surveillance from every corner of the room, my heart started looking for an emergency exit. I told Angel we had too much to lose, including our visits. But then the lights went down, he lifted the hem of the tablecloth with his foot, and pushed me under.

Beneath the table, in a private world, I sat hugging my knees, feeling lost and uncomfortable. The Inmate Committee, in charge of all forms of entertainment, had transformed the space under the table into a low-ceilinged motel room. We had a foam mattress, two arsenic-green blankets, and a pillow, upon which someone had placed a long-stemmed rose. My mouth felt dry. How was I going to give Angel that blow job? I longed for those lozenges and thought about the editor from *Elle* who'd phoned a few months ago asking for reminiscences of "my most embarrassing sexual encounter" for their Valentine's Day issue. I'd been unable to come up with anything, but now, as I sat composing the story in my head, I concluded a guard must have seen me and apprehended Angel. I would be forced to wait it out under the table until such time as they chose to humiliate me publicly; precisely the ending I needed for my date from hell for *Elle*.

I felt a hand go over my eyes, then (the smell of him!) Angel began kissing me all over my face and head, sniffing my hair along the part line. When he took his hands away from my eyes, I saw he was wearing dry clothes.

"I went back to my house to change," he said, laughing, taking off his jacket and draping it over my shoulders. "Your dress is soaked," he said. "Wear this, too." He began to unbutton his shirt.

He peeled back the blanket, gave me his dry shirt, and made me get under the covers. I told him he was the first man I'd been to bed with who tried to make me put more clothes *on*, and he told me I was the first woman who could make him hard and make him laugh at the same time. He wanted to know if all Canadian women could do that, and I said as far as I knew there'd never been a poll.

We kept our voices low. The room, too, grew quiet as the credits began to roll. "Are you sure this is safe?" I whispered. "What if a guard saw us?"

"No one saw us," he said, as he pulled off his undershirt. For the first time I saw the hollow place in his chest. It looked as if his heart had been excavated, like the ruin I once visited in the remote Yucatán. Everything of value had been dug out and taken away. Only a pit remained, which, over the years, had been reclaimed by the jungle.

"I was born with this. . . ." He took my hand, curled it into a fist, and placed it in the little hollow. "My mother used to say by the time I died it would have filled up with the tears she would shed for me during her lifetime."

I laid my head on the pillow, waiting for the table to be pulled out from over us. It took an effort of love to get in the mood, staring up at the words Property of Corrections Canada Morgue stamped on the underside of the table. I shut my eyes tight as Angel picked apart the rose, then laid the cool crimson petals on my eyelids.

"You're not like any woman I've ever known," he said, pressing his nose in my armpit and edging one finger under the elastic of my bra.

"What's that like?" I shook the petals away.

"Uuuummmmmmmmm," was all he said. I wanted to undo his zipper and take his cock in my mouth, but something made me hold back, an old memory, perhaps, of my first "most embarrassing date" in the old boathouse smelling of high tide, fish, and water rats. I was twelve and Dick Wolfe (not his real name, but close) showed me how to set a banana slug on fire, how it would melt into a pool of sticky stuff if you had the right touch. Then he undid his pants, and I remember it looked so eager, so trusting, as he said, "Put your mouth on it," and when he came, I thought I'd cut him with my tooth, the crooked one my parents could never afford to have fixed. I believed I had a mouthful of his blood but did the polite thing, I thought, and swallowed it. "I've cut you," I said, thinking we'd have to go to the hospital and how was I going to explain cutting a boy "down there"? Then he said, his brown eyes more open to me than ever, "That wasn't blood, sweetheart."

"It's been a long time," Angel said, as I lay still, dreaming, half listening to someone at our table tuning a guitar. My arm was going to sleep, and I shifted position. The movie had begun, and the man who'd been tuning his guitar began strumming on it so passionately that Angel and I could no longer talk. Then the projector shut down and the lights went back on. The voices up above us grew louder, as if an argument were taking place.

"Something's up," said Angel. "It sounds like there's a problem with the projector."

"The lights have come on," I said. "How are we going to get out of here without someone seeing us? What sort of person will they think I am?"

"No one is going to blame you," Angel said. "The guards will just think I corrupted you. They think all inmates are criminals."

He put his arms around me as if to reassure me. Then he saw the watch I was wearing and asked if it was a gift. He didn't say "from another man," but I could hear it in his question. I unstrapped it from my wrist and said yes, a gift for him. It was guaranteed to be shockproof and never to lose time.

"I've never owned a watch that didn't break down," he said. "I think watches get nervous being on my wrist."

I pushed him back so I could move my pillow away from the end of the table, where a pair of knees was invading our love nest.

"This one comes with a lifetime warranty," I said.

Angel settled his body back alongside mine and blew a strand of hair out of my face. He shifted again so his chin rested on my shoulder blade. The person with the intruding knees began tapping his feet and calling for more music.

It was growing stuffier under the table, and neither of us had enough legroom. But I'd waited long enough: I slipped my arms out of my dress, pulled him close to me, and kissed him, for a long time. It didn't matter that up above us there was a world of men and women arguing and laughing. (The film, I learned, leaving the social, had turned out to be *Carne*, sadomasochistic pornography, not *Carmen* the opera, and the guards axed the show.) We were alone in the new world of our flesh, and the occasional appearance of the toe of a running shoe under the hem of the tablecloth, or a hand slapping the tabletop, no longer felt like an intrusion.

"But will you still respect me after this?" I smiled.

He took my hand and guided it to his cock. "My respect for you knows no limits."

I unzipped his trousers. Erotic texts from ancient India claim there is a definite relationship between the size of an erect penis and the destiny of its owner. The possessors of thin penises would be very lucky, those with long ones were fated to be poor, those with short ones would become rulers of the land, and males with thick penises were doomed always to be unhappy.

For now, I was destined to make Angel happy. I began licking the end of his cock, which was already swollen. I thought it was going to burst as my tongue busied itself.

"I'm going to die," he said. When I looked up at his face, across the nut-brown expanse of his body, he smiled back, that slow smile, and I took his cock in both my hands. I could barely get my fingers around it. Its head had a ruddy glow and was grinning. It glistened. I kissed it. Sniffed it. Sucked it hard, taking as much of it into my mouth as I could, then licking it again, making a lot of noise while I sucked and licked.

"I'll come if you keep doing that," he said.

Then he pulled me up so I lay next to him and reached inside my panties. He said my cunt nuzzled up to his hand like a horse's soft mouth when you feed it sugar. He moved down between my legs, pulling my panties aside, sliding one finger inside me, sliding it out, sliding two fingers in, then sliding them out, then sliding three fingers in. I arched my back, spreading my legs wider to give him better access, and he tugged gently upward on my pubic hair, baring my clitoris. Then he began licking me, slowly, teasingly, moving in small circles with his lips and tongue, his kisses falling on me, gentle as the scent of rain in a lemon grove. My body strained against his face, and when he looked up at me, his skin was alive with my juices.

I sat up and pulled him down on top of me.

"I don't have any protection," he said.

There are some exquisite moments from which we are not meant to be protected. I slid him inside me, achingly. I had never had anything so hard inside me. I held my breath as he kept coming into me, we were breathing and then not breathing in unison, and I brought his hand up to my mouth to cover it, suppress any sound, and then I began sucking his fingers, one at a time, then two at a tie, then three. His fingers tasted of salt, of my own sweat and juices. "Suck," he said, and pushed into me, harder still, as if by trying he could disappear up inside me and escape forever into the rich orchid darkness of my womb. When he came his face became contorted as if it hurt him to come so hard, then we lay quietly for a while, and then he began licking me again, making me come with his own come, with his tongue, his lips, and his fingertips. I cried when I came, and doubled up, curling into myself. He began kissing me, from my toes up along my legs and the insides of my thighs, over my belly and breasts, up my neck and onto my face and in my hair. He said this was his way of kissing me hello and goodbye at the same time.

Afterward, as I lay on a bed of bruised rose petals, licking the drops of sweat that had rolled down his chest and collected in the hollow above his heart, Angel said coming inside me was like coming on velvet rails. And later when we'd crawled out from under the table and were standing alone once more in the slanting rain, we kissed again. We kissed as if to seal our fate, to finish a life together we hadn't even begun.

Years ago, on an island in the tropics, I had been lured from my bed in the night by the air pregnant with the scent of vanilla. I found giant, cauldron-like cactus flowers opening in the moonlight and thousands of tiny sphinx moths fluttering from one pod to another. In the morning, when I came to show them to a friend, the flowers had disappeared.

I missed the next visit because I had a deadline to meet (a piece about these cactus flowers that bloom one night a year, conduct their whole sex lives, and vanish by dawn) and the one after that because the prison was locked down. There'd been a stabbing, and a hostage taking, and rumblings of a hunger strike. I wrote to Angel, concerned about his health. He wrote back, worried about mine. He hoped I wasn't pregnant, for though he liked the idea—that way part of him had already escaped for good—he didn't want to leave me with a burden.

Angel must have sensed it: visits weren't the only thing I'd missed that month. I made a doctor's appointment. In the evening I tried to phone Angel, but good news was not enough of a reason to bring an inmate to the phone. I asked to book a Special Visit to see him the next day. An officer informed me that Special Visits were granted for death or bereavement only. So I had to save my news until I could sit across from Angel in the visiting room and touch his face, let him take my hand under the table and stroke it with his thumb.

But the next time I saw Angel, he was in the news. "Two men are dead after today's daring escape attempt from Toombs Penitentiary," was all I heard; my heart began to pound to the staccato beat of a police helicopter, a throaty thwap thwap thwapping. I moved closer to the screen and turned up the sound. "Earlier this afternoon two Colombian nationals tried to climb aboard a waiting helicopter that had landed in the prison yard. . . ." There was a shot of the dead line where Angel and I had walked, then a file-photo close-up of his face.

Life can be shorter than you expect. Consuelo and I rode the bus to the prison in the rain. She said Angel hadn't confided in me, hadn't been able to tell me about his escape plan, out of respect . . . *my respect for you knows no limits* . . . but that he'd been insistent: he would send for me when it was safe. My good news—that I wasn't pregnant—seemed like sad news now. All of him had escaped for good.

Mr. Saygrover asked Consuelo to sign for Angel's property, which fit in a gray plastic suitcase. Consuelo looked inside, then handed it to me. Angel, she said, would have wanted me to have everything. He had left his battered *Pocket Oxford*, a key chain with no keys, a toothbrush, an unopened bag of Cheetos, and $2.37 in change. And, he had left me. So much for respect!

A service took place in the prison chapel. A handful of fellow inmates gathered to pay their last respects, the chaplain mumbled a few words and asked us to pray. Consuelo said Angel wouldn't have wanted hymns, so she sang a song from their childhood, "*Si me han de matar mañana, que me maten de una vez*": "If they're going to kill me tomorrow, they might as well kill me right now."

I wanted, for a moment, to kill him myself, all over again, until I saw him lying that still in his gray Styrofoam coffin. I tried to hold one of his hands—awkward because of the handcuffs—then stroked one of his thumbs instead. He wore the watch. I could hear it ticking.

I moved my hands down over his body, saying hello to Angel, saying goodbye. And when I felt the leg irons at his ankles, I wanted to rip open his shirt and let my tears collect in the hollow place in his chest.

But I didn't weep. Through the bars of the chapel window I watched the slow rain falling on the fake-fur trim of the guards' brown jackets, and thought how lonely it would be, how cold and cramped the earth Angel was going into. In this world, I knew, there was an unending supply of sorrow, and the heart could always make room for more.

೮ಿ FULL METAL CORSET ೮ಿ
Anne Tourney

AILEEN CALLS THE ROOM WHERE SHE WORKS the fluorescent nunnery. All day the breath of machines stirs her hair; she suspects she is dying fast in this climate. The skin on her breasts and inner thighs has grown tough. Her hair is dry and won't reflect sunlight.

She supervises thirty women who enter data from endless reams into their computers. Aileen sees the hieroglyphic fingers everywhere. Data stream out of wine bottles, turn up in her food, and pump out of her husband's cock.

At her desk, Aileen can make herself come in twelve seconds. She can make her cunt muscles pulse in and out like butterfly wings until her vulva clenches in four creamy spasms.

When she isn't masturbating, Aileen watches the employees. A new typist has caught her attention. She gazes at the ream with mystic concentration, as if the data were a formula for ecstasy. Aileen doesn't like this woman. She doesn't respond to Aileen's progressive attitude. She wears smocks that whoosh around her, raising dust. Except for her speeding fingers, she moves with a nun's slow serenity.

Aileen prefers the girls who make crass jokes in the restroom, sneak soda cans under their desks, and fake car trouble so they can stay home an extra hour in the morning and fuck their boyfriends.

— ✣ —

"It's Laurie, isn't it?"

The girl stands before the bathroom mirror, clenching her teeth as she adjusts something under her smock. Aileen washes her hands rapidly.

"Lily. The name was given to me."

Of course it was given to you, idiot.

Suddenly the girl lifts her smock over her head. Aileen stares. She feels an unexpected twinge between her legs. The girl is wearing a cruelly elaborate corset, laced so tight that her waist disappears between her bulging hips and bosom. The fabric resembles black leather, only it is much less yielding. The top covers the girl's breasts, slicing into the flesh, but holes have been cut out to expose the nipples. The laces, which cross at the front and tie in the back, obviously restrict breathing. The material creaks as the girl reaches back to loosen its fastenings.

"Could you help me?" she whispers. "I've got to take this off."

Aileen reminds herself that she is hip. She has seen porno magazines. She knows about S&M. But she doesn't move.

The girl finally releases herself and lets the contraption fall. She winces, rubbing the network of red lines across her torso. Marks from a series of pointed studs inside the corset pepper her waist.

"That's barbaric," Aileen breathes.

"Oh, no," the girl protests. "It's beautiful."

"What the hell would possess you to wear something like that?"

"It was given to me."

Aileen is getting angry. "That's the sickest thing I've ever seen!" she exclaims. She has forgotten that she is cool, open-minded.

The girl smiles. "Why don't you try it on?" she suggests. "I won't lace it all the way. They never make you do that the first time."

Aileen wants to scream, but she reminds herself that she is tolerant. She is also a practical supervisor. This girl never misses a day, arrives five minutes early every morning, and does the work of two ordinary typists— all while wearing a garment straight out of a torture chamber. Aileen recalls the expression on the girl's face as she enters the mounds of data. She moistens a paper towel in cold water and presses it to her forehead.

"Back to work," says the girl cheerfully. She hoists the corset off the floor and refastens it. While the girl envelops herself in her blue smock, Aileen stumbles into a stall. She wants to vomit, but between her legs she is thoroughly wet.

Aileen now despises Lily. With the other employees Aileen is friend-lier than ever, using their slang and chatting with them about their sex lives. The girls laugh at Aileen's jokes, then mock her behind her back.

When Aileen accidentally glances at Lily, she sees the corset. When she hears Lily sigh, she knows the girl is in pain.

One morning Aileen's phone rings. All the women look up. She motions for them to go on with their work, but they keep staring. Aileen decides to entertain her audience. She poses on her desk and picks up the receiver.

"Hell-looo?" she says smokily. The women giggle.

"I'd like to speak to Lily," says the voice. It is a man's voice, smooth as a plum.

"Lily?" Aileen recoils. "Employees can't receive calls here," she says coldly. "Talk to Lily on your own time."

"It's essential that I speak to her."

The voice gives Aileen no alternative. Lily has already risen from her desk. When the girl takes the phone, Aileen snatches her hand away. The girl listens for a moment, then puts the receiver down.

"I have to go," she says. Her tone is conspiratorial, as if Aileen should understand why Lily has to depart at the summons of a phone call, with no prior notice, in the middle of the morning. Aileen won't let her leave.

"I'm sorry," says Lily, walking toward the door. The other women stare after her.

The company has given Lily an unprecedented raise. She will return tomorrow, five minutes early, and she will continue to do so, except when a voice on the telephone orders her to do otherwise.

Aileen is furious. She sits at her desk and tries to look over some documents, but she can't read. With shaking hands, she yanks a pack of cigarettes from her purse and stalks out of the room. She lights one in the hallway, then enters the restroom.

Sitting on the floor, propped against the wall under one of the sinks, is the corset. The sinks have new, ultramodern faucets; water flows, without the help of knobs or handles, whenever hands are extended for washing. Beneath these water-saving miracles lies the corset, a medieval nightmare.

Aileen reaches out to touch it. The material is untextured and cool, but Aileen pulls her hand away as if burned. She drops her cigarette in the sink and lifts the corset with her fingertips. It is lighter than it appears, but heavy enough so that it would eventually become a burden.

She strokes the studs lining the garment, then pulls the corset experimentally around her waist, noting the sharpness of the metal teeth. A strap dangles from behind; apparently, this fits between the legs and fastens in the front. Repelled, Aileen realizes that her crotch is damp again. She should take this thing to the incinerator. Better yet, she should take it to the cops. Instead, she finds herself laying the garment down and undressing.

Standing nude, she laces the front and pulls the strap through her legs, buckling it above her crotch. She can still breathe comfortably, and the studs' pointed tips barely sting. She pulls the laces tighter and rebuckles the crotch strap so that it really digs into her. Undulating her hips, she groans at the combined sensations: the edges of the corset biting into her flesh, the studs pricking her waist, the strap abrading her pussy lips. With her palms, she rubs her exposed nipples. She grasps the strap between her legs and jerks it up and down until she comes—so intensely that she soaks her thighs.

Aileen wears the corset back to her desk, certain that someone will see the black garment through her ivory blouse. She sits down, but she can't work. The pain has worsened. The studs pierce her skin, and the stiff garment won't let her breathe. She panics; she has to remove it.

I can't stand it. Oh, God, I can't stand it.

Then she thinks of Lily, with her beatific expression. She forces her body to accept the pain. Closing her eyes, she gives in to it, becomes it. She focuses on the agony of the strap cutting into her pussy. Soon she is excited again.

She tells the typists she is leaving early. Indifferent, they continue typing. Aileen leaves without her jacket or her purse. She can't imagine why she would need them.

In the streets she walks stiffly, but with an undefinable urgency. Walking in the corset brings her to a new level of pain and arousal. Soon she has to stop. The agony is unbelievable. Leaning against a parking meter, she breathes deeply, but the studs are fiery points against her rib cage. Her entire torso is blistered and raw. The strap between her legs feels excruciating.

A car pulls up at the meter. Someone gets out and lifts her, putting her into the car.

Inside, hands remove her clothing and work at the corset. As each lace is unfastened, Aileen takes a drink of air. She has never felt anything as sweet as the removal of that garment.

"You fastened it too tight," her rescuer chides her. "The first time, you should lace it no more snugly than a life preserver."

The car's interior is large, lush, and dark. Tinted windows guard her from the outside world, and another window separates the backseat from the front. Her savior strokes ointment into her flesh. His fingers tell her that, though he is now ministering to her pain, he can also inflict it. His face is scarred and pitted; he has earned his privileges.

His touch arouses her. She leans against the seat and is preparing to ride to orgasm when he stops.

"From now on," he says, "you won't take pleasure before I do. Whenever I want you, wherever you are, you will come to me."

"What if I don't?" Aileen starts to ask, but the look on his face makes her say instead, "What if I can't?"

"If you disobey me, I'll find you and weld you into the corset. No instrument can cut through that material. It can't even be burned. It's indestructible. Can you imagine how it would feel to be trapped in the corset?"

"Yes," she whispers.

"You can't go back now that you've put on one of my corsets. You do want to wear it, don't you?"

She can only answer yes.

"You'll continue your life the way it's always been, with two exceptions. First, you will interrupt any activity when I summon you. Second, you will allow no one but me to touch you."

His face is triangular, with silver eyes—a wolf's face. A face that demands worship. Aileen bows her head.

He unzips his leather trousers, and his cock leaps out, radiating heat. She sucks lightly on the tip. Grasping her hair, he directs her to move faster, and she takes the whole shaft into her mouth, using her muscles to massage his cock to the beat of its pulse. She tastes the ripe flavor of groin sweat. When she feels him swell suddenly, she produces a steady pressure with her lips, tongue, and throat. She accepts the explosion, all salt and cream.

He turns her on her back. Still erect, he rams into her, coming after a few bullish thrusts. He sits back and replaces his cock in his trousers. Aileen moans, wildly unsatisfied.

"Do you remember what I said?" he asks. "I'll please you only when I want to."

Her cunt walls clench like a fist. Rebelliously, she tries to touch herself, but he takes her hand away.

"This time, I'll reward you," he says.

He seizes her knees, spreads them, and leans down to cleave her lips with his tongue. Removing his tongue from her steaming hole, he spears her clit with it. She comes in seconds.

"There's a war against this kind of worship," he says when they are finished. "The corset won't just transform you, it will defend you. Whenever you wear it, you're free to surrender yourself to me. No one can prevent you. I'm giving you a rare opportunity."

He eases the corset onto her and laces it around her nude torso so that its studs barely caress her wounds.

⛧ A FIRST TIME FOR EVERYTHING ⛧
Rachel Kramer Bussel

"ARE YOU SURE YOU WANT TO DO THIS?" Chip asked me.

"As sure as I'll ever be," I said, feeling surer even as the words came out of my mouth. After all, what kind of a tease would I be if I backed out of the bukkake party I'd organized for myself?

It all started with Truth Or Dare. I'm a wordy girl and will always pick Truth over Dare, even though I consider myself pretty gutsy. But without truth, without words, without syllables spilling out into sentences, dares don't make any sense; they're just reckless actions of the sort performed by drunk boys in late-night race cars, rather than the magnificent grace of a tightrope walker or bungee jumper. I want to be the daredevil superhero girl of sex, boldly going where few, if any, of my peers have gone before. If I go with a dare, it's of my own making, one that really does push me right up to my limits, not just where an envious partygoer would like to see me go.

The truth is, I'm a thrill seeker. I'm the girl who's been there, done that, and gone on to relish telling the story over and over again. I've had sex with men and women, in groups, in public, in dungeons. I've had all manner of sex toys, real and improvised, shoved into my pussy. I've been fucked underwater and spanked on camera. I've said yes to things simply to shock other people. I've used a violet wand and a Magic Wand and a TENS unit. I've had all my toes shoved into a greedy bottom's mouth, and I've sucked two cocks at once. I've made a girl profess her love to me the first night I met her, all because of the way I wielded my fist. I'm only twenty-four, but let's just say I get around. I prefer being single because it gives me room to play the field without worrying about hurting anyone's feelings. I like to come home at six A.M. once in a while, do the quick two-hour catnap, shower, and change, using the memory of the night before to fuel me when the lack of sleep threatens to kick in. I'm the one my friends call on for advice, even referring me around to curious but shy friends: "Oh, call Caitlin, she'll know." Yes, that's me, the girl who's done just about everything (and everyone), whose little black book is actually a massive journal scrawled with names and stories and phone numbers and Polaroids, a glorious jumble of limbs and cocks and breasts and lips, ones I've never sought to try to untangle into a neat, tidy chronological history.

Sex has always been the starting point, never the end, to any inquiry about who I am. It's the gateway drug to, well, more sex, to finding out more about how I operate, what buttons I like having pushed and which I set permanently to caution. This utterly carnal lifestyle is balanced by the hours-days-weeks-years' worth of fantasies that must jumble together until I'm compelled to act. I'm not just an ethical slut, I'm a thoughtful one, too. The time I spend thinking about sex, pondering its every nuance and possibility, far exceeds the time I spend engaging in it, and I'm perfectly happy with that uneven ratio.

So when Sally asked me what my deepest, dirtiest, darkest fantasy was during what had, up till that point, been a rather tepid game of truth or dare (bra size and taking one big bite of everything in the refrigerator among the highlights), I told her—and the whole room. "I want to do bukkake. I mean, be on the receiving end. I want to be lying naked on the floor and see a circle of cocks, all pointing at me. I want a round of boys to want me so badly they'll get naked in front of each other, press their dicks up in my face, while I beg them to come all over me. I want them to take turns shoving their cocks down my throat, slapping them against my lips, rubbing them on my skin, in my hair, doing whatever the hell they please. Maybe I'll be tied up, though then that would deprive me of the pleasure of giving two hand jobs at once. I don't know exactly how it would work, but it's been a mainstay of my fantasy life for years."

I paused, mentally highlighting the vision in my mind where they all started to spurt at once, barely giving me a chance to open up and say, "Aah." I swallowed hard and blinked rapidly, trying to get back into the present. "Yeah," I finished quietly, breathless, my eyes closed, almost ready to cry. Some fantasies are too primal, too out there, too real to ever admit— even to ourselves. But it was true; just thinking about all those anonymous cocks close enough to taste, close enough to smell, close enough to swallow, had my panties soaking wet.

I wasn't the only one who was intrigued with the idea. Everyone started asking me logistical questions, their eyes lit up, the tension in the room palpable, but I shushed them. "It's just a fantasy. You asked for the truth and you got it. If you really want me to go through with it, catch me next time I say 'dare.'"

I didn't mean to sound so haughty, but then again I hadn't meant to reveal something so intimate when everyone else was only sharing the most superficial of details. I hugged my arms to myself, beyond blushing. What does it say about a girl that she dreams of jizz raining down on her face, dreams of being a sex object in the most extreme fashion in the way that some girls dream of getting married? What does it say about me that after I went home, the idea just wouldn't go away? I'd thought it was one of those fantasies that could never come true, and even if it could, that it would be pushing things, even for me. Whoever heard of women willingly submitting to bukkake outside of porn? Maybe gay men, but that was okay. They'd be pigs among pigs (in the best possible sense of the word, of course). But who would I be in such a scenario? Could I ask men to degrade me and respect me and get off on me, literally, all at the same time?

Apparently I could, because my gay friend Chip called me the next day and tried to sound casual about bringing it up. "God, Caitlin, when you said that, everyone in the room got a hard-on. Even Mikki," he said, referring to our most vanilla, conservative friend, who just happened to be a lesbian (but would never call herself a dyke). "Seriously. It wasn't just that we were getting off on the idea, but your voice got so breathy when you said it, like you were literally seeing yourself doing it in your head, not just spouting off some story you tell all the time to impress people."

"Thanks, I guess," I said, wondering what kind of can of worms I'd opened up. "But it's nothing, really. It's a fantasy."

"But what if . . . ?" His voice trailed off.

"What if *what*?" I hissed.

"What if you could actually do it? What if I found you hot, straight guys—big cocks guaranteed—who were into it? I'd so do that for you. All I'd ask is that I get to watch."

"Whoa, whoa, whoa . . . slow down there. You? Watching me? And where would these guys come from?" I was supposed to be suspicious, supposed to protest, but I was intrigued and knew from the pounding in my pussy I wasn't going to stop the thoroughly filthy path this conversation had taken.

"I know people, Cait, guys who'd love to jerk off over your pretty face."

"Like who?" I just couldn't imagine anyone we know would actually volunteer for such a task, in the presence of other guys.

"Rob, for one."

"Rob? Hot Rob? Really?" My nipples hardened at the thought of body-builder Rob, always so brooding, silent, and hunky, being naked before me. I'd tried flirting with him in the past, but he seemed so stiff and quiet.

"Yes, Rob, I already asked," he said.

"What?" The word came out as a yell, but inside I was starting to get totally wet.

"And Rob can bring Jeremy and he said he has at least two other friends who are interested. They've all been tested and are single, so there'll be no jealous girlfriends butting in. And I have another friend, Omar, who wants in on it. I'll arrange everything; you just have to show up."

"Really? You'd do that for me? I mean . . ." I trailed off, not really sure what I meant since I'd never been in a situation remotely like this one before.

"Really, Cait, trust me. And it's not for you. Well, it is, but it's for us, too. Believe me." We hung up and I slid beneath my quilt, letting my fingers plunge deep inside my wetness as I contemplated saying yes to making my fantasy come true. The answer was obvious.

I wound up letting Chip plan the whole thing, and when he was done, in a week's time, he had five guys willing and eager to cover me in their come. It wasn't quite the dozen-man orgy of dick I'd fantasized about, but the fact is, we live in New York, and a twelve-cock circle jerk along with spectators, and me, would probably have been too much to ask for. Five was manageable, a nice, albeit odd number, just slightly above four, which was still a respectable configuration. What we were about to embark on could even be called a sixsome, if that's a word, I told myself, and then Chip.

"Caitlin, let's face it. This is your big slutty night. Whether it's five or fifty cocks, it's still bukkake. Be proud, girl! Everyone I've told about this is totally jealous. You're gonna have the time of your life; don't downplay it. This is your chance to live out a fantasy you never thought you'd get to."

He was right. As his words burned in my ears, I went about cleaning up for what promised to be the party to end all parties. I had a few days, but I'd need them.

The night of the party, I was the perfect host. I prepared a spread of hors d'oeuvres, light snacks like veggies and fruit, some chips, some candy, and laid out soft drinks and a few beers, though I kept the alcohol light. I offered plenty of lube, flavored and not, condoms, in case one thing led to another, and some sex toys, including handcuffs. I'd thrown in the restraints I sometimes get shackled to my headboard with. Yes, I'd decided to do it where I'd be most comfortable, on my bed. Chip was there to oversee things and to get off on the spectacle. "What about this?" he asked, rummaging through my toy chest as only a gay man can, coming up with a red blindfold my ex had gotten me years ago. I didn't even know I still had it.

"But I want to *see* all those cocks," I said, already picturing the guys wanking away just for me. That was the part I liked the best; the men wouldn't just be jerking off, they'd be doing it with a purpose. I'd be the center of attention *and* get to feel wave after wave of hot come splashing across my face. I'd always loved the depravity of shutting my eyes and submitting to that most intense of sensations. Even more than swallowing a lover's spunk, having him grace my cheeks, lips, even my hair with it made me feel at once worthy and degraded. I'd had lovers refuse to do it, unable to see me as the filthy whore I sometimes longed to be. One ex had chickened out at the last minute, able to paint my breasts creamy white but otherwise wanting to come only on my insides, not my outsides. Knowing that men were being handpicked for this activity, men who'd want to be there, who'd know just how much I wanted it, was a truly special thing to contemplate. Utterly perverse, utterly fucked up, and utterly arousing all at once, all the more so because they weren't just horny beasts off the street but men I admired and respected enough to welcome into my home to defile me. Unless you know the thrill of pure submission, those two things may sound like opposites, but believe me, they're not. It takes a special, enlightened, intelligent kind of man to treat a slutty girl like me just right.

"Well, I'd recommend keeping the blindfold handy, both for you and for them. They may not be able to go through with it with you staring up at them. Plus think about how your other senses will be enhanced by not being able to see." I shut my eyes and pictured myself surrounded by cock, pure cock. We were expecting the five guests who'd RSVPed, so that would be five dicks, five sets of balls, and hopefully five hot blasts of come streaming over my lips and the rest of my face. It was like a gangbang, but even better.

"Okay," I whispered, already feeling my body respond to the mere thought with an intense ache.

What does a girl wear to her very own bukkake party? I pondered, flipping through my closet and then my dresser drawers. Nothing seemed quite right, considering, but I didn't want to answer the door naked. I settled for a simple, sheer nightie in mint green, and almost as soon as I'd put it on, the doorbell rang. Chip had been urging me away from my makeup, against my natural instincts (how could I host a party with a bare face?), but now the doorbell had decided it.

The first guest to arrive was hot Rob, wearing basic jeans, sneakers, and a white T-shirt. He'd brought a friend who could've been his twin. Both were equally delectable.

"Welcome," I said, giving a small smile to the newcomer and a flirty wink to Rob. "I'm Caitlin," I said, sticking out my hand.

"Joe," he said, reaching forward and enveloping me in a hug. My body responded to his sheer size, and I wondered if his cock would match his heft.

Rob seemed to want in on the hugging action, and as soon as Joe put me down, he swept me up. "You look beautiful tonight, Caitlin," he said, possibly the longest sentence he'd ever bestowed on me.

"Rob," I said, smirking slightly, "you don't have to butter me up, you know, I'm a sure thing, tonight anyway."

"Look, I know that. And if you want the truth, I'm a little nervous. I've never been in a room full of cocks before."

"Well, if it makes you feel any better, neither have I," I said. Well, that wasn't strictly true; I'd been to orgies and sex parties where naked couples abounded, but none where I would be so close to dick, and I couldn't wait. "And . . . I've been especially looking forward to seeing what you've got under there," I said to him, lightly running my fingers over his package. He stirred beneath my touch and as a reward, I lowered the nightie so my boobs popped out. Rob leaned down and began sucking one nipple while I moaned. The doorbell rang, but I figured someone else would get it. I wasn't sure about proper bukkake party etiquette, but that seemed like an oxymoron if I'd ever heard one!

We continued to kiss and fondle each other, and I just shut my eyes and focused on Rob. That lasted all of a minute or two, until Chip was pulling me aside. "Save some room for the main course," he whispered. I giggled, then winked at him as I twirled around before clapping my hands and calling everyone to attention.

"Okay, boys, I guess we're ready to get started. I just wanted to thank you all for coming *(ahem)* and tell you how excited I am." With that I paused and made eye contact with each of the men whose cocks were soon going to be right up in my face. "The only rule I have tonight is that we're all here to have fun, and I want to make sure you're all comfortable. Does anyone have any questions?"

One guy, Jaime, raised his hand. "Can we come anytime we want?"

This was something I hadn't considered; I'd sort of assumed that they'd all jointly have the urge to splatter me with their jism . . . just like in the movies. But the question also granted me the power to answer, and thereby control his orgasm, and my pussy responded to this unexpected opportunity. "No." I looked directly into his eyes, then walked toward him, reaching under his shirt to twist his nipple. He whimpered, and I smiled. "No, Jaime, you're all going to come when I tell you to. Just because I'll be lying there aching to suck, lick, and feel your cocks doesn't mean I'm not in charge. If you want to stay at the party, you'll have to learn to wait."

The collective mood in the room went from excited to practically orgasmic as we all realized that this wasn't a prank but that we were all about to engage in something we'd only dreamed of. "Okay, then, I'll give you a few minutes to get naked. I'll be right over here," I said, pointing to my room. I wasn't sure how they wanted to handle that process, so I let them be while I slipped out of my lingerie and looked down at my naked body. The slight curve to my belly felt sexy, and I slid my hand down over it to my mound, which sported just a few tufts of pubic hair.

I walked over to my bed, the scene of the crime, as it were, and lay down on my back. Chip placed the blindfold and a bottle of water near me, then kissed me on the cheek. "All those cocks are soon to be yours," he whispered to me, and I opened my eyes long enough to see that his own cock was extremely aroused. I began playing with myself, lightly stroking my clit, then running a finger along my slit, trying to be patient. As I glanced at the men as a group, they ceased to be individuals distinguishable by voice and looks and conversation. They were all equal, their cocks together forming a whole that would transport me into another dimension, or so it felt. I let myself sink fully into that fantasy, losing whatever shreds of propriety I was clinging to in order to make the most of this momentous opportunity, for that is what it was.

The first man to saunter over was Jaime, and I immediately felt a frisson of arousal as I looked at his cock. It was already hard, and fat and delicious-looking. I smiled at him, then rolled over to the edge of the bed, turned onto my side, and brought my mouth within sucking distance by way of greeting.

Without saying a word, he offered me his dick. Well, the head of it, anyway. His fist was wrapped around it and he fed it to me slowly. As I took the rounded tip in, then let my lips move down over the crown, I shuddered. Nothing makes me more aroused than wrapping my mouth around a man's hard cock. Today it didn't matter whose cock it was or what he thought of me or even how he was feeling. For once, it was okay for it to be All About Me, though I was sure the men would enjoy themselves as well. I immediately had to keep stroking myself as I swallowed Jaime's cock, his hardness making me frantic. Before I could really start bucking up and down though, he wrapped his fingers in my hair and pulled me away. His forcefulness combined with my now-empty mouth turned me on even more.

"Baby . . . if you want me to not come, you can't suck me like that. I'm only a man, after all," he said, taking a step back. I looked up at him, begging with my eyes, running my tongue over my lips, but he shook his head, seeming to take delight in withholding it. "Later," he murmured, and when I turned onto my back, I saw that another man was next to him and three more on my other side, perched on the bed so they could be close enough. They were each stroking their cocks, almost tentatively, as if waiting for a cue from their comrades that they could go faster. I'd given up trying to distinguish whose cock was whose, because at that moment it just didn't matter.

I moved so I was facing the trio, my back toward Jamie and his pal. I opened my mouth and two men brushed their cocks against my tongue. I looked up and all I saw was dick, dick, dick, literally, as another one appeared near the others, trying to get inside, though as talented a fellatrix as I am, that would've been impossible. I could hear heavy breathing and pumping on the other side and Chip clapping in delight. "Give it to me," I said, stretching my mouth as wide as I could so those first two cock heads could fully enter my mouth.

This was much farther than I'd ever gone before, for even the largest cock I'd swallowed, and there had been some that had made me truly stretch my mouth, gag, and strain, didn't come close to having two dicks jockeying for position. Soon I pulled back and kissed the three tips. I took the dildo I'd placed beside me and began working it into my pussy. I had lube nearby, too, but found that I didn't need it. I knew this wasn't the traditional version of this kind of gangbang, where the men's pleasure was paramount, but since I'd orchestrated this scenario, I wanted to reap the rewards. Far from being humiliated, I was overjoyed at getting to arrange this affair to my exact specifications, and the wetness I found between my legs proved it.

I was torn between closing my eyes and focusing on the feel and smell of so many cocks and seeing them in action. I sat up on one elbow, dildo inside me, and we all jerked off communally, grunting and grinding, hands flying over skin, slamming and jerking, violent words for harsh actions yielding dizzying results. I'd always found it to be true that a light touch may as well be a tickle; I need firm, steady pressure, and gazing upon these men with cocks in fists, apparently they did, too.

Under my observation, the men seemed to jerk their cocks faster, moving in sync almost. Someone crawled behind me and I lowered my head down to the sheet so his penis could rub against my forehead. That gave the others entrée to slide closer, hover directly on top of me, and slap their dicks against my face. I fucked myself with the dildo, wishing I had a vibrator because soon my hips were rising and crashing down against the mattress, my eyes tearing in ecstasy as all those penises suffused my senses. I turned my face slightly to the left and took the nearest dick into my mouth, easily swallowing its long, swollen length. Just then, I felt the first jet of cream land on my back, and I whimpered as best I could with a mouth full of cock. I looked up into the eyes of Rob, and he cradled the back of my head gently in his hand as I sucked him. This may sound crazy, but it felt spiritual to me, a moment of bonding that went far beyond the mechanics of sex. Or maybe I'm just the rare girl who can have a holy moment with five gorgeous cocks surrounding her.

I gave everything I had to Rob, slamming the dildo so deep inside me it bordered on pain, the best kind of pain, as I let him invade my mouth. I'd wanted this invasion, asked for it, negotiated it, and now I delighted in it, all of it. I moaned against his mouth, urging him to come down my throat, and my man of the moment obliged. The stream of hot liquid surged into my mouth and I swallowed, my cunt contracting around the dildo at the same time. Rob's release freed me to lean back and simply let the men take over. I surrendered to the glory of this unique situation and watched as one, then another, then yet another dick let loose until I was coated in sticky, white, beautiful come. I reached up and smeared it all over my face, and kissed whoever's lips moved forward to kiss mine. I didn't want to get up just yet; this sex spell was too beautiful to be broken. I lay there and smiled up at my suitors, my good-time guys, my bukkake boys, a grin covered with come, basking in pure bliss. It sure beat the hell out of most of my other sexual firsts. Chip winked at me, and I winked right back, reaching out my hands for whoever wanted to grab them.

Contributors' Notes

MATTHEW ADDISON is a writer living in Northern California. His work has appeared in *Fishnet* and *The Best American Erotica*.

ERIC ALBERT has been an interpreter for the deaf, computer scientist, teacher, crossword-puzzle constructor, sex researcher, stock-market investor, editor, and writer. He's now back in grad school, studying to become a licensed psychotherapist. He lives in a suburb of Boston and longs to be wholly used. Eric would like to thank Sia Stewart, Deborah A. Levinson, L. E. Robbins, and Julie James for their help with "Inspiration."

KATYA ANDREEVNA's erotic fiction has appeared in a number of anthologies, including *The Best American Erotica 1996, Best Lesbian Erotica 1997,* and *Pillow Talk: Lesbian Stories between the Covers.* Her work has also been published in Norway and Denmark. After all these years and many, many shoe-shopping forays, she is still looking for the perfect pair of pumps.

PAULA BOMER's short story collection *BABY* debuted in 2008 from Impetus Press. Her fiction has appeared in numerous journals and anthologies, including *Nerve, Open City, Mississippi Review, Fiction, The New York Tyrant,* and *The Best American Erotica.*

SUSIE BRIGHT is the editor of this volume as well as the author and editor of multiple best-sellers on the themes of sexual politics and erotic literature, including *The Best American Erotica* series, *Full Exposure,* and *The Sexual State of the Union.* She blogs on sex and politics every day at susiebright.com and hosts the weekly audio show *In Bed with Susie Bright* at Audible.com.

RACHEL KRAMER BUSSEL has edited twenty erotic anthologies, including *Best Sex Writing 2008; Yes, Sir; Yes, Ma'am; He's on Top; She's on Top; Rubber Sex; Spanked: Red-Cheeked Erotica;* and *Naughty Spanking Stories from A to Z* (vols. 1 and 2). Her work has been published in over a hundred anthologies, including *The Best American Erotica,* Zane's *Succulent: Chocolate Flava II* and *Purple Panties, Everything You Know about Sex Is Wrong,* and *Desire: Women Write about Wanting.* She hosts the In the Flesh Erotic Reading Series, wrote the popular Lusty Lady column for the *Village Voice,* and has contributed to *AVN, Bust, Diva, Fresh Yarn, Gothamist, Huffington Post, Mediabistro, Newsday, New York Post, San Francisco Chronicle, Time Out New York,* and *Zink*. In her spare time she blogs about cupcakes at cupcakestakethecake.blogspot.com.

ROBERT OLEN BUTLER has published ten novels and five volumes of short fiction, one of which, *A Good Scent from a Strange Mountain,* won the 1993 Pulitzer Prize for Fiction. His new book, *Intercourse,* comprises one hundred short short stories arranged in fifty couples. Some of these Little Fuckers, as he affectionately calls them, appeared as poetry in places like the *Kenyon Review* and the *Virginia Quarterly Review* and as fiction in *Playboy*. Butler teaches creative writing at Florida State University.

GRETA CHRISTINA has been writing professionally since 1989. She is the editor of the annual anthology series *Best Erotic Comics,* and of the anthology *Paying for It: A Guide by Sex Workers for Their Clients*; she is the author of the erotic novella *Bending,* which appeared in Susie Bright's three-novella collection *Three Kinds of Asking for It*. Her fiction and nonfiction writing has appeared in numerous magazines and newspapers, including *Ms., Penthouse,* the *Chicago Sun-Times,* and the *Skeptical Inquirer,* as well as in several anthologies, including *The Best American Erotica* series. She blogs about sex, atheism, politics, and other polite topics at gretachristina.typepad.com.

ERNIE CONRICK is the pen name of Richard Connerney, a religion and philosophy scholar who recently returned from India as a Phillips Talbot Fellow studying the influence and impact of religion on Indian life and society. He is the former senior editor of *Tricycle: The Buddhist Review,* and the author of *Safe in Heaven Dead*. One of his previous erotic short stories, "The Queen of Exit 17," was published in *The Best American Erotica,* and had the distinction of being Hunter S. Thompson's favorite story from the series.

SUSAN DIPLACIDO is the author of four novels: *24/7, Trattoria, House Money,* and *Mutual Holdings*. Her short story "I, Candy" won the Spirit Award at the 2005 Moondance International Film Festival. Her short stories are included in *The Best American Erotica 2007, The Mammoth*

Book of Best New Erotica (vols. 6 and 7), and Zane's *Caramel Flava*. Visit her online at susandiplacido.com.

MICHAEL DORSEY is a mental health and chemical dependency counselor in Washington state. His eclectic and influential background includes stage actor, writer, editor, and father of two beautiful kids. He can be found at midorsey.com.

CORWIN ERICSON lives in western Massachusetts and works as a writer, editor, and college instructor. His work has appeared in a number of publications, including *Harper's Magazine* and *The Best American Erotica 1995*. He is the coeditor of the *Illustrated Anthology of Classic Erotica* (2008).

MARTHA GARVEY's fiction has been published in *The Best American Erotica, Exhibitions, Glamour Girls, Strange Pleasures 3, Salon, Clean Sheets, Bust*, and *November 3rd*. Her essays have appeared in the *New York Times* and *Killing the Buddha*. She is also the author of two pet health books, *My Fat Dog* and *My Fat Cat*.

R. GAY is a writer and doctoral candidate living just past the middle of nowhere. Her work can be found in *The Best American Erotica 2004*, several editions of *Best Lesbian Erotica, Best Women's Erotica 2008*, and elsewhere. She can be found online at pettyfictions.com.

SHANNA GERMAIN is a poet by nature, a short-story writer by the skin of her teeth, and a novelist in training. Her work has appeared in places like *The Best American Erotica 2007, Best Bondage Erotica 2, Best Gay Romance 2008, Best Lesbian Erotica 2008*, and *The Mammoth Book of Best New Erotica 2007*. Visit her online at shannagermain.com.

DAMIAN GRACE, a scientist who lives in the Chicago area, has been writing erotic fiction under the name DG for four years. Many of his stories can be found on free Web sites sprinkled throughout the Internet.

SUSIE HARA lives and writes in the San Francisco Bay Area. Her play *Lost and Found in the Mission* (written and directed with Rowena Richie) premiered in San Francisco in June 2007. Her stories have appeared in several anthologies, including *Stirring Up a Storm, The Best American Erotica*

2003 (under the pen name Lisa Wolfe), and *Best Women's Erotica 2007*. Writing erotic fiction is the most fun she's ever had with a laptop.

P. S. HAVEN was raised on *Star Wars*, comic books, and his dad's *Playboy* collection, all of which he still enjoys to this day. He has been writing erotica for over fifteen years. His short stories have been published in *The Best American Erotica* series, *Taboo: Forbidden Fantasies for Couples*, and the *International Journal of Erotica*, among others. His work has also been published on the Web at scarletletters.com, cleansheets.com, ruthiesclub .com, as well as at his own Web site, pshaven.com. Haven peddles his smut from deep within the Bible Belt, where he fights a never-ending battle for truth, justice, and the American Way.

VICKI HENDRICKS is the author of the noir novels *Miami Purity, Iguana Love, Voluntary Madness, Sky Blues*, and *Cruel Poetry*, her darkest novel, entwining sex, drugs, obsession, and murder in Miami Beach. Her stories have appeared in *The Best American Erotica 2000, Miami Noir*, and *Hell of a Woman: An Anthology of Female Noir*, among other collections. She lives in Hollywood, Florida, and teaches writing at Broward Community College. Her Web home is vickihendricks.com.

SUSANNAH INDIGO is the editor in chief of CleanSheets.com and the founding editor of the literary journal *Slow Trains*. Her books include *Sex & Spirituality, Sex & Laughter, Oysters among Us*, the series *From Porn to Poetry*, and her newest collection, *Geishas Don't Eat Nachos*. For further information, see susannahindigo.com, cleansheets.com, and slowtrains.com.

NICHOLAS KAUFMANN is the critically acclaimed author of *General Slocum's Gold* and the collection *Walk in Shadows*. His fiction has appeared in *Cemetery Dance, The Mammoth Book of Best New Erotica 3, City Slab, The Best American Erotica 2007, Playboy*, and elsewhere. His nonfiction has appeared in *On Writing Horror, Annabelle Magazine, Fantastic Metropolis*, and *Hellnotes*, among many other publications. He has also served on the board of trustees for the Horror Writers Association. Nick lives in Brooklyn, and can be found at nicholaskaufmann.com.

TSAURAH LITZKY writes erotic fiction because she has a perpetual case of steamy stockings. She hopes her stories will steam your stockings, too. Simon & Schuster published *The Motion of the Ocean* (2004), Tsaurah's erotic novella included in *Three the Hard Way*, edited by Susie Bright. Tsaurah's prize-winning course "Silk Sheets: Writing Erotica" is now in its eleventh year at the New School in Manhattan.

MARCELLE MANHATTAN is the author of the blog Sexegesis, at sexegesis .blogspot.com, which combines fetish erotica with sexual politics. She has received critical acclaim and media attention, including mention in the *San Francisco Chronicle* online and speaking engagements such as with Rachel Kramer Bussel's "In the Flesh Erotic" reading series. "Second Date" is her first published work of fiction. Marcelle holds a master's degree in literature and nearly received her PhD but was saved by a desire to write smut in New York City and run around wearing a lot of vinyl.

The late ANITA MELISSA MASHMAN, from the San Francisco Bay Area, was a beloved activist in fat-liberation politics, particularly with the National Association to Advance Fat Acceptance (NAAFA). Her work appeared in projects of Paradigm Press, *Largesse*, and *The Best American Erotica* before her untimely death from cancer.

ELLE MOLIQUE lives in the Kansas City area. She has a master's degree in music. She likes to cook and sew at home, and scream metal, improvise jazz, and shred classical music in clubs and concert halls. She writes erotica of all kinds. Halloween is her favorite holiday. She keeps a cheese log, a diary of all the cheeses she has found worthy of description.

MONMOUTH is a London-based gentleman of pleasure, and prolific blogger, who captivates his audience at monmouth.blogspot.com.

LISA MONTANARELLI is the coauthor of *The First Year: Hepatitis C*, whose second edition has just been released. She also coauthored *Strange but True: San Francisco* and *Strange but True: Chicago*, and her fiction has appeared in *The Best American Erotica*, and *Whipped!* She has a PhD in comparative literature from the University of California, and can be found at LisaNY.com.

PEGGY MUNSON is the author of the poetic and raunchy novel *Origami Striptease* and a new collection of poetry, *Pathogenesis*. Her work has been included in *The Best American Poetry, The Best American Erotica, Best Lesbian Erotica*, and in *Tough Girls, On Our Backs*, and many other publications. Peggy was born in Normal, Illinois, and she can be found at peggymunson.com.

SUSAN MUSGRAVE is an award-winning British Columbian poet, novelist, columnist, reviewer, editor, and nonfiction writer. She has published over twenty books and writes as a critic for the *Vancouver Sun* and *Ottawa Citizen*. Recent books include *Dreams Are More Real Than Bathtubs, Forcing the Narcissus*, and *Musgrave Landing: Musings on the Writing Life*. Her short stories have been anthologized in *The Norton Introduction to Literature, Fever: Sensual Stories by Women Writers, Without a Guide: Contemporary Women's Travel Adventure, The Best American Erotica 1995*, and *Best American Poetry 1995*. Her books of poetry include *Things That Keep and Do Not Change*. She can be found at library.utoronto.ca/canpoetry/musgrave.

BILL NOBLE is a writer, poet, and community activist hiding out in a liberal/progressive/sex-positive/environmental wilderness preserve somewhere north of San Francisco. His work has appeared in print several hundred times, including multiple manifestations in *The Best American Erotica* and *The Mammoth Book of Best New Erotica*. His honors include selection as author of one of the "erotic stories of the decade" in *The Best American Erotica 2008*, the 1999 Looking Glass Prize for poetry, and recognition by the SouthWest Writers Conference. Talented (he earnestly believes) beyond mere wordsmithing, his skinny butt and endearing mug have graced the feature film from Comstock Films *Bill & Desiree: Love Is Timeless*. Somewhat fewer body parts are on display in Joani Blank and Libido Films' *Orgasm: Faces of Ecstasy*. He is a longtime fiction editor at CleanSheets.com.

LISA PALAC is the author of *The Edge of the Bed*.

CAROL QUEEN is a writer, journalist, speaker, and activist—an influential and dedicated sex educator whose work has touched millions. She is the founder, with her partner, Robert Lawrence, of The San Francisco Center for Sex and Culture. Her books include *Real Live Nude Girl: Chronicles of a Sex-Positive Culture, The Leather Daddy and the Femme, Whipped, Exhibitionism for the Shy, Five-Minute Erotica*, and *PoMoSexuals: Challenging Assumptions about Gender and Sexuality*. Her Web site is carolqueen.com.

DONALD RAWLEY was an award-winning author, poet, journalist, and successful screenwriter. He began his studies with writer and UCLA professor Kate Braverman. His short stories, poems, and articles appeared in numerous magazines, including *Yellow Silk Journal of Erotic Arts*. He was nominated for the Pulitzer Prize and the Faulkner Award. In 1996, he won a Pushcart Prize for fiction. Rawley passed away in 1998.

DONNA GEORGE STOREY enjoys saying yes. Her erotic fiction has appeared in numerous anthologies, including *The Best American Erotica 2006* and several volumes of *The Mammoth Book of Best New Erotica* and *Best Women's Erotica*. Her novel set in Japan, *Amorous Woman*, was published by Orion in 2007. Read more of her work at DonnaGeorgeStorey.com.

Finding herself uninspired to write her doctoral dissertation, CHELSEA SUMMERS began writing her award-winning blog (prettydumbthings.blogspot.com) in March 2005. Since then, her work has appeared in *Penthouse* magazine in the United States and in *Scarlet* and *New Woman* magazines in the United Kingdom, as well as in several erotic anthologies. Currently, Chelsea is working on a book on the secret life of strippers. Chelsea lives and writes in glamorous New York City. She has gleefully abandoned the world of academia for the writing life.

DOUG TIERNEY is from a long line of police officers in Virginia, and a lover of ghost stories. He went to MIT, then took root in Boston. "The Portable Girlfriend" is his first published work of fiction. In his other life, he writes tech manuals for nuclear reactors, rides (and occasionally wrecks) motorcycles, plays bass guitar, and cooks a mean Thai supper plate.

ANNE TOURNEY is an erotic romance author, daydreamer, fidgeter, blogger, and wannabe photographer. She is the author of the novels *Lying in Mid-Air, Head-On Heart, Taming Jeremy*, and *Kiss between the Lines*, and has been anthologized in *The Best American Erotica, Best of Best Women's Erotica, The Mammoth Book of Best New Erotica, Shameless: Women's*

Intimate Erotica, Best Fetish Erotica, and *The Unmade Bed.* Her Web site is at annetourney.com.

PAM WARD is a Los Angeles native. Her debut novel was *Want Some, Get Some,* and her short story work can be found in *The Best American Erotica 2002, Scream When You Burn, Grand Passion,* and *Men We Cherish.* Her poetry appears in *Catch the Fire!* and she is the recipient of a California Arts Council Writing Fellowship and a New Letters Award for Poetry.

SALOME WILDE is the pseudonym of a feminist academic enjoying the artistic pleasure of writing erotica. "God's Gift" is part of her *Secret Sex Lives of Inanimate Objects* series. Wilde's fiction, poetry, and essays are published in diverse online and print magazines and collections, including *Clean Sheets, The Erotic Woman,* and Susie Bright's *The Best American Erotica 2006.* She is currently at work on a BDSM-themed fantasy novel featuring every gender, orientation, and consensual kink she can envision. Visit Salome at salomewilde.net.

Born in Cornwall, IRMA WIMPLE currently lives in the Upper Peninsula of Michigan with her seven cats and one tame cougar. A former community college professor, she is a pastry chef by day; at night she is transformed into a torrid and prolific romantic fiction writer. A veteran of five marriages that she considers successful—in that they are over—Irma devotes her nonwriting time to gardening, ice fishing, reading, and hiking.

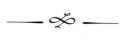

Credits

"Gifts from Santa," by Tsaurah Litzky, © 2007, first published in *Merry Xmas Book of Erotica*, edited by Alison Tyler, published by Cleis Press, 2005.

"Second Date," by Marcelle Manhattan, © 2007, first published in http://sexegesis.blogspot.com, September 15, 2007.

"Five Dimes," by Anita Melissa Mashman, © 1992, first appeared in *Largesse*, vol. 3, edited by Anita Melissa Mashman and Linda Jayne, Paradigm Press, 1992.

"Footprints," by Elle Molique, © 2007, first published in *Leg Show*, published by MMG Services, 2007.

"Parts for Wholes," by Monmouth, © 2005, first published in http://monmouth.blogspot.com, published by Monmouth, October 2005.

"Loved It and Set It Free," by Lisa Montanarelli, © 2003, first published in *Best Lesbian Erotica 2003*, edited by Tristan Taormino, published by Cleis Press, 2003.

"Fairgrounds," by Peggy Munson, © 2004, first published in *Best Lesbian Erotica 2005*, edited by Tristan Taormino, published by Cleis Press, 2004.

"Valentine's Day in Jail," by Susan Musgrave, © 1994, first published in *Fever: Sensual Stories by Women Writers*, edited by Michele Slung, published by HarperCollins, 1994.

"Salt," by Bill Noble, © 1992, first published in *Wet: More Aqua Erotica*, edited by Mary Anne Mohanraj, published by Three Rivers Press, 2003.

"Low-Cut," by Lisa Palac, © 1994, first published as "Four's Company," in *BUST*, vol. 1, no. 4, 1994.

"Sweating Profusely in Mérida: A Memoir," by Carol Queen, © 1993, first published in *Logomotive*, vol. 3, 1993.

"Slow Dance on the Fault Line," by Donald Rawley, © 1993, first appeared in *Yellow Silk*, vol. 11, no. 4 (Winter 93/94), 1993.

"Must Bite," by Vicki Hendricks, © 2006, originally published in *Dying for It: Tales of Sex and Death*, edited by Mitzi Szereto, published by Thunder's Mouth Press, 2006.

"Yes," by Donna George Storey, © 2007, first published in *He's on Top*, edited by Rachel Kramer Bussel, published by Cleis Press, 2007.

"Cold Ass Ice," by Chelsea Summers, © 2006, first published in http://prettydumbthings.typepad.com, August 4, 2006.

"The Portable Girlfriend," by Doug Tierney, © 1995, first published in *Selling Venus*, edited by Cecilia Tan, Circlet Press, 1995.

"Full Metal Corset," by Anne Tourney, © 1993, first published in *Future Sex*, no. 3, 1993.

"A Clean, Comfortable Room," by Pam Ward, © 2000, first published in *Gynomite*, edited by Liz Belile, published by New Mouth from the Dirty South LLC, 2000.

"God's Gift," by Salome Wilde, © 2005.

"Electric Razor," by Irma Wimple, © 2007, first published in *Best Women's Erotica 2007*, edited by Violet Blue, published by Cleis Press, 2006.

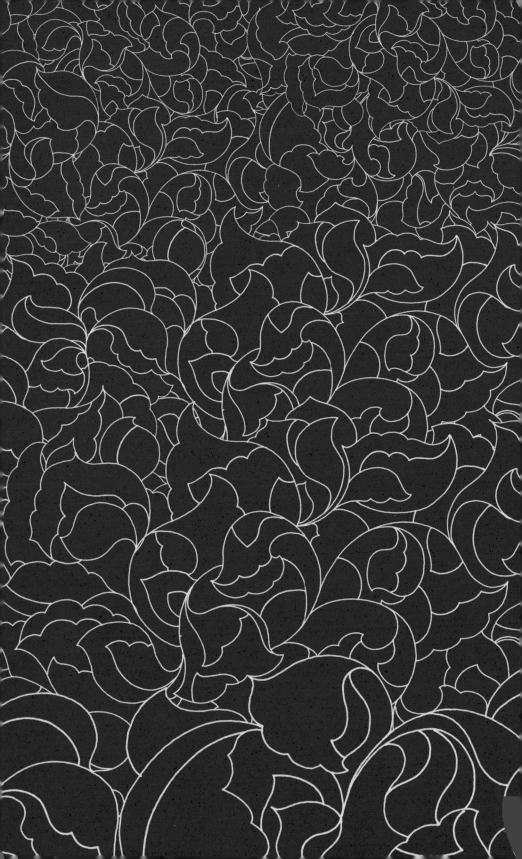

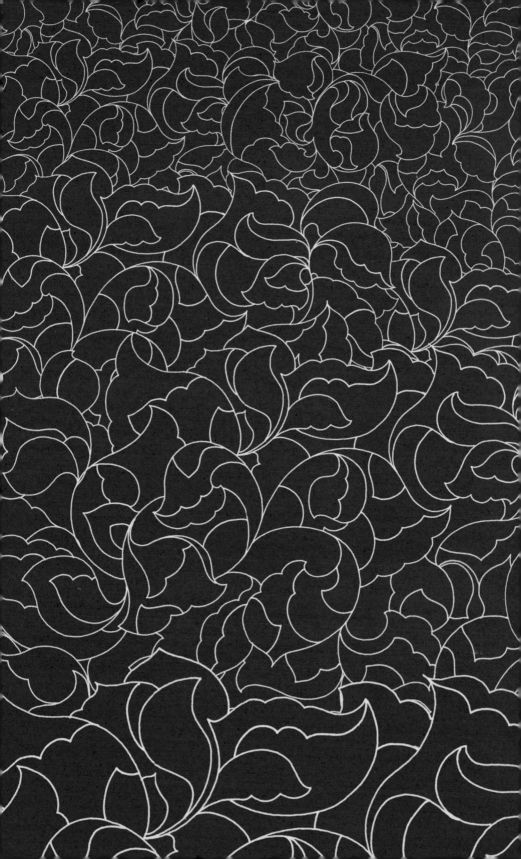